Adele Parks MBE was born in North Yorkshire. She is the author of 23 bestselling novels including the *Sunday Times* Number One bestsellers *Lies Lies Lies* and *Just My Luck*. Over five million UK editions of her work have been sold and her books have been translated into 31 different languages. Adele's novel *The Image of You* has just been released as a major motion movie and she has several other titles optioned and in development including *One Last Secret* and *Both of You*. She is an ambassador of the National Literacy Trust and the Reading Agency: two charities that promote literacy in the UK. Adele has lived in Botswana, Italy and London and is now settled in Guildford, Surrey. In 2022 she was awarded an MBE for services to literature.

Find Adele on X @adeleparks, Instagram @adele_parks, Facebook @OfficialAdeleParks, TikTok @Adeleparksauthor or visit www.adeleparks.com.

FIRST WIFE'S SHADOW

ADELE PARKS

ONE PLACE. MANY STORIES

HQ
An imprint of HarperCollins*Publishers* Ltd
1 London Bridge Street
London SE1 9GF

www.harpercollins.co.uk

HarperCollins*Publishers*
Macken House, 39/40 Mayor Street Upper,
Dublin 1, D01 C9W8, Ireland

This edition 2024

1
First published in Great Britain by
HQ, an imprint of HarperCollins*Publishers* Ltd 2024

Copyright © Adele Parks 2024

Adele Parks asserts the moral right to be identified as the author of this work.
A catalogue record for this book is available from the British Library.

ISBN HB: 9780008586270
ISBN TPB: 9780008586287

MIX
Paper | Supporting
responsible forestry
FSC
www.fsc.org
FSC™ C007454

This book contains FSC™ certified paper and other controlled sources to ensure responsible forest management.

For more information visit: www.harpercollins.co.uk/green

This book is set in 10.6/15.5 pt. Sabon by Type-it AS, Norway

Printed and Bound in the UK using 100% Renewable Electricity at CPI Group (UK) Ltd, Croydon, CR0 4YY

This one is for Chris Worwood and Ian Johnson
You really should have had one dedicated to you before now.
Love you both.

PROLOGUE

The body was pinned up against the tree. Dead. Obviously dead. No RIP here. The detective didn't see many RIPs in his line of work. He saw tortured souls; people who had endured violence – brought down by their own hand or the hand of others – disaster or just plain old bad luck. With disaster and bad luck there wasn't even anyone to blame. It was nuanced, and the fifty-plus, portly copper who had seen it all continued to wrestle with the question of which was more brutal, more devastating: not having anyone to blame or having a poker-hot focus of fury.

The body was mangled from the waist downwards. The glassy eyes had seen everything they were ever going to. All that was going to happen in this life, had. For good or bad, it was done. The DC imagined he could hear the screech of tyres, the crunch as metal twisted, the sound of glass shattering. Nonsense, of course. All that had occurred hours before he arrived on the scene. If there had been frantic honking, horrified realisation, determined destruction, that was finished now.

Now, it was a matter of first responders, flashing lights, debris scattered, a stunned silence.

As they slowly rolled the car back, the body slumped forward over the bonnet. Something flickered on the face, just the hint of early-morning light. No life, or afterlife. The detective did not believe in ghosts. He knew people could be haunted, though. He saw plenty of that. People tormented by their past, the mistakes they'd made, the opportunities they'd missed, the people they'd hurt. And maybe worse still, the DC knew that some people lived their entire lives haunted by their future. Fearful of the mistakes they might make, the opportunities they might miss.

1

February

Emma

I believe in routine. Discipline. Hard work. It makes me unfashionable but successful. So I say, forget the haters. I have rules and routines for a reason. When they are abandoned, things start to fall apart. Children of alcoholics know this better than most.

I get up at 5.08 a.m. every day of the working week, and it takes me nine minutes to dress, get downstairs, turn off the alarms, swallow a vitamin, fill my Hydro Flask with water and unlock the front door before my feet hit the path. I run for the remaining forty-three minutes of the hour, which means I normally run five miles. The average woman runs at a rate of 6.5 miles per hour. Do the maths. I run faster than average.

I run in all weathers, all seasons. I live in woodlands, so a treadmill can't compete. Fresh air in my lungs; the slap, sting or spike of the elements makes me feel alive. Obviously, running in the summer months is a delight – who doesn't love a sunrise? – but I run in the dark months too, when the sun seems never to rise, but instead, at best, only manages to resentfully loll somewhere behind the clouds of a gunmetal sky. My friends say that running through a forest in the pitch black alone on a February morning is stupid. I like to think of it as an opportunity. What doesn't kill you makes you stronger, right?

Once back at my house, I check the headlines, then spend twelve minutes practising sun salutations because cardio is vital for the heart but I don't want my bones to crumble and yoga helps with strength. People think I'm extreme. I'm not, I'm balanced. I shower, perform all the ablutions necessary to try to keep the ageing process at bay, and check the social feeds for mentions of AirBright, the wind harvesting company of which I am chief executive officer. I dress, then prepare a kale, celery and parsley smoothie. It tastes awful but it's full of vitamins. I scan my emails but don't open them unless it's something from my chief financial officer or public relations director. Maybe, if there's time, while drinking my disgusting green gloop at the breakfast bar, I'll read any private texts or messages. My friends, Heidi and Gina, often send me one-liners letting me know what their kids – my godchildren – are up to. That always brings a smile to my face. On days when I need to go to the London office, I'm out the door by 6.32 a.m. I drive to the station – it's on average a nine-minute journey, but I allow some flex for tractors on the narrow lanes – and catch the 6.49 train. I aim to be at my desk in London by 7.45. Seventy-five minutes before I'm contractually obliged to be there, ninety minutes before any of my exec team show up.

This has been my routine for as long as I can remember. There has been some variation on the length of the commute and the flavour of the smoothie. The seniority of my position in the companies I've worked for has evolved, but in essence

– the runs, the arrival at work before other employees – those things have been a constant. I stick to this routine even on my birthday. I am forty-seven.

This statement apparently surprises people. They gasp and say I don't look forty-seven. Really they are thinking, 'Shit, all that effort, all those years, is it worth it?' because most people are a bit lazy and incredibly undisciplined and like to get by doing as little as possible; my routine horrifies them. They don't say what they are thinking out loud, though, maybe because people are generally quite polite or maybe because most of the individuals I mix with work for me; everyone wants to stay on my good side. They don't have to say that they think I put too much energy into everything; I see it on their embarrassed faces: a complicated mix of pity that I try so hard and resentment that it works. The thing is, I'm very realistic about the hand I was dealt and I play. I'm not special, I'm not exceptionally clever or good-looking. I don't have an amazing talent like painting, or writing, or dancing, or singing that might make me stand out from the masses. My talent is my discipline. I'm rational, thorough, careful. I earn a healthy six-figure salary as a result. Lucky me.

As I'm never openly challenged about whether the relentless effort and focus is worthwhile, I haven't really had to consider what my answer might be. It *is* a lot of effort for thin thighs, I admit, but I'm also investing in my future: notably a longer, healthier one. Not being a mother or a wife, I can't assume (or even hope) that there will be someone to look after me when I age. I will have to pay for care, and so being as healthy as possible is just a wise choice.

But. Well. Last night.

I shake my head. What am I thinking? One swallow does not make a summer, and equally one shag does not make a future. Although technically it was not *one* shag, it was three. And he did talk about our future. And it was not simply a shag, it was . . .

I have no idea how to finish that sentence.

If I say special, I am unrecognisable even to myself.

The fact is that this morning there was something new that interrupted my routine. Before I slipped out the door, I popped back into my bedroom and looked at the man sleeping in my bed. He was lying on his stomach, clutching a pillow, which sounds more effeminate than the reality. He's a big, hairy, muscular man and his masculinity – which is almost brutish, certainly exotic, in my bedroom – caused me to silently gasp with surprise. Is it ludicrous to think there might be someone who will look after me in the future? Someone I can look after? I watched him breathe in, out, in, out. My air. His. He's a miracle. He's a big, sweaty, sometimes brilliant, sometimes stupid, agreeable, argumentative, sexy, stubborn miracle.

And now he's mine.

2

January

I became the CEO of Britain's biggest wind harvesting company, AirBright, seven years ago. When I was awarded this position, some people in my industry muttered that hiring a woman to run the company was not much more than a PR stunt, a cynical move by the executives to look modern by ticking a diversity-hire box. Fifty-one per cent of the UK population are female; despite this fact, women are considered to be diversity hires in positions of power. I trained as an accountant but still struggle with that maths.

Whatever. People can say what they like. In childhood, having an alcoholic dad and then after everything that happened, I learnt that people talk about me regardless of my behaviour, actions or even the truth, so I decided long ago to do what works for me. It's the only way to stay sane. What works for me right now is getting on with doing my little bit to save the planet. I like to think I was the best candidate for the job and I do it well. End of. I'm a hands-on boss but I'm also respectful of the expertise of my heads of department. It was the director of marketing who suggested my face ought to be seen more, which is how I find myself, on this cold January day, standing in an enormous, echoey conference centre in Edinburgh, shaking hands with numerous climate-concerned delegates, underneath a branded sign that reads: *Wind Energy is Big Clean Energy.*

I notice him at a molecular level immediately. That in itself is interesting.

He's tall, over six foot, and has great teeth and a mop of dark curly hair. He's unequivocally attractive: symmetrical, a strong chin. Some people find that off-putting; I'm not as subtle. Obviously handsome works for me. He's wearing faded jeans that suggest they are faded through wear, not bought that way as a fashion statement, and a thick-knit navy jumper. He is carrying a battered leather rucksack, good quality but aged. There's a hole in the shoulder of his jumper. I can see his flesh peeking through and I have to fight the urge to lace my finger into the hole, to touch his skin. This is weird, and especially weird from me; I'm not a tactile person. Despite his height and good looks, there is something about him that doesn't quite fill the space in the way he is surely entitled to. He has a level of reluctance, an air that suggests he leans away from life. That sense of reservation is as interesting as his good looks. His eyes whip above my head; he reads the ill-considered marketing slogan and smirks involuntarily.

'Don't bother with the flatulence jokes. I've heard every possible one already. You're better than that,' I say, before he has the chance to offer a word.

I know my comment is ballsy. Flirty. I am always the former, but finding myself being the latter is a surprise to me. *You're better than that*. A blatant seal of approval. An invitation. To what? He's at least a decade younger than I am, possibly more. What am I thinking? Yet there is something vibrant between us. At least, I hope it is between us. Surely this can't be a one-way thing. I can almost touch it, taste it.

These are nebulous thoughts for rational, sensible me to have. I'm normally a fan of the quantifiable; however, there is something here that I'd forgotten existed. I gave up dating two years ago. I was too busy with work, and besides, I was exhausted with shoddy encounters that generated nothing other than a confirmation of the fact that people lie. I became bored by the countless, endless disappointments: men who turned out to be shorter, balder, fatter or – worse – duller than advertised, so I turned off that part of my life, that part of me. Even before that, this sort of raw animal attraction was as rare as hen's teeth. I think I can count on one hand how many times I've experienced it. Yet here it is. Loud and clear. A warm swell of interest, attraction. Lust.

'I won't make jokes about your marketing if you don't make jokes about this.' He points to the *Access All Areas* pass that he is wearing on a lanyard around his neck.

I don't smile, although I want to. It's a good retort. And yes, I think he *is* flirting with me, but the AAA pass means he is press. I have shareholders and board members to answer to, employees that I need to offer a role model to; I must watch my step. A man as attractive as this one will know how to turn on the charm to get a story. Most likely he's angling for an exclusive profile piece; he's probably writing something about women in power. I'll look like a prize fool if I'm too friendly and something I say is taken out of context. I've seen peers make shamefaced trips to HR, forced to make abject public apologies, being trolled or cancelled, not because they did something illegal or malicious but because of a careless word. Joking that I'd like to access all his areas would be momentarily amusing but professionally suicidal. I'm always very careful about what I say and how I behave. I'm considered by nature and cautious by necessity. Suddenly this outlook seems an inconvenience, a shame. I want to flirt with him.

I don't. I keep my face impassive.

If he is disappointed by my cool demeanour or concerned that he has crossed a line and his joke has landed badly, he doesn't acknowledge it. He smiles pleasantly, shoots out his hand for me to shake. I want to feel the weight and warmth of him. I want to know if his grip is firm; will he linger a fraction of a second longer than he ought?

It is.

He does.

Lovely.

'Matthew Charlton,' he declares.

'Emma Westly,' I reply.

He throws out a fast smile. 'Really, you don't need to intro-duce yourself. Your face is on half the conference marketing. You're the keynote speaker.'

I like it that he owns up to knowing who I am. Some people are shy about doing so, and that creates an unnecessary barrier of complexity. He is confident enough to admit he's impressed by me, or if that is going too far, too quickly, he is at least aware of me. Also lovely. I do a lot of keynote speaking. I spoke at the UN Biodiversity Conference in Montreal last year. I'm on an advisory committee that steered the 77th Session of the UN

General Assembly on Environmental Matters. I've spoken at the last three COP conventions – Bonn, Madrid and Glasgow – in front of prime ministers and presidents. I know my stuff; I believe in what I'm selling. A future for us all.

'You're speaking at three-thirty this afternoon, aren't you?' he says. 'I'm looking forward to it. In fact I'd go so far as to say you're the reason I'm here. Wouldn't miss it for the world.'

Public speaking does not intimidate me, so I'm surprised to note that suddenly I'm nursing a rare lick of nerves. The thought of his eyes on me as I stand on the stage causes a whisper of something to flutter in my stomach.

I want to impress.

3

When I walk onto the stage, I feel and hear the auditorium hum with excitement, scepticism, challenge and support. A thousand delegates are in attendance. I can't see beyond the first three rows; after that there is just blackness. He is sitting on the second row, fourth chair in from the far left. Keen. He wants me to see him. My eyes rest on him for a moment. I don't change my expression or acknowledge him, but he knows I know he is there. Is this a little cat and mouse? I think so, and although I'm out of practice and have arguably never been especially good at playing games, it seems natural to me. This is necessary to make the beginning of something – anything – notable, fun.

Outwardly, I deliver the speech with my usual calm confidence, infusing it with the necessary sense of urgency when required, tingeing it with threat but ultimately leaving things on a note of positivity. That's my style. My belief. We can make a difference. Saving our planet is going to require hard work and effort; however, if we all work together – by which

I mean *everyone*, from country leaders to coffee drinkers, heads of industry to those in post rooms – then there is hope. It's a matter of collective responsibility. I tell my audience about the initiatives my company are fast-tracking, how we're contributing towards the aim to be net zero. That's what I am here for, to willy-wave about my company's part in saving the world; it keeps the share price buoyant. It's necessary to start with the horrors – the floods, the melting icecaps, the deforestation, the famines. We're a population used to binge-watching streamer shows; we expect a lot of drama in the first ten minutes of a performance. However, I never want to terrify and alienate. That would be unhelpful. So I highlight positive steps that are taking place across the globe: the initiatives of other companies and governments that are committed to change. As usual, I conclude by promising that there is a future for our grandchildren and even for their grandchildren if we act quickly enough.

As I leave the stage, there is resounding applause, some people stand up. He's on his feet before anyone else and creates the momentum for the standing ovation. He seems animated, electrified. I don't let my gaze linger on him, and I remind myself that the ovation is for my company's work, not me personally. I'm a cog, that's all. Still, it's a buzz. I don't have children or grandchildren, but I might be a tiny part of saving the planet for those who do, and that is massive.

The delegates and speakers are invited to a drinks reception that starts in half an hour's time and is designed to soak up the couple of hours before dinner. When I first saw this on my agenda, I decided I would give it a miss. I know how those things generally go. At best, I'll be cornered by an earnest ecowarrior who wants to preach to the converted; at worst, I might encounter an aggressive climate-change denier. It is far wiser and more time-efficient to return to my hotel room and plough through emails. I'm not a networker, I'm a grafter. There is little to be gained by pressing flesh, rubbing shoulders and appearing accessible. Better to leave the delegates with the stormy, solid impression I made on the stage.

But now I feel differently.

I know that if I go to the bar, Matthew Charlton will find me, and I want exactly that. It's curious behaviour for me, but maybe I deserve a treat. I've been working really hard recently. We're buying a company that needs to be amalgamated into AirBright. The restructure will have an impact on systems, staff and physical space; it's a lot, and we're just at the beginning of the process. I want to indulge the undeniable frisson of excitement he's sparked, just for fun. I use the thirty minutes to dash to my room to freshen up and check emails marked urgent, then I'm back in the bar at 17.05. Not what anyone would call fashionably late, but I hope not excruciatingly obviously keen either.

He is leaning against the bar, gaze trained on the entrance. Our eyes clash immediately and I head towards him.

'I didn't know what to order for you,' he says, waving at two glasses of sparkling water. I like this. He presumed I would join him for a drink, but he didn't presume to do anything cringey like order a glass of champagne. Don't get me wrong, I enjoy drinking champagne, but not at work and not with men I've just met.

'Water is perfect.'

'Shall we find a seat.' It's not a question as such, more of an imperative. He immediately picks up his glass of water and his rucksack and steps away from the bar, glancing about, looking for a table. I've been on my feet all day, and although high heels at work are thankfully a thing of the past, I would like to sit down. And yes, I can't deny that being ensconced away from the throng and with him sounds ideal.

We find a small round table and two comfortable chairs in the far corner of the room. Most of the delegates are clinging to the bar and therefore it's quiet here. Perfect.

'So you're press? Who do you write for?' I ask, the moment we sit down. I need to know so I can evaluate what he wants. A story? Me?

'I don't write for anyone. I'm not press as such, I'm a free-lance photographer. The Access All Areas pass is something a friend blagged for me. I understand it entitles a person to a free drink at dinner tonight and the right to jump the queue in the canteen.'

I'm relieved. If he's not press, he doesn't want a story. I want to beam, but instead I say sardonically, 'Great perks. Have you exercised the queue-jumping privilege?'

'No, I'm too polite.'

I smile. 'So who are you freelancing for? What's your brief?'

'No one has commissioned me to be here. My plan is to take some great shots and then try to sell them to any of the papers, or put them on the websites that let people buy images for presentations and so on. You know Shutterstock, Getty and the like.'

I nod. I am aware of those services. My own marketing department often uses them. It's immediately apparent that Matthew isn't earning big bucks.

'Have you taken any great shots?'

He reaches into his rucksack and pulls out his camera. After a few clicks and whirrs, I find myself looking at images on a 5x3 cm preview screen on his SLR. Matthew leans close to me as he flicks through the photos he's taken. His body isn't touching mine, but I can feel the heat of him, smell his aftershave, and under that a note of sweat that I find strangely appealing. They are good, clear shots. Vibrant. They capture the subject's emotion and animation whilst managing to be flattering – not an easy task. Often a photograph of someone speaking makes them look like they've entered a gurning competition.

I am the subject. There are at least a dozen photos of me delivering my speech.

Just as I'm beginning to feel uncomfortable and wondering if he's a crazy stalker, we come to photographs of this morning's speakers: Gina McCarthy, a renowned specialist on air quality who served as the first White House National Climate Advisor, and Jim McNeill, a British polar explorer. There are at least nine or ten shots of each of them, which negates the stalker concern. There are also many others of delegates looking earnest, interested, sceptical or even, in one case, thoroughly bored. 'Is he napping?' I ask with a laugh.

'Yes, but don't worry, that wasn't taken during your lecture. I promise your audience were rapt.'

'You have some great shots. A cut above the usual conference photographer.'

He smiles, but not easily; it's a tight expression and I regret my comment. It sounds patronising. I am genuinely impressed. I'm usually rather unpleasantly surprised by images of myself. I always look a little older than I expect to. A little more worn in. In these shots I look strong, determined, authoritative. It's impossible to say as much without sounding oddly vain.

A silence falls across the table and I want to shoo it away. I consider asking him how he chooses which conferences to freelance at, but it all seems a bit impersonal, and that's not the note I want to strike with him. I'm grateful when he makes the next comment, even if it is still work-related.

'You were really impressive up there on the podium.'

'Thank you.'

'It must be quite something to be part of the solution.'

'It certainly makes going to work more compelling.'

He shakes his head in something like awe, certainly admiration. 'You seemed so relaxed when presenting. I'm not sure I could do anything like that. I like hiding behind my camera.'

'I'm normally very relaxed, yes. I believe what I'm saying about working towards a smart, decarbonised, decentralised energy system. I know my facts, so I don't have to rehearse.'

'Normally?'

I had slipped the word in because it was honest, but also as a small play. I wanted him to pick it up. 'I confess I was a little nervous today.' I take a sip of water.

'Because the delegation was so large?'

'Because you were in the audience.' I meet his eyes and smile slowly. 'I wanted to make a good impression.'

'Mission accomplished,' he says with a grin, sitting back in his chair.

4

After that, the conversation flows effortlessly. We talk about the TV shows we both know, the podcasts that interest us. I tell him how much I enjoy running, and he says he likes hiking but doesn't do it as often as he used to. When I did make the effort to go on dates, it was still with a mental checklist. Is he a psychopath? Is he a bigot? A *Star Trek* fan? These are all red flags for me. Everyone has a list now. It saves time, but it does kill chemistry.

We have chemistry.

The glorious strangeness of knowing someone is interested in that particular way – not because they have trawled countless profiles swiping left, left, left, then right, based entirely on a selection of static (often filtered) images – is exciting. I feel lit up, and consequently I become more sparkling, funny, confident. We make one another laugh by recounting our worst experiences of meeting people at conferences. His stories centre around being relentlessly pursued by those enthusiastic delegates whose goal in life is to have their photo in the local paper.

'One man wanted a more edgy corporate photo at an insurance conference and insisted the delegates recreate a mosh pit. To his credit, he'd given it some thought: he arrived with whistles and smiley-face T-shirts that he wanted people to wear.'

'That sounds fun,' I say, smiling. 'Certainly not problematic.'

'Right, that's what I thought at first, but he wanted to crowd-surf. We had to do about ten takes and people got tired. They dropped him.'

'Deliberately?' I gasp.

'Not sure. Anyway, he refused to be derailed from his aim. He insisted I travel with him in the ambulance and "carry on snapping".'

'Did he make it into the local paper?' I ask, laughing.

'I hope so. He deserved to after all that.'

'My worst experience was when I was mistaken for my PA, Edward, and Edward was mistaken for the CEO. I guess the speaker was listed as E. Westly,' I confess.

'And the conference organiser made the assumption that the man must hold the more senior role,' Matthew guesses.

'Correct. Despite Edward being twenty years my junior.'

'And when was the mistake identified?'

'When they tried to push me off the stage and drag Edward on.'

By talking about the worst experiences of meeting people at these types of events, we are of course telling one another that *this* experience is pretty good. One of the best. We swap to wine, sharing a bottle of Cloudy Bay Sauvignon Blanc. Matthew tells me that he's recently moved back to the UK from New York. He was born in New Zealand and brought up in South Africa. 'My dad was a diplomat.'

'Wow, that sounds glamorous.'

'I suppose it does.' He grimaces slightly theatrically, in a way that suggests he's often told this story and knows how to counter the suggestion that he was brought up in an overly privileged way. 'As a kid, I just remember wishing my parents didn't have so many functions in the evening, that they'd stay home, maybe read me a story, tuck me in like other kids' parents did. Plus, I really wanted the same accent as everyone else at school.'

'You don't have an accent at all,' I comment.

'That was the point. All the other kids sounded like they were New Zealanders or South Africans. My parents wanted me to sound BBC English. It was hard.'

I try not to react. I have learnt how to hold my face in an impassive expression, not to judge people's childhood resentments. Experience has shown me that most people have a minor gripe: they felt another sibling was favoured; they weren't allowed a TV in their room; they were made to play sport to an exhausting level to realise a parent's unfulfilled ambition. I can always trump it. I wish I couldn't.

Matthew continues. 'I longed for a sibling. Maybe if I'd had one, I wouldn't have felt so lonely.' He sighs, and I do feel a tiny bit sorry for him. I can empathise with loneliness, but I'd have given anything to have parents who dragged me from one country to another. 'Do you have siblings?' he asks.

'A younger brother.' I don't offer any more. I hope he moves on. If he doesn't, and if I'm honest, then the mood is going to be ruined.

'And what about your parents?' It's an open question. I could dodge it, but I decide it's best to get it on the table and out of the way, although I am aware I'm about to land the least flirtatious sentence in the history of dating.

'They're dead.'

'Oh, I'm so very sorry. How sad.' He doesn't look away embarrassed or mumble. I'm impressed that he's offered two sentences rather than the more usual two-word platitude people generally manage. 'When did they die?' he asks.

'I was twelve and my brother was ten.'

'How?'

'A car accident.' I take a large gulp of wine and glance around the room. I should be used to telling this story. I've delivered this fact about my life on dozens, probably hundreds of occasions. Over time, I've taught myself not to show any emotion about it, as I find that if I do so, it embarrasses whoever it is that has stumbled into the conversation about families. I'm so British that even when talking about the death of my parents, my greatest concern is making other people feel comfortable with it. I usually say something like 'Oh, it was a long time ago'; sometimes I even joke, 'Why are you sorry? It's not like you planted the tree they ploughed into, did you?' Gallows humour.

'There was this crazy woman who stepped out into the road. Dad swerved to avoid her but ended up ploughing into a tree. He died immediately. My mother died eight hours later in hospital.'

Matthew does not do what most people do. He doesn't look at his feet, turn away or turn the conversation. He reaches out and squeezes my fingertips with his own. His hand is warm; my fingers are always cold.

'That must have been horrific. I'm sorry to hear you went through that, I really am. Dealing with the death of your most loved people at any age is horrendous, but I can't imagine what it must have been like to endure that as a child.' Tears unexpectedly nip at my eyes. I'm blindsided by his sincerity. 'I get it,' he adds. 'I really do.'

'You've lost your parents?' I ask.

'No, not my parents. My wife. She died last year.'

I draw in a sharp breath. Despite years of being on the receiving end of people's response to such bleak news, I find I'm not sure how to handle it. I'm disappointed in myself, but the truth is, the thoughts going through my head right now are not for sharing. Matthew is in his mid-thirties, I'd guess. His wife obviously died before her time. It's a horrible story. Awful. Completely tragic.

So it's totally inappropriate that somewhere deep in my brain a little voice is saying, 'This does mean he's single, though. Every cloud has a silver lining.'

An outrageous thought.

5

The two-hour drinks reception flies by. I get this odd sensation that I want to somehow grab time physically with both hands and dig in my heels to slow things down, but time can't be manipulated at will.

At dinner, we are seated at different tables, too far away from one another to make eye contact. I'm so tempted to mess with the seating plan, but as my guests are sponsors of the conference, they deserve my full attention. It would be undisciplined and out of character of me to prioritise this flirtation. I resist. By the time the food is eaten and plates are cleared, I discover Matthew has left the dining room.

The next morning I get up at 5.08 as usual. I am dependent on street light. The yellow electric light slips through the gaps between buildings like paint spilt. It is peculiar running through a city rather than the woods. A totally different experience. My muscles still ache, the sweat gathers in my eyes and on my back; the difference is there is no space. I miss my black treelines, punchy against the opaque quiet country light that stretches across the boundary of my land. I run in loops, dodging people hurrying, head down, to or from early or late shifts; traffic cones, buses, bikes, pools of vomit – a badge of someone's revelry the night before. Despite the unsatisfactory nature of the exercise, I enjoy my limbs stretching, my lungs burning. I'm in a great mood.

I shave some minutes off my usual routine as I settle for a shop-bought smoothie. By 6.10, I'm ready to check out. I'm planning on leaving a message for him with reception. While running, I mentally composed something friendly but not exposing. The age gap looms like a tall wall, but one I think I can scale. On the hotel notepaper I scribble a request for copies of the photos he took, but when I ask if I can leave the note for Mr Charlton, I'm informed that he has already left.

'No message for me?' I ask, hoping to sound breezy. Almost certainly I don't, because the receptionist grimaces sympathetically as she shakes her head.

Right.

There's no refuting the brutal fact that my romantic opportunities have diminished exponentially with every passing year since I turned thirty, so I'm no stranger to disappointment. However, his vanishing without swapping numbers or even saying goodbye after our great chat in the bar last night stings. I straighten my shoulders, take a deep breath – literally and metaphorically sucking it up – and head to the airport. From there I catch a plane back to Heathrow and a Tube to the office. This is why I love my job. There's always a to-do list waiting for me. It is reliable.

I'm not the sort to constantly think about a brief encounter with a man; my mind is absorbed by bigger things. That said, I find my thoughts wandering. I think of his eyes, which were revealed slowly as his lids rested half closed, giving him a relaxed vibe. I think of his body. He's clearly fit, with the sort of leanness that promises a six-pack; he has good forearms. I decide I will allow my mind to drift his way for up to five working days. That's it. Tops. Within that time it is perfectly possible that he'll reach out to me. I'm easy to find if he wants to, and if he doesn't, well, so be it. Despite this resolve and faux-serenity, I catch myself living with the shameful wait that others have described to me but I haven't experienced since being in my late teens. Waiting for his call, waiting for an email, waiting for a request on Instagram or LinkedIn. I've always tried to stay above this sort of nonsense.

Early on the morning of the fourth day of this self-imposed deadline, my marketing director runs into my office looking openly stressed. He's currently very wrapped up in the project of rebuilding the company website. It's dated and not especially user-friendly. The new site will feature an introduction to the executive team; the aim is to present us as approachable in a time when everyone distrusts everyone, and energy providers most of all. Even green ones. A lot of people dislike getting their photo taken. I've heard several people on the exec team express concern about how jowly or old they look. I say people, I mean women. The men – notably more jowly, notably older – do not seem bothered by the idea of their image being captured for posterity. For that reason, I've refused to utter a single word about my qualms, although I have them too. I do not want to perpetuate the narrative that whether I am judged to be attractive or not is relevant. I'm a conscious feminist.

It's exhausting.

The employees concerned about their wrinkles and excess pounds want serious, straight-to-camera black-and-white photos, assuming they're more likely to be flattering or certainly easier to Photoshop. The marketing team have argued that as the brief is to present us as an approachable company, candid colour photos must be the order of the day. A guy with his hair tied into a casual topknot explained to us what he was hoping for. 'You know the sort of thing, head thrown back, an irrepressible laugh escaping, hashtag trustworthy.'

Hashtag really? I kept the thought to myself and suggested that we brief the photographer to take two sets of images. Today is the day the exec team are to have their photos taken, but the marketing director is panicked, as the photographer has phoned to say he's sick. 'Can't we just postpone the shoot for a week?' I ask.

'No. The website launch will slip, and coordinating diaries to get everyone in the office has been the absolute worst. We need a replacement, but what photographer of any calibre will be available at short notice?' He looks frazzled. I tell myself I'm just doing him a favour. I have no vested interest.

'Long shot, but look up a guy called Matthew Charlton. His work is excellent. Tell him we'll pay three times his usual rate if he can work today. I'm pretty sure he needs the money, so the offer will be too good to miss. If he has anything in his diary, he'll most likely cancel.'

Matthew is in the office by 11 a.m. I'm not sure what sort of reception to give or expect to receive. When all's said and done, we had a few drinks and a chat. I have no way of knowing whether he's that polite, interested, interesting with everyone he meets. He probably thought of me as safely older and therefore he was excitingly direct because there was no sexual attraction on his part. None whatsoever. Bleak thought. It's most sensible to simply remain professional and a little aloof. A little aloof is never a bad move. I'm the sort of person who would prefer to be underdressed than overdressed at a party. However, when it's my turn to go to the boardroom, which has been turned into a mini studio for today's purposes, I nip to the loo and zhuzh my hair.

He seems delighted to see me, which is a relief. I thought I recalled him clearly, so I'm shocked to discover how vibrant he is in the flesh. Even bigger and better and brighter than I recalled. The attraction I felt instantly reasserts itself. Damn. This is only good news if I get something back from him to suggest he feels the same.

He's running late. It quickly becomes apparent that people like to linger around him. He smiles a lot; he tells funny stories, cracks jokes. His jokes aren't delivered in an oppressive, give-me-all-your-attention manner; he appears naturally witty and gregarious in a low-key way. It's obvious he wants to make people feel relaxed, and he succeeds. He has an endearing habit of throwing out gentle little compliments.

'I like your earrings. The way they catch the light makes it seem as though they're winking at me.'

Elizabeth, head of sales, reaches up to touch her earrings. 'Oh, these. My husband got them for me for our last anniversary.' She smiles. Click. A photo that will no doubt capture her recalling her wedding anniversary.

'Mate, great skin-fade.' Raj, who leads the digital division, shyly runs his hand over his shaved head and grins. Click. A photo that will capture the pleasure felt when someone appreciates the effort you've made.

Finally it's my turn to be photographed, and he says simply, 'Ah, I've saved the best until last.' And there it is, something extra for me. 'How've you been?' he asks.

'Good, good. Fine. Busy,' I reply unimaginatively. He starts to click the camera.

'Thanks for giving me this work.'

'We were stuck.' My response isn't especially elegant, although it is true. Matthew laughs.

'Well, I'm grateful.' I smile at the camera and say nothing. I'm not being coy; I just don't want to be captured mid-sentence. Matthew continues. 'Because I've been racking my brains for an excuse to get in touch. I've been wondering whether there's a partner in the background, and if there isn't, whether you would be interested in going out. Maybe dinner?'

'No, no partner.' I beam broadly back at him, relief and delight flooding through my bones.

Click. 'I think that's the shot,' he says with a confident grin. 'And my answer.'

6

March

'So, you're alive then,' Heidi says as she picks up the bottle of wine that stands glistening in the ice bucket on the table. The bar is loud with the sound of chatter and laughter, good times, but still I can hear my friend's disapproval and frustration in me. I throw her what I hope is a winning smile. She pours a generous measure of wine into the third glass; the other two are less than half full, underlining the fact that I'm late. Matthew was on the phone, and I just lost track of time. So unlike me. I'm not even sure what we were talking about. Nothing, something, everything.

It was Matthew who pointed out, 'Hey, I thought we weren't seeing each other tonight because you're going out with your friends.'

'That's right. I'm meeting them at seven-thirty.'

'Have you seen the time? You're going to be late.'

Gina stands up and leans over the bar table, offering me a hug and a wide beam. She's the easier-going out of the two. Heidi doesn't move from her chair; she's sulking with me but that's not the reason she doesn't hug me. She knows me better than anyone and she knows that I'm not really the hugging type. I do it occasionally, because other people seem to expect it and feel slighted if I don't, but she gives me my space.

'We thought you'd fallen off the edge of the planet,' she mutters.

'The planet is round, Heidi, and there's gravity, so you don't have to worry about that.' I stick my tongue out and pull a daft face so she knows I'm trying to be funny.

'Smart arse.' She clinks her glass against mine. I'm forgiven.

Heidi and Gina are my best friends. Honestly, they are my only real friends. Of course I have endless friendly colleagues, but I think those relationships might be situational. We find ourselves thrown together at industry events and have a chat and a laugh because we have a lot in common. Heidi, Gina and I have very little in common nowadays. They are both married stay-at-home mums. Heidi has three teen kids: Troy, her eldest, is at uni, Fifi and Aaliyah are still at school. They live in Woking, Surrey, and have for twenty years. Gina lives in Kingston, also Surrey. She and her husband, Mick, started their family later. They have an eight-year-old, Lottie, who we all dote upon as the baby of the group.

My best friends spend their time doing school runs or pick-ups from parties, drunken experimental ones in nightclubs or ones with fairy cakes and bouncy castles (either way, the parents know the party is over when the guests start to throw up or cry). They worry about school league tables and their kids' friendship groups. I spend my time in meeting rooms worrying about profit and loss and carbon emissions in the FTSE 100 supply chains. Yet despite the fact that our day-to-day experiences are not at all similar, we *are* best friends. We trust one another completely, tell each other everything, and we have history. If ever either of them rang to tell me they'd killed their husband, I'd reach for a shovel and jump in my car. Not that it is a scenario that's likely to be tested: they both have husbands who make them happy.

Heidi and I met at Birmingham University almost thirty years ago. She was the first black friend I ever had. I studiously avoided the subject of colour with her for months because I thought that was the least prejudiced thing to do – ignore our differences, pretend there weren't any. But she put me right when she explained that her life experiences in no way mirrored mine, and pretending they did wasn't especially helpful.

She told me that teachers at school often commented on her 'unruly' hair, which was in fact a completely natural afro, and insisted she 'crop it'. When she refused, she was excluded from school. This happened twice. She explained that when browsing around shops, she was often trailed by security guards. Once when she was on a train, reading *The Catcher in the Rye*, she heard a middle-aged woman say to her husband, 'What's she reading that for?' The husband responded, 'I'm surprised she can read at all.' Shocking, right? Yes, if you're white. Apparently not if you're a person of colour. It happens too often to still shock.

'This is the low-grade stuff. You should hear what my dad and brother deal with,' she told me. 'You'd never guess how many times they've been stopped and searched, pulled over in allegedly "random" car checks, the aggression they face on the street, at work.' She broke off at that point. I got the sense there was more but she couldn't bear getting into it. I told her it sounded awful, that I had no idea, that I burnt with fury that such arseholes were out there wallowing in ignorance, spreading hate. She said she appreciated my anger. 'The thing is, it's just sadder being me. Not because I am black – I'm proud of that and who I am. It's sadder because I've known how crap the world is from an early age and most people of colour have the same experience. You whities get to live in la-la world for far longer. Sometimes indefinitely.'

Then I told her about being orphaned.

Not the fast, edited account, but the messy truth. My family situation was not something I had ever spoken of to my friends at school, and I hadn't planned on breaking my rule of reserve at university, but she'd been so brave in revealing her vulnerable moments to me, I wanted to show her the same respect. 'My dad was driving drunk. My dad was often drunk. I didn't grieve for him because I hated him for being so bloody stupid and selfish and weak and destructive.' I was panting as I confessed this, the words exploding out of me like bullets. 'My paternal grandparents weren't people my brother and I had been close to, either physically or emotionally. They'd found their son an embarrassment and so had given up on him and cut him off before he even met my mum. Something they maybe regretted. Anyway, they offered us a home, of sorts, after the accident. I was sent to an all-girls boarding school, my brother was sent to one for boys. They simply thought that was the proper thing to do. Or maybe the easiest thing to do. I don't know.'

I admitted that I had fared better than Tom. Yes, I was lonely and isolated, but I threw myself into my schoolwork. People said he was attention-seeking when really he was grief-stricken. He made friends with whoever caused the most trouble at school. Too much cash and time, not enough direction, age thirteen he and his mates were all taking drugs. By eighteen he had visited the Priory three times. He was generally considered, by anyone who could be bothered to express an opinion, a lost cause. 'Very much like his father' was the verdict. There is a big difference; I love Tom, although even I admit he's not easy.

'My grandparents allowed us to go to theirs in the holidays, but they didn't go so far as to make themselves available. Instead they timed their trips to the French Riviera, Barbados and Aspen to coincide with the summer, Easter and Christmas breaks. My brother and I stayed with staff, paid to monitor us.'

When I finished telling Heidi about my childhood, her eyes were like saucers. I'm still not sure if that was because she was impressed with my grandparents' holiday locations or horrified by my life. 'It's a conundrum which of us has it worse,' she commented drily. 'The black kid with loving parents who is irrationally hated by strangers and consequently will have limited economic options, or the rich white kid who has every financial advantage in the world but isn't loved by anyone.'

It was such a shocking thought to articulate that all we could do was laugh out loud. 'Why are we laughing?' I asked as we rolled about on the thin, cheap carpet in her small student bedroom; helpless, barely able to breathe.

'Because of the old adage, if you don't laugh, you'll cry, I guess.'

Heidi has the widest smile and always wears bright red lipstick. She did then and does now. It's her signature look. She was laughing so hard, little bubbles of saliva popped on her teeth, and I felt such fierce love for her. That Easter she invited me to her home for the holidays. I've never been alone at a holiday since.

Heidi and I met Gina when we were twenty-five. Heidi was trying to tone up for her upcoming wedding to Leon, and so we'd started to go to fitness classes at the local sports centre. The classes were run by an instructor who hadn't updated her routine since the early nineties. There was a lot of energetic side bends and jumping jacks, she constantly bellowed things like 'No pain, no gain, ladies!' It was probably something to do with evolution and survival instinct, but we habitually set up our mats in the same spot, at the back of the hall, as far away from the instructor as we could possibly get. Gina always set up a row in front of us. She was, from the off, comedy gold. This is in part because she has absolutely no clue which is her left and which is her right. Heidi claims she once wet herself laughing at Gina's earnest, hopeless attempts to T-step to four counts and round the world, knee lift, clockwise.

A plain-speaking northerner, Gina would provide a no-inhibitions running commentary, often piping up with things like 'My leg does not go there and wouldn't even for Keanu Reeves', 'I'm dying, you sadist' and once, most memorably for the subsequent formation of our little gang, 'Sod this for a game of soldiers, I'm off to the pub.' Then she left, mid-class. The brilliant thing is, Heidi and I shared a glance and followed her. Heidi saw that Gina was a soulmate. I'm the yin to Heidi's yang, but we are not alike. There was space for Gina in our friendship.

We are a strong threesome. We love each other equally but differently. Like the legs of a stool, we need each other and offer support without any of the ugly jealousies or insecurities that women are so often – and so unfairly – accused of. Gina and I were both single until ten years ago. We discussed dates, analysed texts, offered advice when things were going well and then shared negronis when things fell apart. I'd assumed that we'd stroll into old age together, keep one another company on bank holidays. Gina used to say she was looking forward to going on Saga cruises, where we'd eat our body weight in chocolate gateau at the all-inclusive buffet. 'No one can resist one of those. Even you,' she'd tease.

However, ten years ago, the boy she had dated at sixth form got in touch out of the blue. He had moved to London and didn't know anyone there at all. He said he didn't know how to go about making friends outside work. The two of them met up. Gina was expecting to share a list of restaurants and bars worth a visit, perhaps give him some instruction on how to pronounce Marylebone, Southwark and Ruislip so he didn't come across as a tourist. As it happened, they shared a long-buried chemistry and were engaged within six months, married within a year. I'd tried to hide my unbecoming frustration at the fact that as I'd gone to an all-girls school instead of the local comprehensive, I didn't have a childhood sweetheart to fall back on. 'Fall back in love with,' Heidi corrected me when I mentioned as much to her.

I fake-groaned and admitted what I was thinking. 'You're happy that she's joining your married-people gang. But you have a doting husband and three kids. You don't need any more company. I'm doomed to be an old spinster, and I'll be doing that all alone.'

She wouldn't indulge me. 'This isn't about you, Emma.'

'I know. But what am I to do now?'

'Buy an expensive gift and slap on a smile. That's what friends do.'

I followed Heidi's advice, of course. When Gina asked me to be bridesmaid, I acted as if it was all I'd ever dreamed of. I threw her a fabulous hen party: chocolate fountain, a life-drawing class with a hot naked guy as the model, and a cocktail-fuelled afternoon tea. It was the right call, I knew it then when I struggled with it and I know it now, a decade on, when I see she's a happy wife and mum.

We meet in central London once a month. I missed last month's get-together because, frankly, I just didn't want to get out of bed as I'd finally just got in there with Matthew. We had nine dates, over four weeks, before we had sex. He said I was his first lover since his wife had passed. Part of me wished he had bashed out his grief with three or four meaningless hook-ups before we'd met, but as he hadn't, I was aware that when we climbed into bed it would mean something to both of us. Once we got there, it fast became my favourite place to be. I realise blowing out Heidi and Gina goes against the catchy maxim 'mates over dates', but I can't tell you how many times they have blown me out because one of their kids had football practice or felt unwell or because their husbands hadn't got home from work early enough to take over on the childcare. As you get older, you realise there isn't a snappy little rhyme to explain that priorities change.

'So work's been busy?' Gina asks as I reach for my wine glass. I take a couple of large gulps. They'll appreciate the fact that I'm trying to catch up; it demonstrates my commitment to our evening. I can't resent the fact that she assumes my absence is due to work. It usually is. However, I see the pair of them share a look that feels exclusory, and it chafes. I can't quite discern the exact nature of the look. I think maybe it is one of pity, or boredom, or duty. It infuriates me that they might pity me for having such an exhilarating, purposeful career, and it hurts me that they might think it's a boring duty to listen to me talk about it. Although, to be honest, I often feel a little that way when they start talking about school catchment areas or the change in swim club instructor. I just try not to let it show. It's rare that we draw battle lines that flagrantly highlight that we're on separate paths. I know their hint of irritation is the result of my being unavailable recently. I have been very wrapped up in my own world. I want to defuse any tension that might be brewing by talking about something that I know will grab them in a way my work doesn't.

'I've met someone,' I announce. Their eyes bounce to my face. I'm grinning.

'Someone you like a lot!' exclaims Gina, reading me correctly.

'Details,' demands Heidi, instantly gripped.

7

The getting-to-know-you stage of a relationship is – if you believe the romcoms – a delightful ensemble of fun dates, chock-a-block with deep and meaningful conversations, stargazing and laughter. My actual experience of dating has exposed that the reality is far from that. It's tricky, not least because we all have our secrets and habits. I am not keen to reveal how often I dye my grey roots or the time I spend reading the deplorable sidebar of celeb gossip. Plus I snore; I know because I have woken myself up doing so. Yet even accepting all of the above, I maintain the guys I dated before Matthew were still getting the better part of the deal. Men, as they start to approach their forties, just don't bring it to the table. They are often boring, lazy, messy or sullen. I don't think I need to elaborate. Those who have been there get it, those who haven't wouldn't believe it. Safe to say the getting-to-know-one-another stage is often fraught, sharing bathroom space is awkward, finding common interests is rare, and sex is seldom orgasmic.

However, with Matthew the romcom vibe is there in all its

glory. Our dates have been thrilling. We've been to concerts, a mixologist class, a circus skills workshop and several bottomless brunches, not just a coffee in the local dreary chain. He took me to a filthy old pub in the East End that he promised was 'the real deal'. It was. There he taught me how to play darts and we ate jellied eels, which don't taste as bad as they sound. We've been to a trendy neon-lit bar where we played ping-pong while we drank espresso martinis. He thinks my snoring is sweet and says it's really more of a purr, which is a lie but a kind one.

And the sex? The sex has been good from the get-go and has continued to get better and better. We've tipped into the needy erotic stage. The filthy, fascinating, fleeting part of a relationship when you want each other even when you're in the company of others, even when you're bone-tired, when you're watching TV, or at a restaurant, or driving. My body craves his.

Possibly even better yet, the conversations we have on these fun and hot date nights are meaningful and careful. Despite his tragic loss, or maybe because of it, he is emotionally available and talks to me about how he thinks and feels about a myriad of subjects. Actually, he is more 'in touch' with his feelings than I am with mine. We are living in an era where it's fashionable to constantly talk about mental health, but I often find I'm out of step. I would have done well in the 1940s, when the stiff upper lip was the order of the day. Since my father drove my mother into a tree, people have been asking, 'Do you want to talk?' I don't, I never do. Why would I want to talk about that?

'Becky always wanted to talk,' commented Matthew when I made it clear that baring my soul isn't a priority for me. 'She wanted to sit and define love and life and look at what it all means.'

'That sort of thing embarrasses me,' I admitted.

'You don't feel things like she did,' he mused aloud.

'You're saying she was deeper?' I tried to keep the hurt out of my voice, but I felt somehow judged and lacking, in comparison to his more profound, passionate late wife.

He rolled his eyes and laughed. 'No, I'm saying she was more trouble. More work.'

I shouldn't be thrilled by this; it's verging on the misogynistic view that all women are mad if they are deep, that they are trouble if they feel. But this confession – this total honesty – was a relief. The thing is, dating Matthew is wonderful, but negotiating the presence of a dead ex is a new experience for me, and oddly a little tricker than negotiating the presence of a live one. A dead wife can do no wrong. I've learnt to live with the fact that dating at my age means there is usually a significant ex lurking in the background; often there are children and even ex-in-laws to contend with. Normally I can rationalise, accommodate, understand. If they were happy with the ex, they'd still be with the ex; as they are not, they can't have been happy. In this way, even a divorcee can be viewed as a clean slate. A fair chance. However, it's not the same if the spouse died. In Matthew and Becky's case, they'd still be together if they could be. I'm second choice, not a second chance. I'm make do and mend. I'm cross with myself for having these thoughts, which are self-indulgent, absurd. But I have them all the same.

I was glad I'd kept them to myself when he added with a grin, 'I'm much more of an actions-speak-louder-than-words sort of person too.' Then he slipped his hand up my skirt and his fingers quickly edged my knickers to the side. I felt things for sure at that point, real and physical things. I don't know if she ever felt the same things. For a few minutes, I just didn't care.

It's been a while since I've dated and longer still since either of my friends have, so it would be mean to stint on the details. I tell them how we met, and all about the fun and varied dates. I show them his website. They're impressed by his work and the photograph of him.

'Oh, very nice,' says Heidi. She says 'nice' in a way that sounds dirty. We all laugh loudly, drawing the eyes and attention of others in the bar as we're so joyful and raucous.

Gina adds, 'He looks gorgeous.' She rolls the word playfully around her mouth. I tell them that he not only looks gorgeous, he *is* gorgeous.

'How so?' asks Heidi, her interest pricked. I've never been the sort to wax lyrical about relationships. I'm normally cautious, not especially optimistic. Matthew has got under my skin in an unusual way. In a good way.

'He's thoughtful. Reliable,' I reply happily. 'He texts when he says he will, and he calls more often than texting anyway.'

The calls are sometimes long and rambling getting-to-know-you chats. Charged with glee that it is going so well and fear that it might go wrong. Other calls are more prosaic, centred around who is picking up supper. We've catapulted at a rate of knots into a steady relationship. No games. No miscommunication. No second-guessing.

'He's so straightforward,' I tell my friends. 'So wonderfully uncomplicated.' I'm grinning broadly. I perhaps do too good a job of making him sound brilliant, because Gina and Heidi look for the catch. Gina asks, 'Is he married?'

'No.'

'Really, though?' probes Heidi. 'You can tell us.'

'We won't judge,' Gina assures me.

'We will, but with a level of compassion, keeping in mind your previous good character,' clarifies Heidi.

'He is *not* married.'

'So divorced then, with kids. A Kardashian-size family, and each and every one of them a nightmare?'

'No.'

'How old did you say he was?'

I hadn't. 'Thirty-six,' I admit.

'So this is a non-exclusive thing, then? Considering his age, he must have a harem of hopefuls,' says Heidi.

'No, he's all in. He's explicitly said as much.' I can't help grinning.

Heidi narrows her eyes, suspicious. 'Solvent?'

'Not wealthy, but doing fine.'

'His own hair and teeth?'

I laugh and nod but feel a throb in the back of my head. Of course, they're right, there *is* a catch.

'He's a widower,' I announce.

'His wife's dead?'

'Yeah, that's what it means, Gina.'

She blushes and looks uncomfortable. 'No, I know. Obviously. I'm just saying, you don't expect it, do you?'

I shake my head. No, we don't expect it here in the buzzy, busy pub. We're a generation brought up on a constant stream of affirmations that insist happiness is within our grasp, that it will be ours if we are simply kind or focused or drink enough oat milk lattes, but the truth is, life can be horrible.

Sad. Obviously, I've known this longer than most. It always surprises me when other people expect life to be forever fair and fun. It seems so naive.

'How long were they married?' asks Heidi.

'Ten years. They were together six before that.'

'Wow, that's a long time, and since they were young.'

'Yes.'

'That takes some getting over,' chips in Gina.

'If you *ever* get over it,' points out Heidi.

They both look at me with concern. I know what they're thinking. They're worried for me now. They're already making assumptions, judgements, drawing the conclusion that I'll never be the love of his life. The dead wife, the first wife, will always hold that position.

'I think he's focused on getting on with it. That's the most he can do,' I say, determined to fill my usual space, that of being sensible.

'When did he lose her?' asks Gina.

I inwardly roll my eyes at the expression. Matthew didn't mislay Becky, like a pair of reading glasses or a wallet. She *died*. I am not a fan of the euphemisms that people sink into around death. I try not to show any prickliness when I answer. 'Ten months ago.' I know what's coming.

'Less than a year,' Heidi interjects with a splutter of disbelief. She tuts and shakes her head. It's a familiar gesture; her teenagers are often on the wrong end of it, as are tardy serving staff in restaurants. The condemnation is loud and clear.

I probe. It's like pulling at a loose thread on your favourite jumper. You know you shouldn't, because the whole thing will unravel, but you do it anyhow. 'What's your point?'

'Is he definitely ready to move on? It's just that rebound relationships are fun, but they never last, do they? You seem unusually excited about this. I just don't want to see you get hurt.' To be fair, she does look as though it pains her to say this. Still, I bristle.

'It doesn't feel like a rebound thing.'

'So didn't he like her much?' she asks bluntly.

'He loved her deeply,' I'm embarrassed by how heavy that sentence is. He loved her deeply and he still does, but she's gone. The thought causes a tightness in my throat. I force myself to say, 'We've only been seeing each other a few weeks. It's not a big deal. I'm just having fun. I was simply explaining why I've been unavailable.' I feel disloyal talking about us in this way. Backtracking, making out it's not as important as I think it is. We have in fact been seeing each other for two months, and it feels longer. Still, my lie works. Heidi looks relieved.

'Understood. We can't compete with new-relationship sex,' she says with a grin, willing to let me off the hook. She doesn't want to think I'm heading for trouble. Besides, she knows I'm always calm and assured around men. I can look after myself.

'All those lovely orgasms,' adds Gina. 'I really can't remember when I last had one for real. I'm so tired all the time, I just fake them to get Mick to get on with it so we can go to sleep.'

Heidi laughs, but doesn't go into detail about her orgasm situation with Leon. Instead she starts to tell us about the latest row she's having with her youngest, Aaliyah, who aged fourteen is outraged by the suggested curfew time of 11 p.m. Gina then vents about an ongoing row she's having with her neighbour about planning permission for her kitchen extension. Our conversation mooches around how tricky it is to get a dentist appointment, how incredibly convenient it is to renew prescriptions on the NHS app, and the latest MP leaked text scandal. I don't join in much. Largely I stay in my head.

Where Matthew is.

When the night has bled away, we split the tab. It's a shame that this process always creates a moment's tension that we each studiously pretend to ignore. I could easily pay the bill, and I itch to offer to do so, but experience has shown me that it's best not to. Only rich people say money doesn't matter.

As I stuff my arms into my coat, Gina pulls me into a big hug and asks, 'So how did the wife die? You never said.'

'She fell off a ladder at work. She was a theatre set designer, a really talented one.' Those were Matthew's words. 'She did lots of big Broadway shows.'

'Broadway?'

'They were living in New York at the time. Had been for about four years. She was working late one night. The show was about to open, but they were woefully behind schedule. Everyone was under pressure. Matthew thinks she was most likely tired. Exhausted.' My friends wear masks of polite sympathy, the sort of expressions that confirm a death is always tragic, but reveal that they can't get heavily involved because they didn't know her. 'They think she noticed a problem with the chandelier. Not a real one, a prop, part of the set design. They deduced as much because a bulb was out.'

'She was on her own?' Heidi asks.

'The rest of her team had gone home. She'd urged them to. Apparently, that was very like her. Diligent, hard-working to a fault.' I repeat these compliments Matthew has bestowed on Becky. I've heard many. His conversations are littered with them. She apparently was 'incredibly funny', 'could tell a story brilliantly, had people hanging on her every word', 'was very aware of other people's feelings. You know, watched them closely.' With every positive review he gives her, I smile back widely and nod.

Once I pushed myself to say, 'She sounds like my sort of woman. I bet I'd have liked her.' But my generosity was not enough. Matthew replied, 'Of course. Everyone did.'

As we step into the cold, black night and pull the door of the pub behind us, shutting in the good-time noise and adjusting to the comparatively quiet street, I reveal something else Matthew told me about Becky's death. 'They didn't find her until the next day. If help had come sooner, they might have saved her.'

'Tragic,' murmurs Gina, shaking her head solemnly.

'Yes, yes, it is,' I agree.

For Becky.

8

I live in Hampshire. I moved out of London when I turned forty, which was the same year I became CEO of AirBright. I had wanted to live in the country for many years, but I wasn't quite brave enough to make the move. I clung to London's grubby, vibrant streets to ward off something that people might call loneliness but for me was more of a fear of being direction-less or unnoticed. Forgotten. My twenties had been a whirl of long hours clawing up the career ladder, and when I wasn't working, I dashed from brunches to lunches, to matinee movies, to cocktail bars and nightclubs. I worked equally long hours in my thirties, but my recreational time became more about attending lectures at the Royal Geographical Society or going on marches and demonstrations highlighting environmental concerns; evenings were spent at theatres, concerts and jazz clubs. There is always something to do in London, something to amuse and distract. Time flew by. I felt busy, full. I worried that if I moved out of the capital, I would lose that.

Becoming CEO was the badge I needed that unequivocally

announced I was a grown-up, and that even though I did not have a partner or the fecundity that necessitated a bigger home, I was successful in terms of my career and did not need to cling to London to provide a sense of meaning. I had purpose, and I knew that would move with me, emanate from me, no matter where I lived. What I needed next was a space to think, to strategise, to grow. I wanted a home that reflected my values, status and achievements. It was satisfying to realise that being settled was not a matter of settling down or settling for.

I bought a plot of land in a remote part of Hampshire, the county where I was born and lived until my parents' deaths. On some level I was 'going home'. I recognised the names of familiar towns and villages on signposts, and the curve of some roads; I remembered being driven along them by my parents. I hired an architect and set about building my own state-of-the-art eco-friendly house on the edge of the New Forest. I called it Woodview. Not the most imaginative of names, but I am not the most imaginative person. Far from it.

My beautiful home gives me so much emotional satisfaction. At the time of building, Heidi and Gina referred to the house project as my 'baby', which wasn't entirely inaccurate. I certainly lavished money, time and attention. It was important to me that the build was as efficient and sustainable as possible. To cut down on the carbon footprint and to support local industry, I insisted that all the materials and workforce were sourced from within a forty-mile radius of the property. Wherever possible, I opted for natural, non-toxic, sustainable materials. The energy is all solar- or wind-generated. I installed systems to allow rainwater harvesting and used the latest innovation in wall insulation.

The house is sparsely furnished, mostly with salvaged 1950s wooden pieces; the soft furnishings reflect the environment outside, a series of calm neutrals or verdant green fabrics. I invest in art and sculpture, but no one would know. Most people assume my Hockneys and Dalís are posters. I don't have curtains. The floor-to-ceiling windows are vacuum-glazed, so there's no need in terms of warmth, and as I don't have neighbours for a few miles, there's no issue regarding privacy. I like clean, fresh, straight lines. No fuss. Where other houses might have internal brick walls, I have mostly glass ones. These glass walls and the enormous windows allow me to enjoy spectacular views of the woods. After years of being concerned that I might find the remoteness lonely, I realise I like it. Having attended boarding school, where I was forced to share my space but learnt to keep my thoughts to myself, I now value privacy and am comfortable in my own company. I enjoy feeling closer to nature.

Matthew is away this week, in Snowdonia. He has a three-day job with the tourist board taking scenic pictures, and he's tagged on an extra couple of days to go hiking. I'm encouraging him to pick up his hobby again. He hasn't explicitly said, but I think he stopped hiking when he moved to New York with Becky. He didn't have any of his kit here in the UK, so I surprised him by buying him an entire wardrobe of Patagonia base layers, shell jackets, merino wool layers, trousers and boots. I miss him, but I have plenty of work to keep me occupied, and midweek Heidi calls me and says she'll pop over and stay for the night. We occasionally have 'just the two of us' evenings.

Later, I will cook and we'll share a bottle of wine, but the first thing Heidi likes to do when she arrives is hop in the pool. She's a great swimmer and appreciates the change from swimming in water that is fifty per cent urine, fifty per cent chlorine, which she swears is the case in her local council-run pool. She's exaggerating, but I agree that standing on someone else's discarded foot plaster in a communal changing room is the worst.

Heidi is happy to pootle along, swimming for miles if she has a good true-crime podcast playing through the speakers. I can't do endless lengths in a pool. I get bored. I swim thirty lengths at speed and then get out. 'I'll spend ten minutes in the sauna, then shower and start prepping supper. You stay in as long as you like. No rush,' I tell her.

'I am not in any,' she says with a big grin. I love having Heidi here as a guest because I know she treats the place as her own and that's the biggest compliment she can pay me. We're utterly comfortable with one another. I realise I'm incredibly lucky to have a private pool and sauna. Both are solar-powered, and the sauna was built with the sustainable forestry seal, something I remind myself every time I feel a twinge of guilt about having this level of luxury to myself. I like both things better when someone is here sharing them with me. I guess it's one of the many benefits of having Matthew around so often. I've never felt lonely in my big home, but I've often felt spoilt, and that's equally uncomfortable. As though Heidi is reading my mind, she yells at me, 'You've worked hard, you deserve this space.'

'Thanks for the reminder.' I smile at her and leave her to her lengths.

In the small room near the pool, I step out of my wet costume and leave it dripping from a hook, then slip on a cotton robe. I always have Jo Malone myrrh and tonka diffusers in the sauna, and between the heady scent, the warmth and the darkness it is impossible not to feel wonderfully swaddled the moment you enter. I scoop a ladle of water out of the bucket and douse the rock heater to produce a burst of humidity. Then I place a big fluffy towel on the highest bench and lie flat on my back.

Normally I listen to some chill-out tunes when I'm in here, but the sound system is such that I have to listen to the podcast Heidi is playing in the pool. It destroys my vibe, because listening to details about gory unsolved murders is not conducive to relaxation. This particular podcast is about a husband who brutally murdered his wife and then buried her in the garden. She wasn't discovered until years later, when he sold the house and the new owners began to build an extension. He is still at large. The couple who bought the house were so upset by the incident that the wife had a breakdown, they ended up divorced. I really do question Heidi's choice of entertainment. I'm sure I've heard this podcast before, or maybe they're all about husbands murdering their wives. I make an effort to block out the words, and instead think about Matthew. It's not hard; recently I've found my difficulty is *not* thinking about him.

When he kisses me, he often cradles my face. I love that; it feels so purposeful. Then his fingers slowly move down my neck, lingering for the longest time just above the swell of my breasts. I had no idea how erotic that part of my body was until he started spending time there. I untie my cotton robe and let my fingers trail across my body, following the route he would take if he was here with me. My fingers move through the film of sweat, the silky slip of my touch made even better as I imagine his. I've never been into masturbation. It takes a bold teen to discover her own pleasure in a dormitory of seven other teenage girls. Besides, I don't have the necessary vision. I've never indulged in fantasising, imagining or projecting about anything in life; I prefer to concentrate on practicalities, realities and facts. I guess this insistence on staying with what is accountable is a form of self-protection, an attempt to create an emotional barrier against chaos, since chaos was the mainstay of my childhood. However, since I've met Matthew, I find I'm more open to both self-pleasure and daydreaming. He is making me feel more secure than I have before.

Safe in the knowledge that Heidi will be in the pool for ages, and anyway she's famously loud and I'll hear her coming long before she arrives, I close my eyes and let the darkness and heat ease me into some delicious, sexy thoughts. As I'm having great and regular sex at the moment, I find it isn't difficult to reach a breathless and exciting place. For some minutes I imagine his kisses, his touch, his tongue on my hips, tits and clit. I feel the swell of lust and joy that he always pulls out of me. My body shivers and quivers as waves of pleasure flood through me. My breathing quickens. I feel a jerk of excitement low in my abdomen, I shudder.

Spent, I stroke my sticky skin and stay flat on my back. It's hot in the sauna, and after coming, I know that if I move too quickly, I'm likely to feel a bit dizzy. I wait for a couple more minutes, just luxuriating in the afterglow, then slowly sit up.

The air has tipped from pleasant to prickly. It feels hotter in here than usual. I suppose that might be something to do with how I've been amusing myself. I move to the bench closest to the floor, as it's generally cooler, and take a deep, slow breath. However, it isn't at all refreshing. The air is arid, and my nose and mouth feel tight and closed. The podcast continues to drone on. Words such as *dental records, blood loss, fractured skull* float around the room. It's unsettling. I check the thermometer. Could it be broken? I set the temperature at 75 Celsius and it currently reads 85. I guess Matthew must have nudged it to a higher point. Since we've been dating, and he's spent more time here, I have noticed little things like that occasionally. He leaves windows open that I would close, he moves my reading glasses or the remote to places I think are illogical. Those things aren't important, but the sauna temperature is too much for me. As predicted, I do feel a little light-headed. I want a cold shower and something to eat. Time to go.

I push the door, anticipating the relief of the cool air outside. It doesn't budge. I push it again, harder. And again. It still doesn't give. There is a lock on the sauna. I wasn't going to bother with one, but I had visions of my godchildren coming in here unaccompanied and I wanted to avoid an accident. When they were younger, I used to lock the door from the outside if they visited, but I haven't done that for a while. Lottie has no interest in going in on her own – she prefers to stay wherever there are the most people – and Heidi's three are old enough to behave responsibly if they do want to use it. The lock requires a key. The key is not kept in the door; it is kept in the small room that leads into the pool, the place where people change into their swimsuits. It's hung on the antlers of a wooden carving of a stag head, along with the keys to the bifold windows and the outhouses. It doesn't seem at all likely that the door has been accidentally locked. It must simply be stuck.

I start to push hard, banging my shoulder and throwing my whole weight against the door. I begin to feel a little sick and breathless. I knock loudly and call for Heidi, but I know she won't be able to hear me. The pool is quite a distance from the sauna, and besides, her podcast is still playing; that alone will drown out my yells. *Shallow grave . . . neighbours on record . . . stench became overwhelming.* I block out the details. Glancing again at the thermometer, I am surprised to see it now reads 88 degrees. Panic slams through me. I have been in here for at least fourteen minutes, my normal practice is to stay for ten at a temp of 75 degrees. I try to remain calm by reminding myself that other people stay longer and in hotter conditions. I'm not in danger. Yet. But I am uncomfortable. Scared.

I don't waste any more energy banging on the door or shouting for help, but I do try, three more times, to get the door to budge by ramming it with the full might of my body. When nothing gives, I look around to see what I can use to help me get out. There is nothing in here other than the towel I've been lying on, the scented diffuser tucked in a corner under a bench and the wooden bucket and ladle. I sip some of the water. I feel better seeing that the bucket is about a quarter full; I guess I have half a litre to drink if I need it. Am I overreacting? That's something I always try to avoid. Should I sit still for a few more minutes? Surely Heidi will come to find me. I breathe shallowly, trying to ignore the mounting fear that is creeping through me. I catch what is being said on the podcast. Oh no, I think this is a new one. The presenter is now talking about a serial killer. Someone who liked to bury his victims alive. Heidi must have decided to stay in the pool; she might not come to find me for another thirty minutes. The temperature on the thermometer now reads 94 degrees. Something must have gone wrong with the electrics; why else would it still be climbing? How high might it go?

I wrap the towel around my arm and use the wooden ladle to bash at the small glass window in the door. I'm not hopeful that I'll crack the glass, as I know it's toughened to withstand heat and impact, but I'm hoping the entire pane might be dislodged. Never before have I wanted shoddy workmanship, but if it hasn't been sealed especially well, I might have a chance of extricating it. The ladle is substantial, hand-carved from a single piece of wood, but it doesn't make any impact. The room is now swaying and swelling around me, blurring. There is a buzzing in my ears. I'm dripping with sweat; my skin feels as though I'm being dried out like a cured ham. There isn't enough oxygen. Am I going to faint? How long have I been in here now? Twenty minutes? More? Could it be as much as half an hour? I drop the ladle and use my elbow to hit the glass instead.

The first thud does nothing other than send a brief and particularly excruciating shaft of pain through my body as I catch my funny bone. I curse and think how inappropriately that bone is named. The pain is temporarily useful; everything feels sharp for a moment, and I'm galvanised. I bang my elbow into the small window again and again. The fourth time, I hear the wood around the pane creak. A fifth shove and I definitely hear it splinter. I hammer my elbow over and over, ignoring the aching there and in my shoulder, until the pane of glass finally falls to the floor. Cool air whooshes in. It's not a lot, but it's enough. My panic subsides and I slump to the floor. But the physical effort and heat take hold; my vision shimmies, and then there is blackness.

'Jesus, Emma. What happened?' I can hear the urgency in Heidi's voice, but feel too weak and out of it to open my eyes.

I feel her hands, cool and wet from the pool, hook under my arms and drag me out of the sauna onto the cold tiles outside, my cotton robe gaping open. 'My God.' She disappears for a short time and then dashes back with water. 'Take some sips.' She holds the glass to my lips. I gulp at it, ignoring her suggestion to slow down, just needing to rehydrate. She runs back to the kitchen and returns with more fluids and a towel soaked in cold water, which she lays on my body. My skin prickles as though I've been stung repeatedly. 'Did you faint? What made you stay in there so long?' she asks, concerned.

'The door was locked. I couldn't get out.'

She looks at me in confusion, but doesn't say anything other than 'How do you feel? Do you think you need medical help?'

'No, just a cold shower.'

While I shower, Heidi insists I leave the bathroom door wide open in case I 'come over funny' again – her words. Despite this drama, we manage to settle down and have a lovely evening. She offers to make supper and I let her. She says I shouldn't drink alcohol because I must be dehydrated. I laugh and tell her not to make a drama out of a crisis. I crack open a bottle of white wine that I've been looking forward to sharing with her.

'I'll have to get someone in to check the heat control panel on the sauna,' I comment. 'And to fix the window.'

'So tell me what happened,' says Heidi. She turns her face towards me, concern and curiosity radiating from her. We have eaten and cleared away and we are now sitting in the main living room, in front of the wood burner, which Heidi has lit. She has her feet up on the sofa and her toes are curled under a blanket. I'm as far away from the fire as I can reasonably be. I don't feel comfortable near the heat. I'm not burnt exactly, but I feel scorched, not unlike someone who has had too much sun. 'You said the door was stuck.'

'Locked,' I correct. 'I tried it loads of times.'

'No, it wasn't locked. It must have been stuck somehow. I opened it easily when I came to look for you. Walked straight in.'

'I don't understand. I pushed it over and over again, it wouldn't budge. And the temperature was over ninety degrees. I don't usually have it set that high.'

Heidi shakes her head. 'It's reading seventy-five now.'

'What?'

'I checked just now, while you were refilling your glass. And the key is hung up on the antlers.'

'That's so odd,' I mutter. I'm totally flummoxed as to how to explain what she is saying.

'I guess if you were feeling unwell, you might have misread the thermometer.'

I shake my head. 'I don't think I made a mistake, and that doesn't explain the door being locked.'

'Stuck,' she murmurs gently. We sit quietly for a moment or two. It feels oddly like a stand-off, but it can't be. Why would Heidi not believe me? She coughs, as though clearing her throat. 'Emma, I know this is going to sound odd, but as your friend, I'm going to ask. Did you have anything to drink before you went into the sauna?'

'What?'

'Like alcohol. I mean, it was after six,' she says hurriedly.

'No.'

'I just thought maybe you poured yourself a quick glass of wine or something. No one would judge you if you had.'

'But I didn't.'

'Right.' Heidi doesn't meet my gaze, but instead stares out of the window into the dark night. It's raining, a relentless thick and heavy downpour driving against the windows, water gathering in pools on the patio and decking wherever there is a dip and running in rivulets towards the sheds. It's been a wet March. Despite this, I suddenly feel like taking a walk, I want to be outside and have the cold and wet soothe me, calm me. I don't bother to suggest it. I know Heidi won't agree. She would think the idea of walking in the rain at night is barmy. Maybe it is, but I feel it might ease the knot of anxiety that is tied in my stomach.

I see the woods as either restful or playful, always wonderful and comforting, no matter what the element, season or time. Heidi enjoys them well enough during a bright sunny day – at least she did when her kids were a bit younger and spent hours charging through them, beating brambles with sticks, running off the energy that in her suburban terrace could never be fully expended. She's liked the big windows and the view from them less as time has passed and the kids started to use the woods to hide from her, to experiment with vaping and drinking. I think on a subconscious level she resents the fact that her children have to grow up, but it's easier to resent the woods. At night she thinks of them as spooky. She often talks about threats, intruders and being watched. I always laugh at her fears. Now she follows my gaze and comments, 'I wish you would at least buy curtains or blinds. I hate looking out on the blackness and wondering who's looking in.' She says the same thing every time she visits.

'Who would be looking in? I have no neighbours,' I reply, as I always do.

'Anyone could.' She shivers, even though the wood burner is still glowing.

I laugh. 'This fictional peeping Tom would have to be very determined. Unless I buzzed them in, they would have to leave their car at the electric gate, scale it, then walk the half-mile to the house. You need to stop listening to those scary podcasts. You're terrifying yourself.'

'Maybe,' she mumbles, but her lips are pulled tight, strained white like knuckles, rather than forming the huge red beam she normally wears. We both fall silent. Unusually, we have nothing to say to one another. Instead we listen to the rain thrum on the roof and drip from the eaves. It sounds like someone is knocking to get in.

9

April

I have two principal commutes. AirBright's main wind plants are in Scotland, and I sometimes need to travel there if a Zoom call can't suffice with expediting whatever business I'm tackling; and I generally need to be in the London office at least three days a week. Late-night events sometimes necessitate a stopover there. I used to resent the London jaunts, preferring to secrete myself away in my beautiful country home. Since I've been dating Matthew, all that has changed as he lives in the capital.

I've started to enjoy the hotels more. Before Matthew, I stayed at a Travelodge or a Premier Inn. Practical, clean and functional. Nothing more luxe than two cartons of UHT and a packet of non-branded ginger biscuits. Those rooms aren't the sort that lend themselves to passionate lovemaking sessions; they're more suited to half an hour of TV-watching at low volume, then lights off to settle in for a decent night's sleep. Recently I've started booking myself into more resplendent, indulgent places. One Aldwych near Covent Garden; the Ned in the financial district of the City; the Mondrian in Shoreditch.

We get a kick out of meeting in the lobby or bar before we go to the room. The moment the lift doors glide closed behind us, we fling ourselves at one another, like filings to a magnet. We practically run along the corridor, frustrated with the moments needed to open the bedroom door. A little green light. All systems go. Sex in hotel rooms is, I find, especially uninhibited. Particularly candid and satisfying. Maybe it's because I don't have to think about laundering the sheets, maybe it's because it feels like a holiday even after a long day in the office.

Or maybe it's him.

It's really rather special now. The sex. It's the sort that makes me resent the moment it is over, even while I'm still shuddering and glowing. It's the sort that makes me want to see him every day. I now actively look for opportunities to visit the office and stay in town. I know I'm making it convenient for us to meet regularly, taking away the potential obstacle of distance. Making myself readily available would be pathetic except for the fact that he is equally accommodating. Besides the meet-ups in London, he's very willing to travel to Hampshire and stay at mine, which he does most weekends. It nets out that we see each other three or four nights out of seven. We are dating exclusively. There's no room or time for anyone else. More poignantly, there's no need or desire either.

'I don't want to be out there in that mad world of dating,' he explained when I brought up the matter. 'After Becky, I never thought I'd want to be with anyone again. Then you came along.' He kissed me, and I could feel his smile in the kiss. I tried to think about that and not the words 'after Becky'. The fact is, she came first. I am second to her. Nothing can be done about that, and wishing something in the past was different is a fool's game. It could drive you mad.

At the weekend, I set the alarm for 6.08, allowing myself an extra hour's sleep: I don't have to be at my desk, but I still like to make the most of the day. When the alarm went off this morning, Matthew groaned and insisted that I'm out of my mind to want to get up so early, so instead of me going on my run, we had sex. It's a good workout, but not as energetic as a five-mile run. I will have a level of pent-up energy lingering all day. A bird in a cage. I try to explain to Matthew why it's so important to me to run every morning, and he says, 'Babe, you don't need to exercise. You have a brilliant body. You're so slim and trim.'

'It's not about staying slim,' I point out. 'It's about the power of knowing I'm fit, strong and fast. I work long hours. It's easier to do that if I'm fit.'

'You really should try and relax, babe.'

People have told me this all my life. I've never listened. He leans in to kiss me and then sets about teasing another orgasm out of me. I'm left quivering, and for the first time I consider that he might have a point; maybe relaxing suits me. At least, this sort of relaxation. I am so chilled that I don't even bother to tell him I'm not especially keen on the endearment 'babe'. I'm aware that it's infantilising and basic-level sexist. I'm not a tiny being, helpless or naive; I don't need him to look after me, far from it. But the thing is (whisper it), part of me does rather like him having a special name for me. It's sort of wonderful. I've never been a fan of pet names (even the term turns my stomach), but every time he calls me 'babe', I find I inwardly smile. 'Hey, babe, how's your day going?' His voice breezy down the telephone line. Or the endearment sprinkled through his texts. *Babe, I was wondering, do you want to go to . . . Babe, have you ever read . . .* It's delightfully strange.

I wonder what his pet name for Becky was.

This invasive thought about her is unwelcome. It tinges my current joy with a streak of something rotten. All my pervasive thoughts about her do that, and yet they keep coming, as annoying as uninvited visitors knocking at the door just when you're settling down to watch TV. Might he have called her babe too? I don't like that idea, but worse still is the thought that her pet name might have been something deeper. Something *more*. He probably called her 'my darling' or 'my love'. I won't ask him, because he will tell me; he's scrupulously honest and straightforward, a characteristic that sounds more appealing than it turns out to be in fact.

A few weeks ago, I asked him how they met, and while it turned out to be in a very standard way, through work, when he spoke of their first meeting, his face lit up as though a switch had been flicked somewhere deep in his head, and his eyes sparkled on full beam. The intensity was disarming, and I stupidly asked, 'Was it love at first sight?' I posed this question without sincere conviction, because that's not a real thing, is it? It makes no sense. Real love must be based upon mutual respect, common ground and shared experience. It can't be instantaneous. I was really asking was the attraction immediate, mutual? I should have been more disciplined. I shouldn't want to know.

His face softened as he recollected. 'I think it was, yes. I think that's how it would be judged. Certainly I've never felt like that before or since. She consumed me from the off.'

I was made uncomfortable by the intensity of his response. And yes, I was peeved by it. Was it necessary to add 'or since'? In a fated effort to hide my awkwardness, I blurted out a second question. 'And did she feel the same?'

'I'm not sure she did, no.' He grinned nostalgically. 'I proposed within a year of us meeting, but she turned me down.'

'So you proposed again?'

'And again, and again.'

'So when did she finally accept?'

He looked a little startled by my tone. I suppose I might have sounded exasperated, or irritated, or envious. Not great.

'I had to work quite hard for a few years to persuade her to marry me,' he said carefully.

His response gave me a painful insight into their relationship. I was embarrassed for him, mortified that he had done the running. In our case, he hadn't had to do much running. Any at all. I wanted to be caught by him. This fact makes me feel less important, less interesting and challenging. I wish I didn't always feel less in comparison to her. I'm not used to it. Until I started dating Matthew, I was very firmly OK with who I am, what I contribute to the world, what my worth is. I'm frustrated that she hadn't matched his devotion. But if he'd told me she was equally enamoured with him as he was with her, would that have been better? Would I want to think of their reciprocal unparalleled passion? I don't think so.

I tried to keep my tone jovial as I probed. 'How did you eventually woo her?'

He laughed out loud. 'The traditional way. I maxed out all my credit cards.'

I am ashamed to admit, even to myself, that I want to find

fault with his poor dead wife. I conclude that his relationship with Becky was obviously transactional. Basic. But even that isn't as comforting as I'd hoped. He doesn't spend a lot of money on me. We both know I'm far wealthier, so I pick up the tab for the hotel rooms and the dinners. He doesn't buy me gifts. What's the point? I can buy myself anything I need or want. I've never wanted him, or any man, to buy me things. Being jealous or irritated of something I don't want is irrational; I don't like being irrational. Thinking of her usually makes me feel frustrated, angry, sad or defensive. Always something bad.

I've googled her. Naturally. I couldn't stop myself. Becky Charlton and Rebecca Charlton. The search results were dominated by a TV presenter of that name. I discovered there are several Becky Charltons, but none of them is obviously identifiable as Matthew's dead wife. Even when I tried to narrow down my search by age, profession, obituaries, I didn't discover any definitive information or images. I suppose she might not even have been called Charlton; she might have kept her own surname. I don't know what that was.

Matthew hasn't volunteered a photograph, and I can't bring myself to ask him to show me one. It's undignified. It's a giveaway. He'd know I'm thinking about her. Fixating on her. Not knowing what she looks like drives me wild. Was she white or black or brown? Tall, petite, athletically built or voluptuous? I imagine her in endless, various incarnations: authoritative sleek dark bob, cool room-owning afro, romantic soft blonde curls, dynamic peroxide pixie cut. My own hair is shoulder length, it's a mid-brown colour, made a little bit more exciting by professional highlights. I don't have a fringe. I sometimes wear it in a ponytail, nothing more adventurous than that.

It's the sort of hair many women around my age have, hair that's not quite as glossy as it once was. I wonder if Becky had piercings, tattoos. She was arty, so either or both are probable. Does he find me dull by comparison? My skin is devoid of ink. I have my ears pierced once and wear discreet gold studs. I waste time wondering what sort of clothes she preferred. Was she all about sleek monotones or a colourful statement dresser? Perhaps she made her own clothes, or bought exclusively in vintage shops; both styles intimidate me. That's madness, right? I run a company with a multimillion-pound turnover, and I'm intimidated by women who wear aqua crimplene day dresses.

I am not myself.

Is this love? Losing yourself? I don't know. Past partners have never crawled under my skin. Until recently, my big, enduring passion has always been work. This is the first time I've been willing to be overwhelmed by a person. I want this.

I can't focus my attention; I can't be logical and sensible. Because I don't know what I'm looking for, I imagine echoes of her in every woman I meet. In every version of her that I conjure, she is beautiful. Show-stoppingly beautiful. And young. Or at least younger than I am, by over a decade. Therefore vibrant in an ephemeral, inimitable way. Of course, Matthew is young too. They matched. He knew her intimately, but I wonder, does he still do the same, constantly scan faces, hoping to recognise her in other women?

A new thought occurs to me that I haven't had before. Perhaps he sees her in me. It is possible he has a type; maybe that's why he committed so quickly. That thought alarms me more than all the others. I'm just her, but second best. Less. I am infuriated with my irrationality. I don't know her, I never did and I never will, so how can I compare myself? Why do I put myself through this?

Still, I asked, 'Did you remain as in love throughout, all those years you were together?' I wanted to hear that it had waned, I suppose. That it was hard to maintain the passion.

'I've never stopped,' he muttered.

'Well, that's good,' I said, not certain it was, at least not for me. 'It must be a comfort.'

'The last words I said to her were "I love you, you sexy bitch."' He laughed to himself, pleased by the memory.

So yes, he's scrupulously honest, disarmingly frank, and I will not ask about her pet name. It's here and this moment that counts. From this point on, to protect myself, I'm only going to ask innocuous questions.

'Have you ever been to Lyndhurst?' I say. 'It's a beautiful little town, stuffed full of antique shops. Do you like antiquing? I know it's not everyone's thing.'

'I love poking around antique shops,' he says with glee. 'Becky loved it too, actually. We used to go all the time. She had a great eye. I've missed it. Come on, let's get cracking.'

As Matthew sings in the shower, I tell myself it's a great thing to have a shared hobby and that he's so enthusiastic about doing something I enjoy. It doesn't matter at all that Becky had a great eye.

And I reconsider what might be defined as an innocuous question in our particular situation.

10

Maybe Becky did have a great eye for antiques. Matthew certainly does not. He seems to be drawn to anything ugly, damaged or dirty. A fact we both find amusing rather than annoying or embarrassing.

'These are fun,' he says, pointing at a collection of gut-wrenchingly ugly Toby jugs.

'They're absolutely awful,' I declare with a grin. He shrugs good-naturedly and moves on.

'But this is rather nice, right?' He's landed on an elaborate dragon ornament. It's supposed to look like a wooden carving but is clearly moulded. 'What would you say, late eighteen hundreds?'

'Nineteen eighties reproduction, more like. And hideous.' I laugh. Matthew puts the dragon back on the shelf and shrugs again.

'What do I know?'

It's a bright April day, spring at its best. There is a sense that the world is creeping back to life after a long, dull winter.

Daffodils and crocuses are bravely sprouting on the grass verges. The little artisan shops have their doors wedged open, welcoming in customers. Dog-walkers slow down for a chat, giving me a moment to pet their dogs. We buy hand-made fudge from one shop, get excited about chilli and orange marmalade in another, and enjoy a glass of local cider in a tiny café. All morning, I get the feeling eyes are on us. We draw smiles and nods from strangers. I guess people like to see others walking hand in hand, laughing, chatting.

My favourite shop in Lyndhurst is an enormous antique shop that spreads over three floors. It's not the sort of place that sells elegant eighteenth-century Italian furniture; it offers a mishmash of clutter: stamps, jewellery, lamps, chinaware and musical instruments. Some would think the place is full of junk, but I believe in the adage 'One man's trash is another man's treasure.' I am gratified when I lead Matthew into the shop that he stops dramatically in the doorway, looks around and smiles appreciatively at the curious and varied offerings in this dusty paradise. He inhales deeply, taking in the particular smell of grimy books and maps, the shadow of something lingering in objects that have been handled, worn, loved, lost. His eyes bounce around the store before he heads upstairs to where the antique maps and books are housed. I like to start in the basement. It's cold and draughty down there, a little dank, and as a result people rarely linger. That's where traditionally I have uncovered something special, something overlooked. I head to the treasure cave.

The shop is almost empty, as is often the way with antique shops. Ambling about dusty rooms looking at things that are obsolete, the original owners long dead, doesn't appeal to everyone. Personally, I like the peace. When I'm in an upmarket antique shop, I sometimes spot things that remind me of being in my grandparents' home. It wasn't somewhere I felt especially happy or loved, but I knew I was safe and that counted for something. They had beautiful furniture: a George III flame mahogany secretaire, Japanese silk screens from the eighteenth century, and a number of Regency long clocks with enamel faces that counted out my lonely minutes. When they died, I couldn't see the financial or emotional value in the pieces. I let the executers of the will sell off everything in a hurry; Tom was once again in rehab and I had enough on my plate. All the beautiful things vanished. I find myself keeping an eye out and occasionally buying the odd small piece that reminds me of something they owned that I think might fit in my home. I'm not exactly sure why.

Today I get lucky. In among the chinaware, glass decanters and rather run-of-the-mill watercolours, I discover a pair of splendid Victorian hand-blown glass taxidermy domes. My grandparents had a similar pair that housed a collection of bright blue butterflies. The butterflies were suspended as though in flight in a way that as a child I thought was magical. I feel a shiver of mounting excitement in response to a thrilling find. The glass is bright and shiny and free from cracks; there are the usual tiny nibbles to the edge, but they are only detectable to touch, not to the eye. The handsome domes are about sixty centimetres tall and just less than thirty in diameter. The little cardboard label dates them circa 1880, which I think is accurate. They are sitting on black ebonised bases lined with the original claret velvet. The cloth is slightly sun-worn, but that only adds to their appeal as far as I'm concerned. I like things that are weathered and have endured. My heart lifts a little. This is the reason I enjoy antiquing; you never know what you are going to unearth.

It's silly of me, but I feel a swell of competitive spirit. Once I spot something I want, I always fear that there is someone else in the shop who at the very same moment might see the charm and value in the pieces I've earmarked. Statistically this is unlikely, but still, I don't like the thought of being so close to the domes and then missing out. It's tradition to play a little bartering game with the vendor when making a purchase. However, as I'm always concerned that someone else might swoop in and steal the item from under my nose, I'm generally a fast negotiator. Today, whilst the shop is almost empty, I cannot shake the feeling that I'm being watched. I look about and realise I am – by the woman rearranging the merchandise downstairs, who is obviously keeping an eye out for light-fingered types desperate to nab a Wade Whimsy ceramic turtle.

'I want these,' I tell her. 'I can't carry them both up the stairs at once. If I take one up, will you keep an eye on the other one for me, please?' She nods but doesn't appear especially interested in my purchase and doesn't offer to help me carry them, which would have been useful. Some traders are like this; they seem almost reluctant to make a sale. I guess they get used to seeing their pieces around the store and become unreasonably attached.

I slowly carry the first dome upstairs, and place it on the counter at the front of the shop with care.

'What have you found?' Matthew asks when he notices I've reappeared.

I beam at him. 'This. Isn't it fabulous. There are two of them.

It's rare to find a pair in such great condition.' He nods, but doesn't come to the till for a closer look. His eyes are trained on a leather casket that is about half the size of a shoebox. It's adorned with gilded embossing, with a knotted carry handle and brass escutcheons. I move towards him to take a closer look. It's a decent piece, complete with original ornate working key. The lid opens on a spring to reveal two dainty glass ink bottles, each housed in its own blue velvet section.

'It's really beautiful,' I assert. I'm happy to be encouraging after dismissing his previous choices.

'Yes. It is.'

'Let me buy it for you,' I say impulsively.

'No, no, that's OK.' He shakes his head, practically backing away from the casket.

'Honestly, I'd like to. A little souvenir of the day.'

'It's expensive,' he protests. I haven't checked the price tag. My guess is it will be between £200 and £300.

'It doesn't matter.' I pick it up and take it to the till point.

'No, really, don't. I don't want it.'

'But you couldn't take your eyes off it,' I say with a smile. I roll my eyes playfully at the man behind the till, who is waiting patiently to see what we are purchasing. He is in his sixties, balding, pleasantly plump. There is evidence of his breakfast on his tie. Fried egg. He looks at me over his glasses with a conspiratorial grin. I'm aware that I'm performing for him a little. I want this small, delightful domestic scene to be witnessed and appreciated. A generous girlfriend indulging her partner.

But then Matthew says, 'It caught my eye because Becky collected inkwells. I know she would have loved this.'

'Oh.' I feel instantly deflated. As though someone has doused me in freezing water.

'Not me, I don't love it especially,' he clarifies. He seems embarrassed, but not as embarrassed as I am. I nod, feeling foolish. If I buy this, I'm effectively buying a gift for his dead wife. My face burns. I quickly put the casket back on the shelf.

'I'll go and get the other dome,' I mutter.

I'm not sure exactly how it happens. I guess I'm flustered about the inkwell misunderstanding and therefore rushing. I do urgently want to get out of the shop and away from the vendor who witnessed the embarrassing rejection. That's how it feels. Like a rejection. Or worse, a testament to how little I know Matthew. I want to leave the scene behind me. I hastily grab the second dome and turn back towards the stairs. I think my bag, which is hoisted over my shoulder, must have knocked against something. Suddenly there is an almighty clatter as several items fall to the floor and smash. Shards of glass and pottery skitter across the tiles. I feel a splinter bounce on my leg. The woman who was keeping an eye on the dome for me says nothing, but casts me a withering glance.

She leaves the room; I presume to fetch a dustpan to clear up. I am embarrassed and unsure what to do, so just continue back upstairs. It's only when I get to the till that I notice I'm bleeding. A thin line of blood tracks down from my calf to my ankle. I apologise profusely for the chaos I've caused and offer to pay for everything I've broken. Matthew and the male shopkeeper go back down into the basement to assess the damage and ascertain how much I owe. There's not much room down there, evidently, and so I don't join them. I wait, my cheeks burning.

'It's not as bad as it looks,' says Matthew cheerfully when he comes back upstairs. 'A glass decanter, a couple of teacups, a little art deco clock. We've settled on a price tag.' He winces. 'Does three hundred and fifty sound fair to you?'

It sounds a lot to me for what he's just described, but I'm far too mortified to argue my case. I pay for the damage and for my domes; it seems to take an inordinate amount of time to wrap them. We leave the shop as quickly as possible; I hold my shoulder bag close to my body, trying to avoid another accident.

11

The romcom blueprint also demands that there are successful meet-ups with quirky friends and loving family members who are all utterly delighted that the lead has finally met the One. They demonstrate their approval by sharing knowing grins and nods. We haven't done this yet. Matthew's family lives in New Zealand, nearly all of mine are dead, and whilst Tom is currently not in a drying-out clinic, he's not in the country either. My brother yo-yos from one extreme to another, and at the moment he is on a year-long spiritual retreat in the Himalayas. He's vegan, makes clay pots in the mornings and practises yoga in the afternoons. Apparently he can now do the side crow and is working towards a headstand. I don't know when he'll meet Matthew. However, I am excited to introduce Matthew to my chosen family: Heidi and Gina and their clans. Heidi has asked us all to hers for Sunday lunch, something I do regularly, although admittedly not as regularly since I met Matthew.

We ring the doorbell and listen to their dog, Bella, barking excitedly and the kids yelling at one another.

'You answer it.'

'No. I'm busy, you go.'

As heavy footsteps thump towards us, I identify Leon's broad, muscular shape through the frosted glass on the door. There is perspiration on Matthew's upper lip. He looks pale. 'You OK?' I ask.

He nods. 'Yeah, of course. It's just meeting them en masse. You know. It's a lot.'

'It's like pulling off an Elastoplast. Better to do it quickly,' I say, kissing him briefly on the lips. Breaking away, I grin and add, 'Honestly, they are like family. They love me, so they'll—'

'Grill me,' he cuts in. I laugh. He's funny and I like that. Humour demands confidence, and I appreciate confidence.

I'm still smiling when Leon flings open the door. 'So this is the man,' he says, pumping Matthew's hand up and down before pulling me into a hug. 'I have a brief questionnaire that I'd like you to fill out so we can assess your suitability,' he jokes.

Matthew looks momentarily horrified, then his face breaks into a wide grin as I laugh and say, 'Ignore him.'

I've had countless Sunday lunches here over the years, and I have always enjoyed them, even when the kids were young and threw tantrums or threw up – tummy bugs or just too much ice cream. They're always fun, a joy. I slip into the family's stride; no one puts on their best manners for me. It is authentically welcoming. I'm barely a guest, I'm just part of it all. Usually we eat and drink a little more than we should and laugh more than most people get to in a week. So the bar is set high. Despite all this, as I chase the final gravy-smeared roast spud around my plate, I take a moment to acknowledge that this Sunday lunch is the best by far. The experience feels fuller, more complete. I can't really explain why I think this, as I've never believed anything was missing before. My gaze drifts towards Matthew. I feel emotionally replete. I want to say to people, 'Thank you. This is sufficient.'

Matthew makes me feel so proud. Of course I have introduced other men to my friends and some of them have been perfectly fine. That's how Heidi has described them, *fine*. Damning them in a syllable. I used to want to be angry with her, yet I know she is discerning and was in fact simply articulating what I felt but was reluctant to say. Sweetly, she's always insisted that she's just picky because 'It's going to be hard for me to think anyone deserves you.' I watch her watching Matthew. Surely she can't fail to see that he is the undoubted star of the show today, clearly far above fine.

Throughout lunch, he's shown interest in all the kids, and they appear to be interested in him in return. Heidi's three have entered animated conversations, above and beyond the expected monosyllabic responses that they usually throw out just to avoid their mother ticking them off for being impolite, and Lottie is practically zipped to his side; she is desperate to tell him about her Pokémon card collection, which she's holding in her hot little hand. He's flattered Heidi and Gina by not challenging their position of importance in my life, the way more territorial men might, instead deftly deferring to their superior knowledge when matters of my taste or history crop up. He jokes with the husbands. He's chatty and entertaining, he asks questions of everyone and provides a few anecdotes of his own, but he isn't overbearing. He's talked with pride about my work and the hours I'm putting in dealing with the restructure, proving he's interested in my days in the office. He's a textbook boyfriend.

After lunch, Heidi, Gina and I settle in the sitting room, leaving the men in the kitchen. As soon as the meal was over, the older kids dashed upstairs, ostensibly to finish their homework. We adults are sceptical, but we pretended to believe them because none of us want to play Monopoly, and if we made the kids stay with us, that would be the cost. The spring sunshine floods into the room, and although it hasn't brought any heat with it, it is glaringly bright and bleaches away all signs of colour; we appear like two-dimensional people on a sepia photograph from the seventies. Lazy and content. We each have a coffee; I'm also still holding my wine glass, which someone refilled just before we left the table. There's a tub of Quality Street chocolates balanced between us. Gina is laying into those despite the fact that just ten minutes ago she swore she was stuffed and couldn't eat another bite. I'm not judging; I said I'd had enough to drink. The men are stacking the dishwasher. Their chatter drifts through to us; although the words are indistinct, the tone is pleasant and punctuated with laughter.

'So do you still think he's too good to be true?' I ask. It's a prompt. I want to hear my friends heap praise on him.

'More than ever do I think so. I'm certain he's a figment of our collective imagination, he's that good,' says Gina. 'But as he's managed to coerce Mick and Leon into clearing up after the roast, I believe we should all go with it. Let the magic happen.' She grins.

It's true. Usually we follow a more traditional 1980s pattern and it's the three of us in the kitchen clearing up while the two dads might, at best, be kicking a football about with the kids. I glance at Heidi, waiting to hear her affirmation. She pops a strawberry cream into her mouth. This is how well I know Heidi: her favourite Quality Street is the toffee penny, but she eats those last because she knows no one else in her family likes them, so she can leave them, safe in the knowledge that they will be waiting for her when all the other choices have gone. She initially eats the ones she likes second or third best, which may or may not be other people's favourites. It's a pretty selfish move, but it makes me laugh as it's her one and only failing as a person, and therefore forgivable.

'I'm so glad you like him.' I beam.

'Do you get on with his mates?' Heidi asks, the moment she's swallowed her chocolate.

'I haven't met any of them yet. We thought we'd tackle you two first.'

She nods, and then probes, 'What's his flat like?'

'Why do you ask that?' I reply, avoiding giving a direct answer to her question.

'Well, he was saying how much time you both spend at yours, and he's clearly impressed by your place. I just wondered if you like his.'

I have to sidestep again, which is a bit awkward. I sip my wine and then comment, 'You know, I really like the way he is openly impressed by my success and Woodview. He doesn't struggle with any macho nonsense of being intimidated by everything I have.'

'Yeah, sounds like he makes himself at home. He expressed clear admiration for your enormous wine fridge, not to mention your indoor swimming pool and sauna area. I heard him

79

tell Leon we should invest in one – a wine fridge, that is, not a pool. Not that we have even enough for the fridge.' She makes a show of feeling down the back of the sofa. 'Just hoping to find a spare five grand lying around.' She chuckles sardonically. There's something in her tone that suggests she doesn't think Matthew's open admiration for what I have is as wonderful as I do. For me, it's a relief. I prefer it to a sense of awkwardness or resentment, both of which I have encountered in the past. I can't explain to her how tiresome that is, because it's not just boyfriends who feel intimidated by my wealth.

At that moment, the three men and Lottie drift into the sitting room. 'What are you talking about?' asks Lottie in her usual direct way.

'Emma was just saying she'd like to see Matthew's place,' replies Heidi.

All heads swivel towards me. On the spot, I feel myself colour a little. I hadn't even confessed to not seeing it. Heidi has just deduced as much. 'I wasn't saying that, not exactly,' I mutter, reaching for my wine glass again and taking a big gulp. Then I offer the chocolates to Lottie to try to distract her and move everyone on to another conversation. I feel the weight of Matthew's eyes on me.

'You would like to see it, though, right?' says Heidi. Part of me wants to throw her a silencing glare, but the thing is, she's correct, I *am* curious about where he lives. We've been seeing each other for a few months now; we meet up several times a week. I'm often in London, and yet he's never invited me to his apartment. Instead we meet in the hotels I book. I try not to think that this is weird. But it's certainly uneven. I am suddenly struck by how little I know about the day-to-day workings of

Matthew's life, and it embarrasses me. How can we do the things we do to one another in bed, make one another think and feel the way we do, and yet I remain unaware of his living arrangements? I can't quite shake the feeling that he's keeping me out, keeping me at a distance, and now I realise that my friends are thinking the same.

Matthew mock-winces, 'She'll need a tetanus shot before she stays at mine. I mean, it suits me, but by comparison to her place, it's a dump.' He reaches for the chocolates and takes ages before he selects a toffee penny. He unwraps it slowly, and I wonder whether Heidi will ask him to put it back.

She doesn't; instead she says, 'I thought you probably lived in a shithole.'

Lottie gasps theatrically, the way she always does whenever she hears an adult swear. 'You shouldn't say shithole, it's a really awful word,' she says primly.

'Sorry, Lottie,' responds Heidi. She doesn't apologise to Matthew, though, which I think maybe she should. She adds, 'Leon and I were speculating as to why you've never asked Emma there. I said it would be a shi— a dump, and he suggested maybe you live with your mum and are a total saddo.' Everyone laughs as though she's joking; I roll my eyes, give her a playful shove, but in fact she's making me uncomfortable. I don't like the way she seems to be challenging Matthew publicly. We were all having such a lovely time. The fun atmosphere feels strained and stained now.

Leon asks, 'Where is your flat?' His tone is not in the least loaded. He's just making conversation. Men ask about people's addresses as a staple form of small talk, along with journey routes and commuter train times. Leon won't have any idea that I'm just as keen as he is to hear the answer to this question.

'On the river. Nearest Tube Bermondsey.' Matthew comes to sit on the sofa next to me. He has to wiggle into the space, inching his bum left to right. Heidi slowly takes her feet off the sofa to make room for him. He reaches for my hand, puts it on his thigh.

'Do you own your flat? Is it where you lived with Becky before you went to New York?' Gina enquires. Her tone is conciliatory, conversational. Still, her question makes me yet more uncomfortable. It's as though by naming Becky, she has just brought her into the room with us. I feel her presence, shadowy yet insistent.

'No. We never bought. We moved around too often to know where to put down roots. The money I've thrown away on rent.' Matthew winces. 'Right now, I share with two postgrad students. It's really not dignified at my age. I'm a bit embarrassed to take you there, frankly. I mean, I do my best to make it look presentable. I'm constantly fixing things.'

'He's really handy,' I chip in. 'I've had some problems with electrics recently. My lights kept blowing a fuse and we were constantly being plunged into darkness. Matthew fixed them.'

'What do you do with yourselves when you're plunged into darkness?' says Gina with her signature warm, dirty laugh.

'You've always been really good with DIY. I hope you're not letting down the sisters by feigning inability just to flatter Matthew,' says Heidi, her tone distinctly icy.

'I have no idea about electrics,' I point out.

Matthew lifts my hand to his lips, kisses the knuckles, and for a moment it feels as though there's no one else in the room;

I'm all that counts to him. His gaze drops, and after a beat he says, 'There was a time when I couldn't work. You know, straight after . . . I just couldn't find the energy. I let clients down and contacts go cold, so I really struggled financially. My photography work is not especially lucrative at the best of times; you must have noticed that commissions are few and far between.' He shrugs. It's not a dismissive, careless shrug. The way he brings his shoulders to his ears, and then lets them tumble down his back, explicitly states, 'And there you have it. That's what I am.' I realise he thinks he's sub-par. How oddly we look at ourselves. I squeeze his hand. I want to tell him that my friends are concerned he's too good to be true.

He looks me in the eyes and says earnestly, 'I hadn't realised you thought it was odd that you'd never been to my place. That it was a subject of discussion.'

'No, it wasn't that, as such . . .' I break off, unsure how to finish the sentence. I want to bounce back to the playfulness that abounded at lunch. I wait, hoping someone will leap in and discuss whatever sport is playing this afternoon. No one says anything. I don't know if it's because they're all stewing in a food coma brought on by Heidi's excellent Sunday roast or because they're rapt at Matthew's explanation.

'How much do you pay in rent?' The question is out of my mouth before I really consider what I'm asking. I'm a CEO. I simply like to know the value of things. I'm curious, nothing more.

Matthew blushes, but smiles good-naturedly, names a figure. It's been such a long time since I rented, I'm out of touch as to what the market rate is. The amount he pays seems reasonable to me. A little less than I spend per month on cleaners and the pool guy. 'And I pay for storage too, for my furniture,' he adds. 'The shared flat is furnished, you see. Storage costs are crazy, and while nothing I'm keeping is of much financial value, in other ways it's . . .'

'Priceless.' I finish his sentence. I think of the chairs, tables and sofas that Matthew and Becky must have owned together. The trips they must have made to IKEA and John Lewis. I think of their bed. I imagine their home, full of their things, their memories. Them. He's struggling financially, but the possessions they acquired throughout their married life hold unquantifiable sentimental value, so he pays for storage. He isn't ready to clear out Becky's belongings. Undisputable evidence that he's simply not prepared to let her go. His unwillingness is understandable, but it leaves me feeling exposed. If he's not ready to tidy her away, is he ready to be messy with me? I know we're approaching the first anniversary of her death. I want the date to come and go, to be behind us. But a year isn't a long time. Is this all too hurried? I must wear my concern in my expression, because Matthew asks, 'What? What is it?'

'Nothing,' I assure him.

'Yes, there was something. I saw it in your face. You looked sad.'

'Oh no, not at all.' I can't confess what I was thinking; instead I blurt, 'Look, Matthew, if you need some money, you only have to ask. Your rent doesn't seem high to me.'

'What?'

I feel everyone in the room sharply inhale. The moment the words are out of my mouth, I realise that they're ludicrous, insulting. I would have been better confessing that I was halted with raw jealousy at the thought of their bed, and stung once again by the pain of living with the fact that this man would not be in *my* bed if his wife hadn't died. He hasn't chosen me; he's settled for me. But I couldn't say that, so I said the stupid thing about money. Face burning, I try to fix things.

'I don't mean as a gift. I mean as a loan.' Matthew's mouth drops open. 'I mean, a gift is fine too, if that's better for you,' I add, unsure how to interpret his look of astonishment. I continue to thoughtlessly gabble on. 'I'm just saying, don't go short, I have plenty. More than I can spend and no one to spend it on. You know.' I stop talking, but it's too late. The hurt radiates off him, putting me in mind of a damaged nuclear reactor. He's shimmering with pain and embarrassment. Maybe there is a little anger too. A dangerous energy.

'What do you think I am, some sort of toy boy?' The expression is comical, and under other circumstances I might have laughed, but the atmosphere is so taut it feels as though it could shatter, like glass. 'I don't need your money, Emma,' he says with a stiff smile. He is always polite, dignified. He's that now, but steely cold too. 'I don't need it or want it.' I nod, drop my gaze from his, too embarrassed to find a way into an apology. 'I can manage perfectly well on my own,' he adds defensively.

'Right. Yes, of course. I never meant—'

But he doesn't let me finish. 'I did before you came along and—' He snaps his mouth shut. It lingers, the unfinished sentence, the implication: *and I will after you've gone.* He doesn't think we are forever. I hoped we might be. I hoped he thought that too, but I've ruined that with my careless talk about money.

'Don't worry, Auntie Emma, you can spend *all* your money on me. *I* don't mind one little bit,' says Lottie, with a girlish

85

giggle, oblivious to the nuances the adults around her are drowning in.

Heidi stands up. 'Can I get anyone another coffee?'

Gina and Mick are on their feet too, saying they must go. Lottie is practically carried out of the room, so keen are they to get away from the awkwardness I have created. Matthew digs out his mobile, reads something on it, or perhaps just pretends to. Then he says, 'Right, sorry, but I've got to head off now too.' He holds the phone aloft. 'Loads of work to do. I need to sort through Friday's shoot, bin the photos where the client blinked and share the file with them as soon as poss. They're chasing me.'

I don't believe him. He hasn't mentioned any work he had to do this weekend. I assumed he was coming back to mine tonight; I was looking forward to it. I jump up and head for the hall, reaching for my coat.

'Right, well, I should be on my way too,' I mumble.

This stops Heidi in her tracks. 'You can't drive.' She sounds concerned. 'I thought Matthew was driving. I thought that's why he didn't have a drink.'

Matthew looks increasingly uncomfortable. 'I was abstaining because I had this Photoshop work to do.' He rubs the top of his head and frowns. 'Heidi makes a good point, though, Emma. You've had too much to drink to attempt driving. When I saw you knocking it back, I thought you must be staying here.'

I ache for him to call me babe. Emma sounds so stiff and formal. How did I let this wonderful afternoon collapse into such awkwardness? I am always more conscious than most about drink-driving, obviously. I know I can't drive, as I've drunk over half a bottle of wine. How much over, I'm not sure.

86

But plenty. I wouldn't call it 'knocking it back', though. Like Heidi, I'd assumed Matthew was coming home with me and that he would drive. I think he would have, if I hadn't publicly offered to bankroll him and therefore totally humiliated him in front of my friends. I wait a beat for him to suggest we head over to his. He doesn't.

I know that Heidi will feel duty-bound to step in, offer me their sofa for the night. I've borrowed her knickers and PJs often enough in the past, but embarrassment creeps up through my body, I'm pretty certain it will be evidenced in a vivid red blush on my neck. I rush to head off her pity. 'I can get the train home. I'll pick the car up tomorrow. Will you pop a visitor's parking permit in it?'

Heidi nods, her gaze bouncing between me and Matthew. A train back to Hampshire tonight and then back here to Woking again tomorrow is a big inconvenience. Surely he sees that.

'Good plan, better safe than sorry,' he comments, glancing again at his phone. He shouts goodbye upstairs to the kids, kisses Heidi on the cheek, shakes hands with Leon.

'Food was delicious.'

'Must do this again.'

'Soon, soon.'

'Thanks for coming.'

'Thanks for inviting me.'

'Travel safely.' The barrage of pleasantries does nothing to disguise the discomfort of my clumsiness, his rejection.

The door slams shut. The spring sun has dipped behind a cloud and the air feels damp and threatening. We're alone, and for the first time since we met, this doesn't feel like a good thing. He's distracted and distant, I feel riled and rebuffed. By the time we're at the end of the street, it's started to rain. A relentless drizzle. Neither of us has a hood or an umbrella. Matthew puts his collar up and we both walk at speed. The inclement weather washes away the opportunity to chat and reconnect; we dash to the train station in silence. I don't understand how this journey home is so dissimilar to the journey to Heidi's. Then, my body was wet with desire; the day held promise. More, we felt as though *we* held promise. Now we are going in different directions. We stand on opposite platforms with the track between us. His train comes first. I watch him board. His gaze is nailed to his phone. He doesn't look up.

12

I'm wet and cold by the time I put my key in the lock, but it's not the sort of cold that can be fixed by popping on another jumper. Lunchtime drinking has left me with a heavy feeling in my head, and the fact that Matthew hasn't come home with me has left me with a heavy feeling in my heart. I am overwhelmed by a sense that it's not going to work out. My money always ruins things. Not the worst problem to have, I know, but a problem all the same.

I blink back the dreary hangover that is brewing behind my eyelids and head upstairs. I'm showering when I hear it. One crash, then another five or six in quick succession; a pause and then more crashes. Maybe ten or a dozen in total. The noise is coming from the living room, just below me. I freeze.

It's here. It's happening. The thing Heidi is always warning me about, the thing I never believed would occur. Someone is in the house. An intruder. Immediately I see what could unfold. I can visualise the burly, dangerous man who will hurt me. I don't want to think about the ways he might hurt me, this unknown man, but there are many. Taking my stuff is far from the worst thing that can happen. Every woman knows that. The horrifying knowledge lurks in our collective subconscious. The seed of fear planted when you're just twelve or thirteen and some man makes an inappropriate comment about your budding breasts. A seed that sprouts when your first date calls you a prick-tease, insists 'everyone knows no means yes', when it doesn't. It never does. Fear takes root when a gang of men on the street – maybe workmen fixing cables, maybe suited and booted office workers congregating outside a pub – allow their gazes to slide over you, inside you, their tongues on their lips. Flicking. Dogs on heat. Tendrils of fear climb like veins through your body when you hear the vile words that can only be fired at women, and you are voiceless because there are no male equivalents to the vitriolic single-syllable insults. The fear blossoms when you are followed home, cold keys between your knuckles, in the other hand, a rape alarm. Every woman knows the threat is potent and prevalent.

And real.

Swiftly I step out of the shower and lock the bathroom door. I leave the water running. If he has heard me showering, it is safer to pretend I'm still in there. I grab a towel and dry myself ineptly while looking around for my phone, which I soon realise is on my bedside table. I weigh it up and think that if it is a burglar, I'd be much better off allowing them to take whatever and go on their way. Tackling someone is far too risky. I could easily be overpowered; there might be more than one intruder. I hurriedly rummage in the dirty linen basket and find knickers, bra, jeans and jumper. I feel a bit safer dressed. I wait and wait. After some minutes without hearing anything more from downstairs, I carefully, silently, turn the lock and then, millimetre by millimetre, emerge from the bathroom.

I'm terrified I'm going to find myself face to face with the intruder. My eyes are wide, almost to the point of straining the sockets, but I don't see the burly man I fear. I don't see anyone, yet I'm certain someone has been in my bedroom; it smells different from when I went into the en suite. The thought that he was so close makes my stomach lurch.

I try to identify the smell. I can't, not quite. It's earthy, dank, not exactly the smell of drains, but something close. Something decaying and unsavoury. I'm surprised by that. I expected the odour of aftershave, sweat or maybe cigarette smoke. What I detect doesn't seem quite human, let alone specifically male. I stand statue-still and listen for more movement. I can hear my own breathing, and it is loud and too fast. I try to quell the fear. I have a panic button next to my bed that raises a silent alarm; pressing it prompts an immediate telephone response from a private security team. If I answer that telephone call, there are code words that trigger a physical response, and security could be here within fifteen minutes. If I don't answer the telephone call, help comes regardless. I must get to the button.

Carefully, silently, I inch towards the bed. My hand quivers as I stretch for the red button. I press it and count the seconds until the telephone rings. One, two, three, four . . . It's the longest eight seconds of my life, but soon my home phone trills through the house. My instinct is to answer it, snatch up the handset and scream for help, but there is a chance the intruder is still here, and if so, it would be a mistake. I have to trust the system. If I don't pick up the phone after activating the alarm, help will come.

The phone falls silent.

I stay deathly still. The only movement is my chest rising and falling. My mouth is dry, and even when I run my tongue over my teeth, I can't create any saliva. Unwelcome thoughts smash their way into my head. I try not to think of all the times my friends have said that by living in the woods, I'm isolated; by living in a glass box, I'm exposed. I wait.

13

'Are you OK, ma'am? Are you injured?' The security guard is in his late thirties. He is thickset and has a determined, capable air about him. I stare at him in relief and shock and try to react appropriately to what he is saying. I'm frozen. Since I pressed the panic button, I've stayed silent and absolutely motionless. It seemed essential to my survival, and now I don't know how to shake off that paralysis. 'Can you confirm you're not injured?' he asks. His tone is controlled but insistent. I nod. 'Can I approach you, ma'am?' I nod again. This time with more impatience. It feels a little woke that he's asking for permission to approach me. What if I was bleeding and in desperate need of emergency care? Plus I think he's being a little patronising by calling me ma'am. I'm not royalty or ancient. Then I pull myself up. He's just doing his job. I take a deep breath.

He starts to ask other questions. Was I the one to press the alarm? Did I do so because I suspected an intruder? Did I see an intruder? I answer him yes, yes, no. I don't elaborate. He informs me that he and his colleague have checked the house.

They haven't found anyone, but there are signs of a disturbance. He asks me to come downstairs with him so I can verify. 'Do you have any shoes up here that you can put on? You'll need them.' I slip on a pair of trainers and then follow him, mentally anticipating what might have been stolen.

The security guard walks me downstairs, through the hallway, the kitchen and the dining room space; they all look exactly as usual. Then he directs me towards the living room area, where the second guard is waiting for us. I look around, confused. I have six impressively large indoor plants; the sort that interior decorators refer to as 'statement' or 'architectural'. They are all planted in tall white concrete pots. Or rather they were. Every one of the pots is smashed and overturned, soil is spilling out onto the floor and the plants are broken, snapped off at the stem. To smash the concrete plant pots someone would have needed to use great strength, or even a tool, such as a hammer. Yuccas, palms and small fig trees lie ruined, the trunks broken and leaves wrenched off. Then I notice that the two Victorian domes that I bought yesterday have been smashed to smithereens. Thousands of tiny diamond-size shards of glass glint under the electric light.

'I hadn't even unpacked those,' I mutter. The security guards look quizzical. 'They were still in the bubble wrap and tissue paper that the guy in the shop packed them in,' I explain.

'What were they? Like drinking glasses or something?' one asks.

'No, taxidermist domes.'

He looks nonplussed. 'Were they valuable?'

'Not compared to many things here.' I shake my head, confused. 'They were special, though.'

The guards ask me to check the house for any missing property or other damage I might note. An extensive search reveals there is none. Nothing is missing. My tech, art and jewellery are undisturbed. There are no signs of a break-in. No broken windows, no forced locks, nor are any of the doors or windows unlocked or open. We find the bubble wrap and tissue paper in the bin. The bubble wrap is neatly folded, the tissue paper scrunched into tight, deliberate balls. I offer to make tea, and while the kettle is boiling, I ask, 'What sort of intruder tidies away the packing?' I'm mystified.

The guard who found me upstairs replies, 'So you're certain you didn't put these dome things on display? You didn't damage them or any of the plants yourself?'

'No, of course not,' I retort indignantly. It's a strange question. 'Why would I?'

'And you don't know who did damage them?'

'Will you check the grounds?' I deliver it more as an instruction than a request. I use my imperious voice so that I don't betray how bewildered and spooked I am.

One of the guards goes outside, the other stays with me. He accepts the tea I offer but doesn't sit to drink it. He stands, swaying left to right, changing the balance of his weight from one foot to the other. A pendulum swinging. The second guard reports back: there are no footprints on the garden beds, paths or tracks, despite it being wet and muddy. They ask if they can check the security camera footage. I have cameras trained on the paths and gateways. The footage shows me and Matthew leaving this morning in my car, me returning via taxi alone and the security guys themselves arriving just twenty-five minutes ago. There is no sign of anyone else arriving or leaving the property.

'I don't understand,' I mutter. The guards shrug and exchange a look that says things could have been much worse and a few broken plants doesn't warrant too much concern. 'Do you think it's a disturbed robbery?' I ask.

'That was my first thought,' comments the thicker-set, older man. 'But since we haven't picked anyone up on the CCTV footage and nothing seems to be missing, I'm more inclined to think it's a kids' prank. Locals. High or drunk. Mindless vandals. Jealous, most likely, of this place. Got in the house and now vanished into the woods.'

'You think?'

'What else?'

I nod, because I don't have any ideas of my own. 'Actually, that is probable. A while back, the light bulbs in my outside garlands were smashed by vandals.' I hadn't thought much of it at the time but now the incident comes back to mind.

'It happens. Do you want to call the police? You can, but . . .' He trails off. The implication is clear: it seems like a bit of a fuss. What could the police do, since nothing has been stolen? I wasn't harmed, there are no leads.

I see the security guards to the door; they say they'll write up a report to help with the insurance claim. Once they've gone, I start to clean up. I carefully place the larger pieces of glass and concrete on newspaper, wrap them up neatly like little gifts, even though they are the opposite. Next, I get out a dustpan and brush, and sweep up most of the soil before vacuuming. I fill a bucket with scalding-hot water, then mop the floor. There are no footprints that need eradicating and the vacuuming picked up all the soil, yet my home doesn't feel cleansed. I am exhausted. All I want to do is crawl into bed and sleep for a long time. However, I don't want to be alone. I consider calling Matthew. I'm holding my phone in my hand, internally debating, when his name pops up onto my screen as if I manifested it. I answer immediately.

'Hey, you. I fancied a break and wanted to call you.' He sounds warm and right and simply like himself once again. Not at all like he sounded when I left him at the station, vague and preoccupied. My shoulders melt down my back. I am so relieved. I thought I'd lost him. I can hear the sound of a police or ambulance siren, and someone shouts at him to 'get out the effing way'; basically the symphony of London streets. It seems bustling compared to the silence of the countryside. I normally treasure the tranquillity, but tonight it feels solitary.

'Oh, I'm so pleased to hear from you,' I gush. I tell him what has happened.

'Could it be the wind? Did you leave a window open?' he asks.

'No. I didn't leave a window open. Besides, even if I had, you know how big and sturdy the plant pots are, right? How could all six of them have blown over but nothing else be disturbed?'

'Could an animal have got in? A fox or a badger.'

'I didn't have any windows open,' I repeat. I know I sound exasperated; I am. Matthew doesn't seem concerned. In fact, his tone suggests he thinks I'm making an unnecessary drama. 'Plus the bubble wrap was folded and in the bin.'

'What a strange thing,' he murmurs.

It feels like it's more than that. It feels dangerous and threatening, rather than strange, but I don't say so because I don't feel his engagement, and whilst I have shared a special couple of months with him, I've been self-sufficient for years. I'll process and manage this on my own if I must. I'm not in the habit of asking for help, and clearly I'm not good at it. I would take it, though, if it was offered. I wait to see if he suggests coming to stay tonight.

He yawns, and then starts telling me about his evening and the work he has managed to get done. After ten minutes or so he says, 'Well, perhaps you should get to bed. I'm sure it will all seem less of a mystery in the morning.' I don't see how that will be the case, but as he's clearly not going to offer to come here, I suppose I have no choice but to follow his advice.

Once again I check all the doors and windows are securely closed and locked. I set the alarm, take a couple of Temazepam and get into bed. As I pull the duvet up to my chin and sniff the air, I can still smell it, the strange, moist matter that I don't recognise and can't quite identify. Something like antique shops, or wet dogs, or damp woods. The cloying smell sits in the back of my throat.

14

When I wake the next morning, my first thought is that the Temazepam must have had quite an effect, because the light coming through the windows is solid and open, suggesting it's about 9 a.m. rather than 5.08. I must have slept through the alarm. I grab my phone to check the time. It's 8.42. I have a Zoom at 9.00 and I look far from presentable. 'Crap,' I say aloud. I'm in the habit of talking to myself. I sometimes wonder if I should get a pet to fill the void. I leap out of bed and almost throw myself into Matthew, who is standing in the doorway of my bedroom holding a breakfast tray. I curse again and jump about a foot in the air. 'You scared me!' I yell.

'Good morning, babe,' he says with a gentle smile. His voice is almost a hum, as though he's soothing an infant. 'Sorry, sorry. That was thoughtless of me. I didn't think you were awake. I was planning on gently rousing you.'

'How did you get in?' I demand.

He looks embarrassed. 'After we spoke on the phone last night, I felt awful. I realised you'd been through something and

I hadn't got it. Can I?' He signals to ask permission to place the breakfast tray on the bed. I nod. The tray is loaded with toast, freshly squeezed orange juice and black coffee. I sniff the air. The strange stench from last night has been replaced with the tantalising smell of coffee beans, and under that, notes of freshly baked bread. Am I imagining that?

'Did you make this bread?' I ask. There are a lot of questions to be answered. I'm not sure why I lead with this one. My head is fuzzy and I'm aware I need to get a move on; my meeting starts soon.

'I noticed your breadmaker at the weekend. I thought it was criminal that I'd never seen it in use, so I decided to make some for you.'

'But that means . . .'

'Yes, I arrived last night. After we spoke, I felt like a prat. I wasn't kind to you. Babe, I have this thing . . .' He looks awkward. 'Some might say I'm an emotional cripple. It's just that I prioritise crises. I grade them. You know, after . . .'

'Becky,' I say flatly.

'Exactly. You said you weren't hurt and nothing of value had been stolen, so my first thought was that you didn't need any help. The whole incident felt like a storm in a teacup.'

I feel the hairs on my skin rise. Yesterday they had done so out of fear; today it's more irritation. What is he saying? If I'm not actually dead, then I don't need help? At least he seems to notice my annoyance, because he puts both hands on my shoulders.

'I'm so sorry. I was wrong. Bad call.' I relax into his touch a fraction, somehow relieved to feel known and accessible. I hadn't realised I wanted to be either thing until I became both to him. The annoyance melts further as he continues. 'I started to think how scared you must be feeling following a break-in and being out here on your own in the woods. I realised I'd got it all wrong, so I got the train back to Heidi and Leon's and collected the car. While I was there, I asked Leon for the spare key to your house so that I could just let myself in.'

'You told Leon and Heidi what happened?' I wonder why Heidi didn't call me.

'Heidi wasn't about. She was out walking the dog, I think. I just spoke with Leon. He's a great guy, isn't he? Anyway, I explained to him that there might be a chance you'd be asleep.' He glances at the bottle of Temazepam on the bedside table. 'I know you take those sometimes. I didn't want to be hammering on the door in the middle of the night giving you a scare. Another one.' He smiles, tilts his head to one side and stares into my eyes. Seeing if I'm with him, seeing if I think he made the right call. He goes on. 'Although as things turned out, even if I had tried hammering at your door, I'm not sure I could have roused you. I sneaked up here last night hoping to crawl into bed with you, but you were out cold. I guess taking Temazepam on top of all you'd had to drink really had an effect.'

I look at the floor, discomfited by the thought that he might not have been able to rouse me. I try not to feel judged, but I'm not used to people noting all my habits. Since I hit the perimenopause, I've slept poorly; about once a week I resort to Temazepam. It's not ideal, but I'm busy and I have to function, which is hard on broken sleep. I hadn't realised Matthew had clocked it. I don't want to have to explain all this to my younger boyfriend. It would draw attention to my chaotic hormones, my age, something we don't often discuss. A sense of awkwardness that feels a lot like shame crawls through my body.

Reading me correctly once again and trying to make me feel better, he rushes to add, 'You don't need to be embarrassed. Maybe it had nothing to do with that; more likely the shock just took it out of you.' I smile at his kindness. 'Anyway, it seemed weird sneaking into bed with you when you were unconscious but I wasn't ready to sleep. That's when I got the idea of making bread. I slept in the spare room. I just wanted to be here for you. You know.'

He stops talking and smiles shyly at me. I feel spaced out and a step behind, but I do accept he's made a huge effort here. Who bakes bread? The breadmaker was a gift from Gina. She handed it to me saying, 'What do you buy the girl who has everything?' Even she didn't seem hopeful that I'd use it regularly. I've used it precisely once.

'Well, this is all really nice,' I say, eyeing the tray. I notice he's even put out a napkin: ridiculously thoughtful. 'However, I don't have time to revel in this lovely treat. I'm running late. I have a meeting in a few minutes. I slept through the alarm,' I explain.

'No, actually, I turned that off and I cancelled your meeting.'

'What?' My delight at seeing him and his sweet breakfast tray is clouded by another wave of confusion. I'm not sure how I feel about his interference.

'I called Edward.'

'You called my PA?'

'Yes. I explained that you'd had a break-in and that you had things to sort. I didn't say you were sleeping or hung over.'

'Well, I wouldn't say—'

'He's going to push back all your morning meetings. You can start work at noon. I knew you'd hate the idea of taking a whole day off, but I thought you needed a bit of a break. Babe, I know you're not used to being looked after, but maybe it's time you were.' I must look nonplussed. 'Hell, I hope I haven't overstepped.'

He looks mortified, and I consider. Has he?

I sit with the emotions that are swirling through my head. The fact that he's cleared my morning meetings but not the entire day's commitments chimes for me. He's right, I'd be apoplectic if I found myself with a day of idleness. Workaholics don't relish the thought of holidays, and sick days are out-and-out resented. But considering that without an alarm to wake me I slept until almost nine, I can concede that my body needed the rest. *Has* he overstepped, or is this just the most romantic thing I've ever heard? I know Heidi would think it was the former. Gina would be certain it was the latter. I don't know what to think.

'Look, babe, can you just get back into bed, eat some toast, drink the coffee. It's going cold.' He picks up a slice of toast and bites into it, muttering, 'I, for one, am starving.'

'Me too,' I admit, play-snatching the slice from him and taking a bite of my own. I crave my regular kale smoothie, my run and routine, but I climb back into bed. I might as well, since the status meeting has been cancelled. Matthew gets in next to me. He's fully dressed and I'm in pyjamas, yet it feels cosy and comfortable. We eat peacefully, both drinking from the single coffee cup and orange juice glass. It's intimate, and I feel happy. I often feel fulfilled and purposeful; I'm not sure how often I feel outright happy. So this is nice.

Good.

Unexpected.

'I really am sorry about yesterday. I was a dick when we spoke.' I don't contradict him. 'I'll buy you some replacement plants.'

'You should have seen the mess,' I mutter.

He misunderstands me. 'I'll buy you plastic ones, no mess.'

'I hate plastic plants. What's the point of them?'

'Greenery.'

'Fake. Plants are supposed to give us oxygen.' I realise I sound harsh, so I turn to him and kiss him, saying, 'I don't understand dildos either.'

He laughs, but disentangles my arms, which I've weaved around the back of his neck, not taking my cue on how I'd like to use this unexpected free time. 'I had a lot on my mind yesterday,' he says.

'Yeah, you said you were busy.'

'I did have some work to do, but it wasn't just that. Not really.'

'What, then?' I ask, using my forefinger to wipe a smudge of butter from the corner of his mouth. I suck my finger. I wonder if I look at all tantalising or just plain silly.

'That stuff I was telling you about my crappy accommodation, it was only part of the story.'

'So what's the problem?'

'The landlord has discovered asbestos in the roof,' he says.

'Oh my God. Has it been disturbed? It's carcinogenic.'

'Indeed. I'll have to move out straight away. I feel for the guy I rent from. He'll lose income and I'm certain the necessary work will come at a cost.' Matthew is such a sweetheart, always thinking about others. He's facing health risks and is without a place to live, but is worried about his landlord.

'So the obvious solution is that you move in here.' The thought rushes out of my mouth before I can overthink it. Matthew looks shocked, not the ideal response. Have I just made the same mistake as I made offering the loan? I rush to retract or at least soften the impetuous suggestion. 'I mean, if you like, if it's convenient. Not forever, just a short-term fix. Or mid-term. Whatever.' Now I sound like I'm pleading, and that's just as bad. Worse, probably. 'You've been doing a lot of backwards and forwards, commuting between here and London. It's not good for the environment.' I smile. He does too. 'What I'm offering makes financial sense.'

'I don't want to do it just because it makes financial sense.'

'Of course not. That's not what I meant.'

'I want to move in with you because you want me here, because I want to be with you.'

'Yes.' I beam. 'That. Exactly that.'

He pauses for a second. I barely breathe. 'In which case, yes, I'd love to.' We grin at one another, pleased with ourselves, and then we sort of remember to kiss. It sounds silly to say that we have to remember to do that, but we have not yet established rhythms, patterns. I see Heidi and Leon, Gina and Mick move around one another in such relaxed harmony that it's like watching tides responding to the moon's wax and wane. I suppose those habits are developed over time. Time we might now have, as he's moving in. I can hardly believe it.

'I haven't lived with anyone since boarding school. I don't know what is normal for other people,' I blurt. A warning. An explanation.

'Does anyone know what is normal for anyone else?' asks Matthew with a shrug.

'No, I suppose not.' I like his answer. I hadn't thought I was looking for anyone to provide answers, but maybe I am. 'When would you like to move in?'

He glances about him. The house gleams invitingly. The expensive fixtures and fittings shine and sparkle. 'I could drive to London and pick up my things now if you lend me the car. I don't have much to collect.'

It would also mean I don't have to sleep here alone tonight, or any night. I nod and giggle.

Actually giggle.

15

Recently, I've noted that when I communicate with Heidi, I often end up wishing I hadn't bothered. Misunderstandings between us pop up like mushrooms on a waterlogged field. One moment we're laughing, the next we're tetchy and it feels like I'm fending off an interrogation. The misunderstandings and the interrogations tend to centre around Matthew. It's unsettling, annoying. For this reason, I've found myself cancelling our plans to meet and instead limiting our interaction to phone calls and texts. At least that way she can't see me rolling my eyes or biting my tongue. On our last call she opened with 'Have you met any of his friends yet?'

'We're dispensing with hello now, are we?' I asked, not totally hiding my irritation.

'Hello. So have you?'

'No.'

'Don't you think that's odd?'

'No.'

'Does he have any siblings?'

'No, he doesn't.'

'Are his parents still alive?'

'They are.'

'Why haven't you met them?'

'I've told you. They live in New Zealand.'

'That's convenient.'

'Obviously, it's anything but.' I sighed.

She asks a lot of questions about him. It's gone past excited wonder or even nosiness; now it feels like something a little more insidious. If not full-blown mistrust, then certainly scepticism. When we text one another, some messages seem loaded, while some go unanswered for days or her replies are just emojis rather than the long, in-depth messages I used to receive from her. Previously we've gloated about being the last people on the planet to still use correct spelling and grammar in texts – we even use semicolons – but in the past few weeks I've found myself googling things like 'What does the slanty-mouthed emoji mean?' Just yesterday she sent a text that began, *What are his colleagues like?*

I responded, *He freelances. Doesn't have regular colleagues.*

Do you think he's ☺ *with his career?*

Happy?

I mean, does he have any ambitions to do anything more?

More?

Else, anything else. Not saying it's not enough.

She is, though. Even though he's a good photographer, she thinks I should be with a captain of industry. Somebody with a career the size of mine. A bank balance the size of mine. It's crazy. Those types of men don't want career women for wives. They want women who will manage their social life, book their holidays, cook their meals and launder their clothes. Of course, because doing those things is a full-time job too. Matthew has no ego and can fit in around my world. It's enough for me that he's passionate about something, that we share beliefs and goals. It's hypocritical of Heidi, as she doesn't work outside the home. Leon is a solicitor and they manage on his salary. There is an inherent inequality in her thinking. Our friendship was founded on a shared sense of displacement and buttressed with subsequent laughs and loyalty. Understanding, positivity and honest conversation between us have rarely faltered. Now, though, the first two have gone, and while she'd probably argue that she's still being honest with me, I'd say she's being blunt, even belligerent. Wounding. In the past I've valued our unique willingness to be totally frank with one another, but that was when our thoughts were aligned. Our views on pop songs, people and politics developed in parallel; we rarely disagreed; we were never at odds. Until now.

Recently, I've been giving a lot of thought to the saying 'It's who you know, not what you know.' I've never believed that. I've always believed it *is* what you know. But now, since I've met Matthew, I realise that yes, it is who you know that counts, though not in a cynical way. I don't believe knowing Matthew will give me a leg up in my career or get me invited to fabulous parties or put me in contact with politicians so that I can lobby them on issues that are important to my work. No, of course not, he isn't that sort of person at all. But knowing him somehow makes me better, my world glossier, my life more energetic. Knowing him *counts*. I realise how dopey that makes me sound, and sometimes I'm gripped with shame and panic that I'm an idiot and making a fool of myself because no one expects to fall in love so deeply at my age. And certainly not with a younger man. Yet I have.

Because I think this *is* love.

Can you believe that? Can you imagine that? Me? Someone who has never looked for love or prioritised finding a partner. I can't decide if it's unseemly, insane or incredible.

However, I haven't told Heidi any of this. I feel shy telling her I'm in love. Anxious. She will judge, dismiss. I haven't even told her Matthew has moved in. I plan to, this evening. This sort of momentous news is best delivered face to face. She'll be happy for me, right?

I spot Heidi and Gina at a table in the corner. I wave with the sort of enthusiasm that suggests a level of mania. I bite the bullet the moment I sit down at the sticky pub table. 'Matthew has moved in,' I blurt.

Heidi's eyes grow as wide as saucers. 'Are you mad? You hardly know him. That's so fast,' she says directly.

'I'll get a bottle of champers, should I?' I offer, not acknowledging her comment but instead battling the flare of disappointed annoyance I feel towards her.

'I don't think they sell champagne here,' mumbles Gina apologetically. It's the sort of London pub that makes you think you've walked into a Dickens novel. The smell of decades of beer spillages is ingrained in the carpet; beer mats curl at the corners. She's right. They sell draught beer, spirits, and Coke on tap. Ordering house wine is considered fancy. We picked this place because it's close to the station and convenient.

'Well, Prosecco then, cava. Just bubbles. They might have a dusty bottle stashed somewhere for special occasions.'

Gina grins. 'Worth asking.'

I send a pleading look Heidi's way. I want her to get on board with this monumental thing and celebrate it.

'No thank you, it's only just five-thirty. A bit early for me. Besides, I'm having a few days off the booze,' she says.

'Cleansing?' enquires Gina.

'Not as extreme, just looking after myself.' Heidi eyes me meaningfully. I sigh and want to ask why she agreed to meet in a pub then. We could have done something different: a meal, a gallery, a games café. London has everything to offer. I doubt she is off the booze; she's protesting.

'I'll have a glass with you,' says Gina. I nod at her gratefully and then push my way through the crowd. I lean on the bar, spreading my elbows wide, taking up more space than usual, keeping people further away. I concentrate on the bottles of gin and whisky glinting a welcome, and the colourful stained-glass windows that throw smatterings of jewel-coloured light. Odd that Victorian pubs and churches chose to decorate in the same way. I guess there are commonalities. Enough people worship at this altar of alcohol. I keep my eyes on the server and push down my sense of disappointment at Heidi's response.

Matthew and I have been living together for a couple of weeks now and it's going brilliantly, better than I could ever have hoped. He does have a habit of moving my stuff around, and it's sometimes odd to reach for something in the fridge and find it finished. Odder still that he uses my body moisturiser, a fact I didn't discover until I found the tub empty. I hadn't realised how clumsy he is until I started living with him. He dropped a fork down the waste disposal unit and didn't even realise he'd done it. He knocked over my Venetian glass bedside lamp and again didn't notice; he must have barrelled in and out of the room without realising it had toppled. Still, these minor inconveniences are tiny and unimportant.

Our habits and routines have quickly aligned. I've got very used to his presence in the house, and it's wonderful to eat and sleep, talk and watch TV with someone. With *him*. We're constantly discovering things about one another, as we urge each other to try our respective speciality dishes, or listen to a track that is a favourite, or watch a movie that one of us deems a 'must see'. Side note: our film tastes are not similar, I like to watch gritty dramas or documentaries. He prefers blockbuster movies and, most extraordinarily, musicals. I like our gender-stereotype-defying preferences. We go to country pubs and eat fish pie among hill walkers; we go to art galleries and afterwards drink tea and eat cake in the café, sitting next to fiercely educated grey-haired ladies. I'm slowing down, working less, eating more, relaxing, just like people have always told me to. It's wholesome and adult. Sensible. He exudes dependability and I feel extraordinarily content. Shouldn't all of that please my best friend?

I order a vodka shot and down it at the bar. I had thought I'd probably drink a little more than is wise tonight, but in a celebratory manner; now I neck the shot as a form of Dutch courage. Sweat gathers under my armpits and I feel tension skitter up from the base of my spine to the crown of my head.

I return to the table with a bottle of cava, two wine glasses and a Diet Coke. Before I can even sit down, Heidi asks, 'Why did he come back to the UK after his wife died? Why not stay in the US with his friends or go back to New Zealand and be with his family?'

'I don't know, but I'm glad he did.' I plonk myself down,

feeling heavy. I pour the fizz and clink my glass against Gina's, but it's a habitual gesture and doesn't hold any real *joie de vivre*.

'The thing is, Emma, friends and family are part of the deal with a partner. They prop you up when you need it. And at some point or other, everyone needs it. You have to look at a partner as a package, and you don't know his package,' comments Heidi.

'I think she does,' Gina says, with a dirty laugh. She winks. I appreciate her attempt to lighten the mood, but Heidi won't be distracted. She stares at me, her huge brown eyes glinting with a cold, steely determination. The pub is noisy. Everyone around us seems to be having a good time. Fleetingly I wish I was in another group. One where friends were simply chewing the fat and knocking back the booze.

'As I don't have a family to speak of, I'm not that concerned about his package.' I pronounce the word in a way that clearly communicates my disdain for her theory.

'Is he still in touch with his dead wife's family?'

It's never crossed my mind to ask. 'They live in South Africa, so he can't exactly pop by for tea.'

'Everyone is so very far-flung, aren't they? His family in New Zealand, hers in South Africa, friends in America.'

I sigh. I know that Heidi is like a Rottweiler when she gets something between her teeth. A dog with a filthy, briny bone. One that she occasionally buries in the garden but always goes back to and unearths. I know I must face her down. 'What's your point?'

'I don't have one.' She does. She always does. We stare at one another, a Wild West stand-off. Eventually she sighs, sags like an airbed that is being deflated after the guests have departed. 'It's odd that he hasn't introduced you to anyone. It just seems like he's getting his feet under the table fast,' she murmurs. Maybe there's some sympathy in her tone, but I fear it's pity and I bristle.

'Getting his feet under the table.' I repeat her comment with incredulity. 'What an especially twentieth-century thing to say.'

'Why the rush? You never do anything rash.'

'I'm forty-seven. I think maybe it's time I did.'

'And that's another thing. The age gap,' she states flatly.

'I don't think anyone would comment if it was the other way round. If he was eleven years older than I am, people wouldn't raise eyebrows.'

'But it isn't the other way round. It's this way round.'

'I never realised how sexist you are.' I try to laugh, but the sound gets swallowed in my throat, not authentic enough to battle its way into existence.

'It's not a matter of being sexist. What if he wants a family? Babies? Have you even talked about that?' We haven't, but I can't bring myself to admit as much, because she'll point out that we should have, we must. Matthew knows the facts. He knows my age; he must have given the matter some thought. I suppose it is a conversation that has to happen, but I freeze when I think of having it, because if he says he does want children, then he's basically saying we're not forever. I don't want to hear that. I think Heidi sees all of this in my face, because her body softens an infinitesimal fraction and she adds, 'The thing is, Emma, you've always said you were quite happy on your own.'

'Well, I was, but I'm *deliriously* happy now.' I throw back my cava and, simply for something to do, pour another. 'I'm not saying it's long term. It's just he had to move out of his last place in a hurry, and we thought, why not? It will be fun. And it is. Just that, fun.' I break off, hating myself for downplaying how splendid we are. How special it is.

Heidi has the good grace to look a bit embarrassed, but pushes forward. 'I don't want to be the one to say it, but is he rushing things because he's in a bind over his accommodation, or because he's lonely and he just needs someone, or—'

I shake my head quickly, denying the thought, eradicating it if possible. I don't want my best friend to articulate my worst fear. The noise of the pub seems to rise and fall like waves crashing on a shoreline. Heidi reaches across the table and squeezes the tips of my fingers. I put my hand on my lap, out of her reach.

'Is he just lonely? Is he really over her?' Her voice is almost a whisper. And yet it is a roar.

'What? How would I . . . How would I know?' I stutter. I am annoyed at myself for displaying this vulnerability, asking for her advice even when she's saying everything I don't want to hear. But I ask anyway, because I've always trusted her.

'How often does he visit her grave?' she asks.

My mouth is parched. I could do with some water, but there isn't any. Instead, I throw back another glass of cava. It does the opposite to quenching; my throat rasps. I take a deep breath and rationalise what is going on here. Heidi should be welcoming Matthew with warmth and enthusiasm. Friends ought to support each other. Isn't that what she told me to do when Gina got engaged to Mick? There is only one explanation I can think of. She's jealous of him. The thought crushes me like an avalanche of snow tumbling down a mountain; it gathers momentum, and within a swift second it buries me. Fatally.

Heidi has never had any competition for my affection or time, and now she does. Since meeting Matthew, I haven't been available for all our meet-ups, which must annoy her. Occasionally I have let her phone calls go through to voicemail, and maybe she too feels the distance of lingering, unanswered texts, because that's not just a one-way thing. When her texts are impertinent or irritating and stuffed with ambiguous emojis, I sometimes make a silent protest by being slow to respond.

This is jealousy. She wants to keep me for herself. For her convenience. This isn't about what's best for me. It's about what's best for her. I pour myself another drink. I don't top up Gina's glass, as hers is still full. Both women are staring at me, examining me. The room droops.

'Steady, I bet there was a huge mark-up on that plonk,' Heidi comments.

Why is she always talking about money? Why doesn't she want to see where this might go with Matthew? I've always said she and her family are my chosen family. I'm generous with them. Very. In fact, last year I made a will, and apart from the bits I've left to charity, my godchildren are the main beneficiaries. Who else have I got to leave it to? My brother is well taken care of; he doesn't need it. Is she worried that if I reprioritise my affection – if I fall in love – I might change my mind about the will? Momentarily I lose my bearings. The world slows, voices echo and slur. It's like I've dived into an icy lake, plunged too far underwater, and it takes a great effort to come back to the surface, back to reality. I stare at Heidi and she glares back.

'Girl, I'm on your side. You know that.' But for the first time since we met, I'm not sure she is.

'Shall we talk about something else now?' I say coolly. 'How's the revision going?' It's a general enough question. She runs with it, sharing details about colour-coded revision cards that I find I don't care about. I don't even know which child is revising, but one of her kids is always studying for some set of important exams. I finish my drink, and when the glass is drained, I say I need to get home.

'Already?' comments Gina.

'I have some work to get through.'

'You always have work, but you never slink off this early,' she points out. Then she beams at me, 'Truth is, you're itching to get back to the lovely Matthew and his package, aren't you?'

'Nothing stays the same,' I mumble.

'Nor should it,' she says, standing up to hug me. At least she gets it.

Heidi says, 'Text me when you're home.'

'I'm a big girl, Heidi.'

'I know, but bad things happen to girls of all shapes and sizes.'

16

Despite dashing to the station, I miss my train by a matter of minutes, and I have to wait another fifteen for the next one. I kill time drinking a glass of house white in the station bar. I don't really remember making the decision to order a second, but when I pay, I realise I have. I'm agitated and hoping that alcohol will soothe. It doesn't. A wave of dreary sadness washes over me as I pass through the ticket barrier. I'm not just upset that Heidi might be jealous of my relationship with Matthew or stung that she doubts his commitment to me. The truth is, sometimes I can't provide her with the answers to the questions she asks. Maybe she's right and I don't know him as well as I should. Throughout my career, I've maintained that there is no such thing as a stupid question. I'm known for asking the things no one else wants to ask but everyone ought to. It appears I have not transferred this skill to my private life. Should I have? Or are the two things entirely different? The thought confuses me after what I've drunk. I wish I'd bought some water.

When Matthew and I are together, we exist in an almost

surreal immediacy that make the past and even the future seem irrelevant. There's an urgency and a completeness to our every moment that doesn't allow room, or even harbour a need, for anything other than what he offers me. Isn't it better to stay in the moment, forget what's gone before, don't worry about what is yet to come? Isn't that the mantra we're all supposed to live by? Being with him is like being in a deep, contented state of meditation. The here and now is enough. More than enough. Yet when I am away from him, for example when I'm with Heidi and she's probing, I become unsettled and uncertain. I guess that leaves me two choices. I should know more or I should be apart from him less.

The train is busy with commuters. I squeeze into a seat and text Matthew to say I'll be home by 8.30.

He texts back. *What, already? That was a short night xx*

Missed you xx

He responds with a smiley face and then: *I better clear out the other woman xx*

I send a laughing face. Funnily enough, texts with emojis between the two of us don't aggravate me at all. It's aways been our language and I'm always sure what he is implying, unlike when I'm texting with Heidi.

He asks, *Have you eaten? Xxx*

No. I'm starving xxx

I could eat you xxxx

Despite this silly exchange, my mood doesn't clear. I stare out of the window. The rain makes everything look grey, flat and exhausted. I watch as stations whizz past, in and out of sight, eternally remote, boasting nothing more exciting than uninviting waiting rooms and public toilets.

I carry the regret of my evening with Heidi and Gina with

me, and the moment I stumble through the front door, before I have even taken off my coat, I blurt, 'Where is Becky buried? You never said.' I regret the question as I hear myself ask it, although it is arguably a smidge better than 'Do you want kids?' which is also preying on my mind.

'Hello, babe.' He walks over to me. Kisses my forehead. I know I smell boozy, which I'm not proud of. I clamp my mouth shut, try not to breathe near him. He's holding a spatula that's dripping with a thick red sauce. I watch warily, in case any of the sauce drips onto my dark wooden floors or my coat. Matthew doesn't appear aware of it in his hand; he just seems delighted to see me. He beams. 'I'm making dinner,' he adds, not answering my question.

'Oh, let me wash my hands and I'll help.' I dash upstairs, splash water on my face and gargle with mouthwash before returning to the kitchen. I like cooking with Matthew. I've prepared and eaten enough meals alone to know that this ritual is special, valuable. I enjoy creating something with him; it's not babies, but it's something. We are both decent cooks. We learn from one another. Tonight he has prepared a staple, spaghetti bolognese. The smell of the basil, tomatoes and garlic is delicious, and my mouth waters. Carbs are just what I need to soak up the alcohol before I go to bed. I don't want a cracking hangover in the morning. I can't afford that, as I have an early start and a busy day. The restructure at work is demanding a forensic approach to budgets. Salaries are the biggest cost, meaning redundancies are inevitable. Tomorrow I'm meeting the CFO to identify who we need to lose. I sigh. I shouldn't have gone out with Heidi and Gina; I should have kept my head in the game.

'I am not someone who insists that my bolognese is the best outside Italy or anything hyperbolic, but I do know I make a reliably good one,' says Matthew with an endearingly modest smile. 'The trick is to let the sauce simmer for as long as possible so that the flavours of the beef and sausage mingle and reduce. I prepped this at four this afternoon.'

'But you thought I was eating out,' I say.

He smiles at me. 'I had a feeling you might come home to me. At least, I hoped you would. I wanted to be prepared if you did. Besides, if you had stayed out for a raucous time with your friends, I would have popped it in a Tupperware box for tomorrow. It's just as good on the second day.' He looks shy about admitting to being so thoughtful, so domestic. I smile encouragingly, and he adds, 'But I thought that maybe you'd decide being here is just the best.' He pauses, makes eye contact, and my stomach hiccups. 'And I was right.'

See. There it is. Evidence that we know each other so well.

Matthew is wearing a crisp white shirt and a pair of jeans. He looks handsome and vital. He clocks my eyes roaming up and down his body, grins. 'What?' he asks.

I can hardly confess to marvelling at how attractive and sexy I think he is, so instead I say, 'I'd never risk making bolognese in a white shirt.'

He laughs and holds up an open bottle of red wine, offering it to me. The bottle is almost empty. I feel a sense of relief that he's been drinking. I didn't have to surreptitiously gargle. I can be comfortable with him. Of course I can. I move to the hob to inspect his cooking. We stand side by side and he dips the spatula into the sauce and brings it to my lips. I taste it and nod my appreciation. When he answers, it takes me a moment to understand what is being said.

'In America, where we were living at the time. That's where she's buried.' I'm glad that I don't have to look him in the eye now. What might I see there if I did? Pain? Grief? Love? I know he still loves her. That's natural. Yet difficult. I should have remembered he always answers every question I put to him. His solid, matter-of-fact response shames me, rather than reassures me. I shouldn't be quizzing him, checking up on him, it's beneath us. 'We had so many friends there, it seemed right that the funeral was in New York so we could say goodbye together. Besides, the idea of her on a plane, in a fridge or whatever it is that they do . . .' He shivers.

I place my hand on his forearm. 'I see. Makes sense.'

'Anyway, I couldn't have afforded to have her flown anywhere. Not to South Africa, where her parents are, or here, even though I knew I'd be coming back to the UK in the long term.'

'Aren't you sad that she's so far away?' I ask. 'Wouldn't you like to be able to put flowers on her grave? Aren't you worried that no one is doing that?'

'She's dead, Emma, what does it matter?' Matthew snaps.

I gasp at the abruptness of his response. Normally he's so patient and unflappable. However, I also accept that my questions are clumsy, unkind. Heidi has got under my skin. It's idiotic of me to push this matter. I'm glad we don't have to visit her grave together, that we don't have a physical presence hanging over us. As it is, I sometimes feel the ghost of her sitting between us. Not literally, of course, I don't believe in such nonsense, but metaphorically she haunts me.

He puts his hands on my shoulders. 'That sounded harsher

than I meant it to. Sorry. All I mean is that I carry her around in my heart, in my head. I don't need to visit her grave. She's with me always.' And now I really wish I hadn't asked, because his words land like slaps. She's with me always too. 'OK, enough of this talk.' He claps his hands together and looks about him. 'I'm going to put on some music. I just need to find the portable speaker thingy. This house is so large, I keep losing things. Then we can enjoy this delicious meal I've slaved over for you.' He grins. 'Will you make yourself useful, put on the spaghetti?'

I keep spaghetti in an embossed Fortnum and Mason biscuit tin, but when I reach for it, I find that it's empty. Behind the kitchen, just past the utility room, is the larder. I rummage around in there for a new packet of spaghetti. It's not on the shelf where I keep pasta, although there is a bag of farfalle and another of rotini. Certain that there ought to be a packet somewhere, I get down on my hands and knees and root about behind tins of black beans and cannellini beans in the bottom cupboard. Finally, I'm successful. I grab the packet triumphantly and return to the kitchen.

I don't understand what I'm faced with.

My beautiful, serene state-of-the-art kitchen is decimated; it has turned into a 3D Jackson Pollock. The bolognese sauce is everywhere. I don't mean the pot has been upended – I don't know how that would happen anyway, as it's a chunky Le Creuset that I struggle to pick up. It's still on the hob, but it seems that someone has scooped up the blood-red sauce and thrown it over the walls, smeared it across the surfaces, the breakfast bar, the floor. There are splatters on the sink, the splashback, the draining board.

I stare at the act of vandalism and my confusion meta-morphoses into fury. What the hell? Who the hell? Why the hell? The tomato and mince look like blood and crap. It looks like a protest in a prison. Something I've seen in a movie or a nightmare. But before I can fully process my fury, it dissolves into fear. My lungs harden and my breath sticks in my throat. The plants and globes being destroyed was bizarre enough; now this. I've been wanting to tell myself that there isn't a problem, but I know that's not true. Whoever did this might still be in the house. I feel a chill; suddenly the room seems eerie and dark. The air is not as it was. It is wet and drained of oxygen, of health. I can't explain what I feel, because it is unlike anything else I've ever experienced. I am not alone, I'm sure of it. Am I having a panic attack? 'Hello?' I call out. No one replies. Had I expected anyone to?

'What have you done?' I jump, look up and see Matthew coming down the stairs carrying the portable speaker. He glances around at the mess and then at me, at the spatula in my hand. He shakes his head sadly.

'I didn't do this.' I can't recall picking up the spatula, and yet there is sauce trailed down my hand to the elbow of my shirt. I drop it. It falls into the pan and makes another splash on my clothes. I notice that his white shirt is still immaculate; it's the only thing that remains clean. My cheeks feel like they're being squeezed together, squashing my nose and eyes; not painful exactly, but uncomfortable and disorientating. I know I'm a little drunk. The thought is in one way a relief – because when I am totally sober, this will all seem less weird, it will make more sense, surely – and yet being drunk is simultaneously a problem because drunks are unreliable, unreasonable. 'It's vandals again,' I explain. 'We must check the house, right now. We should press the alarm.'

Matthew immediately moves to the back door, wiggles the handle. It's locked. He turns to the bifold doors that run the length of the house and checks those; they are all secure too. He dashes upstairs and although I'm nervous that he'll encounter someone, he would be able to manage himself so I don't try to stop him. For a few moments I remain exactly where he left me. He returns to the kitchen and says, 'Nothing. No one. All the doors and windows are locked.'

'I don't understand.' I break off. Matthew looks equally confused, and embarrassed too. He stares at his feet. He doesn't think anyone has been in the house. 'I didn't make this mess,' I insist.

He nods, but without conviction, then starts to carefully examine the chaos. The sauce is trailed in thin lines in some places as though it has been flicked; the effect is like a painting Lottie once presented to me with pride. She'd blown several different colours of paint through a straw. At the time, Gina and I commented that the classroom must have been chaos. In other parts of the kitchen, the mess looks as though it's been ground into the rugs and smudged onto the surfaces. More of a finger painting.

Matthew looks perplexed. 'I wonder how they got in if all the doors and windows are locked?'

'Well, it must be someone with a key,' I reason. 'It's the only logical explanation.'

'If you think that, then you need to write a list of people who have keys.'

'It's a short list. The cleaners, the pool guy, Heidi and Gina.'

I shudder. It's horrible and exhausting. 'I have to fire the staff.' Matthew runs his hand through his hair, looking pained. 'How can I trust them? All of them are from a local agency; I'm going to be absolutely hated around here. Word will get out. I'll have to get the locks changed, because I don't know if they'll make copies of the keys before they hand them back. I can give Heidi and Gina new ones.'

Matthew nods again slowly, but he looks uncomfortable. I'm used to making hard decisions on staffing. He will never have had to do anything similar.

I see that my phone, car keys and laptop are all still here on the kitchen table, exactly where I left them when I went to the larder. Nothing has been stolen. 'I'm not going to call the police. I'll call the security company tomorrow to report it, but it's been a long day; shall we just get on with cleaning up?'

'You're sure?'

'Yes.'

Matthew sighs and heads upstairs to change into a T-shirt that will be more appropriate for the task. I don't bother, I'm already a mess, sauce splattered all over my shirt. I snap on rubber gloves, fill a bucket with steaming-hot soapy water and start to scrub.

17

Neither of us fancies eating anything by the time we're finished scraping and scrubbing food off rugs, barstools, kitchen surfaces and floors. However, I don't feel ready to go to bed.

'Shall we just have a glass of wine and watch some TV?' I suggest.

'Well, the wine sounds like a brilliant idea. Why don't you sit on the sofa, I'll open a new bottle and then you can tell me what went on with your friends this evening that put you in such a bad mood.' I gaze at him, mouth slack, surprised that he's not only realised as much but remembered to circle back to it after all the drama of the vandalism. I smile as I accept the glass of red wine that he's offering. 'Did you argue?' he asks as he sits down next to me. The sofa lets out a sigh to welcome him, or maybe that's me.

'No, not as such.'

'Well, something made you lose it.' I don't think asking where his wife is buried classes as losing it, but I guess that's just a figure of speech so I let it go.

'Heidi was a bit cool about the news that we'd moved in together. She thinks we've rushed things.'

'Fair enough. I'm sure from the outside we do look a little speedy. She's only looking out for you. She's a good friend.'

I wish she could hear how kind and reasonable Matthew is about her, a marked contrast to how suspicious and wary she is about him. 'I'm looking forward to meeting your friends. You know, when it happens,' I say, carefully. It's true, I am looking forward to meeting them, even if they were all Becky's friends too. At least then I'll be able to report back to Heidi that I've done so, to shut her up. I don't want to sound pushy but can't stop myself adding, 'I have a work trip in New York coming up in late summer. Maybe we could book you a flight and you could come along. We could tag on a few extra days as holiday. You could catch up with your old friends, introduce me to them.'

'I'm not keen, to be honest,' he says, looking away from me, through the window that faces onto the woods. It's half past eleven, so it's pitch black. The sort of dull, solid blackness that seems to swallow life. As the room is lit, only our reflections shine back at us; it is impossible to see what's out there. It's a peculiar thing to be watching us having this conversation. I get a strange feeling that I'm observing our relationship rather than participating in it. That is mad. I am here. Right next to him.

'Why aren't you keen? Are you ashamed of me or of them?' I ask this in a jokey tone, trying to hide the fact that that's what I'm worried about. Mostly the former.

'No, of course not. You're gorgeous, perfect.' He turns to me, wearing a solemn expression. 'They're great too. My friends. Really sparkling. Attractive, clever, solvent, you know all that.

That's the problem. They'll all point out that I'm punching, and you'll realise they're right.' He smiles, kisses the tip of my nose. This scenario seems unlikely; it's unusual for a man to pick a partner more than a decade older than him. His friends are much more likely to point out the issues we might encounter as a couple, as mine did. They might make the case that by choosing me he's opting out of a family. They probably have younger women they want to introduce him to, now that he's back on the market.

A fox or deer, maybe even a badger, darts between the trees closest to the house. I don't get a look at it, but the sense of movement pulls my gaze away from Matthew. He puts his hands either side of my head and turns my face gently back to his so that we are staring into one another's eyes. 'You're bound to think at least one of them is a way better bet than I am, and you'll want to trade me in.'

Is he joking? 'I never would,' I murmur.

'I can't risk it.' He smiles and pulls me into a long kiss. His hands caress my jaw, my neck. His thumb massages the spot just below my ears. My stomach rolls with pleasure. I want to give in to the kiss, drown in it, but I gently pull away. My body only just cooperating with my brain's instructions.

'Seriously, Matthew, what is the issue?' I ask. 'You've met my close friends and even some of my not so close ones and colleagues. Isn't it time I met yours?'

He sighs, frustrated. Is he frustrated with me for breaking away from the kiss and shelving the hope of us having sex? Or worse, for asking this question? But when he speaks, I realise his frustration runs deep and has nothing to do with me. He pinches the bridge of his nose and screws up his eyes. 'When

I came back to the UK, I thought I'd pick up with old colleagues and contacts, maybe even my old uni mates, but it didn't pan out that way.'

'Why not?'

'I'm not sure. Maybe too much time had gone by. Or . . .'

'Or?'

He shrugs, sort of retreats in on himself. 'People are strange after a death. They don't know how to behave. So many of my old buddies gave me a wide berth when Becky died. It was painful. Extremely so.'

'Of course.' I nod carefully. The way I always am, always must be, when Becky is mentioned.

'Some people tried, but they said the wrong thing as often as not. There was a lot of "she's in a better place now". It just didn't help me. Others kept telling me she wouldn't want me to be sad.'

'Would she have wanted you to be sad?' I ask.

Matthew grins. 'She was very jealous and protective of our relationship. She'd want me to be totally and absolutely fucking miserable. Inconsolable. She definitely wouldn't want me to find happiness again.'

'Really?' I'm shocked. How is that love?

'Yeah, she wasn't the generous type.'

Then he laughs as though this is the funniest thing ever, rather than a bit sad and negative. Yet I laugh too and our lips find one another's again. Our lips, our tongues, our hands. I edge onto my back and he climbs on top of me.

As we make love, I keep my eyes on him. When I do allow myself a glance at our reflections in the window against the black night, I find he is doing the same and we lock eyes there too. We look good together and sometimes we like watching ourselves. I keep my gaze fixed on his eyes and try to dismiss the thought that someone else is watching us too.

Afterwards, I put my knickers back on and we head upstairs. I'm exhausted but need to shower before I go to bed. Getting up at five in the morning only really works if you're asleep by ten. It's almost 1 a.m. now. I think I'll skip my run tomorrow.

I turn the shower up to the highest setting, so that the water is pummelling me aggressively, and speedily soap my body. My thoughts about the day cascade as quickly as the water. One moment I'm grinning to myself, caught up in the recollections of exactly what we've just done to each other, the fabulousness of the gentle kisses and the tender caresses that ultimately accelerated into something harder and more animalistic. The next moment, my mind clouds as I get flashbacks to the bolognese sauce splattered around the kitchen. An act of vandalism, an act of hate. Why? Who? Then I remember Heidi's coolness earlier this evening. Perhaps motivated by something as ugly as jealousy or greed. Her muted response to my news that Matthew has moved in has left me feeling strangely deserted. Alone.

I need to sleep. Everything will be clearer in the morning.

Because my head is whirling and the water is gushing, I initially don't quite catch what he is calling through to me from the bedroom. He was chatting about the fact that he'll talk to the cleaning agency about getting new staff, how he'll check all their references, manage the whole thing to save me stress. 'Or I could do the cleaning myself if you're not comfortable with the idea of strangers in your home. I'll sort everything out. I'll call the locksmith.' There's a pause, and then he starts again, 'Do you think we should . . .'

Something, something, something. I turn off the tap to hear him properly.

'Sorry? What did you say?'

'Do you think we should get married?'

It feels like the world shudders to a halt. I stare at him in the bathroom mirror. He's in the doorway now; I am still in the shower. Naked, wet. His eyes find mine, and then the world judders on. Keeps turning. Like the sun coming up.

I let the words sink in. In fact they don't sink in so much as lift me up off my feet. I am hovering. Walking on clouds. I could turn to him, be direct, but I daren't move, I don't want to change anything, not even the air between us. I don't want to disturb this moment. This unimaginable thing. He looks pensive, as though he's asking my opinion on the matter, which is a slightly different thing to asking me to marry him per se. I am speechless. We only met in January. If I put my mind to it, I could count how many times we've seen one another. I could probably take a good guess at how many times we have had sex. If I can still keep track, then surely it's too early to be talking about marriage. Is he serious?

He *looks* serious. 'Is it an awful idea?'

'No, no, it's not,' I mumble.

'I'm good at being married. I like it. I think you'd like it too. They say those who have the best marriages are always the first to remarry after the death of their beloved partner. People don't always understand that. But if you think about it, it makes sense. You're unlikely to rush to remarry if your wife has been a bitch or had an affair with your best friend; if your husband has been violent or controlling. But if your spouse was loving, thoughtful, interesting, fun, you'd want to find a way of re-creating that. Bad marriages don't promote marriage. Good ones do.' He pauses. 'Does that make sense to you?'

I'm not sure this is the proposal of any woman's dreams. I'm soapy, with wet hair, and he's just told me he's proposing to me because his first wife made him happy. Shouldn't there be a mariachi band, red roses, a big diamond? At least a declaration of love? And yet this feels truthful and solid. It feels real because it is devoid of clichés. Everything he has said is about love. True love. Enduring, nurturing partnerships, not three slick little words.

'What we have feels very special, doesn't it?' he asks.

'Yes, it does. It does, but . . . Well, no buts. It does. But three months,' I stammer.

'Well, three and a half, to be exact.' The shower is dripping slowly, *tap, tap, tap*. I can feel soap bubbles popping in my hair, *pop, pop, pop*. I feel my breath drum through my body. 'If Becky taught me anything, it's that life is too short to waste time. Why wait if something feels right, and this does, doesn't it? It's not just me who thinks that, is it?' He looks nervous, vulnerable. 'I'm a straightforward sort of guy. What you see is what you get. And you strike me as a straightforward sort of woman. So what do you think, should we crack on with living?'

I consider what it means that even my proposal is entangled with her, his first wife. He wants to seize time with me because he lost time with her. Here's the thing. From the moment we are born, every pop song, novel, film and TV show tells us that we need a special someone, that we are incomplete on our own, that there is a better half out there. Until recently, I never bought into that argument. I could happily dance alone. Think alone. Achieve alone. Live alone. Grow old alone. But then he came along, and you know what? It *is* better. Just that. My life is better with him in it. End of.

'OK, then. Let's,' I say.

'Yeah?'

'Yeah.' I'm laughing now. I step out of the shower and move into his arms. My wet, slippery naked body pushes into his warm, firm, clad one, and it feels like a fit. A perfect fit.

18

May

It's Saturday, but instead of looking forward to a weekend filled with chatter and sex, maybe a long walk, I wake up feeling a buzz of annoyance at both my friends. When I told them about the proposal, Heidi didn't even bother to hide her disapproval.

'I'm your best friend, so I'm just going to say it. You're a really rich woman.'

I tried to shut her down. 'I am not going to hear he's marrying me for my money.'

'Look, I can understand that he's keen. As your oldest bestie, I know all the things there are to love about you, Emma. You're smart and honest and loyal and hot, but . . .' She didn't finish the sentence. Or maybe she did. Maybe she wanted to leave it on the *but*. Then Gina suggested a prenup. I guess it was to break the tension, but I was stunned.

'It's a genuine solution. Heidi is saying that him rushing things might be questionable and you're saying you're rushing things because you're impossibly in love. Asking him to sign a prenup will clarify the issue,' she said with a smile.

I'm furious with them both. Gina for suggesting the prenup in the first place and Heidi for calling me every few days, ostensibly to talk about the wedding plans but always in the end because she wants to know whether I've called a lawyer yet. What was Gina thinking? Normally she is the tactful, careful one. The peacemaker. I thought when I announced my engagement that she'd talk about 'knowing when you know'. I expected her to shush Heidi and encourage me. A prenup seems like a chilly suggestion from her. How am I supposed to ask him to sign a piece of paper that will highlight the fact that he has less money than I do? A contract that suggests I don't trust him. However, every time I say as much to Heidi, she points out, 'If he loves you, he won't mind at all, will he?'

The *if* hurts. She doesn't need to say *if*.

I am seeing Heidi and Gina next week. I know they'll demand to know what the prenup status is, so I've decided today is the day. After my run, I will grasp the nettle and just get the matter out of the way, long before the actual wedding. My skin prickles and my palms sweat just thinking about the necessary conversation. I mentally fling little darts of fury at Heidi and Gina, but in the end, my more rational self wins out. Deep down I know they are looking out for my best interest. A prenup is sensible. I'm always sensible. I just don't want to be sensible about this.

When I finally stutter out my request, my embarrassment seems to spring like a flea, instantly transferring from me to Matthew, which turns out to be even more awful to endure.

'Of course. My God, I'm sorry. How mortifying.' He has turned puce, the blush shimmying up over his chest, neck and face to the tips of his ears. I curl my toes and wish we were an hour further ahead, beyond this awkwardness, or that it was ten minutes ago and I could have chosen not to say anything at all. However, time seems to stick like tar in this moment. 'I don't have much money, as you know, so,' he tries to laugh, 'so a prenup hadn't entered my mind. I've never thought about this from your point of view. I guess that's the issue, isn't it? I don't have money and you do.'

He glances to the floor, and I feel a shift in the air. I can touch it, smell it, practically taste it. It's like someone has flung open the windows and doors and let out all the heat between us, which was tremendous: passionate and exciting. The draught subsequently created brings an influx of distrust – or more accurately, the chill is the decisive moment where *he* feels mistrusted, even though that is not the case. *I* trust him completely, I do.

'I'm sorry,' I mutter.

'No, no. Of course. I should have suggested it to you. I just didn't think. You know. I'm not very materialistic,' he explains. Then, more coolly, he adds, 'It's just not a thing, not a *driver*, for me.'

I try not to feel stung or criticised by his remark. Money isn't something that drives me either. Yes, I have lots of it, but I'm not materialistic. I'm all about reduce, reuse, recycle. The most important part of my job is not my remuneration, but the respect I command, the change I can create. If I were materialistic, I wouldn't have chosen to marry a man who earns below the national average salary, would I? Obviously I can't use that line of reasoning as my defence; it would be beyond tactless, even if I had the opportunity, which I don't, because Matthew hasn't paused to let me say anything at all.

He's filling the space between us with repeated comments such as 'A prenup, of course. Of course, you were bound to require one. No problem. I see. Neither Becky nor I had any money to speak of. Didn't give it a thought. This is a different world, but yes, obviously, if a prenup will put your mind at rest, we'll do it right away. Where is it? Do you have something drafted up?'

He looks around the room as though he expects a clutch of lawyers to jump out from behind the sofa and present him with a legally binding document there and then. He's talking too quickly. Probably trying to swallow down the hurt or drown out the awkwardness, but I hear it anyway. I try to close things down, move on.

'No, I don't have anything drawn up. I wanted to talk to you about it first. I'll call my solicitor and ask how to approach it. I'm certain it's a pretty standard thing. No biggie.' I've never used that expression before, and it sounds alien on my tongue. The request for a prenup sits uneasily, quite obviously a 'biggie'. I want to turn the conversation. Engaged couples ought to talk about wedding cake or wine choices. Fun things. I try to pick up on a conversation we started a few days ago. 'I just love the idea of going to the Champagne region and tasting some of the fizz made in the smaller houses to pick one for the wedding reception. I think discovering a favourite is a little more intimate than serving Taittinger or Veuve. Do you agree? Should we base ourselves in Reims or Épernay?' I ask.

Matthew has turned away from me. He's looking out of the window, past the short lawn and into the woods. I see that the back of his neck and the tips of his ears are burning scarlet. I think of hot embers in a fire late at night when the glorious warmth of the lick of flames is gone but the spitting embers can still scald. He replies, 'I'll leave that to you. I imagine you know both regions, and *all* the champagnes, better than I do.'

'Well, Épernay then,' I mutter. He fishes his phone out of his pocket and starts stabbing at it. 'Work?' I ask.

'No, I'm messaging my mum. I want some advice on something,' he replies.

I wait patiently as he spends about ten minutes swapping messages with her. I want to say something like 'Send her my love', because that seems like a normal thing for a daughter-in-law-to-be to say, but as we haven't had so much as a Zoom introduction yet, sending love seems a bit forward.

When Matthew finally slips his phone back into his jeans pocket, he grins at me and asks, 'Do you want to wear my much-loved grandmother's engagement ring? It's rather lovely. An emerald, encircled by a number of little diamonds.' I hesitate, and he adds, 'It's worth a decent amount.'

'Did Becky wear it?' Damn, the question comes from my gut, straight to my tongue. It should have checked in with my brain first.

'Yes.' He beams a little wider, as though this is a great thing.

'Then no. I think it's maybe a bit . . .'

'Odd.' He finishes the sentence for me, and I'm relieved.

'Yeah.'

'Mum said you might think that, but I wanted to offer. You know, I didn't want you to think I wouldn't want you to wear my grandmother's ring.' There are too many negatives in that sentence for me to be certain that we have landed with a positive. He then adds, 'I want to treat you the way I treated her.' I see that his insistence on parity comes from a good place, but inwardly I sigh a little. I want him to see us as different and separate. I want to be his wife, not just his second wife, but that is tricky because I *am* the second wife. Fact. 'And I wanted you to wear something you could be proud of.' I shrivel inside. He's clearly worried about how to pay for an engagement ring of note. 'Do you have your mother's ring, maybe? Would that be suitable?' he asks.

I shake my head and resist articulating the fact that I don't want to wear a dead woman's ring. Any dead woman's. I want a ring that represents a fresh start.

'Let's go shopping,' I suggest. 'Right now. Let's go to London.'

19

I can't take my eyes off it. I repeatedly hold out my arm, stretch my fingers wide and admire my engagement ring. When I'm not staring at it, I discreetly touch the band with my thumb. Just checking it's there. We picked a round solitaire set on an eighteen-carat band. Modest by Tiffany standards, but even so, not something Matthew could afford. I slipped my Coutts card across the glass counter without either of us commenting.

Now we're sitting in a smart bistro having a light lunch. Or at least giving that impression. I'm too excited to eat. Matthew is flicking through his phone, reading the weekend papers online. It strikes me that just a few months ago if I'd walked past this café and spotted a couple looking so harmonious, I'd have had to fight a twinge of jealousy, disquiet. It's wonderful to be this side of the glass. It's so peaceful that it seems exactly the right moment to bring Matthew up to date on my thoughts about the wedding. When I do so, he looks shocked.

'So you're saying you want a church wedding?'

'I do.' I giggle at the two little words, which carry so much significance and will change the course of my life, alter the very fabric of my existence as I transition from a single woman to a wife. 'Or at least I *might* want a church wedding. I want us to consider the possibility before we dismiss it.'

'Wow, right, well, OK. Let's think it through. I have to say, I'd assumed you'd want to get married in a smart hotel. So do you believe in God and all that? You're a scientist. I think of you as so logical.'

I shrug. This shouldn't be a difficult conversation to have with the man I'm going to marry, and it's probably one that most people have before they get engaged, yet here I am. 'For me the desire to marry in a church isn't really a religious thing, it's a personal continuity thing. Just a nod to tradition. My parents are buried at St Adelaide's in Hodstone. Do you know Hodstone? It's where I was brought up. It's in Hampshire, about twenty-five miles from where we live now.'

'I think I've seen signposts to it. Twenty-five miles. We can hardly call it our local church.'

'No, but it's so pretty, and because of my parents, I thought it might be the right place.'

'I see.'

I think for a moment he's going to refuse. I bite my tongue and don't tell him that St Adelaide is the patron saint of second marriages. A fact I learnt as a child. It meant nothing to me then, other than getting a house point at school when we had a quiz about local history. Now it seems pertinent. Important. 'When we got engaged, I emailed the vicar and asked if he'd consider marrying us there.'

'Will he do it? Even though we're not churchgoers?'

I don't mention that I made a sizeable donation to the church restoration fund. I don't want him thinking I bought my way into a pretty backdrop, not considering the awkwardness of the conversation about the prenup this morning. 'Yes, I think he will. He asked to meet us.'

Matthew's Adam's apple jumps as he swallows. 'Well, if it means so much to you, then of course. You should set up a meeting at some point.' He plays with the handle of his empty coffee cup.

'I've already done so, as it happens. This afternoon, five p.m.' I glance at my watch. 'We'd better get moving if we're going to be on time.' My fiancé blinks slowly. 'You know me, I'm nothing if not efficient.' I grin broadly, trying to convince both of us that my actions are reasonable, simply those of an excited bride impatient to plan her wedding. Of course they are that, but they are also actions that have left us oddly exposed. He didn't expect this from me, a desire to marry in a church, and I didn't anticipate him objecting. Heidi's words ring somewhere deep in the back of my head. *You hardly know him.* 'Do *you* believe in God?' I ask.

He shakes his head emphatically, just once. So sure his opinion is the right one that he doesn't feel the need to elaborate or protest too loudly. The epitome of being quietly confident in his own reasoning. 'I wish I did. I think it must be great to believe that something can be changed or solved just because you wish it to be.' His tone is subdued.

'I prayed a lot when I was a child,' I admit. 'It soothed the sense of helplessness and anger I felt when my dad was drunk, and then, you know, after the accident . . .' I wait. Matthew doesn't talk about the details of his life after Becky's death. I think we must have passed the one-year anniversary now. I have no idea how he marked the day. I don't know how to approach the subject. We're planning a wedding and yet he's still grieving for his first wife. I tentatively edge towards the subject of grief and remembrance in case he wants to open up to me.

He meets my eyes; he appears to be searching for something too. I'm not sure what exactly. Maybe a sense that life goes on, maybe a feeling that I understand his loss. Whatever it is, I think he finds it, as he nods slowly. 'OK.' He reaches for his coat. 'I'd better meet your vicar then.'

I can't resist excitedly texting Heidi. *We're going to St Adelaide's this afternoon. Thinking of marrying there. Will tell you all when we see one another.* I add the church emoji. The grey ticks turn blue, but she doesn't respond. Not even with the bride, groom or wedding bells emoji.

After my parents' funeral, my grandparents scooped me and my brother into a waiting black Rolls-Royce and we were taken directly to our respective boarding schools. From then on, my time was split between school and my grandparents' home in Scotland. Even though I bought land and built a house in the county I was born in, I only visit Hodstone once a year, to lay flowers on my parents' graves on the anniversary of their deaths. I'm really hoping to oust the hard memories and make happier new ones by marrying here.

The village itself hasn't changed much since I was a kid. As well as the church, there's a pub and a post office squashed between higgledy-piggledy thatched cottages and workers' terraced homes, the type that have front doors that open directly onto the street. It's the sort of village that tourists drive through and gasp at, commenting that time has stood still here. They say it must be charming to live somewhere so unspoilt, but they don't stop, they keep on driving to the next town, where there are shops and restaurants.

We didn't live in the pretty part of the village. As my father had been cut off from his parents' wealth and was too much of a drunk to hold down a job, we managed on my mum's salary, but we didn't have the sort of money that could buy charm. We lived in a less aesthetically pleasing 1980s new-build on the outskirts. The sprawling suburbs have trebled in size since I was a girl. Matthew and I drive through a mass of red-brick semi-detached houses. It is neither impressive nor off-putting; it's unprepossessing. It's where I came from and I'm fine with that. Everyone comes from somewhere and that's not what a person should be judged on. What can be a cause of shame is where a person ends up. Matthew constantly looks from left to right, his head swivelling as he takes in saggy, tired old ladies sitting on benches at bus stops, and hunched, hooded youths milling aimlessly along the street.

I wonder when we will get to New Zealand. I am looking forward to mooching around his childhood town, meeting his mum and dad. There's room in my life for parents, even if they are only parents-in-law. I'm ready to embrace a brand-new family. I hope they feel the same about me. I wonder if my in-laws were close with Becky. Was she the daughter they'd never had, or did they resent the fact that she took their son across the world? What will they think of me?

The church dominates the village green, but the first thing I direct Matthew's attention towards is the pub. In the late-afternoon light, the white pebble-dash looks closer to grey, the hanging baskets are empty and no one is sitting at the tables outside. I ask him to imagine the garden decked with sparkling fairy lights on a warm summer evening, the sky glowing amber as the sun sets. 'There's room for a marquee. We could have a live band, and there's a catering company just up the road that has an incredible reputation.'

He interrupts. 'You're thinking of having our wedding reception here at this pub?' He looks horrified by the idea.

'It's one thought. I did wonder about putting a bus on and taking everyone back to mine – ours.' I quickly correct myself. 'But then we'd have to clean up afterwards.' I'd thought he'd like the simplicity of a pub reception; it's consciously understated. Seeing that he doesn't look at all happy with the suggestion, I say, 'There's also a stately home a couple of miles away that does weddings. We could possibly hire that.' Truthfully, Grange Hall has seen better days. The splendid glamour it once possessed was spent a century ago, and now it's scratching about for a living. Acquired by a chain of hotels that clearly bulk-bought moulded mock Louis XIV chairs and pink tablecloths but didn't have the funds to invest in updating the heating systems or fixing leaks, it's far from a dream venue. I decide to tackle the issue of the venue after we've met the vicar and there's a green light on the church wedding.

The church, a Grade I listed building, is undoubtedly, unequivocally beautiful. Dating from the twelfth century and made of coursed limestone rubble, it has everything a person imagines when they think of an English village church: belfry windows, parapets, pinnacles and gargoyles that give the later addition – the fifteenth-century tower – a classic Gothic appearance. Matthew and I stop at the lychgate. 'Do you like the look of it?' I ask.

'It's very traditional,' he replies. I raise my eyebrows. I expected more enthusiasm.

He tries again. 'It's as expected.' I realise he has just articulated my thoughts but it doesn't sound like a compliment when he says it this way. I push open the little wooden gate and step inside.

For a moment I don't think he's going to follow me. He is pale, wide-eyed. His skin is almost waxy. Beads of sweat sit above his lips; there are two spots of colour high on his cheeks. Rose-red blotches, like a curse in a fairy tale. I lead him towards the church, breathing deeply, letting the warm air fill my lungs. I feel hopeful, positive as we reach the low porch that houses a statue of some sleeping long-dead noble. The large wooden doors, ornate and beautifully carved, are wide open, an invitation. I glance excitedly at Matthew, but he looks far from happy. 'Are you OK?'

'OK?' He repeats the word back to me. Not an answer, more of a question.

'Are you unwell? You look flushed.' I put the back of my hand on his forehead to see if he feels feverish. He pulls away from me. His eyes are flashing fear, panic even.

'I can't go in there,' he states flatly.

'What?'

'I can't go into the church.'

I gently tug at his arm. I assume he's joking, but there's nothing about his face that suggests he is. 'What is it, Matthew? What's the matter?'

'It's Becky.'

'Becky?' I am instantly seized by a sense of complicated unease – anger and pain. 'What about Becky?'

'I should have said something earlier. I'm sorry. Look, I can't do this.' He turns away and heads back up the path.

I chase him, pull at the sleeve of his jacket. 'Matthew, slow down. What's going on? You can't do what? Explain it to me.'

He's at the lychgate before he stops. I watch his shoulders rise and fall, his head bowed, his back hunched. I wait until he turns to me. 'Becky was religious. Very. We had a church

147

wedding. In a place very much like this one, actually. It was beautiful and big. We had hymns, prayers, blessings, the lot. For all the good it did.' He looks pained now, as though he is physically hurting. I can almost imagine I hear a heart crack, although I'm not sure if it's his or mine. 'And I haven't been inside a church since I buried her. I don't think I can again, and I certainly don't want to be married in one.' He's quivering from head to foot now, and I wonder if he's having a panic attack.

'OK, OK,' I say calmly, soothingly. 'I had no idea. Don't worry. Take a deep breath.' Again I feel swamped by a sense of how little I know about his history. Now that I do know how he feels about churches, I ought to feel closer to him; new information should make the bond between us stronger. Yet all I feel is resentment that once again Becky is influencing my life. Should marrying in this church be such a problem for him? After all, it's not the same church, even if it looks a bit similar. I buried my parents in this exact church; that's why I want the service here, to feel closer to them. Shouldn't that take precedence?

While I encourage Matthew to take long, slow, calming breaths, I try to be logical and reasonable. I can't get frustrated with him. Everyone is different in the way they cope with grief. My parents died thirty-five years ago. Matthew's loss is still fresh. Are my friends right? Are we rushing this? Should we be taking longer to get to know one another? I feel panicked, gripped with fear that he is going to say as much. That would be unbearable. The sun is settling low in the sky; light flickers and sparks through the treeline, like strobes at a rave. I think carefully about what I should say next.

'It doesn't have to be a church wedding.' I take hold of his hand, weave my fingers between his and then kiss his knuckles.

'I don't care where we get married. We have plenty of time to think about it. We're only just engaged.' He doesn't look at me. His eyes are darting around the churchyard. He looks like a trapped animal. One that is prepared to chew off its own foot to escape. I can't allow that. 'Hold on a minute. Wait here.' It's stupid, but I imagine him driving away without me, disappearing altogether. Vanishing from my life as swiftly as he landed in it. I couldn't stand that. I feel reassured to know the car keys are in my bag. I run into the church and find the vicar. I hurriedly explain that Matthew doesn't want a church wedding and apologise for wasting his time. He is polite; he seems used to rejection. 'Are you popping in on your mum and dad while you're here?'

It takes me a minute to compute. 'Oh yes, of course,' I assure him, more as an honourable exit from the conversation than out of any real desire to stand at my parents' graves.

Matthew is waiting for me at the end of the path, and a surge of relief almost knocks me off my feet. His hood is up and he's hunched, but I'm glad to note his breathing has slowed and he seems far less agitated now. I sense the vicar's eyes on my back and feel duty-bound to follow his suggestion. 'Will you come and see my parents' graves?'

'Right, yes,' Matthew says. 'Of course.'

We walk through the ancient graves that cluster closest to the church, towards the plot further afield where there are fresh mounds of earth, fresh flowers too. I pay a gardener to tend my parents' graves, as I can't stand the idea of them becoming neglected, even more forlorn. Years ago, I invested in a range of bulbs and plants that ensure a bed of colour throughout most of the year. The gardener visits once a fortnight to clear litter, weed the plot and polish the marble. He sends me photos from time to time, so that I know he's doing his job. I don't ask him to do so, I trust him, but I find it quite reassuring – comforting, I suppose – to see the plot looking cared for, kempt. That's why I can't compute what is in front of me.

'Oh my God. What the hell?'

'Moles?' asks Matthew.

No, not moles; their mounds are neat and natural. The earth in front of me has been hacked at, dug up in a random, aggressive way. The heads of the tulips have all been severed, the jaunty pouts snatched, crushed and scattered. I stare at the disturbed soil, where worms are burrowing through, pink and blue, translucent and alien. I don't want to think about worms. The air no longer smells clean and fresh; instead it smells of filth and decay. It's not just the soil and foliage that have been disturbed; there is red paint splattered over the headstones. A lot of it. It is still wet and dripping. It rolls down the white marble, lingering in the engraved letters that spell out my parents' names, catching in the curves of the vowels, secreted and staining the consonants. The paint rolls closer to my foot. I take a step back. I look about me, but the nearby graves are all undisturbed. Totally peaceful and proper. This is targeted.

'Who would do such a thing?' I ask.

Matthew looks aghast. 'We need to report this. Whoever has done it must be close by. The paint is still wet,' he says.

'Yes, yes, we should talk to the vicar,' I mumble.

'And the police,' adds Matthew.

20

June

Matthew thinks I need to talk to Heidi and Gina about what happened to my parents' graves, and of course the change in wedding plans. 'You have to tackle it, babe. You know you do.' I'm not sure which is the harder conversation to make my way into; both seem impossible. I do nothing about seeing them for a couple of weeks, and then he surprises me by inviting them and their families for a walk and lunch at ours on Saturday.

'Oh, how lovely,' I comment when he tells me. Although I'm not sure it is. 'I didn't know you even had their numbers.'

'I swapped numbers with Leon that Sunday we went to theirs. I called him and asked for Heidi and Gina's deets.' He beams. 'This is what couples do, babe. They support each other. I'll cook. It will be awesome.'

It's a hot day. Too hot. Sweat is sliding down the back of my legs and I've changed clothes twice. I feel unusually nervous, and not all that excited about meeting my friends. I know Heidi hates it when it's too hot. 'It will be cooler in the woods,' says Matthew with a reassuring smile.

He makes a good point, and so when everyone arrives, I discourage settling in the garden and instead put on my walking boots, pointedly discussing the route. I feel a walk might be more successful than sitting around. People can find space and have private conversations. That might be more diplomatic.

'All right, we're coming,' mutters Heidi when, for the third time, I comment that it would be good to get going to avoid being out in the glaring sunshine at midday.

Despite my intimate knowledge of the area, the men have taken it upon themselves to lead the party; Matthew, Leon and Mick set the pace. The three girls trail behind. Fifi is wearing her earbuds, listening to her own private world and locking the rest of us out as much as possible. It's not personal, it's her age; we're boring to her right now. By contrast, Aaliyah and Lottie chatter constantly, competing with the birdsong by frequently calling out to us to settle a matter of fact or recollection, or just to laugh at their jokes. I'm glad of the younger two girls. They disguise the silence that has settled between Heidi, Gina and me. We three are walking between the two groups. Our conversation is more stilted. I want to think it's the heat. I know it's that I am stressed about what I have to say. Matthew doesn't know my friends as well as I do. No matter how lovely his patatas bravas and calamari tapas lunch is, I can't think that today is going to be 'awesome', not considering what needs to be said.

I launch in, knowing the longer I leave it, the more tense I'll become.

'On reflection, we've decided to keep it small. The wedding.' I hope my tone sounds casual; I fear it sounds defensive.

'How small?' Heidi demands, instantly antagonistic.

'Tiny. In fact we're going to do it abroad, on a beach some-where. No formality. No speeches, no suits or long dresses.' The words tumble out, rough, almost belligerent, because I'm trying to avoid sounding apologetic.

'What? No, no way,' Heidi counters firmly. She stops dead, and as we are on a narrow single-file track, I nearly bump into her.

'It's her wedding,' points out Gina. 'She can do whatever she likes.'

'Thank you,' I say with a hint of exasperation.

'Although Lottie was looking forward to being bridesmaid,' she adds in a whisper. 'I'm not sure we should tell her today, at least until not after lunch. You know, so as not to spoil things.' I glance behind me. Lottie waves enthusiastically, her thin limbs tapering like ribbons on a maypole. I feel a dollop of guilt at the thought of disappointing her by not having a big wedding and allowing her to wear the floaty bridesmaid dress of her dreams.

I try to explain. 'You know I told you we were going to visit St Adelaide's in Hodstone?' My friends nod in unison. 'Matthew reacted really badly.' Now I find I'm the one lower-ing my voice. The men are about ten metres ahead of us; it's unlikely they can catch our conversation, but I don't want to embarrass Matthew as I explain why we've made the decision we have.

'In what way?' Gina asks.

'Like a post-traumatic stress thing. He sort of froze.'

'Matthew did?' Heidi makes sure her intonation communi-cates her surprise at this; more, her two-word question implies that he had no right to get upset there in particular.

'He just wouldn't cross the threshold and go to talk to the vicar as planned. Well, when I say planned, it was my plan really. I sprang it on him. My bad.' I don't know why I feel the need to justify, but I do. 'He's explained that it's all mixed up with his feelings about Becky – their wedding, her funeral. He says that he no longer associates churches with anything good.'

'Wow.' Gina lets out a low whistle.

'But you were OK with it being there?' Heidi clarifies.

I know what she's thinking. 'I buried my parents years ago,' I mutter. Despite the shade of the trees, I still feel uncomfortably hot. Sweat is pooling at the back of my knees and under my arms. Come to think of it, everyone looks a little flustered. I focus on taking a drink from my water flask.

When we pick up the pace again, Heidi says, 'Well, it doesn't have to be a church wedding. Hardly anyone does that any more. It doesn't mean you have to elope. You can have a civil ceremony in a hotel or stately home or something.'

'Yes, we could. We talked about all the options, but on reflection, I'm forty-seven, I'm not sure I want a huge fuss.'

'You do,' she insists.

She's right, I do. I stopped expecting a wedding when I turned thirty-five, I stopped hoping for one aged forty-five. It's been fun thinking about a big party, a Jenny Packham dress, flowers, champagne, a choir, menus. But it's not the be all and end all, is it? Matthew is right.

'I didn't enjoy it the first time around, if I'm honest,' he explained. 'A big bash was something Becky wanted, so I went along with it, but I've always thought it's about the marriage, not the wedding day.'

We'd come home from Hodstone exhausted and confused

after tidying my parents' graves. I'd talked to the vicar; he and the church warden both expressed great shock and sadness. They'd offered to help me clean up the plot, but Matthew and I managed on our own. We drove to the B&Q on the outskirts of town, bought a bucket, some turps, more topsoil.

'People get carried away; they spend a fortune they don't have on just one day. Becky and I couldn't even afford a honeymoon after we'd overextended ourselves to pay for the wedding. We were back at work the following Monday.' He wrapped his arms around me and kissed the top of my head. 'I'm guessing you'll feel the same,' he murmured. I didn't want to contradict him; it's lovely that he assumes we think alike.

I melted into his chest, feeling safe and thrilled at being favourably compared to extravagant and profligate Becky. The fact that he had a big wedding when he married her and didn't think it was the ideal route gives me an opportunity. So I didn't point out that money is not really an object for us. Instead, I said, 'I think the perfect solution would be combining the marriage with a holiday. Going somewhere hot and exotic. Coming back with tans and rings.' I made myself sound enthusiastic, almost giddy.

'Oh, that's a brilliant idea.' His face lit up; relief and joy oozed from every pore. 'You work so hard. You're always under a lot of pressure. You do need a holiday. Where were you thinking?'

I had seen an advert on the side of a bus the last time I was in London. It had stood out like a beacon of serenity amongst the London crush and chaos. 'The Maldives.'

'Love that plan. Let's do it. Soon,' he added with a wide grin. He tilted my face towards his and kissed me. I thought we'd make love then, but instead we made plans. It thrilled me how much he wanted to formalise what we had. Make me his wife as quickly as possible.

'But when you say you're eloping, you don't mean just the two of you?' Heidi asks me now. 'We're obviously all coming along. And you'll give us plenty of warning. Time to save up for the flights and accommodation, right?' Her voice quivers with uncertainty on the word 'right'. It's not like us to feel unsure of one another. It's not like us to lie to one another either, but somehow I can't bring myself to tell her that the first-class flights are already booked. We're going next week. Alone.

I shrug and fudge, 'We haven't absolutely finalised everything.' This is clearly going to be a situation where it's easier to ask for forgiveness than permission. When I come back from the Maldives as Mrs Charlton, Heidi will deal with it. She'll see I'm happy and that will be all that matters to her. Won't it?

21

Lottie pushes past us as she heads towards her dad in an excited rush to tell him a joke that Fifi has just told her. Unfortunately, as she does so, she steps off the path and into a patch of nettles. She reacts badly to the stings, raw red bumps erupting all over her shin. She starts to cry, partially through pain but mostly because she doesn't like the look of it. Mick hoists her onto his shoulders, and although we've only done about a third of the planned walk, we decide to head back to Woodview.

Matthew finds his way to my side and asks, 'Have you told them our wedding plans?'

'Mostly. Not the detail about timings.' He raises his eyebrows. 'I think that will be fun to keep as a surprise,' I add.

I drop back to walk with Leon and nervously watch as Matthew, Heidi and Gina form a cluster. I hope he doesn't mention the date of the wedding. Whatever he does say makes them glance my way. Leon nudges me in the ribs. 'I guess they're plotting your hen, right?'

The three girls hop into the pool as soon as we arrive home.

I encourage everyone to join them, as I feel the overwhelming heat of the day is creating an undefinable sense of irritation, even malaise. It turns out none of the adults have brought swimwear. Matthew says he can loan trunks to Leon and Mick – they're all about the same size, and I bought him a few pairs from Paul Smith in preparation for our trip to the Maldives. Heidi clocks the fact that the tags are still attached and reads the price. I feel judged. I don't offer my swimwear to Heidi and Gina; we're not the same shape or size. Gina is tall and very long in the body, and Heidi has huge boobs that require supported swimwear that she refers to as her 'boulder holder swimwear'. We know our figures are different; it's never an issue, none of us care. I get the feeling that today it might be an issue. Heidi has been complaining that she's piling weight on just looking at food, and I think she's feeling more self-conscious than usual.

Matthew thoughtfully suggests we sit in the garden, leave Mick and Leon to supervise the swimming while he fixes drinks and puts the finishing touches to lunch. 'What can I get you ladies to drink?' he asks, the perfect host. 'I have rosé chilling. Or maybe an Aperol spritz?'

Rosé is Heidi's favourite tipple, Aperol is Gina's. He checked with me yesterday.

'I'm having a day off alcohol,' says Heidi. 'It's too hot to drink. I'll fall asleep if I do.'

'I promised Mick I'd drive home,' Gina adds. 'He'll have a beer, though, when he gets out of the pool.'

'You could have just one,' I suggest, aware that Matthew has made an effort to get their favourite drinks in, and also aware that a glass of something might make everyone a little more relaxed.

'No, that's stupid. She's driving a child,' snaps Heidi. 'I think we can all cope with one day off alcohol, don't you?'

I'm not driving anywhere, and in fact I was looking forward to a crisp glass of rosé, but her tone is so definitive that I tell Matthew I'm happy with sparkling water.

Matthew starts to bring out some of the food he has prepared. He emerges with tuna tartare and king prawns with garlic and chilli. I'm glad we opted for a tapas-style lunch, so we can all pick at it casually rather than sit formally around a table. With food in front of us, we seem to find a cordial groove, and some of our usual energy and verve. My friends talk appreciatively about the dishes. 'This seafood is yummy. You really live your life like you're in a magazine,' comments Heidi.

'Well done for finding a man who can cook,' adds Gina.

Once we are settled with the first round of plates, I expect Matthew to peel off to join the men and kids in the pool. He doesn't. Instead, he sits next to me and takes my hand, which is sweet but makes eating tricky. We are opposite Gina and Heidi. 'There's something else Emma has been wanting to talk to you about,' he says. 'Some weird things have been happening and she needs your support.' My friends stop discussing which salad is the perfect accompaniment to garlic and chilli prawns and give me their full attention.

Matthew's formal introduction to the topic isn't how I would have approached it, but once I start speaking, the words flow freely. They already know about the plant pots and globes being smashed. Like Matthew, they suggested extra security cameras and being more vigilant when alone. I didn't tell them about the bolognese sauce. It's not that I wanted to hide the incident from them, it's just that Matthew proposed the same night and *that* became the big news. Then we got into the prenup thing, so I never got round to telling them about the strange vandalism that was so upsetting. But now I must. Matthew holds my hand throughout. I realise he's trying to show support and solidarity, but my palm is sweating and generally I'm the sort of person who uses my hands when I talk. I feel bound, restricted.

Heidi and Gina listen carefully, not interrupting, which leads me to reveal more than I was planning on saying. I tell them that I often get the sense I'm being watched; that sometimes I think someone else has been in the house. I am certain – OK, almost certain – that between us we'll find an alternative explanation, something sane and probable. Something less devastating than the current ideas that are swilling around my mind.

'Is this why you had the locks changed and sent us new keys?' asked Gina. I nod.

'What gives you that impression that someone has been in the house?' asks Heidi stiffly.

'Sometimes the place smells different – it's a weird wet-dog smell. Sometimes something has been moved or is missing. My laptop vanished for a day and then reappeared the next. Two mornings in a row I wanted to go for a run but could only find one running shoe in the cupboard. At the end of the day, the second one was back in the cupboard again. Tell me that isn't weird.'

'Matthew, would you mind getting me a glass of rosé after all? I think I need it now. And maybe if you could prepare Gina an Aperol, a weak one.' Matthew nods, happy to accommodate the request. That's because he doesn't know Heidi the way I do. I instantly know she's getting him out of the way. Whatever she wants to say, she doesn't want to say it in front of my fiancé.

The moment he's out of earshot, she hiss-whispers, 'Not much of a mystery. Do you actually need me to articulate it?'

We stare at one another. I knew this would be her first thought. 'It's not him. He was in London when the globes were smashed, upstairs when the bolognese was spilt, and with me when the graves were vandalised.'

'Desecrated,' she corrects. I squirm. I've considered that word too but tried to avoid it. It's too much. It's too bleak, cruel and threatening. Heidi, however, seems happy to embrace the darkness.

'He loves me, Heidi. We're getting married. Why would he ruin my stuff?' I ask quietly and firmly.

'Classic gaslighting,' she pronounces emphatically. 'All of these strange and cruel things have happened since you met Matthew. It's blatantly obvious.'

'No it isn't,' I rebut. 'It's only gaslighting if he says it's not happening. He's as worried as I am.'

'OK,' she concedes. 'But if it's not him, then it's something to do with him.' Her tone is ominous, dramatic.

'Here are your drinks, ladies.' We all nearly jump out of our skin.

'That was quick,' comments Heidi.

Matthew has in fact brought a tray with all the bottles and glasses on it. He pours Heidi's wine and preps Gina's Aperol. He clearly didn't want to leave me alone with them; he's trying so hard to support me. I notice that he hasn't brought out a glass for me, but I don't mention it. If I do, he'll think I'm trying to get rid of him too.

'Are we talking about the vandalism?' he asks. His straightforward manner is uplifting.

'Yes.'

'Any theories?'

'Well, the timing would suggest that this aggravation is something to do with you,' comments Heidi boldly.

'I agree with you.' Matthew nods, holding her gaze. I know she won't blink, so I interrupt.

'I've given it a lot of thought. I wondered if it could be a friend or relative of Becky's who is unhappy with Matthew moving on. Someone who really doesn't want us to be together.'

My friends don't dismiss the theory. I almost wish they would. I want to believe the vandalism is just a matter of bad luck, down to bored, mischievous kids. Not a real threat or worry so much as a nuisance. But how many bored kids are there in the world, and why do they all seem to be getting their kicks from destroying my property? Invading my space.

Gina nods. 'It's possible. Matthew, can you think of any likely candidates? Someone sad and mad enough to do this.'

'No one comes to mind. Most of our friends live in New York. Her family are in South Africa. But I agree someone is trying to cause trouble, put a wedge between us. I just don't think it's one of Becky's friends.' He is still staring right at Heidi. It's impossible for any of us to ignore his challenge. I really wish I had a drink right now. Something to help me slip through this awkwardness. I want to keep my gaze trained on the oily plates on the table, but I know I must force myself to look my friends in the eye. Gina first, she's easier. Her cheeks are pink, but I know immediately that she's embarrassed, not guilty. Embarrassed for who? Me, or Heidi? She knows what he's saying. It appears they both do.

'Are you for real? Are you accusing *us* of doing these batshit-crazy things?' Heidi yells. My attention snaps to her.

'No, no, of course he's not. We're not,' I reassure quickly. And we're not. Not exactly. When Matthew first mooted the idea that Heidi might be responsible for this hate campaign – that's how he described it – I laughed. He quickly retracted the thought as preposterous, but since then I've racked and racked my brains and I can't think of anyone else who might have a problem with our relationship. I'm simply not close enough to anyone else for them to care what I do with my life. 'But you did just accuse Matthew of gaslighting me. That wasn't very supportive, was it? You're not his biggest fan,' I stutter. It's a hard thing to say. The truth often is.

'You have known him for about *five* minutes. You've known us all your adult life.' Heidi's eyes are so wide I think they are going to pop out of her head on springs, like in a cartoon.

Matthew puts an arm around me. We're a unit. He says, 'I think since we've met there has been a sense that you feel you're losing Emma, that I'm taking her away from you, and I just wanted to clear that up. Let you know that there's room for us all to love her.'

Heidi jumps to her feet. Her thigh bangs into the table and upsets a wine glass. Gina starts mopping up the spillage, but I don't think a couple of napkins can absorb the mess that's pooling between us.

'I'm just saying I have always rather got the feeling that you don't like me.' I feel so awful for him in that moment. I think of the effort he's gone to today. He has been shopping and prepping for two days, he's bought three tubs of ice cream to cover each of the girls' favourite flavours. He's trying so hard.

'We don't *know* you,' corrects Gina carefully, her voice soft.

I feel a sense of dread creep through my body. I keep my eyes on Heidi. I'm trying to read her. It's ridiculous to suspect her of doing these terrible things. She loves me. But that's the point. She loves me and she doesn't like him, not at all. She doesn't trust him and she doesn't want the balance of our intimate friendship altered in any way. Love makes people do extreme things. Silly, illogical things. Also, I know that Heidi's mantra in life is 'Sometimes the end justifies the means.' She first said it to me when she set off a fire alarm at uni, to cut short a tedious lecture because we wanted to make our train as we were going to a music gig. More recently, she reported the headmaster of her kids' school to the governors for having an affair with his PA. She said he was morally unfit to speak at school assemblies. I don't know if that really was her objection, but I do know that he hadn't accommodated Fifi's GCSE choices and she'd had to take French instead of Spanish. Heidi was delighted when he was asked to resign. There have been dozens of other occasions when she's muttered this mantra.

I am aware that Leon and Mick and the girls have emerged from the pool. I'm not sure if it was because they were hungry or if our shouting drew them out. Fifi and the men look concerned. They stand dripping, their faces wary. It's time for me to show Matthew my loyalty, support and trust. He is my fiancé. It's even more painful saying this in front of an audience, but I must.

'It appears to be someone who knows my movements and

it's most likely to be someone who has a key.' Then I drop a bomb on our long friendship. 'You two are the only people with keys to my new lock.'

Heidi's eyes flash with fury. She marches through the garden and into the kitchen. Everyone follows her. Her bag is lying on the breakfast bar, where she habitually dumps it whenever she visits. She reaches for it and scrabbles about until she retrieves her key ring. It's a Tiffany screwball key ring that I bought her for her last birthday. She efficiently identifies my shiny new key on the bunch of seven or eight and then removes it. She slams it down. 'And now it's just Gina. Girls, get your clothes, we're going.'

She doesn't even allow them time to get dressed; she bundles them into the car in their wet costumes. Leon is stunned but does as she directs. As their car pulls away, I hear her bark instructions. 'Sit on your towels.' I feel saddened by the thought of their journey in wet clothes.

Gina looks like she is in physical pain. Torn as though she's being split in two. Mick ushers Lottie into the wet room and emerges a minute or two later. Lottie is at least in her clothes, although her hair is dripping. After a beat, Gina says, 'I'm going to go after her. I'll call you tonight, OK?' I nod and try not to think that Gina has chosen Heidi. I know she's just trying to help make peace. She puts her hands on my shoulders. 'Just don't do anything rash, OK. Take a breath.' I nod. 'We'll sort this,' she assures me.

I turn away from her and bury my face in Matthew's chest. He rubs my back. 'It's OK, we'll be OK,' he murmurs.

22

We marry within forty-eight hours of arriving in the Maldives. The ceremony takes place on the beach at ten in the morning, before it gets too hot. The morning sun spreads across the sand, making it look like buttercream on a birthday cake; the ocean is disconcertingly blue. Sunlight dances on the water's surface; I find it hard to look at the sparkles and flashes popping like fireworks. The scene is idyllic. If I was the sort to run a personal social media account to showcase my perfect life, I know I'd be able to post the most stunning little tiles to make our friends sigh with longing and envy. As I think this, the horrible words 'What friends?' flip into my mind. I push them away. That is not a helpful thought on this day of all days. Anyway, I only have a work account on Instagram, which is run by the marketing team, so I won't be posting anything. I am excited at the thought of our wedding photos, mounted in silver frames, dotted around the house. I'm already looking forward to looking back on this day.

I wear a white crocheted kaftan that I bought in a hurry at

Heathrow, and an orchid in my hair. Matthew wears shorts and leaves his linen shirt open. He's accessorised with a panama hat and looks unfairly cool. The photographer and hotel staff are our witnesses. After the ceremony, we eat freshly caught lobster under a silk canopy; we drink piña coladas and laugh about how we both think the naff nature of the cocktail and its sweetness is made all the more delicious because we are suiting ourselves and no one else. It feels like we are floating in a bubble. A private, delicate, iridescent bubble.

Of course, all bubbles pop.

When we return to the UK, I am busy at work, playing catch-up for the sudden, unexpected time away. I have to visit Scotland for a few days to make some in-person redundancies, which is hard, and even when I'm back down south, I spend most of my time in the London office, practically chained to my desk, barely looking up from my screen. It doesn't make sense for Matthew to come into London with me, as I'm too busy for dinners out, let alone long sessions in sexy hotels. I go back to staying in Premier Inns when I finish late and can't face the commute. It's a relief to know he's in Hampshire, looking after Woodview. Keeping it safe.

I'm glad to be busy; it helps me avoid thinking about the fact that this is the longest period of time Heidi and I have ever gone without speaking to one another. Her silence is loud. Deafening. I also don't want to think about the fact that there have been no more incidents of vandalism since we last saw one another, when she handed back her key. It kills me to think the two things might be related. I get a searing pain in my chest that leaves me breathless.

Gina and I have swapped some messages; she knows I'm

married. She asked if there was a prenup in place before it happened, and although I think the question is impertinent, I assure her there was. I choose not to take offence because I can't bear the thought of losing her too. When I do find the time to visit her, I'm laden down with an abundance of colourful sarongs and hand-made jewellery, gifts for Lottie from the Maldives. I cleared out the expensive hotel boutique and bought all the crafty bangles and pendants I could. I also give her a string of freshwater pearls. Even as I handed over my credit card, I knew the necklace was inappropriate for a child, but I bought it anyway.

Lottie accepts the gifts with a quiet formality that doesn't hide her disappointment at not getting her big day. It isn't intended to. I wonder whether she ever will forgive me, or whether I'm doomed to a lifetime of dark scowls and monosyllabic answers.

Gina asks the right questions about the wedding, but as there weren't any guests to chatter about, readings to pass opinion on or food to judge, our conversation dries up rather quickly. The main event was the spectacular sex we indulged in. The sort that made my body stretch and flex, my muscles ache. Not a conversation that can be had in front of Lottie. When she goes upstairs to practise her guitar chords, I expect the conversation to turn to the joyful sex; however, as soon as we're alone, Gina's first question is 'So have you seen Heidi?' I shake my head and feel cross that she looks at me in a way that suggests I am at fault. 'You can't really believe she's the one who vandalised your home and your parents' graves?'

'I don't want to believe it, but she had opportunity and motive. She was there when I was locked in the sauna, and she knew I was going to St Adelaide's that day.'

'You sound insane. You are not a detective. She is not a criminal. You are best friends. This is nonsense, Emma, think about it. The pair of you have to talk this through.'

I admire Gina for trying to mend bridges. I've sometimes wondered if she's ever felt like the third wheel, but her generous efforts show that she values the friendship between Heidi and me as much as we do. More, right now.

'She's made it clear she doesn't trust Matthew and she wants to split us up.'

'No, she just wanted you to be careful, cautious.'

'Why? Because she thinks he's only interested in me for my money? Can you imagine how offensive it is to hear that?'

Gina nods. 'Of course, that's awful. But that's not what she meant.'

'I think she liked having me to herself, at her beck and call. An extra pair of hands with the kids. Deep pockets. It's ironic that she's worried that Matthew only wants me for my cash,' I mutter.

'What do you mean?'

I'm angry with Heidi. Hurt, too, and I need Gina more than ever, which is how I justify breaking confidences. 'Well, I paid for Fifi to go on that school ski trip last year and for Troy to go on a cricket tour to South Africa when he was in sixth form. Heidi and Leon couldn't afford the holidays and I didn't want the kids to miss out. I've often paid for treats: jaunts to Legoland when they were younger, to the Nike flagship store in Oxford Street. I even paid for their dog.'

'You bought Bella?'

'Yes, when we were at the breeder's and Heidi was paying, her card bounced. What could I do? The kids were psyched,

Bella was already on a leash that Aaliyah was holding. Heidi said she'd pay me back. She never did.'

Gina's eyes widen. 'I had no idea.'

'Ask her if you don't believe me.'

'Of course I believe you. It's just you've never spoken of it.'

'It was a private thing. I've never minded, I was happy to help out. But now, since all she goes on about is Matthew liking me for my money, I feel really upset. Maybe that's what she values in me too.' It's such an awful thought to articulate.

'Don't be daft,' says Gina. She squeezes my arm. I think she wants to hug me; if she does, I might cry. It's so unlike me to be emotional, but there's a lot going on right now. Extreme highs and awful lows. It's hard to keep my emotions in check.

I reach into my bag and pull out a bottle of champagne. 'Do you want to toast the bride and groom?' I ask, desperate to change the subject.

Gina glances at the kitchen clock. 'Maybe later.' She fills the kettle and pops it on. Determined, she returns to the subject. 'Well, Heidi wouldn't be the first person to be a bit resentful of a new man in her best friend's life. I still don't believe she would do what you're suggesting she's done.'

'Well, I don't believe Matthew would, which was where she tried to throw shade.'

Gina looks torn. 'I'm not saying that either.'

'And we've ruled out the idea of it being any of Becky's friends or family.'

'Even so . . .'

'Gina, there hasn't been any vandalism since Heidi and I had words.' I say this coolly as I stand up and open a cupboard. I know where she keeps her glasses, and even though she is making more tea and I don't feel much like champagne after that conversation, I need something to do. She is staring at me with a disconcerting intensity. I don't like it.

'Is everything OK, though, Emma?'

'What?'

'I mean, if it wasn't, you know you can talk to me or go to a doctor.'

'A doctor?' I don't understand at all. I've never felt better. 'Do I look ill?'

'No, you look really great and seem happy. I'm glad for you and Matthew, I really am. He seems lovely, but . . .'

'You do know anything that's just been said is cancelled out if there's a but?' I hope she stops talking. I don't want her to say anything we both might regret.

She takes a deep breath and, in a gust, she gabbles, 'You're just not behaving like yourself recently, and you know at our age our hormones are all over the place and it's difficult to be as clear-sighted. I know my moods are up and down all the time and the brain fog is a shocker.'

If it is true that Gina's moods are up and down all the time, I haven't seen any evidence of it. She appears eternally calm, so laid-back she's practically horizontal. Why is she talking about the perimenopause swamp? I stare at her, puzzled. Why would I need to see a doctor?

She goes on, 'You know, I was reading this article and the symptoms that women experience in the perimenopause are far wider-reaching than previously thought. It's not just hot sweats and a dry vag.'

'I don't have either.'

'No, right. That's what I'm saying. There are loads of other symptoms. Like ones to do with mental health. Some women get very paranoid, forgetful; they might make bad decisions or even imagine things. You know, experience actual psychosis.'

'Matthew is not a bad decision.'

'No, but—'

'I didn't imagine the attacks.'

'Right, but—' We stare at one another.

After a long beat, I say, 'Gosh, I hadn't realised it was that time already. I really must get going. I've got a thing I need to attend to.' I gather up my bag and coat. I leave the bottle of champagne on the table. Up until this moment, I hadn't imagined there was such a thing as a forlorn-looking bottle of champagne. I call a hasty goodbye up the stairs to Lottie and then dash out the door.

Gina doesn't ask me what the 'thing' is. Why would she? We both know I'm lying.

23

July

Since the wedding, I haven't once set an early-morning alarm when I am at home with Matthew. I still sometimes manage a run at some point during the day, but the impetus to get out of bed at the crack of dawn has gone. Honestly, I can't really understand why I believed such a strict regime was necessary for all those years. However, this morning, it's Matthew who gets up first. He accidentally wakes me as he's sneaking out of bed.

'Morning, handsome.'

'Morning, babe. I'm sorry I woke you. I wanted to let you sleep. I know you've been working around the clock recently.'

'Oh, that doesn't matter. I'd rather be awake with you than asleep.' I throw back the duvet, revealing my naked body. 'Come back to bed,' I murmur. After years of thinking of my body as nothing more than an efficient vessel to get me from A to B, I now think of it as something much more lascivious and decadent. Something sexy and sexed up. I glow with the thought of pleasing and being pleasured. I crave Matthew's touch. His cold hands on my skin when I'm hot under the duvet, his warm hands when I come home late and he's cosy in bed. Right now, I feel the luxury of a weekend unfurl in front of us. We got back from the Maldives three weeks ago, but this is the first Saturday I've woken up at home since we've been a married couple. I feel alert and ready. Celebratory. I have plans.

So I'm disappointed when he says, 'Oh babe, don't tease me. You know I'm working today.'

'What?' My entire body slumps. I pull the duvet back over me. Suddenly cold, or maybe self-conscious.

'I told you. I'm photographing three young chefs. You remember, the ones who are all ex-prisoners.'

I do recall him telling me about how these men raised enough money through celebrity chef endorsements and crowdfunding to open a new little eatery quite close to the place they used to be incarcerated. The idea being that they will serve excellent food to prison visitors and anyone else brave enough to go to the less salubrious parts of London to be served smashed avocado on sourdough toast for a tenner. He's right, we did talk about it. It sounds an interesting project; I just hadn't appreciated it was happening today.

Matthew goes into the bathroom, and I hear him turn on the shower, then humming above the sound of the gushing water. I can't resent him working at the weekend, considering I often do, and I can tell he's excited about this commission. While he showers, I think about how I'm going to spend my time.

I consider what can be done around the house. It's fun to see Matthew's face when I announce that I've unblocked a U-bend or mowed the grass. 'You dinosaur, women can do these things, you know,' I joke when he comments that he's surprised by my independence and abilities.

'It's just that Becky and I had distinct pink and blue jobs. She wouldn't even take out the bins.'

I get out of bed and follow him into the bathroom. As I clean my teeth, I comment, 'You're clearly looking forward to the shoot.'

'It beats taking pictures of middle-aged white men in suits for their corporate websites,' he replies.

'Excuse me, you are talking about my tribe.'

'Well, last time I looked, you were all woman,' he responds, smiling in that way he has; the way that makes me weak and momentarily happy to be so. He steps out of the shower. Still wet, he leans towards me and lands a long kiss. I breathe him in, and my stomach lurches.

'I need to shower. We could go back in there together,' I offer.

'I'd love to, but I really do have to get on the road. I want to beat the traffic.'

'I'm not going to overthink the fact that I'm standing here naked offering to have sex in the shower and you're turning me down because of the flow of traffic on the M3.'

He grins. 'I'm sorry. You could come with me.'

I shake my head. 'I'll be in the way.'

Downstairs, a gust of wind blows through the house and a door slams shut. I jump when I hear the bang. Matthew wraps his arms around me. 'Hey, scaredy-cat. It's OK.' I laugh. He gently kisses me, and murmurs, 'I wish I believed in some higher power – lucky stars, Cupid, anything – so I could thank them, because my life is great right now. I'll miss you today.'

I beam. 'I'll miss you too.' The words tumble out of my mouth, excited and simple.

24

The gutters are clogged, a consequence of living so close to the woods; leaves and other debris are in abundance. This used to be just an autumn problem, but here I am at the beginning of July still doing the job. Clearing the gutters is a big, dirty task, one that might require a professional considering the height of my roof, but I decide to take a look. At the very least, I can make an assessment as to how much work might be required before I find someone to come and deal with it properly.

I change into a pair of old joggers and a long-sleeved T-shirt, then dig out a pair of rubber gloves and get to work. My workshop smells of bagged manure and sawdust; surprisingly I find this smell quite appealing, one thing suggesting growth, the other industry. I unearth an old plastic kitchen spatula, tarp, a hose and the ladder. It's a heavy extendable thing that I bought a few years ago so I could pick apples from the tallest trees in the orchard. I haul it to the front of the house, getting a buzz out of the exertion required for this manual labour. I've been at my desk too much of late.

Any YouTube video about gutter-clearing will recommend that you have someone hold the ladder for you. That's not an option today, and I'm used to circumnavigating my way around being on my own. I realise I no longer have to – I could wait and do this tomorrow when Matthew is home – but it seems silly to waste our time together doing household jobs. I make sure the ladder is securely propped up against the house and avoid uneven ground. I spread out the tarp and then slowly and cautiously climb the ladder.

As I suspected, the gutters are full to the brim with soggy brown leaves and sticks. I start to scoop out the debris and flick it to the ground, mud splattering in an arc. After painstakingly cleaning the filth to my left and right as far as I can reach, I carefully come down the ladder, move it along a metre or so and then go up again and repeat the entire process. I soon get into my rhythm and find it therapeutic. My mind wanders first to thoughts of mulching the debris, creating compost, and then to work. Every time Heidi and Gina come into my mind, I push them away. Not now.

It happens so quickly I don't even comprehend it has until I'm flat on my face on the ground. The pain of the fall ricochets through my body in heavy, debilitating pulses; everything stings or throbs at once. I take stock, just start to think about what I've damaged, and then a fraction of a second later, the ladder falls on top of me, hitting my back. *Thwack.* This second impact creates a new level of pain; it's immense. I scream out. My shoulders feel like they are about to be split open, my spine and the back of my head hurt so much I think I'm going to be sick. I reach up, expecting to feel blood; a lump is already swelling on my skull.

For a moment, I can't move. I just let my body pulse in pain. After a minute or two my head starts to slowly clear enough for me to recall that I did not have my phone with me when I climbed up the ladder. I'd left it on the porch, worried that I'd drop it from a height. I need to reach it. The heavy ladder pins me to the ground and so my progress is hampered, but I start to inch forward with all the strength I have. My wrist aches and my knuckles are grazed and bleeding. I'm shaking, and I'm not sure whether that's with pain or shock. I need to call an ambulance; this is my last thought as waves of blackness swarm into my head. I taste vomit in my mouth. I close my eyes.

I don't know how long I'm out for. No idea. I'm disorientated and in so much pain I can't think clearly. I feel relief that when I wake up, I am no longer under the ladder. My back is still throbbing with the impact of where it fell on me, but I can't feel the weight of it. Thank God, someone has helped me. Matthew? I look around for him, for anyone; I call out. 'Matthew? Help someone, please! I need help.' My voice cracks with distress. No one responds; there is no one around. I must have crawled or rolled out from under the ladder just before I passed out.

I tentatively start to move my fingers and toes, then push myself up onto my knees so that I can crawl into the house. It's agony moving, or even breathing. I think I might have broken a rib. I grasp the phone and immediately call Matthew, but it goes straight to voicemail. I momentarily wonder whether I should leave a message. I know he'll be terrified if he hears me in such a bad way, so I hang up and then laboriously jab out a text asking him to come home to me as quickly as he can. I don't give any details as to why. I can't say I've fallen off a ladder, not considering what happened to Becky. He'll be insanely panicked and no doubt break speed limits to get to me. That's in no one's interest.

I limp to the downstairs loo, wash the grit out of my hands, chin, knees, all of which are bloody but, on examination, I believe only require TCP, not stitches. It stings to apply the antiseptic and I want to cry. I consider calling an ambulance, but decide that although I'm bruised and battered, my injuries are certainly not life-threatening. I may be diverting it from someone more in need. I decide it's more community-spirited and all-round sensible if I wait for Matthew and he can drive me to A&E. Despite the adultness of this decision, I feel woefully sorry for myself, and it takes all the energy I can muster to limp to the sofa and lie down. I put my feet up on the armrest. There's nothing to do but wait.

Matthew sends a text in response to my plea for him to come home. He doesn't ask any questions; he simply responds, *On my way, babe.* He adds four kisses, and seeing them lifts me a fraction, despite the pain. He's clearly missed me, and no doubt thinks my demand for him to come home quickly is nothing more than a keenness to climb into bed. I track him on Find Friends. I watch the little blue spot that represents his phone and his movements thread slowly through London traffic and then speed up when he reaches the outskirts. I feel enormously comforted. He's coming. Help is coming.

I listen to the car approach, tyres scrunching on the driveway. The car door being opened and slammed quickly, his footsteps – one, two, three – as he dashes up the front step and through the door.

'In here,' I call. Seeing him in the doorway, I start to cry. Now that I can surrender my safety to him, the tears that I've held back fall freely. I'm not even embarrassed, and that's new for me. I've been self-sufficient and self-reliant for years and years, but now Matthew will look after me.

'Hell, babe, what happened?' His face is taut with shock and concern.

I start to explain that I fell off the ladder and then it fell on top of me. I sob as he carefully, tenderly examines my cuts and bruises and then declares, 'I'm taking you to A&E.' He helps me to my feet and leads me to the car. He parked it (or in fact abandoned it) just outside the front door, so I don't have far to walk. I'm limping, my back, head and ribs aching horribly. It's only when I'm settled in the car that I notice the ladder is propped back up against the wall. I'm surprised that he paused to do that. I thought I'd monitored his progress from the car to my side. When did he have time?

'You picked up the ladder?'

He glances at me as he starts the car, then does a three-point turn and sets off along the drive. 'No, I didn't.'

'But it's up against the wall again. You must have.'

He shakes his head slowly. 'That's the reason I'm taking you to hospital. When you said that the ladder fell on you, it made me think you had concussion. It was against the wall when I got back.'

'No, no, that's impossible. It fell on top of me,' I insist. Matthew keeps his eyes on the road and doesn't reply. 'My back is bruised from the impact. I can feel the lump on my head,' I insist.

'Let's just get you to a doctor and then we'll see what's what.'

25

We don't get home until almost 9 p.m. A heavy silence hangs between us. Exhaustion and discomfort tinged with resentment and confusion does not lend itself to chatting. I maintain the ladder fell on me; Matthew is maintaining that is impossible because he found it up against the wall. I too saw the ladder against the wall. I can see why he doubts what I'm telling him. The facts are against me. Doubting my memory, my account, leaves me feeling terrified. Loose in some odd way. I think I understand for the first time what people mean when they say they are falling apart. Normally I am so solid, so upright and firm. Now I feel like I am liquid. I might spill or evaporate altogether. These thoughts are fantastical, I can't underline enough how unlike me they are, yet I am thinking them.

Because our accounts differed, the doctor took me into the consulting room alone, and insisted that Matthew remain in the waiting room. The doctor was younger than me by at least twenty years. He had cool hands that felt soothing against my wrist when he took my pulse, and he asked whether I felt safe.

'Safe?' I repeated the word back to him. I do not feel safe. But

I do not feel unsafe in the way the doctor was suggesting. I'm not scared of my husband. He was in London when this thing happened to me. He is not injuring me or threatening me. But someone is. I am sure of it. I couldn't say this to the doctor. I'd sound confused at best, mad at worst. I forced myself to smile politely; I even offered up a little laugh. But nothing too loud, nothing manic. 'Oh, I see what you're thinking. That's very good of you. Always best to check for anything awful, but that's not what's going on here. No domestic violence. We're newly-weds.' I felt foolish using this term. Partially because being a newly-wed doesn't necessarily disqualify you from domestic violence, unfortunately. But also confessing to such a thing at my age seemed irregular. Yet we are exactly that – how else could I describe us? We're very new to each other.

The doctor's face did not alter; it remained set in an expression that I couldn't quite read. Scepticism, fatigue? He didn't say congratulations, he just sighed and continued with the examination. After a sixteen-hour shift in A&E, I suppose there's only so much empathy and energy that can be mustered. He agreed with me that the severe bruising on my back indicated that something had fallen on me, but later, when he spoke to Matthew, he added, 'Or maybe she fell on her back and rolled over onto her stomach and can't recall this. Either way, she was incredibly lucky.' I felt he'd let me down.

Lucky: concussion, two fractured ribs, a lump the size of an egg on the back of my head, scratches and bruises on my forehead, hands and knees.

The house feels cold when we get back. Unfamiliar. I shiver. I detect that strange smell again, something rotting, dank. 'Can you smell that?' I ask Matthew.

'Smell what?'

'I'm not sure, like wet dog?' That's not an accurate description; there is nothing insidious about wet dog, and this smell is somehow devious, off.

'I bought a new scented candle last week,' he says. 'That's pretty herby. Maybe you can smell that. I think it had cedar and basil. If you don't like it, I can throw it out.'

I stare at my new husband. He's smiling at me, but it's not a wide beam. His face oozes concern. I'm puzzling him. Perhaps even alarming him. I'd bet my house on the fact that all he wants to do is please me, help me, but he doesn't know how to, nor do I. I am wondering how I can explain to him what I want to articulate; the theory that is starting to grow in my head and that doesn't make sense. If I speak of it, it can only cause trouble, but it is the logical conclusion I am reaching. If logical is a word that can be used here. This thing I can smell is not a scented candle. It's the same stench I came across when the plants were smashed, when the sauce was thrown about. I smelt it at my parents' graveside. I don't recognise the not-quite-human smell and yet I'm certain it must be the smell of whoever it is that is targeting me in this peculiar way. It's not prankster kids. Kids are noisy, careless. This threat is silent, precise, focused. I shiver.

'I can't smell anything different,' says Matthew, shrugging. 'It is cold, though. I'll check there isn't a window open.' Yes, the temperature dropping. I've noticed that too.

He checks all over the house but doesn't discover an open window. He turns the heating on and tells me he'll fix supper.

'Thanks, but I just want to get to bed. These painkillers are making me drowsy.'

I go to bed alone and Matthew stays up, says he's going to watch an arty film that he tells me isn't my thing anyway. I thought I'd fall asleep instantly, but I don't. Weird that after years and years of sleeping on my own, it's only taken having a couple of months of company for me to miss Matthew's solid, warm presence. The mattress seems too cool and flat, and I miss the slight dip he creates that causes me to roll towards him. I flick on the bedside lamp, pick up my laptop and start to google my impossible theory. That's how I think of it in my mind. Impossible. Laughable. But I find myself looking anyway.

I'm disturbed by the accounts that make it seem possible, as much as I might have been if there was evidence to contradict it. I would like to share my thoughts with someone, but who? Not Heidi or Gina, obviously, and I don't know how to have this conversation with Matthew.

After about an hour, I hear him on the stairs. My heart lifts when he says, 'I just can't get into the film. It's really boring.' I immediately close my laptop, assuming he's going to come to bed too, but then he adds, 'Would you mind if I popped to the Fox and Crown? I'll take the car, so I'll only have a half. I'm just not ready to hit the hay yet.'

'We have beer in the fridge,' I point out gently. I don't want to be one of those wives who spoils her husband's fun, curbs his social life, but nor do I want to be left alone tonight. It's been an especially hard day.

'I fancy some company, a change of scene. I won't be long. I'll have my phone on the whole time. If you need me, I'll be back in a jiffy, but I know that's unlikely. You're always so plucky.'

Plucky. I let the word roll around my head. The old-fashioned word for determined or courageous appeals to me. It's the sort of compliment I like more than if someone tells me my hair looks great or they like my shoes. I don't want to let him down by appearing anything other than this strong version of me that he has in his mind, so I beam and say, 'Of course you should go. I'll be fine. I really am going to go to sleep now. If you decide you want a pint, just leave the car, get a taxi. You can pick it up in the morning.' He doesn't need my permission to do this, of course, but I want to look encouraging.

I swallow a couple more painkillers and then fall asleep almost straight away.

When I wake, the room feels swollen with a solid darkness that is only possible in the countryside, where there's no light pollution. Matthew is not in bed. I assume he decided to sleep in the spare room, rather than risk waking me up when he came back from the pub. I automatically reach for my phone to check the time: 2 a.m. My head and ribs are pounding again. I count back the hours since I last took painkillers and decide I can allow myself the next dose, although strictly speaking I should wait. I see there's a message from Matthew, sent at 11 p.m., saying his plans have changed. He has forgotten his keys, and rather than disturbing me, he has made friends with some of the locals at the pub and is joining them for a lock-in. He'll see me in the morning, unless I text him to say otherwise. *If you're still up, I'll come home. My guess is you're in the land of zzzzz Don't want to disturb you.* He's added a heart emoji and a sleeping face emoji and a pint glass emoji. No kisses.

I am too new to this wife-ing business to know what an appropriate response is. Honestly, I feel irritated that he's left me alone tonight, but I can't decide if that's justified or not. I was asleep; is there any reason he should be here?

I answer my own question. Well yes, to monitor my concussion.

He's sent me a snap of him with his arm round the publican, shiny brass beer taps in the foreground, colourful optics with spirits in the background. He looks flushed with booze, but happy, and I can't help but smile back at his image. I won't be the only one with a headache tomorrow. I shouldn't feel jealous that he has struck up such fast and buoyant friendships with the locals. Since he moved in, he's made an effort to be part of the community, something I've never really had time to do. He's in a village WhatsApp group that I wasn't even aware existed. He's always texting someone or other, popping out to help programme a boiler, chop wood or pick up litter in public areas. He's been welcomed by the locals in a way I never have. I've lived here seven years and never been invited to a cosy lock-in. Although, to be fair, the only time I ever visit the village pub is in the summer months, when Heidi and Gina and their clans come to stay. We go for long walks that occasionally end with a ploughman's and a pint.

I lie back in bed. Frustrated, my mind whizzing, I can't fall straight back to sleep. I probably shouldn't have looked at my phone; everyone knows screens are detrimental to sleep. Woodview is extremely well built, so the windows don't rattle when the wind blows. I can't hear foxes baying or other nocturnal sounds that might spook me. However, I still feel unsettled. All houses have their own rhythms. Mine might not creak and groan, but it hums and buzzes, and even these familiar sounds – the fridge murmuring, the air filter clicking into action – keep me awake.

This time, it's not the crash of things being smashed, but rather thumps, bangs. I hear them, and freeze. A frigid acceptance of another invasion. The thumps are repetitive and consistent. *Thud. Thud. Thud. Thud.* Evenly spaced. Unhurried. A few seconds apart, deliberate, and all the more threatening for that. Each bang seems to swell around me, through me; I feel frightened and trapped. What should I do? What *can* I do? The noise closes in on me, sucks the air from me. Right here, next to my bed, is the panic button that will activate the alarm. All I have to do is reach out and press it to call for help.

But I don't do that. I can't. I am frozen.

The very name of the button deters me. Am I panicking? Is it possible I'm dreaming? I do feel bleary and dazed, the effects of the fall and the painkillers, no doubt. I hold still and listen again. *Thump, thump, thump.* Maybe it's a heater or a filter playing up. That's more likely, isn't it? My rational self fights for a logical explanation. What if I hit the button and the guards come and there's no one here? I'd look like a hysterical woman. Foolish. Paranoid. Nervous. I'm none of those things. At least, not normally. I'm a strong, independent woman and I was even before the phrase was invented. Even if someone is here, I tell myself it must be stupid prankster kids again – not thieves or rapists – and they'll flee the moment they spot the security guards' car arrive.

I consider going down to investigate whether it is a mechanical fault that's making the noise, but I can't quite shake off the fear of it being a person. Even if it is just bored teens, I don't want trouble. Things can escalate, go wrong. My phone is on my bedside table, within easy reach. I could simply stretch out my arm and pick it up, call Matthew. He wouldn't judge me as foolish, paranoid, overly nervous. Would he? If the intruders do vanish by the time he arrives, he'll simply be pleased that I'm fine. Right? If there are no intruders, all the better.

Yet I do not stretch out my arm. I'm not certain why. Maybe because calling an inebriated man to rush to my rescue somehow goes against the grain. He can't get in the car to come to me, he's too drunk, so it would take him ages to get home. I pull the covers over my head and try to ignore the bangs that are shuddering through the house. I tell myself I'm imagining them. I tell myself they are benign. I don't want to know if they are not. I'm trying to remain logical. I don't want crazy, catastrophising thoughts. But suddenly I wonder: am I mad? If I am a madwoman, do I want anyone to know? The articles I've read online swirl around my head. People talk of not being believed. Being dismissed and derided.

The thing is, people are often afraid of being alone. I've been asked about that a lot throughout my years of being single. There was a lot of self-examination, too. Being an unmarried woman, even today, is often brutally lonely. The world is set to convince you that you are a bleak case, that your life is less valuable as you are devoid of those significant connections a person could have – partner, children, grandchildren. It's insinuated that we are in eternal danger of sinking into egotism, isolation or irrelevance. We are left wondering who will look after us when we grow old, who will remember us or miss us when we die. And we are left worrying whether a life without intimate companionship is a life half lived.

Before I met Matthew, I was often asked whether I was afraid of being on my own. I'm only just realising that there's something to be more terrified of.

Maybe I'm not alone.

26

I don't remember when my body gave in and let me disappear into slumber, but I must have fallen asleep eventually, because the next thing I know the sun is flooding through my bedroom window. A new day. A beautiful day. I take a deep breath. Tell myself it's going to be OK. No matter what I'm facing.

I am not up to a run, obviously, not with my injuries, but I must get up, ensure there is some level of normality, discipline. I am not one for giving in or giving up. The thoughts I had last night embarrass me. I have to forget that childish nonsense; it just can't be. I shower and dress, swallow a vitamin and a painkiller, turn off the alarms, unlock the front door and set out along my usual running path. I do everything slowly and carefully, as my injuries throb, but I want to get out of the house. I see, but do nothing about, the hardback books that are scattered all over the floor in the main reception room. The intruder has picked up each of my gorgeous Taschen coffee table books, huge, weighty tomes, and flung them at the wall. A deliberate, concerted effort. *Thud, thud, thud.* The books are now sprawled wide open like pinned butterflies, linen spines broken, glossy pages torn. Damage done.

I did not imagine last night. Another intrusion. Another attack. My optimism is immediately assaulted. I can't deal with it right now. I know ignoring it is not rational, but I just can't think about it. Instead, I take a walk and hope that by the time I get back to the house, Matthew will be there. If he is, I have to tell him my theory about who is targeting me. However difficult it is to explain.

When I get home, he is waiting for me in the kitchen. He hands me an oat milk latte and kisses my forehead. I glance towards the reception room, expecting to see the books lying on the floor in ugly disarray, but they are not there. He has cleared them away.

'How are you feeling?' we chorus.

'I have a headache,' we both say, again simultaneously. This makes us laugh. I'm so grateful for his presence, his normality. He smells of beer, sweat and cigarette smoke. Not on his breath; the smoke is lingering on his clothes, second-hand. The pub landlord is obviously lax about smoking regulations when he has his lock-ins. Matthew starts to tell me stories about last night's antics. He gives a lot of detail and colour. Recounting various conversations with people he instantly sees as friends. He's a good storyteller, and I can imagine the warm scene full of bonhomie. He laughs a lot to himself whilst describing events, and repeatedly reiterates that 'Everyone asked after you.' He suggests we both go next Saturday, 'If you're feeling up to it.' He also tries to get me interested in joining a pub quiz team. 'That's Tuesday nights. I bet you'd ace the science questions.'

I cut across his chatter. 'I want to check the security footage.

I can't believe I didn't think of it yesterday when we got home from the hospital.' After the first act of vandalism, Matthew insisted that we beef up the number of security cameras on the property. Now, not only do we have them trained on the gates (which are electric, and no one can get in or out of the grounds in a vehicle without passing through them), but we also have them on the front, back and side doors and the outbuildings. Whoever was skulking about yesterday must have been caught on one of the cameras.

But no, yesterday's footage does not show any intruders. My blood slows. I wanted to be wrong. The only sign of life is Matthew leaving in the morning and returning at speed after I called him home. No one else passes through the gates. The cameras are not pointed near where I was working on the gutter, although the front door camera does capture me crawling into the house. It's strange watching the low-res, grainy version of myself in so much pain, vulnerable, alone. I rerun it three times without saying anything, then look up at Matthew, who is leaning over me, watching too.

'What a shame the cameras didn't pick up anyone,' he says with a sigh. 'It looks awful. Poor you, going through that. Maybe you shouldn't keep watching it over and over. It must be traumatising to see yourself like that.' Gently he spins my desk chair around so I'm facing him. He kisses me carefully on the lips.

He hasn't asked how my night was. He hasn't mentioned the books scattered over the floor, battered and abused. I wonder why not; maybe he just thinks I was reading and simply left them out. Untidy and out of character, but not impossible. But that wouldn't account for them being damaged. Then I understand,

and the thought makes my skin prickle with embarrassment and frustration. I remember the first thing he said when he came downstairs and found the bolognese sauce all over the kitchen. *What have you done?* Is it possible that he thinks I'm the one who threw the books at the wall? Is he avoiding the subject in order to be tactful, careful? Does he assume I flung them in temper or frustration, perhaps after he went to the pub, or when I received his text to say he was staying out? I'm mortified. This is so unlike anything I would ever consider doing. Why would he assume I'd destroy my own property, that I'd lose control in such a way?

Is it something Becky might have done?

I am controlled and rational; I would never indulge in that level of chaos. I have to set him straight. He is likely to feel dreadful about last night – after all, he left me alone and intruders once again invaded my home – but he has to know that I did not throw the books; someone was here again. 'Matthew, about the books . . .' I begin.

'Books?' He looks quizzical.

'I didn't fling the books against the wall.'

He grins. 'I would never imagine you would fling books against a wall. What are you talking about?'

'The books you tidied away this morning.' I point to the place where, before my walk, the books were strewn. Matthew looks that way too, but still appears perplexed. 'Someone threw them around the room last night. While you were out. That's why some of them were torn.'

'Hold on. What?' He shakes his head, then says quietly, 'I didn't tidy any books.'

'But you must have, because they aren't there now,' I point out. I'm confused, and he looks concerned.

'Emma, babe, who do you think threw the books?' he asks gently.

'I don't know exactly,' I admit. 'I didn't dare come downstairs to see. But I heard them being thrown.' I want to tell him who I think threw them, but it sounds insane.

'You agree there are no books there now, don't you?' His tone of voice is ridiculous. It's as though he's talking to a child, or a startled animal.

'Obviously there are no books there now. That's why I thought you'd cleared them away.'

He shrugs. Mystified. 'Who could have thrown your books?' It's not a genuine question so much as a firm statement that no one could have, that what I'm suggesting is impossible.

I don't want to sound screechy, but my voice rises with frustration at not being believed. I try to quell the panic of not understanding what is happening. Whatever it is, it's bad and wrong. 'I don't know. The same person who locked me in the sauna, who broke my plant pots, made the mess with the sauce, who wrecked my parents' graves.'

'Do you still think it was Heidi?'

I feel heat rush through my body. I shake my head slowly and sorrowfully. 'No. She and her family are in Spain this week on hols. I saw it on Instagram this morning. It can't be her.' I feel ashamed that I ever thought it might be Heidi doing such destructive things. She is my friend, my oldest friend. Or at least she was, until I ruined things between us. It stung to find out via social media that she's out of the country. Normally we talk about her holiday plans extensively before she sets off; everything from where she should go to what colour she should paint her toenails. Often I am invited to join them.

'But *someone* is doing this to us.' To me. The 'someone' has a problem with *me*. 'I heard the banging.' I realise my voice sounds a bit whiny and insistent. Unsure.

'Did you call security?'

'I didn't want to make a fuss.'

'You always say that.' He shakes his head. 'And this was when?'

'Two a.m. or thereabouts.'

'You probably dreamt it.' His tone is patient, not unkind, but it annoys me. I feel ignored.

'No. I didn't. I thought that at the time, but the books were scattered everywhere this morning.' I turn to him, agitated. 'You moved them.' It isn't an accusation so much as a hope. He shakes his head slowly. 'But you must have,' I insist. 'They were there this morning. I saw them.' I walk to the shelves and run my fingers along the spines. The books are all back on the shelves, in the exact order that I always keep them. Tallest on the left, shortest on the right.

Matthew follows me to the shelves. He kisses me on the forehead again. Paternal, concerned. I wish he'd kiss my lips. 'I'm going to go to bed. It was a crazy night last night. Maybe you need some more sleep too, Emma. It is bloody early. You do know other people stay in bed if they have broken ribs, right?' He's smiling, but his expression is tight and strained, suggesting he's forcing his positivity. 'Then after you have a nap, we can go out for lunch. You need to take it easy.' I can hear the concern in his voice. The worry.

And I think he has cause to be worried.

27

I agree to Matthew's suggestion that we go out for a pub lunch. I agree because the house feels threatening and claustrophobic. I just want to be out of there. This is sad, because for the past seven years, my home has been my sanctuary and refuge. I've always thought of it as restful, wholesome, open. Now the endless glass windows do not create a sense of opportunity and space, but instead make me feel vulnerable, exposed, like an insect under a microscope.

We can't get a table in the Fox and Crown, where Matthew spent last night. 'Probably a good thing,' he says. 'It looked like hell when I left this morning. Stinking, you know.' He tries a few other places, but all the charming pubs nearby are booked up, and in the end we have a very average roast in a draughty, unprepossessing eatery with bad service. There are faded prints of nineteenth-century harvests on the wall that look apologetic rather than bucolic, the loos are smelly and the tables sticky. We both try to pretend we are having a better time than in fact we are. Something that is even trickier to achieve when I order a glass of red wine and Matthew catches my eye, literally raises an eyebrow. I feel judged. 'A glass of red is always nice with a roast,' I explain.

'Right, but should you?' he asks. He orders a Coke, because he's driving and, let's face it, hung over. That doesn't stop him saying, 'The painkillers are pretty heavy-duty. Should you be drinking while you're medicating? Did you have a drink last night?'

'No, I didn't.'

'Are you sure?'

I don't reply.

I don't really enjoy the Merlot; it tastes sharp and sour. The gravy is greasy and creates a slick in my mouth, the vegetables are overcooked. It's the sort of meal that hasn't passed muster since 1995.

'I wish we'd booked somewhere a little fancier. There's a restaurant in the next village that has a Michelin star,' I say.

'We don't need Michelin stars to have fun,' he replies, but it feels like we do when we both decline pudding and coffee and are back in the car heading home after only an hour and five minutes. The pavements are wet, the grass is wet; even the air feels wet, although I can't remember noticing when it rained. The blue has drained from the sky, it's now colourless. The entire landscape looks like a reluctant apology. 'This place must be lovely when the sun shines,' comments Matthew, admitting that it's far from lovely now.

This isn't how I imagined our weekends together as a married couple would be. On the journey home, I rack my brain, thinking of some small talk that might fill the silence, but I am stumped. Too confused to muster the energy. Shouldn't he be the one making the effort? I'm injured and scared. He's the one who spent the night in a pub, leaving me exposed to God knows what. The fact that he isn't making an effort bothers me.

Sometimes I am struck by just how new to each other we are, and it's disconcerting. I have defended the speed of our relationship to everyone: my closest friend, nosy colleagues – even my brother expressed surprise at it via a text with a string of chin-scratching emojis. I realise I haven't got the balance quite right yet. On one hand, I expect Matthew to be polite to me all the time, but on the other hand, I recognise that as we are husband and wife, showcasing best manners eternally is unrealistic. I'm not saying spouses ought to be impolite to one another, but I think they should be relaxed and honest, unthinking. It bothers me that I bite back my words, that I am careful with him, he is careful with me. It's not absolutely right. We should be talking about the books, the ladder and all the other weird unexplained things that have happened. We don't. We don't talk about anything at all. The silence exposes how fragile our alliance is. Shiny and new, yes, but also delicate.

Matthew suggests another early night. He insists I need to relax. Initially I think he is suggesting sex. I am unsure how I feel about that exactly. Am I physically up to it? Am I in the mood, and if not, can I get in the mood? However, before I make up my mind, it becomes apparent that these questions are superfluous. He picks up the culture magazine that comes free with the Sunday paper, so I reach for my laptop.

We read in silence. After about an hour, Matthew turns to me and asks tenderly, 'How are you feeling?'

'My ribs aren't too painful, but my head is still aching,' I admit.

'I was thinking, babe, maybe you should try and drink a little less.' He says this with a gentle smile. The benign expression does nothing to counter the sting of what is behind the words, which I find offensive, wounding. I recoil.

'Excuse me?' I carefully close my laptop. I know the article I was reading by heart anyway; I've scanned the same line at least a dozen times. I was just pretending to read to convince Matthew, and myself, that I'm fine and everything is normal. But I'm not. It's not.

My husband's words feel like an overstep. I follow his gaze to my bedside table, where an empty wine glass stands accusingly. I feel my skin flush. I can't remember bringing it to bed with me.

I just want to relax, or if that's too much of a stretch, then I just want to not think. I put the laptop on the floor besides me and lie flat on my back, tugging the duvet further up my body so that it reaches my shoulders. We sleep naked; normally this is a fact I revel in. I love to roll onto my side in the middle of the night, smudge up close to him and feel his skin against mine. Tonight, I feel oddly vulnerable. I refuse to show as much, and so instead I decide to grasp the challenge. We should be able to have difficult conversations. I don't want to have to walk on eggshells. 'You think I drink too much?'

'I didn't say that.'

'By suggesting I should drink less, you did by implication.'

He looks wary, and then with a sigh says, 'I just think the drink might be the reason you're getting things confused recently. Look, don't take this the wrong way, but did you have a glass at lunchtime the day you fell off the ladder?'

'I'm sorry. What are you saying?'

'I'm not looking for a fight.'

'You might have stumbled upon one anyhow,' I snap. I shoot him a look that would cause a weaker man to crumble.

He reaches for my shoulder and gives it a little squeeze. 'You know if you had a problem I would be there for you, I would support you.'

'If I had a *problem*?'

'If there *was* a problem,' he corrects himself. 'You know, with alcohol. I'd understand. Your dad and your brother . . .' He trails off.

'There *is* a problem. I'm being victimised by some unknown person or thing.'

'Thing?' He looks quizzical. It wasn't wise of me to add that. How can I tell him my latest theory after what he's just said? It sounds mad even to me.

'Do you think I was drunk and smashed my own plant pots?' I demand. He doesn't respond. I'd have liked him to come back with a firm no. 'Do you think I threw the bolognese around the kitchen? The books around the living room? Of course you do, you've just said you think I was pissed when I fell off the ladder.' He still stays silent. 'Oh my God, you *do* think that.' I feel punched by the unfairness of the suggestion. 'Someone pushed me, then threw the ladder on top of me.'

'We checked the security cameras, Emma. We have done after every incident. There has never been anyone around. Not once.' He sounds as sorry as I feel. 'I'm not judging. I want to help.' He pauses for the longest time. 'So last night, were you drinking on your own again?'

I shake my head, denying his suggestion and also trying to dislodge it. I don't want that thought – that accusation – settling. Drinking on my own *again*. It's upsetting and I resent it. I resent him. I'm not a big drinker. Am I? True, I probably nudge above the recommended fifteen units most weeks: work dinners, receptions where glasses of white wine and similar are regularly served. On our date nights I usually start with a G&T, then we share a bottle. He generally has two glasses, I have three. But I'm never *drunk*. He got hammered last night. Isn't this a bit hypocritical of him? I certainly wasn't drunk when I fell off the ladder or when I found the books this morning.

'You have a high-powered job, a lot of responsibility and stress; it's not surprising you drink to relax. Maybe you should try to meditate or something. Forest bathing? I've heard that's good for stress.'

'I didn't do those things,' I say firmly.

He clenches his jaw. 'Well who did then? Tell me that. One minute you think it's local kids, then Becky's friends, someone with a key so maybe the cleaner, then your best friend of thirty years. You've thought all these things and then ruled them all out. Someone has to be responsible. Who?'

'I think I'm being haunted,' I blurt.

Matthew stares at me, shocked. Perhaps even horrified. Then he starts to laugh out loud. His laugh hurts my head. Hurts my feelings. 'You are joking.' I stare back at him, hold eye contact. Resist the urge to crack a smile, pretend I am joking, back away from the bizarreness. 'Wow, you have some imagination.' We both know I don't, not really. I struggle to dress my Christmas tree I'm so lacking in creativity.

'You said yourself we've ruled everything else out. I've spent some time researching it.' I reach for my laptop and quickly find the articles I want to share with him. I've saved a number of sites about the paranormal. 'Believing in ghosts isn't such an outlier thing as you might imagine. In fact, last year a survey of two thousand people was conducted by a reputable market research company, and they discovered that over sixty-three per cent of respondents believe in the paranormal in some form.' I'm gabbling; I don't want to allow a pause because I know he will shoot me down. 'We use the market research company ourselves at AirBright. They are not a dodgy outfit.'

'I'm not questioning the credentials of the researchers, just the sanity of the British public,' he says drily.

'But if so many people believe, then there must be something in it.'

'No, Emma, remember the double-decker Brexit bus. Things that are believed don't have to be true.'

I start to read from the site. 'Forty-four per cent of respondents have even had a personal paranormal encounter of their own. A third of respondents said they've felt a vague "unexplained presence" in their home, whether it was due to flickering lights or strange smells.' I look at him with hope. Surely he'll admit we've had our fair share of inexplicable encounters. Exactly as described here. 'Remember the lights in the grounds going on and off that night a few months back.'

'A fault with a bulb, that's all.'

'And the smell. I'm always telling you about the smell that I detect after each incident.'

'I bought a new candle.'

'We've had objects moving around the house.' Matthew doesn't say anything; he just stares at me slack-mouthed. I continue. 'A further twenty-three per cent of respondents said they don't believe in the paranormal but admitted that they still wouldn't want to "provoke" anything.'

'Those numbers don't add up.'

He's right, they don't. I've read the report a few times and still can't get to the bottom of it, but I assume it's unclear journalism rather than a problem with the research results.

'I've provoked Becky by marrying you,' I conclude sadly.

Matthew shakes his head. 'I'm bewildered, Emma. This is insane.'

I agree it makes no sense that I am even entertaining the possibility that ghosts exist, but I have started to believe exactly this. When I first began researching ghosts online, it embarrassed me that so many people believe in them. They all sounded unhinged, and I fought the idea of throwing my lot in with them, these irrational nutters who don't have a decent grasp on reality. I started reading bonkers sites that giddily declared, *Don't wait for Halloween to use a ghost-hunting app. It's a thrilling thing to do at any time, alone or with friends.*

Creepy basements are a great place to talk to spirits.

Dark woods are the spot to look for apparitions. Who knows what you'll find lurking there.

Ghosts can be company, if you don't have a pet.

I laughed out loud. I was glad that my first foray into entertaining the possibility of something paranormal was so ludicrous, because I wanted to dismiss the idea. I like being rational, clear-sighted. Believing that I'm being haunted isn't very me.

But then nor was falling in love aged forty-seven, and that happened.

The more I researched the paranormal, the more convinced I've become. It's the only answer. 'I think she's haunting me,' I continue. 'I think she did all the disruptive things around the house, but now it's escalating. She shook me from the ladder and then threw the ladder on top of me. She wants to hurt me. I'm really scared, Matthew. I think she wants me dead.'

Slowly, sadly, Matthew shakes his head. 'Emma, don't you see, if you think that's a rational explanation, there really is a problem. I don't know if this is connected to your drinking.'

'What?'

'I just don't know what to say to you.' He said he'd help. He said he wouldn't judge, but now he says, 'I'm sorry, I'm going to sleep in the spare room tonight. It's a lot to process, you know. My new wife accusing my dead wife of trying to kill her.'

And with that, he gets out of bed and strides out of the room.

I bet Becky's ghost is laughing.

28

Becky

*S*he's *lost it.* His text is stark and to the point. No kisses, I notice. We don't do that. They do. I've seen her phone often enough to know as much. There's always at least one, often a string of them. It's pretty infantile. Mortifying, considering her age.

I type my response. *That was the plan.*

I wait. He is online. I can see that. I wait for the word 'typing' to appear. It doesn't. Fucking WhatsApp. It's hell on earth. If he was standing in front of me, I could read him. I could make him elaborate, answer me. I hate the fact that the whole world can hide behind devices now. We've cultivated new levels of passive-aggressive polite deception. True, I know I sometimes use it to my advantage, but fuck, it's frustrating. I send a single question mark to nudge him. He knows me well. I'm not someone who likes to be kept waiting. I don't like being on the outside of the action. He better give me details, quickly. He does.

She thinks you're haunting her.

I mentally punch the air. *What?!!! That's perfect. Batshit crazy is better than alcoholic.*

Again I wait, sighing my impatience out through my nose. God, he really is annoying recently. I think he actively enjoys making me hang around, stay on the periphery. It's more than damned rude, it's a power kick. And it was never this way before. The problem is, he doesn't think about what it's like to be me in all of this. I decide I'll count to ten and then I'll . . . well, I don't know. I'll call him, I suppose, or send another text, or switch off my phone so he can at least see that I'm not waiting about for him. I'll do something, that much I'm sure of. I'm not having this.

When I'm at nine and three quarters, he sends another message. *Can't talk now. She's right next to me. See you tomorrow.*

I snap off the phone and throw it against the wall, aggravated by the thought of the two of them lying in bed together. I'm developing a taste for throwing things, smashing things. The phone bounces and lands on the bed. I don't check to see if it's broken; if it is, I don't care. Soon I'll be rich. I'll buy the latest iPhone. I won't have to put up with this crappy out-of-date one. I won't have to put up with anything. Money guarantees that. I'll get everything I'm due. Finally.

Spoiler alert. I'm not dead.

I'm not a theatre set designer either. I've never lived in America. My parents are not from South Africa. I'm not even married to Matthew Charlton. I never have been.

I know, right, you can't trust anything anyone says these days, can you? Especially men who seem too good to be true. Take note, they always are.

The being married part is the smallest lie. We are engaged.

More or less. We're going to get married soon. As soon as he isn't married to her and the money comes through. We're practically married on many levels. We've been together forever. Sixteen years, almost my entire adult life, and as I don't count my childhood as actual living, you can call this forever. We did meet at work, that much is true. At a fashion show. I was modelling, so was he. Although I called myself a model, he called himself an actor and said he was just doing the model-ling to make some money between jobs. He made it clear that modelling was a bit beneath him. I didn't take offence. I admired what I believed to be his ambition.

It took me a little while to discover that he was often between jobs; in fact he hadn't even finished drama school. It took me longer still to understand that his ambition was not so much admirable as delusional. He rarely got acting parts, and if he did, they never paid much. The modelling job was one of the better fill-ins; more often he worked in bars and restaurants. However, I was nineteen, he was twenty. Babies. You don't think so at the time, obviously. Our worlds seemed so sophisticated and powerful, full of sex, drugs, hip bones, incomes and agents. He was breath-stealing hot. We looked incredible together, and we were inseparable from the day we met.

I was of no fixed abode; I'd go where the work took me. Back then it was Paris, Milan, New York. Most of the time he came with me. I liked that. Coming back to the hotel to find him (and a line of coke he'd sourced) waiting for me felt like the closest I'd ever had to a stable routine. Mattie often commented that the life he was leading was light years away from the one his parents had led. They couldn't comprehend his world and therefore couldn't offer him any guidance; they didn't try to. My parents were out of the picture. So there was no one to tell us that we were just kids, no one to advise us that we should slow down, calm down, save up, sober up. Even if there had been, I probably wouldn't have listened anyhow. I don't take advice well.

When we met, the attraction was instant and absolute. I can't explain how complete my surrender was. I thought he was everything. A goal to aim for, a reason to live. A rule to live by. A family. Love. I just couldn't live without him, even though all along I had a sense that I was putting the brakes on my possibilities. Sacrificing multiple opportunities to cling tightly to one. But it was what I wanted. It was electric. I didn't believe in soulmates then, and I don't now, but there was a time, those first few years, when I believed in us in that romantic, passionate way young people believe in each other. Before they realise it doesn't matter what you feel; that comes second to what you do, and what you do is all tied up with what you earn. How you live. That's basically growing up. Understanding that.

Sometimes he really bores and annoys me, just because we've been together for so long. Other times I think he's as hot as hell and I want to fuck him in the street. Like when he agreed to this plan, that was one of those times. Because not every man would have the balls. Not every man could pull it off. I'll give him credit where credit is due, he's been very convincing.

Too convincing? The thought shimmies into my consciousness, shakes itself like a wet dog. Annoying.

It was all my idea. So I should be thrilled that he's gone along with it. And I am. Mostly. Of course I am. There is a shitload of cash at play here. A. Shit. Load. I'm talking millions. And more than that too – there's justice, revenge. Call it what you will. The whole nine yards. I'm owed.

I've shared him before, which is possibly why the plan occurred to me in the first place. I think most women would baulk at the idea. Possessive, protectionist, limited. I've had to get past all that. True, the first time I shared him wasn't intentional, and it hurt. A sharp knife slides in swiftly and you almost don't feel it until the damage is done. We'd been together two years. I was at the height of my career. I'd secured a few very big advertising contracts. One for skincare, another for jeans, a third for sparkling water. I was making a lot of money and attracting attention. Occasionally people stopped me on the street, asked for selfies, and sometimes after shows people asked me to autograph their catalogues. Once, someone tried to cut off a bit of my hair. She said it was to take to her hairdresser to get her to colour-match because she wanted to look just like me. Weird shit. I loved it. He was looking for work, not finding any. He had sex with another wannabe actress who, I guess, also needed to feel validated. She wasn't a stranger; she was someone he'd met at drama school, who'd been trying to get her nails into him for a while. I'd spotted her when I visited him once. I knew she was trouble. I'm good at spotting trouble. And causing it too, if necessary.

He confessed everything to me. He rang me up and cried over the phone. I think that was worse than the actual betrayal. If it was a one-off as he claimed, he'd got away with it, I didn't need to know. But he wanted to tell me. I wonder was that part of it for him? Me knowing, me seeing him. I was so hurt, like ripped-in-two hurt. Want-to-vomit hurt. Can't-understand-the-world hurt. And I was furious too. I told him he could fuck right off, that I didn't want anything to do with him and that I never would again. I don't think I even meant it as I said it, but you have to make them suffer a bit. There must be consequences. For weeks, months, he kept calling me. He threw out all the predictable bullshit – told me he was sorry, told me it meant nothing, told me that he'd do anything at all to get me back. That he would do anything for me from now on.

To be fair, he's been good as his word on that.

Obviously I asked all the questions every wronged woman has ever asked.

'Do you love her?'

'Of course not. It was just sex.'

'So was it good sex?'

'No, no, it was just . . .'

'Just what?'

'Different sex.' He was twenty-two. Of course he wanted different sex. 'I love you, Becky. I already know that one day we'll get married. You are my one. This was just curiosity. And I know it was a mistake. I'm sorry. Look, I know it sounds like a cop-out, but I'm a trained actor and I have no – or at least little – world experience. Can't you just think of this as process or something? You know, to help me access my range?'

'How do I know you won't make the same mistake again?' I demanded.

'You don't,' he replied.

I respected his honesty. With himself, with me. It's a rare enough commodity, that level of self-awareness. Look, I was mad about him. The break-up I'd insisted on was hurting me as much as him. I missed him, and if I was totally honest with myself, I found the idea of him having a bit more experience surprisingly exciting. I wanted to take him back. I just had to find a way that was sustainable. Something that would allow me to cultivate self-respect, keeping in mind the possibility – no, the probability – that at some point in the future he was once again going to be curious to know what else was out there. My childhood was such that I had grown up to be self-reliant, unconventional and realistic; I combine that with being passionate, competitive and ambitious. So I gave a lot of careful thought to our predicament. We were kids, but we wanted to grow old together. What were the odds of us doing that faithfully? Slim. And even if we succeeded in being faithful for the next sixty years, I reasoned that it would be so fucking boring for us both.

'How was it different?' I asked.

At first, he was embarrassed explaining it, awkward. He didn't really have the vocabulary or the balls to tell me about their sex, but eventually I wheedled it out of him. I thought it might hurt me more to hear the details, but it didn't. Talking about it somehow demystified the encounter, and then it turned me on. So we started doing the threesome thing – this was fourteen years ago, right? We were very ahead of our time. Points for that, at least.

It was always the same combination: me, him and another girl. Usually I picked the girl, made eye contact in a club or a bar, wherever. I approached her. Two reasons. Firstly, I have higher aesthetic standards. Not really a surprise; for most men every hole is a goal, up to a point, and I couldn't trust him to pick the sort of woman I considered beautiful or sexy. Secondly, if the girl wasn't into it, it was easier for me to pretend there was some sort of mix-up, a miscommunication, and I wasn't seriously propositioning her for a threesome. If Mattie had approached these women, he would have been called out as a creep a number of times. Even if he is super-hot, sharing is just not everyone's thing.

I stayed in control, I managed everything. I had to for my own peace of mind. I never left him alone with the girls I picked up, so they couldn't make any sort of private connection, or worse, swap numbers. I never allowed us to meet up with the same girl more than three times. Three was a good limit. By then we'd worked out where everyone fitted, who was most suited where. A plethora of arms and legs, bums, tits, lips and hips; there's a lot to consider in a threesome, and like all sex, it takes a bit of practice with each person who comes along. People have preferences and physical capabilities that need to be taken into account. It is a carefully choreographed dance. In my experience, if sex is ever going to be good, it's good by the third try. More often than that, though, and there's a risk that good tips into compelling or meaningful. I didn't allow much chat before or after. I'd call her a taxi within ten minutes of him coming.

It went on that way for five years, until he'd got other women out of his system, until he realised that variety might be the spice of life, but fidelity and loyalty are the main ingredients; let's say, the protein that makes you grow. I remember the night he called it quits, said I was enough, more than enough. We were in Amsterdam for his birthday. We'd gone there specifically to tick off a new first: something we could pay for, come by easily, no risk of any follow-up or emotional entanglement. We went for dinner first, just the two of us, and he ordered the taster menu. Seven courses. It took forever to get through them. I kept pointing out that it was getting late, that if we were going to do this thing then we had better get moving. He kept telling me that we had plenty of time. After we'd paid, he slung his arm around my neck and said, 'Shall we just go back to our hotel? Just the two of us.'

'Have you got a headache?' I joked.

'Something like that.'

That was the night he told me he didn't want to share me any more and he didn't want to be shared. He wanted us to be each other's everything. His acting career hadn't amounted to anything. I'm not sure why, he's talented. Maybe he had the wrong representation. Maybe it was just bad luck. He'd got a few bit parts in shows like *Casualty* – who hasn't? Some adverts and low-budget films. He was in a Jane Austen adaptation once. I can't remember which one. He looks good in breeches and he had a line about sandwiches. I think maybe the problem is he's charming and talented but unfortunately these attributes have made him a bit lazy. He'll take whatever falls into his lap, but he doesn't have it in him to relentlessly pursue. His tendency to follow me around the world to my shoots meant he often blew out casting calls. It's not realistic to expect anyone to hand you anything on a plate. I learnt that to be true a long time ago, which is why I've never missed a casting call. His loving but clueless parents hadn't taught him that lesson. He just wasn't hungry enough. Successful actors have to be either extremely lucky and connected or utterly relentless, ruthless and resilient. Mattie isn't any of these things.

That night, on the eve of his twenty-eighth birthday, he told me he wanted to give up the acting dream too. He was scared he was likely to fall into porn or end up playing the part of a medieval executioner at the London Dungeons. I wasn't sorry to let the dream die. It was time for a change.

29

Photographers, agents, newspaper articles, cab drivers and bouncers in nightclubs all said the same thing: investing money in property was the thing to do. We listened. It was our dream to have a home in London, of course; that is the basic model/ actor life map. Mattie wanted us to buy a neat top-floor flat somewhere like Clapham or Fulham. I had bigger plans, and as I was forking out 85 per cent of the deposit, I got the final say. So we bought the Old Schoolhouse. Eight hundred square metres. The mortgage was fucking massive, but we weren't overly concerned about the stretch. I had loads of work, we were young and couldn't imagine anything other.

Idiots.

The Old Schoolhouse was originally a canal-side warehouse, until it was converted into a ragged school for some of London's poorest in 1843. Somewhere kids went as a salve to poverty, overcrowding and disease for a few hours a day of their miserable lives. Once there were enough government schools, ragged schools closed their doors. For the next century, the building went through a variety of industrial uses before falling into disrepair and being threatened with demolition. A developer bought it in the mid-eighties but the boom-and-bust nature of that decade meant he lost all his money and jumped from a bridge to a watery grave before he did anything with it. The history is all very tragic if you think about it. We didn't think about it, or anything much. We bought it from that man's granddaughter. She seemed relieved to get rid of it. 'It's been ruinously expensive, a black hole,' she told us the day we picked up the keys. 'Good luck.' We didn't hear the warning. We hugged one another, drunk on the thought of owning so many square metres of real estate in London.

We had plans to fix the roof, install central heating, bathrooms, kitchens, strip back the floors, sweep chimneys, restore all original features, divide it into four flats. Live in one, sell the other three. We were sure they'd go for upwards of a million each. We'd make an absolute killing.

A week after we bought the Old Schoolhouse, I lost two of my three major modelling contracts. I was shocked by suddenly being dropped, but I shouldn't have been. I was twenty-seven by then. You can't stop time or market dynamics. Getting older in my line of business is the equivalent of a middle-aged president getting a blow job from an intern. In fact, ageing is even more of a crime. My agent suggested I find work on smaller campaigns. I envisaged advertising dandruff shampoo, or slacks in the back of Sunday supplements. It didn't work out. I turned up for countless auditions, only to be told I was too pretty, not pretty enough, too young, too old. The truth is, this sort of work is fiercely competitive. Ageing models and up-and-coming models are chasing the same spots. Besides, the pay was laughable. There are so many pretty women who are happy to do this sort of thing for next to nothing, just so they can say they're models. My agent dropped me. I tried not to panic, told myself that the Old Schoolhouse would offer an alternative income, and as Mattie had given up his dream to be an actor, he could get a regular job and help towards the mortgage. I was sure we'd be fine. There was a fortune to be made. London flats only ever increase in value.

Only we didn't own flats. We owned a draughty, leaking warehouse that flooded every time it rained. The floorboards were rotten; I twice put my foot through them. Woodworm attacked the beams; I feared if I didn't fall through the floor, then the ceiling would fall in on me. We saved up to get architectural plans drawn up, then called in estimates to see how much the conversion would cost. It was eye-watering. Mattie turned pale and said, 'I'm reading that incorrectly. There's an extra nought on the end, that just can't be right.'

'It is right. Well, if not right, it's what they're saying it will cost,' I commented, peering over his shoulder.

We had no idea how expensive everything would be. It wasn't just the materials; the labour was prohibitive too. Mattie said he'd go to college and learn some practical skills so he could make a start on the conversion, or even just the salvation, of the property. The course cost more money and time, and he was far from a natural when it came to building or plumbing or anything practical. I thought maybe he'd start doing some work while he was studying, but apparently the main thing he learnt was that we had to secure the roof as an urgent priority, a job too big for a novice DIY-er. We extended the mortgage, but even so, we couldn't afford to go with the roofer who had presented glowing references. The guy we could afford did a botch job and then disappeared. We resorted to relying on plastic buckets catching the rainfall in at least three places. In order to save every penny we could, we moved out of the flat we were renting. I wasn't willing to spend on rent when we had a roof elsewhere, even a leaky one. It was my decision. Matthew argued, 'Well yes, the Schoolhouse offers a roof, just about, but nothing else. No hot water, no lighting, no bathroom or kitchen.'

'It won't be forever,' I reasoned. 'We can save enough to convert part of it and then live in that. We can develop one flat at a time.'

'But we haven't the money to start on even one flat. We should just sell.'

'But who to? The market has crashed. We wouldn't get what we bought it for, we'd lose what we put in as a deposit. We must wait it out. The market will recover. Property always does in London.'

Only the rats found it comfortable; they settled in swarms.

We lived like squatters in our own property. I got the water and electricity turned on. We managed to reconnect a small kitchenette and a filthy loo and basin that had been installed for builders to use when the space was last going to be renovated in the eighties. In order to do this much, and pay the mortgage, I sold nearly everything I owned. First to go was the Audi A5 convertible, then designer shoes, bags and clothes I'd been gifted on shoots. I didn't wear any of them regularly any more, as we could no longer afford to go out to the sort of place that warranted them. I told myself I didn't need jewellery or even my GHD tongs. Matthew didn't have anything of value to sell. We couldn't afford to install central heating throughout, but made do with a blow heater that was so expensive to run we rarely dared turn on. We used hot water bottles and lived not dissimilarly to the original occupants of the ragged school. I envisaged a day when we'd take up the floorboards and get underfloor heating, and then relay the boards. I was very respectful of the history. Matthew didn't get it.

'The history of this place is fucking miserable,' he commented. 'Poor lice-ridden kids beaten into learning their times tables so they could calculate exactly how many boxes of matches they needed to sell to avoid being evicted from their slum.'

'That's rather a pessimistic view. I like to think we're living in a place where children were inspired through the gift of education.'

'You're delusional.'

He said that sort of thing relatively frequently – 'you're delusional', 'you're ridiculous', 'you're so stubborn', 'we should just sell'. He was wrong, small-minded, lacking in vision. I could see how it could be. How it would be. I could envisage millions in the bank, a stunning property, beautiful clothes and possessions once again. I didn't want to be ordinary. I wanted to be rich. Properly rich. The poverty and grime wore him down because he'd grown up comfortably. I had not, but even I never got used to the broken windows, iced pipes in the mornings, pigeon shit and rat droppings that festered just metres away from where we slept. It was a step back for me too, yet I wasn't prepared to give up on my dream. 'You can walk away if you like,' I'd respond when he said we should sell. He never would, of course. Where would he go? It was impossible to imagine giving up, impossible to imagine a way out. We rowed. Often. The surprise is not that we rowed but that we didn't kill each other. He stopped calling me his beautiful girl and started calling me his beautiful problem.

By then, I had started working at a place called the Concierge. It is an incredibly expensive and exclusive members' club that caters to multimillionaires who want to hang out and behave badly, safe in the knowledge that no one is going to take a sneaky photo of them and sell it to the tabloids. I worked the reception. It wasn't especially arduous; the hardest thing I had to do was smile after doing a twelve-hour shift in four-inch heels. My skill set was niche. I could source an after-hours gift from Tiffany's for a wife or mistress in the event that a client had forgotten a birthday; I could get a bottle of Patrón en Lalique if someone wanted to spend £7,000 on a bottle of tequila, or I could charter a private plane if they had a sudden urge to play blackjack in Monaco. I took all the work offered. Mostly night shifts from 4 p.m. to 4 a.m. It was warmer than being at home, so I didn't mind. Besides, being surrounded by that level of wealth was motivational.

Mattie didn't finish the courses on carpentry and plumbing. Eventually he decided to retrain as a photographer, which meant more student loans and more debt as he spent thousands of pounds on cameras and other equipment.

It was tiring. I am tired.

One of my friend's boyfriends proposed to her through a flash mob dance. That was pretty cool. There was another one whose boyfriend ordered a custom-made fortune cookie from Amazon that said *Will You Marry Me?* Not bad, but honestly if you can get them on Amazon, are they really custom-made?

Mattie's proposal was somewhere on the scale of low-key to grubby. There was no drone above us capturing our special moment, no fireworks, no room full of candles. We'd been together for thirteen years, and one wet Sunday afternoon, we were half watching something or other on TV – *Married at First Sight* or *Say Yes to the Dress* – when he said, 'Do you think we'll ever get married?'

And I replied, 'No, you're too poor.'

He laughed, until he realised I wasn't joking. Then he stopped laughing and got sulky and weird. Mattie is hot, right. Definitely. And I love him and I love being with him, living with him, fucking him, everything, but he's broke, perpetually broke, and he lacks ambition, and it's not what I want out of life. I used to think that eventually someone else would come along, someone wealthier who could buy me nice things, who could buy me *something*, for God's sake. But there is only a whisper of a chance of that becoming a reality. By the time he first proposed, I was already the wrong side of thirty. Now, the only rich men who would look at me are drawing their pensions. That's economics. It's shit that the world still works that way, but it does.

I probably couldn't leave Mattie anyway. Not if it came down to it.

Sixteen years, right; even if he's a disappointment, he is *my* disappointment.

My girlfriends say I'm a bitch to even think the way I do. That I shouldn't be so obsessed with money, that I should just be glad that Mattie is really hot and devoted. They say that because they all have more money and uglier husbands than I do. He has asked me to marry him loads of times since that first time. I always say no, for the same reason. Then sometime last year he pushed back and argued, 'You're poor too, Becky.'

'Yeah, but I don't like it.'

'Nor do I.'

'But I dislike it so much I'd do anything to be rich.'

'So would I.'

'No you wouldn't. Not anything.'

'I would.'

He sounded deadly serious. We were at my mum's flat at the time. It's shabby, depressing and small in every sense of the word, but warmer than the Old Schoolhouse, so we often hung out there. Mattie was in a foul mood that day. He had a bad back from sleeping on the bed settee. The nagging pain was making him short-tempered.

'Like something immoral or illegal or dangerous?' I asked. Pushing.

'Yeah, I would. I'm sick of living like this too. Our life is shit. Have you got a plan?'

I did have a plan. I had a complex long-game plan that would make us millions. When the front desk at the Concierge was quiet, I'd let my mind pore over infinite details. I'd imagine all the problems, complexities and possible dead ends, then I'd finesse the solutions, the insurance, the remedies. I researched what the likely punishments were if we got caught. I imagined how we'd spend the millions if we didn't. I had weighed it all up carefully. So I told him. Not the truth, not the entirety. Because that wasn't the plan. I told him what he needed to know.

30

I'm well aware that the division of labour is very unbalanced here. My part of the deal largely centres around sneaking into Emma Westly's house, looking through her computer and paperwork and getting to grips with her finances. Later, of course, if everything goes to plan, I'll have to do more. I'll have to do the worst. But there's no denying the lion's share of the early part of this venture has rested on Mattie's shoulders. That, frankly, made me nervous in the beginning, because he isn't, you know, always the most reliable. This is a one-shot venture; I can't afford for there to be any mistakes, so I've micromanaged everything I could and Mattie has been fine with that, used to it. In most relationships there's a proactive one and a reactive one. It's a relief that things are working out.

So, she's batshit crazy. She thinks his dead wife is haunting her. Even I hadn't thought of that.

I started following her on social media as soon as my mum told me who she was cleaning for. However, it's an official work account and it didn't give me much. The tone is preachy, patronising, telling us all which bog roll we should use and how ethical purchases might be a 'few quid more' but 'cost the earth less'. Lady, I'd love to have the choice. I can't believe she scores so many likes for that sort of condescension.

Once Mattie agreed to my plan, I started making more comprehensive searches, started to follow her in real life. I got my doctor to sign me off work with nervous anxiety and exhaustion, which bought me a few weeks' research time. I'm not anxious or exhausted, I'm euphoric. For the first time in a long time, I'm getting ahead. I'm on to something big, something I've long since been owed. First I took up guard outside her office – it was the easiest place to track her from. It's where she spends most of her time, as she's a live-to-work type. I positioned myself on the street opposite, sitting in the window seat of a café or standing in a doorway or lingering by the bus stop. It's a busy London street, so no one ever noticed me. It's easiest to go unseen in a busy place.

Her office is as you'd imagine: shiny, flashy. The employees who drift in and out are of a type: self-consciously cool, hip and earnest. They ride electric skateboards or scooters; they leave work wearing bike helmets or headphones; my guess is they listen to zeitgeist trending podcasts. I've never seen one of them go for a post-work drink; they invariably march straight past both the nearby grubby little pub and the trendy bar. If they ever do stop for a beverage, it's an oat milk vanilla latte or a high-protein green spirulina smoothie at the overpriced café I hide in. I imagined that being surrounded by these young people probably made her feel old. That pleased me. I calculated that it would work in our favour when Mattie stumbled into her life. I'm a patient woman, which was useful, as for the first three days, I didn't spot her. Then I did.

She looked different from how she appeared on social media. Her body was as toned and trim, but her face looked nearer to her real age. On inanimate photos she appears smooth, composed, younger. In real life she looked a little more worn in, a little more troubled. I watched and noted how she dashed in and out of the building faster than any of her employees bothered to; they tended to saunter. She arrived earlier than them too, which is possibly how I missed her at first. I quickly understood that she does everything at speed; it is exhausting to watch. I asked myself, what has she got to rush for? OK, she's the boss, but she has hundreds of underlings who are probably doing all the real work; she certainly has loads of staff to manage her home. She can't be that busy. I deduced that her constantly hurried manner comes from a puffed-up sense of her own importance. She wants to give off the 'I'm a very busy and important person' vibe.

I watched her carefully, followed her closely. To and from wherever she was going. I started to understand her habits: which days she came into the office, what her commute route was, what groceries she picked up on the evenings she returned to Hampshire, and when and where she met friends. I worked out what's important to her, her likes and dislikes. I kept notes so that I could thoroughly brief Mattie. She was often on the phone, lots of dull business calls, but some were fun ones to her friends. I've never heard her speak to her brother. My feelings towards her were unambiguous from the off. She's a spoilt bitch with everything I don't have. If I had a brother, I'd keep in touch with him even if he was an annoying addict.

Especially then. She is oblivious to everyone around her. I was able to get close enough to smell her perfume, and I often sat behind her on the train back to Hampshire. She never noticed me.

I saw the conference announced on her company Instagram, where she humble-bragged about speaking at it. Great honour, great responsibility, etc., etc. She really is nauseating. I'm OK with that, though, as I know Mattie likes my sort of sense of humour – sarcastic, fast. I felt confident that he'd find her saccharine sincerity a bit wearing. Good. I don't want him *liking* her. I bought the tickets to the conference, trailed around charity shops in the posh part of London to buy clothes with designer labels that could look like he'd worn them for years. She wasn't the type to appreciate fast fashion, and brand-new clothes would be suspicious. My attention to detail was, if I say it myself, incredible. I briefed him with all that I had learnt about her tastes, beliefs and preferences those past few weeks, so that he knew what to bring up in conversation. I guessed it would be the little details that would seduce her. Women like her like to think they're unique and special and that others have noticed just how unique and special they are.

'She doesn't give money to the homeless on the street.'

'That's tight, she's loaded.'

'Yeah, but she does buy sandwiches and water from Pret and hands those over nearly every day. I have also seen her stop and talk to those annoying people who canvass for charities.'

'You always walk straight past those,' murmured Mattie.

'Well, yeah, I have no money. I'm poorer than most of

the people benefiting from the charities. Besides, although they canvass with extraordinary energy, they're not sincere. They're on commission and earn with each direct debit they secure. I'm surprised she falls for it.'

'Which charities did she sign up for?'

'WaterAid, Trees for Cities, Keep Britain Tidy and Women in Sport.'

'All of those since you've been stalking her?'

'Researching her,' I corrected him. 'It's easy for her to give, isn't it? Fifty quid a month for her is just like a normal person flipping fifty pence.'

'I suppose, but not all rich people are charitable.'

'I also learnt she's not a hugger, so don't go in too tactile.'

'OK. What else?'

'She never crosses the road unless the green man is lit, she jumps at loud noises and then looks annoyed at herself for doing so, she eats lots of noodle bowls from Itsu. She runs every day.' She runs with the kind of grim determination that makes me wonder what she's running from. 'By the way, the doctor won't keep signing me off and I need to be available for you and this project, so I will have to resign from the Concierge.'

'How will we manage?'

'Doing without the regular income is a gamble, but Mum is helping us out and it will be worthwhile when the big payoff comes.'

At the conference, I directed the 'meet-cute'. I told him when to approach her, when to hold back. The moment she'd finished delivering her speech, I nudged him so that he quickly stood up before anyone else and clapped loudly; she couldn't fail to see his enthusiasm. I didn't allow him to join the throng congratulating her as she left the auditorium. 'She'll come to you,' I predicted with certainty. 'You should get a drink in.'

'Shall I get a couple of glasses of wine?' he asked me as we waited for her to arrive at the bar. 'You said she drinks red. That will make me look confident, and she'll be flattered that I guessed her preference.'

I rolled my eyes. 'No, it will make you look reptilian and creep her out. She needs to trust you, and women don't trust men who ply them with alcohol. Get water. Not tap, sparkling, to show some level of effort.'

I found a seat at the bar and told him to take her to the table in the corner when she arrived. I couldn't hear them, but I watched them. As I'd followed her for the previous few weeks, I'd become a bit of an expert on her body language. I'd seen her interact politely with strangers; with them she keeps her back straight, her head high, holds herself at a distance. I'd seen her brush off anyone she considered a time-waster; she can do this with one cold glance. And I'd observed her with her friends. When she talks to them, she practically melds into them; her body bends towards them, curls as though she is caressing the air around them, then over and over again she explodes into loud bursts of laughter, throwing back her head, opening her mouth wide, shaking with mirth.

That first night, she did something similar with Mattie. I knew she liked him from the off. That was a relief. He's good-looking and charming, I've said all that, and when he turns his intensity on you, he's hard to resist, and he really did appear to be upping the ante. It was good to know that the acting classes weren't a complete waste of time. It's lucky I'd seen his act before, or it might have been quite hard to handle watching him tilt his head as he listened to her, hanging on her every word, once or twice touching her arm with the tips of his fingers – nothing too blatant, but enough to show his interest, to send a spark. I guess those years of threesomes were my training for this. Helped me identify when he was disassociating the physical and the emotional. I told myself it was great news that he was managing things so well. That initial meeting had been a significant financial investment. I'd had to shell out for train tickets, conference tickets and the hotel room. We did at least put the room to good use. Got our money's worth when he'd finished up with her. He was under strict instructions to leave her feeling ambiguous about the nature of his attention. It would have been a mistake to so much as kiss her on that first night. Slowly, slowly wins the day.

The next morning, he wanted to leave her a note. I wouldn't let him. I knew this woman; she was confident and independent. If he came across clingy or in any way too keen, she'd run a mile, maybe even smell a rat. He had to leave her hanging. Wanting more.

It was a nervous wait. Just when I was beginning to be concerned that I'd misread her, her marketing team got in touch, some flimsy excuse about needing a photographer at short notice. Could Mattie perhaps go to her office?

Boom, and just like that we were off the starting block.

31

'If you don't fuck her, she'll lose interest,' I told him.

'She won't, actually. She likes talking to me.'

'Yeah, but you'll be friend-zoned, or she'll think you are friend-zoning her.'

I said this in a way that suggested it was no big deal to me and with the hope that it was no big deal to him. He was a little skittish about jumping into bed with her, or at least he had the good sense to pretend that was the case to me. He'd used the grieving widower card for four weeks, but they were dating – just as I wanted, just as I'd planned – but I knew they would have to have sex eventually. I'd signed up to that.

I knew when they had. I could see it in her face the moment she emerged from her house to go for her run. She looked relaxed, joyful. Mattie is good in the sack. I didn't ask him about it like I had all those years ago when he slept with the no-hope wannabe actress. I didn't need any level of specificity in this case. Overthinking it wouldn't help. I didn't want to imagine his lips on hers, on her nipples, on her thighs. I didn't want to wonder about what sort of sex they had. We all know there's a range. Was it good? Bad? Surely bad. Dull, static, ideally. She probably just lay there being useless, not sucking or allowing him to lick or explore. God, I hoped so. But did anyone have static sex any more, or did that die out in the 1950s? I didn't want her to have the sense to even fake an orgasm, and I certainly didn't want to think she didn't need to fake one. All I could do was try to put it out of my head. Generally I'm good at compartmentalising. Best not to know. What you don't know can't hurt you, right?

What I *do* know rips me apart.

I bet she did come.

How much money justifies encouraging your partner to make another woman come? If you'd asked me that when I was nineteen, I'd have said there is no amount in the world. I used to say romantic things like that. I used to believe them. Now I'd say a couple of million will more than cover it. I don't think I'm cheapening him.

I think I could have accepted her joyful expression, but then I saw him whistling. He looked pleased with himself. Very much carrying the air of a job well done. So I unscrewed every one of the bulbs that hung in cheerful festoons throughout her garden and smashed them on the patio. Kids sometimes steal those filament light bulbs; you can sell them on eBay. I could have stolen them so she'd think it was kids, but I wanted her to have to clear up the mess. I hoped she'd cut herself while doing so. Later, when Mattie asked me if I knew anything about the smashed bulbs, I replied, 'Nothing at all.' He probably didn't believe me, but he didn't challenge me. He picks his battles. Wise.

It's annoying to admit, but they are quite a convincing couple. People who don't know them might very well believe in them. They're not as magnificent as we were when we first started dating; then, we literally turned heads. But she is always laughing and talking and I suppose that is attractive if you like noisy, bubbly types. When Mattie commented that she always had something to say on literally any subject, I snapped, 'Of course, she went to a posh private school, didn't she? They teach you that stuff. Small talk and debating and interesting conversation-openers.'

'And she laughs a lot too.' He was smiling to himself as he said this. Men are simple, in every sense of the word; they have no idea how transparent they are.

'I'd laugh if I was as rich as her,' I muttered. I didn't add what I was thinking. *She won't be laughing when we're finished with her.* I went to three different comprehensives before I left school at sixteen. No one ever taught me much at all. I'm not going to give you the sob story. Just believe me, it was fucked. My education and my propensity to laugh and chatter were both fucked. Sod Mattie for being impressed by a posh little prig who had everything handed to her on a plate.

When I wasn't searching through her house, I followed them on their dates. Most of the time I had to wait outside concert halls and trendy restaurants, just imagining the fun they were having learning to make cocktails or master circus skills as I stood on the pavement eating chips. I preferred it when they went to free galleries and museums; at least I could follow them inside then. I didn't tell Mattie I did this. I thought he'd feel scrutinised, and I didn't want him to get spooked and start behaving unnaturally with her. I kept at a safe distance. Out of sight.

Out of mind too, apparently.

I mean, obviously nothing is actually going on with them, in a properly meaningful sense; it's all essentially play-acting, but it's not always easy to watch. To the casual observer, he might seem quite into her. I tailed them on their little antiquing excursion. I knew he was playing a part and I was glad he was doing it so well, but I was irritated by the fact that he has never once accompanied me on an antiquing excursion or any mooch around any shops. They looked like they were having fun. His excuse to avoid shops with me has always been that it's pointless to go shopping because we don't have money to spare, which is true, but you can just look, you don't have to buy. Years ago, I collected eighteenth- and nineteenth-century ink bottles; it was when I was modelling and had spare cash for such fripperies and indulgences. I had to sell the collection when I let everything of any value go. I didn't get as much for them as I paid. I heard him tell her that I collected ink bottles, which surprised me. Pleasantly. Cheered me up a bit. I hadn't expected him to remember.

It is beyond weird hearing him talk about me as his dead wife. The whole grieving widower thing was my idea. I thought it was a better backstory than him presenting as a divorcee or appearing flighty, because at thirty-six, a lack of significant exes indicates a fear of commitment. Plus, we had to have a story that explained why he had no friends or family that she could meet. A lost, isolated widower living away from loved ones is an object of pity and easy to trust. More than that, this story provided a little pinch of something extra. I knew it would create uncertainty about where his affection – his devotion – truly lies. That's a good thing with a competitive woman. I know she's jealous of me. Dead me. She wouldn't be in the least bit jealous of alive me if she knew everything.

The shopping expedition really got to me. They were making goo-goo eyes over tasty treats while I was moping in the shadows, hungry as usual. I followed them from shop to shop. Not going in the smaller ones where I'd be easily spotted, but hanging about outside, waiting for them. When they went into the large antiques emporium, I saw him head upstairs, so I took the opportunity to slip inside and nip downstairs. I didn't know exactly what I hoped to achieve by staying so close to them; it was a compulsion. I mean, what else was I to do with my Saturday afternoon while he played the devoted boyfriend? I told myself I was being vigilant, as sometimes I would overhear titbits of conversations that proved useful. I would tell him what more could be said on a particular subject or what should be said differently. To some extent I guided the seduction by telling him exactly what women – or at least this particular woman – wanted to hear.

I've turned into a regular little Cyrano de Bergerac. You know, the ugly bloke who wrote the letters to the beautiful woman on behalf of the beautiful but stupid man. The question is and always has been, who was she really in love with? I'm not an ugly bloke, but the classical reference pleases me. Mattie often talks about my 'schemes' and my 'tricks'. The word choices seem loaded, a little condemning. My plans are given respectability and currency if I can liken them to classical literature. People think I'm stupid because I was a model and my education was constantly interrupted. I'm not, and it's dangerous to underestimate me. *That* is stupid.

The incident in the antique shop wasn't planned. I couldn't quite stop myself. I'd been watching him all morning; he'd been nauseatingly attentive and had provided her with the perfect day while I was left lonely. Ignored. Less. She wasn't supposed to notice me, but I found it quite insulting that he didn't either. Smashing the trashy stuff and letting her think she'd knocked them with her handbag made him notice me, though. The antique dealer assumed I was just another customer; I think she assumed I worked there. Only Mattie knew who I really was. Everyone was panicked and upset. He looked the most scared of us all.

I just wanted to spoil their day. Silly bitch, trying to buy up the whole shop for him. It was so flashy, so gauche. He should have let her get the ink bottle set, though. I liked it. Arguably, this act was undisciplined of me. I'm not an especially disciplined person, to be frank. I am doing my best in this particular situation to be patient, guarded, but my natural bent is to let it all out. I rate passion. I like to feel and roar. Mattie knows that. I'm not going to apologise for it. It's totally part of the territory. I'm trouble. I always was even as a kid. That's not a big surprise. No one can pretend six care homes and four foster homes while your mother is in jail is ideal. Being bad got me noticed. I prefer being a rule-breaker. People who follow rules, pencil within the lines, must regret it on their deathbeds. It's not that I have no regrets, it's just that I have no lost opportunities.

Look, fuck you, I have no intention of pleading my case.

32

The plan, as I'd initially laid it out to Mattie, was not at all alarming, my strategy being, 'don't scare the horses'. It's basic to liken him to a nervy stallion, but accurate. I definitely didn't want him shying away from the jump. When I first told him about the woman my mum cleaned for, Emma Westly, rich and alone, I simply said she was an easy target to help with our cash-flow problems. I said the aim was to get just enough to pay the mortgage. Keep us afloat. I explained that she had so much more than she could spend, while we had nothing at all. Did that seem sensible, let alone fair? I said we would establish the worth of her valuables in her home and hack her computer to get access to her bank accounts. To do this, I just needed time and her passwords. Him being her 'boyfriend' gave me access to both. He recognised it wasn't an especially honourable path, but he didn't have a better idea.

'Then we can filter some cash away from her,' I told him.

'Won't she notice that?'

'Rich people like to give the impression they're good with

money, but some of them are not; they just got lucky and inherited a shed load. She's that type. Soon, they get so rich they can't even keep track of what is where. We'll probably find she has dormant accounts that she's forgotten about. We can empty them.'

As per the plan, Mattie discovered the password to her computer easily enough; all he had to do was ask for it when he was ostensibly ordering some tonics online at an overpriced artisanal tonic producer (how the other half lives). This meant I was soon able to find a list of all her passwords stored on her computer – for banks, credit cards, investing companies, pensions. She's smarter than most, though, I'll admit that. She stores her passwords backwards to how she uses them. That almost threw me. Almost.

Since I had advance warning about when she was going to be away from home – because she was in London, in a fancy hotel, shagging my boyfriend – my searches of her property were thorough, practically forensic. I used his key to get in and out so there was never any sign of me. It only took me a few visits to quickly ascertain the value of all her assets. I have a good eye, and easily identified the paintings and sculptures that look like kids made them but actually are collectibles. I took photos and sent them to an old friend of mine in the art world, asked for rough estimations, said I knew someone who might be interested in selling. I collated copies of all her bank, savings and investment statements and, where I could, insurance docs or receipts for antiques and jewellery. The lot.

It was never my plan to settle for skimming off the top. Turns out I'm not a bad actor either. I appeared frustrated when I told Mattie, 'Maybe it's just the rich men I met at the Concierge who are lax about keeping track of their money. Emma Westly isn't frivolous with hers, and from what I can gather, she knows where every penny is. She has a spreadsheet she accesses all the time.' I was poring over the statements with an obvious air of despondency. I have hard copies as well as digital ones. I don't want to take any risks. The piles of paper lay between us on the crappy little chipped IKEA table I rescued from a skip. I literally hate everything I own. It's all so pathetic. 'She has so much, but she's so careful.' I said the word in a tone that clearly communicated condemnation.

'I'm beginning to wonder if this will work. Almost three months in and all she's done is offer me a poxy loan,' he said, shaking his head woefully. He's not a completer.

I know he found the loan thing infuriating. Humiliating. He lost his temper the night she mooted it. He sent me texts saying he was quitting 'the whole fucking crazy plan'. He stormed back to the Old Schoolhouse insisting we didn't need to put ourselves through 'this idiocy'. I happened to be at Mum's. Later that night, I went round to Emma's and took out my frustration on her plants and stupid glass domes. He'd riled me. I can't do this without him, and I was genuinely worried that he was going to pull out. It all worked perfectly, as it happened. He couldn't even manage a whole night on his own at the Old Schoolhouse. He remembered just how fucking uncomfortable it is there, and was a little more pliant the next morning regarding my plan to make us rich. Meanwhile, Emma felt scared and needy after my demonstration and so suggested he move in with her, resulting in us gaining more access and momentum. Far from a disaster.

Mattie came up with a suggestion of his own. 'We could steal from her, take all her jewellery and valuables, anything that isn't nailed down. A clean sweep. Why not?' He looked excited about this plan. I could see the appeal. A fast one-and-done. But even while he argued the case, I could see the problems. He continued, 'We could do it while she was away in Scotland on business. She wouldn't even lose out. She's insured to the hilt.'

'But you'd be the main suspect,' I pointed out. 'The handsome stranger who recently came into her life and moved into her home in a hurry, only to move out of it again just as her Rothko vanishes.'

'Well then, you could rob the place on a night when I'm with her. I could hang around for a little while afterwards, a couple of weeks or something, until the heat was off.'

I wondered if his suggestion was simply naive or devious. I'd be taking all the risk. I eyed him, weighing it up, but decided not to call him on it. Instead I pointed out another flaw in his plan. 'And how much money do you think we'd make?'

'We could get away with about a hundred thousand worth of valuables, maybe more.'

'I wonder what that would be worth on a non-legit second-hand market?' I mused. 'Probably a tenth of that. It's not enough to renovate the Old Schoolhouse.' This is why he's not in charge of planning. A break-in wouldn't offer everything I want. It would simply lead to confusion and higher security. Something I'm keen to avoid. 'The thing is, we're even worse off now than when we started this. You know I had to give up my job to support you adequately in this venture.' It was a careful choice of words. I was not manipulating him – it was not as blunt and unsubtle as that – but I did need to guide him round to my way of thinking. Anyone would do the same. 'We've had so many expenses. Travel costs, the new clothes we bought you so you could look the part . . .' I pause. 'Besides, think of the Old Schoolhouse. We've invested so much, Mattie. Not only cash, but years of our lives have been devoted to that place. I worked out how much we've spent on our mortgage, and it's heartbreaking.'

I opened my bag and pulled out the piece of paper with the calculation written on it. We have an interest-only mortgage. We've been paying it for eight years, and have spent over £90,000, and yet we are not one iota closer to owning the property or even making a dent in the actual loan, which is £800,000. It may as well be £8 million or £80 million – it is an impossible amount for us to pay off as a jobbing photographer and an ex-receptionist at an upmarket private members' club. We thought we'd be paying it off as a movie star and a super-model. Then it would have been chicken feed. The world is so unfair.

I had hoped that my detailed searches of her finances, files and life in general might throw up some useful material. Something dark. No one is as good, virtuous and disciplined as she presents, are they? I thought we'd find something dodgy in her inbox: a racist comment that could bring her down, an explicit picture sent to some ex-lover that could do the same, a messy tax return that didn't declare absolutely every stream of income. She loves her job; she wouldn't want to lose it. Blackmail could make us a decent amount.

I didn't find anything. She really does live her life as though the spirit of Mother Teresa is sitting on her shoulder.

I suggested to Mattie that he could take some photos of her. Compromising ones. 'You're perfectly placed to do that.'

'But then she'd know I was the one blackmailing her.'

'She would, obviously. But if you got enough money out of her, would it matter? You wouldn't need her any more.'

He looked uncomfortable. I knew he'd resist this idea. I was banking on it. He doesn't like to think of himself as a bad guy; he wouldn't like her to think of him as such. 'I don't think blackmail would get us the lump sum we need,' he said. 'There is a lot of money knocking about here. As you said in the beginning, there has to be a big opportunity. Let's keep thinking. I'm sure you'll come up with something.'

'I'm sure I will,' I muttered. I already had. It was just a matter of when I revealed it to him.

33

One evening after they'd moved in together, she was in London with her friends and so we had her house to ourselves. He was making me bolognese. There are certain things between couples that from the outside look like one thing but to the couple they mean a whole other thing. We both knew that him preparing this meal showed he wanted to treat me, nurture me. It's my favourite dish of his. He often makes bolognese for me when he thinks I need cheering up, or if he's done something wrong, or if we're celebrating something. It's multifunctional. That evening I wasn't in need of cheering up, and as far as I was aware we weren't celebrating anything; I wondered whether I should brace myself, but decided not to be cynical.

Maybe he just wanted us to have a nice night together. I wanted that.

I stood at the marble breakfast bar, drinking a glass of her wine (I'd picked a dusty bottle from the top shelf that I assumed was a good one) and watching him carefully. He clearly knew his way around this kitchen; I deduced that he must be doing a lot of the cooking for her. He'd never said. I didn't resent the fact that he looked so settled; I wanted him to have a tempting taste of the good life so that he had a crystal-clear understanding of what he was playing for. I'd always believed he would fit into a luxurious environment. It's what I'd expected for us both. He looked like the sort of wealthy husband you see in adverts for expensive watches, and not at all like the wealthy husbands who stumbled into the Concierge. They all had great big bellies, wandering hands. They were inadequate, fumbling, stumbling. I guess a lot of people don't get rich until they are old; it's such a waste, such a problem.

It amuses me that everyone always says that appearances can be deceptive as though it's a bad thing. It can be unnerving but not necessarily insidious. The most fascinating and important thing about appearances is that they can become reality. You only have to consider Instagram and the blistering bouts of FOMO you get over people you don't know – people you will never meet, who are not even having as good a time as they pretend to be having – to know that appearances can become the reality. We all scroll through strangers' posts and feel beaten up, eaten up by envy because they are bikini-clad on a yacht or drinking Dom in a hot-air balloon or are a size eight in an infinity pool (pick your poison). That jealousy is real; the dissatisfaction we feel with our own lives exists. The self-loathing and hatred is a fact. Appearances become the actuality, so I know that what I'm creating here can be genuine too. I never doubted Mattie would fall effortlessly into this world of wealth and luxury. He is in his prime: attractive, sexy, and he looks like he was born to it. What a shame he wasn't.

I sometimes let my mind drift to just how simple and brilliant life would have been if Mattie had just been rich. He comes from a loving home, but they couldn't afford to send him to private school, buy him a car or give us a deposit for a flat. Everything would have been so much easier if that had been the case. Just lovely. I never imagine that scenario for me and my own family, though. It's too close to the bone and yet too wild and painfully impossible at the same time. Fuck it. No matter, I've worked with what we have. I played the cards dealt. I will be successful. I have to be. I must stay focused on the world I've planned. The one where we live in Hampshire while the Old Schoolhouse is being renovated. I'm going to keep her place even when the renovation is complete. It's good to have somewhere in the country as well as London. Mum can live there, not just clean there. That seems fair.

Yeah, news flash. I'm playing for the whole shebang.

Mattie's head was bent over the Le Creuset cast-iron pot. I smiled to myself, delighted that he was ensconced. I was also very comfortable in Woodview by then. I knew all about how the water and room thermometers work, where the key to the sauna room is kept, the code to the alarms, the range of the security cameras, the storage and management of the security data. I'd searched every square inch of the place; it had no secrets from me. I like the pair of us having it to ourselves, playing house; it feels comfy, secure, right. It is important to me that he doesn't have all his good times with Emma and associate me solely with poverty, damp walls, dripping taps and rats. That won't do.

That night, I'd dressed up. I'd helped myself to a ME+EM dress in Emma's wardrobe – we are the same size. If Mattie recognised it, he didn't say so. I'd had a blow-dry too. I can't remember how long it had been since I'd visited the hairdresser. It felt amazing to have someone wash my hair, massage my scalp. I practically had an orgasm over the little biscotti that came with my flat white. I'm allowing myself small treats like a blow-dry now, since I know we're getting closer. I'm putting stuff on a new credit card; it will be easy to pay it off. I look forward to being so used to being pampered that I'll get impatient with the hairdresser for taking too long on the head massage and I'll say no to the free coffee. I bet Emma does both things; she's always rushing through everything. Not grateful enough that her life is worth wallowing in, not aware that she ought to be appreciating every single second. While she can.

Normally I resist lighting the Jo Malone candles that are scattered around the house, but that night I had. Emma wouldn't notice if they were burnt down; she has fresh candles delivered every month. I don't think she even sees this as the epitome of luxury it so obviously is. I think she sees it as a basic, the way the rest of us think about buying loo roll or milk. I was glad to have him to myself; sharing was proving more wearing than I'd anticipated. I was always being confronted with evidence of the sex he had with Emma. The house searches not only threw up details about valuations on art works; I also found massage oil, her underwear lying on the floor, sticky and stained sheets. I shouldn't keep looking, but somehow I am compelled. Even though it turns my stomach, even though it makes me want to smash things, break and burn things. I don't, though – well at least not always. Sometimes I content myself with opening the Velux windows in her bedroom so that her rugs and bedding get soaked when it's raining, or turning off the hot water so that when she returns from work she can't have a hot bath.

Petty stuff. Not enough. The threesome thing, when we were young, hadn't turned out to be the armour I had expected it to be. That was just sex, there was no doubt about it. Brief encounters, recreational, almost clinical. I've asked him to make Emma fall in love with him. It's risky. I know that. But I am prepared to take risks. I have to.

I often stay at Woodview when she is away. It's remote enough that no one ever sees me arrive or leave. I've shown Mattie how to tamper with the security footage; we've both become quite adept at deleting, pausing, editing. We make it look as though he is always on his own, in case she ever checks. I always insist that we sleep in the spare room. I have no desire to sleep in the bed they share; I'm not a masochist. I am always careful not to leave anything behind. I don't want to give her indisputable proof of my existence, that's not the plan. I do, however, burn incense before I leave so she never detects my perfume or our sex. I could burn her expensive candles; they would do the same job. Mattie once asked me why I didn't.

'Why introduce a new smell to the house and risk alerting her?'

'The incense is a more natural smell, woodland and stuff. She won't even detect it,' I replied. This was a lie. I knew there was a strong possibility that she would notice the strange scent; that she might have already. I want to make her uncomfortable. I want her to know something is different in her home but not be able to put her finger on what exactly. It's good that she's confused, disorientated, not quite on top of things.

That particular night, I thought there was a high chance she'd have a drink or two with her friends and then message to say she might as well stay in town because she had an early meeting the morning after. In reality, she didn't have any such thing. I'd put a fake meeting in her electronic diary to try to tip the scales of her decision to stay away overnight, so Mattie and I could be left alone. If she did decide to travel back to Hampshire that night, I'd at least have some sense of satisfaction knowing she'd get up even earlier than usual to travel to her office, only to discover the meeting didn't exist. That would probably put her in a bad mood all day.

These tiny paper-cut wounds bring me great pleasure.

Mattie looked up from stirring the bolognese and suddenly asked, 'Do you think this is ever going to work?'

'Of course it is,' I replied swiftly. I thought we were right on track. He wasn't entirely aware of the race we were running, so he didn't have the same confidence. Let's just say his perspective wasn't as honed.

'What have we got into?' he asked plaintively, running his hands through his hair. He looked desperate. The thing is, whenever he makes a gesture like that, a clichéd epitome of a particular emotion, I can't help but doubt it. You know, like if he throws his head back in laughter, I always think to myself, is he really *that* happy? Or if he's biting his fingernails, is he truly nervous? Right then, I couldn't help but wonder, was he stressed or just frustrated? Impatient? Was he any of these things, or did he just like a drama? OK, that's not the most charitable thing to think about him, but that's what happens when you live with an actor; it's hard to know what is authentic. I've found it's better to listen to his intonation to get a grip on the truth. He gives himself away when his voice gets caught in his throat, when his laugh roars through a room, when he shouts out in ecstasy just as he's going to come. I felt a swell of impatience at his comment; I mean, how stressed could he be in fact? He was going to endless amazing restaurants, he was hanging out in her beautiful home, and he was sleeping with two women. *I* was the one who had a right to be stressed.

Still, I found it in me to calmly reply, 'Good things come to those who wait.'

'But we have waited and waited and nothing much has come our way,' he said petulantly. 'How am I going to disentangle myself from this? I've met her friends now. The more people I meet, the more likely it is that we'll get caught out.'

'Caught out how?'

'There are a million ways. Someone only has to find a hole in my backstory.'

I shot him a quick glance. Wary. 'Did you slip up?'

He tutted, turned away from me. 'No, but I might at some point. This is complex, you know. And it's obvious her best mate doesn't like me.'

'I find that hard to believe.' He is generally very charming. Women like him. I think we've established that much.

'She cross-examined me like she's some sort of MI5 agent. She's jealous of me, I think. Thinks I'm a threat to her relation-ship with Emma.'

'Good to know. We might use that.'

'What if someone recognises me from our real life?'

'That's not going to happen. Her friends live in Surrey, we stay in Hampshire or London. They're older than we are, they have kids and stuff. You don't mix in the same circles.'

'*She* lives here in Hampshire.'

'She doesn't have any friends around here. She keeps herself to herself.' She's a snob. None of us are good enough for her.

'Everyone is only a few degrees of separation from everyone else in the end. Someone somewhere might be connected.' He shook his head slowly and added, 'Plus, I think she really likes me. I don't want to hurt her.'

His voice was quiet. There were no big actory gestures. I kept my face as still as possible. It was important not to react even though he had just told me he liked her. That he cared for her. Because that was exactly what he had said, under the guise of saying the feelings were hers. What was he thinking? She's a decade older than he is. She's obsessed with her work, therefore de facto boring! What can he possibly like about her? True, she has a great body. But she works at it, she must at her age. I've watched her run. She really puts herself through it every morning, sweating and panting and clearly aching. I have a great body and I don't have to do much to keep mine in shape other than smoke and drink a lot of sugar-free Red Bull. She looks a little like me, actually. I should have perhaps factored that in. Who knew that Mattie had a type? We're both brunettes, although I wear my hair much longer, and we're both brown-eyed. Slim, tall. Is that going to be a problem?

'I'm just going to have to finish the relationship sharpish and walk away,' he said firmly. 'It's the sensible thing to do.' A shadow flashed through his eyes. Regret? I hoped he was only regretting the fact that if he did walk away, he'd have to say goodbye to the oyster and champagne lifestyle he'd been enjoying. 'I'll probably have to ghost her. Right?'

He always thinks I have the answers; luckily for him, I always do. We sat in a heavy silence. The clock was ticking, the fridge was humming, birds outside were tweeting, oblivious to the misery, the need and despair unfolding between us.

A dangerous, chaotic combination. Necessity is the mother of invention and desperation is necessity's older, bossier, more insistent sibling. Finally I muttered, 'I suppose we could . . .' I broke off. 'No, that's mad.'

'What, what?' He reached for a lifeline that he was sure I'd supply. A way out. A solution.

'No, honestly, forget it. It's a stupid idea.'

'Becky, we're desperate at this point, more desperate than we've ever been. Any idea at all must be considered.'

So with apparent reluctance, I told him the first part of my real plan. The petty fraud, theft, blackmail had never been that. She is worth millions. Literally millions. There is so much to play for. There is everything. 'You could marry her.'

He laughed, but then he saw I was stony-faced. 'What? Are you crazy?'

It was not the first time I'd been asked this, by him and others. It is a fairly regular charge to be dropped at my door, actually. It always makes me laugh. People say it like it's a bad thing. They'd be shocked if I said yes. If I told them that it is exciting to be crazily ambitious, crazily untethered, crazily immoral. Look, if believing in seizing opportunity with both hands is crazy, then yes, I am crazy. I feel sorry for people who are *not*. It's so much more fun, so much bigger, such a souped-up, vibrant way to live.

I smiled and said encouragingly, 'Think about it, she's mad about you. She's not getting any younger. If you proposed, all her Christmases would have come at once. She'd say yes in a heartbeat. I'm sure of it.'

'You think.' I could see that he liked the idea of her accepting his proposal; his pride had taken a beating these past few years as I'd refused to capitulate to his many offers. Then his face collapsed and he added woefully, 'But marriage is for life.' Now I was the one laughing. What planet did he live on? He looked angry, so I stopped laughing. He clarified. 'I mean, it's not an easy thing to get out of once you're in it. I'd need to be married to her for years to walk away with any proper cash.'

'Well, maybe one or two years, yes. But it would fly by, and you like her company well enough, don't you? It's not actual torture. It's just like a prolonged acting job. It's like being on a soap.'

'And you'd be OK with me marrying someone else? Marrying her?'

I had to handle this with kid gloves, obviously. I didn't want to appear careless. I'm not careless. It has been awful knowing they're together. I've had to shove it out of my mind again and again, put it in a box, lock the box, throw away the key, but there is a bigger picture here. 'It wouldn't be ideal, but I'd get used to it. I'd know it's fake. It is only for a short time. We've waited years to marry; a couple more wouldn't hurt us. It wouldn't change anything between us.'

'Wouldn't it?'

'No, my love, it wouldn't.' I reached for his hand and squeezed it. 'Plus, she works away often enough, and whenever she's away from home, I would come to you. We'd still be together.' I put my hands on his face, stared into his eyes. 'We are above petty jealousy. We are better than that. Stronger than that. I think you'd come away with at least two million. That's a fraction of her wealth, but a fortune to us. We could pay off the mortgage and finish the refurbishment of the Old Schoolhouse. We'd be set for life.'

'How do you know I'd get that much?' I could see he was interested.

I'd done my research. 'I'm guessing, but I bet you could. I was thinking maybe after two years you could tell her you want babies. That you're sorry, heartbroken in fact; you don't want to have to choose, but it's an undeniable instinct. She'd be forty-nine then, chances of her conceiving are minuscule, even if she was keen to try. I'd bank on the fact she loves you enough to grant you a divorce so you could find someone you could have children with.' She's just the sort to do the full-on martyr thing, choosing to live alone with her self-loathing rather than with a man she felt she'd trapped.

He looked uncomfortable. 'I suppose. But two years. It's a long time.'

'Well, the only thing that could speed up the process is if you divorce her. If she was found at fault.'

'She's not the type to have an affair.'

'No, she isn't,' I said carefully. 'But you could divorce her on grounds of her unreasonable behaviour.'

He shook his head. 'That won't work. She's pretty much the most reasonable person I've ever met.'

'She likes a drink, doesn't she?'

'No more than most.'

And this was it. 'That might be true, but we can make it look differently.' I carefully started telling him the details of my plan, gauging how much he might be prepared to hear. 'Now that I have access to her computer, I could change more things in her diary so she misses important events and appointments. People will start to talk about her unreliability and look for reasons behind it.' People can be depended upon for that – thinking the worst, gossiping. It's a rotten fact of life. 'I could move things around the house so she believes she's being forgetful.' I had already been doing this. I wanted her to doubt herself. She's obsessed with being in control; it will be interesting to watch what happens when that slides. 'You can start dropping hints to her friends and colleagues that she's drinking a little too much, that you're worried about her.'

'Gaslight her, you mean?' I could hear the confusion and disapproval in his voice, perhaps with an undertone of disgust. Mattie generally plays things very straight. It isn't that he's especially moral, it's more that he's too lazy for complications.

'I wouldn't call it gaslighting. That's a bit reductive. Didn't she tell you her brother and father were alcoholics?'

'Yes.'

'Well then, her drinking too much should be easy to sell. Just think, I know the exact worth of everything she owns. When it comes to divorce, she won't be able to try to say the value of her estate is less than it is. I'd like to see her try to lie to your lawyer.'

'I don't have a lawyer.'

'We'll get you one when the time comes. One step at a time, hey? You have to marry her first.'

'And you've just thought of this now?' He sounded suspicious.

'Yes, just occurred to me,' I replied firmly. So firmly that he dared not question me further.

Of course this wasn't true. I'd never intended to settle for scraps and morsels, I want the whole feast, but I knew that if I admitted that, he'd get weird about it. Most likely go on about me always having crazy plans, perhaps moan that I take things too far, an accusation that he has levelled at me in the past. Plus, it was unlikely that he'd be thrilled that he'd fallen for my lies; no one likes being lied to, because it makes them look stupid.

I waited. The silence throbbed through me. Weirdly, it felt loud, overwhelming. This was up to him. I couldn't do it without him. I hardly dared breathe.

'OK.'

I wanted him to be crystal clear. 'You'll do it?'

He looked sad. Jaded. Jagged. 'We've started this thing now. We need to finish it.' He sighed in a way that reminded me of when I was a kid and I used to let all the air out of the tyres of my foster dad's car on the days he was supposed to drive me to see Mum in prison. The hiss was sort of desperate and hateful.

There's always a line, and we'd just crossed it.

34

'I asked her to marry me.'

'Sorry, you did what?' I was in my mum's flat when I took his call. I dragged the toe of my trainer over the lino floor, deliberately leaving a black mark, then slammed my hand on the magnolia wall. The walls were decorated so sloppily that the paint covered the light switches and power sockets. The effect this creates is not one of sleek unity, more of a careless insipidity. It's a tight, cramped space. The first thing I always do whenever I arrive is open the windows. My mum complains that I let the heat out, but it's just something I need to do. On some level, being with Mum means I have less air. Hearing his news made the flat feel more claustrophobic than ever. He'd asked her to marry him. What the fuck? It was Sunday evening. I had only mooted the idea of marriage to him on Thursday evening. This was far too rushed, too impulsive. 'That's not what we agreed,' I said sternly. 'I was going to tell you what to say when, in order to get her to say yes.'

'Well, she liked *my* proposal and she did say yes.'

'Oh.'

'Aren't you going to congratulate me?' I could hear the smugness in his voice. The triumph.

'Congratulations.' It stung. No, that's not right. It felt more than that. There were shafts of debilitating pain shooting up through my body. I collapsed into a kitchen chair, slamming my shoulder blades heavily into the wooden back. Everything my mum owns is mean and hard. It hurt. I was glad of the pain that resulted from the physical impact. I hoped it would distract me from the strange shock of hearing my boyfriend was engaged to someone else. *This was my idea, my idea, my idea*, I repeated to myself. It was, but I hadn't expected it to hurt so much.

'So tell me all about it.' I don't know why I asked. It didn't matter. It was done, but I felt a need to keep a grip on the situation. I didn't like him going rogue, but since he had, I needed to understand exactly how things had played out, despite the hurt running through my body like a poison.

'She was freaked out after your handiwork with the bolognese. We cleaned up together, and when we finished, I asked her to marry me. It was totally impulsive; the idea was swirling around my head because you'd been talking about it, and I just blurted it out. You know, a seize-the-day, what-have-you-got-to lose sort of thing.'

What? Hang on. What was he saying? He proposed after they cleared up the bolognese? Thursday. He had waited three days to tell me this news. The news that he was engaged to be married. What the actual fuck? Wasn't that the sort of thing he might have wanted to update me on straight away? He could at least have sent a text. What had they been busy doing for the last three days that the need to pass on this info slipped his mind? No, actually I didn't want the answer to that. I bit down hard on my lip until I could taste blood. Mattie didn't seem to notice my silence; he was too buoyant with the victory of his independent strike to care. Instead he blathered on about 'moving up the timeline', 'striking while the iron is hot', 'no time to lose'. One self-congratulatory cliché mushed into the next. I blinked furiously, trying not to let tears fall down my cheeks. I'm not a crier. Not usually. Kids who grow up in care learn not to show their emotions. I've heard kids who go to posh boarding schools learn the same lesson, so don't get out the violins. I was crying then, maybe, but that was just because I was shocked, not weak or sad or hurt or scared. I couldn't be. It was my idea. I wouldn't allow myself to be.

He was gloating, behaving as though he'd won a Nobel fucking Peace Prize. He kept repeating how brilliant it was that he'd brought the plan forward a few months. 'The sooner I'm in, the sooner I'm out.' He was wrong. We needed to take this slow and steady. If it appeared he was in an unseemly rush, or behaving impulsively, it would ring alarm bells, either with her or with her friends. Someone would start to whisper 'fortune-hunter'. He'd have been better waiting a few more months. Why had he done this? Was he teaching me a lesson, flexing his muscles? He continued, 'I mean, when I first saw the shitstorm you had created, I was so pissed off with you. Did you have to?'

'I was annoyed that she'd spoilt our evening,' I replied honestly.

'That tomato sauce really stains, you know. You ruined her white alpaca wool rug and the sofa will have to be re-covered.

We've put a throw over it for now, I'm going to get it sorted on Monday morning. Get some upholsterers' quotes in. I was thinking like a grey leather cover. At least that way if you go crazy again it can be wiped clean.' He laughed at his joke. I didn't. 'What do you think? Will grey leather work, or maybe cream?'

I thought he should put the damaged sofa in the Old Schoolhouse, say it was beyond repair and just let her buy a new one. Even stained, it was better than anything we owned. But I didn't give him my views on the interior decor. Instead, I concentrated on what he was saying to me and what he wasn't, and tried to make sense of both.

I had been so damned irritated when she sent him the text saying she was coming home early and not staying out with her friends. She got to spend so much time with him and I really resented our night being curtailed. But my irritation turned to fury as I saw his panic; he looked like a school kid caught graffitiing on the teacher's desk. Of course I had to get out of there sharpish, but his fussy urgency was somehow unseemly. He ran around the house eradicating all signs of me, plumping up cushions and smoothing out the indents on the sofa where I had recently been curled up with him; he hastily washed and dried the wine glass I had drunk from and carefully returned it to the cupboard. He rushed upstairs and gathered up my clothes, shouted at me, 'Get out of her dress!' I felt like an undervalued mistress. Used and then nothing. It seemed that he'd temporarily forgotten *I* was his wife, or as near as dammit. Certainly his almost-wife. *She* is the other woman. I didn't want her eating my bolognese, I didn't want her having my peaceful evening with him. He practically pushed me out of the back door as though he was putting out a cat. He didn't pause to so much as flash a regretful smile that our evening together had been hijacked.

I stayed and waited until she arrived home, watched through the arrogant floor-to-ceiling windows as he fussed about her, got her to taste our bolognese, poured her a glass of wine. The wine I had been enjoying.

It was an unthinking, adrenalin-fuelled act, but I don't regret it. I had to do something. I wanted to cause some chaos, wreck things, leave a mark. Some people cut themselves. I'm more outward-facing in my destruction. There's no resisting that feeling when it floods into me, swamps me. All I can do is give into it, bend with it. If I didn't, if I stayed rigid, I might snap. There isn't a choice or a decision. It's a force. A pure, blind fury invades every molecule of my being. I don't see red, I see white. My vision is bleached away, I feel dizzy and sick. The only thing I can do to ease the symptoms is rip and smash and throw and roar. Mattie knows this. He's seen it often enough. He knows it's not really my fault. It's out of my control.

I hung about outside, cloaked by the blackness of the night, and watched her emerge from the storeroom at the back of the kitchen. Her face was a picture when she saw my work. Her shock and horror soothed mine a little. As I saw her eyes widen in panic, her face tighten with fear, I was able to breathe again.

I settled and watched them clean up together. It got cold and I didn't have a coat with me, but I didn't budge. I watched them go to work with rolls and rolls of paper towel, scooping gloop into black plastic sacks and then setting to with buckets of steaming soapy water and mops. I was laughing to myself, seeing how much chaos and confusion I had caused, knowing that I'd spoilt her evening as she had spoilt mine. But then suddenly they were having sex. Just there in front of me. It was disgusting to watch. Worse than anything I'd watched him do before. Worse than I'd imagined it. I wanted to leave so I didn't have to witness it. I wanted to stay and see the act through to the grubby end. Both things at once. I told myself I should stay, that it would reassure me. Like it used to when we did the threesome thing. Back then I could always see that he was just into the sex, not into the woman. He was certainly respectful and decent enough with whoever, because he's not a prick, but there was never a connection. If he looked at them directly, he was always looking at their bodies. If he looked in the mirror, he caught my eye. That was all he was interested in. Their bodies. Or me.

I watched as Mattie and Emma both stared into the blackness beyond the window. For a moment I thought they had spotted me, but no, it wasn't me they were looking for. He searched out her gaze, she found his. Their eyes met.

And now they were engaged.

35

Since he was charging ahead with his part of the plan, there was nothing for me to do but up the ante in my programme to undermine her, destabilise her. So that's what I did. Mattie and I texted constantly and spoke when we could. He did at least have the decency to give me a heads up that they were ring-hunting. At first, he had a stupid idea of giving her a valueless, sentimental ring that had been in his family. The exact same one he once suggested I wear. I told him to go to Tiffany's, reminded him that when this was all over, she might throw the ring back at him. It would be more useful if that gesture was worth twenty grand. *I like your thinking!!* he texted. The double exclamation marks suggested an element of jubilation that I didn't feel entirely comfortable with. He seemed irrepressibly buoyant, a little too close to a happy groom-to-be. Surely this was just because our plan was coming together. Wasn't it?

I didn't like the idea of them having a big traditional church wedding. It felt full on and formal. Meaningful. This isn't that. It's easier to unpick a wedding that hardly anyone else witnesses; wedding guests are more invested. I didn't want people invested in this marriage. When he texted me to say she'd made an appointment with a vicar at St Adelaide's in Hodstone, I immediately knew I had to stop that. It's a great-looking church, just the village along from where my mum lives; it's not inconceivable that Mattie and I will marry there one day. Had he even thought of that? I expected Emma to be spooked once I fucked up her parents' graves. She wasn't. She's as hard as nails. Mattie had to pull out all the stops, come up with some bullshit about being too traumatised by my funeral to want to marry in a church.

I wanted them to do it abroad, with fewer witnesses. I hadn't anticipated how quickly they'd arrange that. Fine, whatever. He was getting cocky. He thought he was in control, but when Emma insisted on a prenup, he instantly fell apart again. Came running to me for advice.

'What are we going to do? I never thought she'd ask for a prenup,' he was yelling, which was stupid of him. We were in the Fox and Crown, my mum's home. People know us here. They don't have to know our business, though. I squeezed his leg under the table. Hiss-whispered for him to calm down, offered to get him another beer. Really? He never thought she'd ask for a prenup? I'd have thought it was obvious that she would. A rich businesswoman like her, marrying a – let's face it – broke younger man whose job is just a small step up from a hobby, of course she'd be wise to put a prenup in place. I had counted on it. For a brief period of time, I had been concerned that she might turn out to be surprisingly sentimental and not her usual practical self with regard to the engagement. It was a relief when her friends stepped in and talked her into it. Without a prenup, how was I going to get Mattie over the line?

I had to think about how much of this I wanted to explain

to him, though. Since I'd watched them have sex that night they got engaged, I'd been even more circumspect about exactly what I should share with him. I love him. I can't remember a time when I didn't love him and I can't imagine a time when I won't love him, but I don't know if I can trust him. Lots of people get confused, believing one thing leads to the other. No way. I wonder what he can cope with, what he will process and support.

I brought his pint back to the table. I'd bought myself a Diet Coke. There was a flask of vodka in my handbag. I rooted around and dug it out. Amazing Graham, the landlord, knew I couldn't afford to pay pub prices for spirits and that I brought my own with me; he turned a blind eye. Men of a certain age are generally kind to me because they still appreciate a pretty face but are terrified of very young pretty faces. Young women now are aware and demanding. They don't accept flirtatious favours – all power to them, they don't have to, that's progress – but I still take what's on offer. I will until I have the agency to tell creeps to fuck off. When I say agency, I mean money.

I poured a healthy measure of vodka into my Diet Coke and thought about Emma. 'She doesn't trust you, Mattie, and honestly, she's right not to, isn't she? I mean, you're not in love with her.' Worth underlining, I felt. I set my face in an expression of concern. 'Well, you have no choice in the matter. You'll have to sign the prenup to prove to her how trustworthy you are, or else she might not even go through with the marriage.'

'No, shit, no. That won't work. She's shown me a draft. If I sign it, we have to be married for five years before I see any decent money. I'm not doing five years.'

I was glad to hear his revulsion at that idea. I touched his arm and murmured soothingly, 'No, of course not. I'd hate that too. But I'm sure it won't come to that. I've an idea. With all this evidence we're gathering, we can change tack.'

'Change tack how?'

'You don't have to divorce her on grounds of unreasonable behaviour. We can get her committed.'

The word spilt across the little table. The old boys on the table next to ours were playing dominoes; was it my imagination or did they pause? Lean our way? I put my head closer to Mattie's.

'Committed? Like in an asylum?' he asked.

'I'm not sure that's what they call them nowadays. That's such an awful word. So loaded. I just mean we could get her put under observation or something. Get her help if she's drinking too much and behaving destructively because of it. Same tactic, we're just looking for a slightly different outcome.'

'She doesn't need help.'

'But we agreed, we're going to make it look as though she does. Right? It's already happening. We don't need to give that more thought.' I had to keep him moving along. 'We've been through this. You're engaged to her. She wants a prenup. You're marrying her for her money; if there's a prenup, you won't get any money when you divorce her, but you have to sign the prenup if you want her to marry you, because she thinks you're marrying her for her money. Is this really so hard to follow?' I was steamrolling him. Of course I was. He has a tendency to look back, check over his shoulder. It's not useful and it's not sexy either, come to that. I pushed on. 'So, you sign, you marry her, and when she starts to appear unstable, you can get power of attorney. Then you will be in charge of her money and we can go back to plan A, filtering off cash. It will be easy, as you'll get legal access to everything. Then, once we have enough, you can divorce her. Or not. I mean, if she's in an institution, you might not want to bother. We would be free to do as we please anyhow.' He stared at me, slack-jawed. 'Are you getting this?' I snapped.

'Yeah, I think I am. It's just . . .'

'Just what?'

'It's just a lot. It's pretty ruthless. I mean, *committed*.'

'The Priory is practically a spa. She'll be fine. We'll be rich, Mattie. Isn't that what you want?'

'Well, yes, but . . .'

'And she'll be out the way. Gone. Keep up, Mattie.'

He gave me a dark look at that comment, but he signed the prenup. It was a step closer.

Obviously I couldn't follow them to the Maldives to watch the nuptials. Instead, I moved into Woodview while they were away. Mum stayed over too, because she didn't want me to get lonely. She understands how hard this has been on me. I caught her going through Emma's jewellery again. She's light-fingered; lost all concept of private ownership when she was inside. Theft is not what she went in for, but prison provides quite the education. Mum went in after a domestic with my dad that ended badly. For him. He had it coming, but while that makes a catchy song line in the musical *Chicago*, it doesn't make much of a defence for murder. She went inside a victim of a crime of passion and came out with a general sense of amorality and specific abilities for theft, fraud, self-defence and God knows what else. Let's just say she's resourceful.

'She wouldn't miss it if I took one or two of the smaller bits,' she said. 'She has so much.'

'You can take one piece,' I said firmly. 'Scatter other bits around the house so she thinks she's mislaid stuff. Put it in weird places, like the fridge, so she wonders how it got there.'

Mum slowly turned to me and glowered. 'I know the plan, Becky. I designed the blueprint.'

The looks she spews are killers. I swear I felt my blood cool and slow. I was born just before she went to prison, and although we were able to be together in the mother and baby unit until I was eighteen months, I have no memory of her at that time, so I don't know if she learnt to glare like that inside or whether it was always her way. I like to think her hardness was born of necessity. It's more understandable that way. Forgivable even. She doesn't have to be hard with me. I'd do anything for her. I am. I get it that she's not in the habit of trusting or being trusted. Who is? She wasn't the only one punished for my father's death. We don't talk about the sixteen years she spent inside, the years I spent in care. I would talk about it with her, but she's never asked. I once mentioned sleeping with a chair up against the bedroom door so no one could get into my room, and she said, 'Living it once was shit enough, why pick at the scabs?' I guess she feels bad that I went through it, that she couldn't mother me. It's not her fault. If it's anyone's, it's my dad's.

I like to think that if she'd never had to go to prison, she would have been the same as other mothers, that she would have smiled and laughed, read bedtime stories to me and made packed lunches every day; maybe she'd even have cut off the crusts. When I was a young kid, I used to make up stories to comfort myself. I'd imagine her winning the mums' race on school sports day, tearing along the track and snapping through the ribbon, everyone cheering. I think I got the image from that iconic picture of Princess Diana winning the parents' race at Prince William and Harry's school.

I must have, because I've never seen my mother run. I imagined her spooning medicine into my mouth when I was ill or booking me dentist appointments, brushing my hair, teaching me how to swim. Mum stuff. No one did any of that for me, but so what? I have great hair, straight teeth. Self-sufficiency is an important life skill and my mum gifted me that.

By the time she got out, I was modelling. Too old to be mothered in the conventional way. We're close, though. Tightly bound by what we missed out on, rather than tied by conventional shared experiences. When she first started talking to me about this opportunity with the rich woman she cleaned for, I felt something I hadn't felt before. I felt protected, looked out for. She knew Mattie and I needed cash, that we were struggling. It's not like she has a cash box under the bed or a trust fund that she can draw on. Sharing this opportunity was all she could do to give me financial security, and all parents want to help their kids out if they can, right?

I watched as she slipped a fine gold chain bracelet into her jeans pocket. Then she spat into a bottle of toner. She shook the bottle and said, 'Don't use that.'

I sighed, bewildered. Spitting into skincare products wasn't on brief. Emma wouldn't be disturbed by something she wasn't aware of. It struck me as a petty, nasty act. Undisciplined. I'm not above petty or nasty, but I like to be effective. On strategy. 'Why did you do that?' I asked.

Mum ignored me and continued to root through the jewellery boxes. I didn't push. I left the room, went downstairs to watch *Love Island*. Sometimes my mum's whole *Game of Thrones* Cersei Lannister vibe is a bit weird.

36

The pub was heaving. It had that particular Saturday-night thrum that is the result of people gathering determined to have a good time, willing to pay for it tomorrow. I was alone in my cloud of apprehension, my eyes trained on the door, waiting for him to enter. We had been in London when he got her message. We drove back together.

'I wonder what it can be?' I'd asked.

He'd kept his head facing forward but his eyes slid to me. 'Did you ask your mother to do something?'

'No,' I said hotly, but I could see he didn't believe me. 'Why would I want to make mischief today and spoil our day out?' I reasoned.

He sighed. Unsure whether to believe me, unsure if it mattered. My mother might have done something whether we'd asked her to or not. Clearly Emma had run into some trouble. She'd texted him asking him to get home as soon as he possibly could.

He drove straight to her place; I was unceremoniously

dumped on the road just before the gates, out of range of the security cameras. Left to make my own way back to Mum's flat. I'd sent him a number of messages asking for an update since, but it wasn't until the evening that he'd deigned to answer. Then he'd told me that he was at the hospital with her, that she'd fallen off a ladder and was concussed. Just like his first wife, I thought, weird coincidence. Although obviously there isn't a first wife. I'm just saying. Others might see a pattern.

When Mattie finally arrived at the pub, he looked full of hell. His first words were 'You've gone too far. The plan was to have her committed, not to kill her.'

'What has this to do with me? I was with you.'

'Where was your mum today?'

'Isn't it possible Emma just fell off the ladder?' I asked.

'I thought so at first, but the ladder was then thrown on top of her.'

'Like, *fell* on top of her?' I queried.

'No, because it was then put back up against the wall.'

'Oh.'

'She certainly thinks she's losing her mind now.'

I paused, gauging how far to go. 'Well, that's a good thing. That's what we wanted,' I reminded him gently.

'You should see the state of her.' He looked shaken and furious at once. His words came out in a snarl, a tiny spray of spittle landing on my cheek. I went to the bar and ordered him a pint and a glass of wine for me, bought some crisps too, as I thought about what to say next. My mother went to prison for killing my father. It's not just possible she's responsible for this, it's probable. I'd go as far as to say a certainty. Mattie wasn't aware of all the circumstances of my father's death, not exactly. I certainly did not think this was the moment to enlighten him.

We found a table in the corner of the pub, as far away from the happy-go-lucky clientele as possible. He took a long draught of his beer, downed almost a third. When he put his glass back on the table, he jumped out of his skin; we both did, because my mother was looming over us. She's not a big woman, shorter than average, in fact, but we were sitting down and so she seemed overwhelming.

'Everything OK?' she asked.

'You know it's not, Susan,' snapped Mattie. 'You pushed her off the ladder and then threw it on top of her. You could have killed her.'

My mum smiled slowly. Honestly, it made my blood turn sluggish. 'Not dead, then,' she muttered.

'You didn't push her off the ladder, did you?' I said, hurriedly interrupting before she could do anything stupid like outright admit it. Mattie snorted with impatience.

My mother shrugged, and they stared at one another, seeing who would blink first, literally or metaphorically. The noise of the pub bounced around us: chatter, laughter, chairs being scraped, some inane pop music from the nineties that I recognised but never liked. So much noise, but we seemed to be stuck in a silent void. 'What was she doing up a ladder anyway?' I asked.

'Cleaning the gutters,' Mattie replied.

'Why? She could pay someone to do that. Maybe she is a bit mad.' It was a weak joke, but I was trying to break the tension.

'Not everyone wants to pay people to do things for them. Some people get a sense of satisfaction by doing things for themselves.'

'They do indeed,' said Mum. Her tone was dark, ominous. Mattie and I shared a look. Neither of us wanted to think there was a deeper meaning behind her words. What was she prepared to do? What else?

'I don't want her dead. We're going to have her committed. That's the plan. You've gone too far,' said Mattie.

Mum hissed her response. I had to lean in to hear it. 'It's not me who's gone too far, it's you.'

'What do you mean?' Mattie asked. He looked flustered.

I eyed them both, unsure as to exactly what was going down. Something was, though. I had a strange feeling that if I stuck out my tongue, I would be able to taste the tension in the air. It would be metallic, like blood.

'Just don't get too cosy with her. I won't tolerate that,' warned my mother. Then she abruptly said she was going back up to the flat to watch television and left. I watched her cut through the crowd. She didn't head upstairs; she headed straight out the pub door. I didn't point out as much to Mattie; he'd just panic. To me, it made sense. Emma was alone in her house; it was the perfect time to pay her a visit.

'Fuck. You're all mad, I don't know who to trust,' muttered Mattie. He laid his head on the pub table and banged it. Not hard, but enough to draw attention. I smiled at everyone who looked our way as though I thought my boyfriend was a really funny man.

'Sit up, pull yourself together,' I instructed. 'Look, Mum might have done us a favour here. You should call her friends. Tell them you're concerned about her.' I stared at him, waiting for him to pull out his phone.

'What, now?'

'Yes. Make out you're really worried. That you think she's in danger.'

'I am,' he muttered darkly. 'I think she is.'

I ignored him, and added, 'Maybe mention you think she had a drink earlier when she was on her own.'

'I just want to get pissed,' he said wearily. It was ironic that his reaction to this stressful situation was to want to drink heavily, the very thing he was going to accuse Emma of – an over-reliance on alcohol, leading to unreliability.

'Go outside, make the calls, I'll get more drinks in.'

37

She's lost it.

That was the plan.

She thinks you're haunting her.

What?!!! That's perfect. Batshit crazy is better than alcoholic.

Can't talk now. She's right next to me. See you tomorrow.

I've been rereading these words all day. They look different now that there's a big crack across my screen. Sort of traumatised, shadowy, not quite real. He said *See you tomorrow*, but he hasn't sent another text since to tell me when he's free. I might have to suggest they get a dog, one that needs to be taken on long walks, then he'll have a convenient excuse to get out the house. She must watch him like a hawk. Jealously guarding his every move. I thought she was more independent than that. I'd thought *he* was. Surely he could find an excuse to get out to meet me. He could say they needed a pint of milk, or that he was going to the tip. He could at least walk into a different room and send a text, for fuck's sake. His silence bothers me, and I can't settle to anything, not food, a book or TV. I pace around the small flat, wearing out the floorboards. Wearing out myself, actually. I tell myself it's excitement that our plan is coming together, but as the day draws on and I hear nothing more from him, it feels more like agitation.

By 6 p.m. on Monday, I give in. His lack of response to my texts means I have no choice other than to go around there. I don't tell him I'm coming. I don't want to spoil the surprise. Mum's bedroom door is closed; it has been all afternoon. She's most likely napping. She might be awake, though. Sometimes she hides away in her room. Her time in prison has led to her valuing alone time. Some days, if she hangs out in the pub for too long, she gets overstimulated, overwhelmed by the constant noise and crowds of people around her. It can make her jumpy. In case she is awake, I slip out carefully, silently. I decide to walk. If I take Mum's car, she'll want to know where I'm going, and I think it's best she stays at home today. Whatever she has been up to at Emma's recently has been effective, obviously, but maybe she's done enough for a while.

Being outside in the fresh air feels good. I'm used to walking backwards and forwards between the Fox and Crown and Woodview now. I always take the overgrown path that runs alongside the well-trodden public right of way, as it's masked by trees and bushes and I'm less likely to be seen by passers-by or anyone who might be looking out of their bedroom window. The route requires a level of attention and dexterity because it is narrow in parts and brambles are trip hazards at various points. Normally I'm careful and nimble. Today I'm in a hurry and don't take as much care. Brambles tear at my jeans and scratch my arms. I rub impatiently at the thin bloody lines and stride on. At one point I disturb a fox and her two cubs. They spring across my path. The mother stops and stares at me. Her eyes flash as though communicating a warning, or even a threat. I suddenly think of the look my mother threw at Mattie on Saturday night. What did she mean when she said *he'd* gone too far? I stand still to show the mother fox I have no intention of hurting her young. She slinks away.

I stay in the woods and watch the house. Waiting for the day to flatten into dusk. I need the dark and the shadows. It's been raining again. The ground is muddy and dank. I'm so stealthy now that birds barely stir when I crouch under the trees. They used to panic and scatter, but no longer. All the lights are on, as usual. She'd justify that by saying her energy is green, I suppose. You have to be rich to install solar panels in the first place, though, don't you? I think of the Old Schoolhouse and the electricity we get because I paid a dodgy electrician to tap into someone else's supply. It's a fire hazard, but it's free. I think of being at my mum's and her constantly barking, 'Turn off the bloody lights, am I made of money?'

Woodview looks like a doll's house with one side lopped off to allow easy access. I've often thought that the design is conceited. Emma Westly is obviously brazen about being exposed. Confident that she has nothing to hide. No secrets. No shame. I can read the house – them – well by now. I know their domestic rhythms. At around this time she is likely to be in her home office, while he is in the kitchen preparing dinner. When he calls her to the table, he pours her a glass of wine, and they clink glasses, eyes meeting. They don't watch TV while they eat. They talk. Laugh. It's nauseating.

While they are absorbed in the meal and the conversation,

that is the time I tend to go inside: move her reading glasses from beside her bed, hide the remote, delete an email or two, open a window, alter a thermostat. I have on occasion taken some garment or other, not to wear but to dump in an outhouse. Once I smashed her bedside lamp. Then I return to my viewing spot and watch as the rest of her evening is marred by these small hiccups. They spend half an hour looking for the remote, which in the end is found in the breadbin; her glasses are next to the wine rack; the trousers to her work suit won't turn up for a day or two. Finally they can curl up on the sofa and watch a film, but they feel too warm downstairs and when they go to bed the bathroom is icy. Perfection stained with her self-doubt and irritation.

Tonight, everything is different. I don't have to do anything at all to ruin the lovey-dovey mood. He is not in the kitchen cooking. He is standing by the window, staring out into the garden, perhaps out towards the woods. He's keeping vigil, but it's pointless, he won't be able to see me. I'm in the shadows. She is upstairs. She's lying on her bed; she's not tapping on her laptop or reading a book. She's not even flicking through a magazine in a half-hearted, distracted manner. She is staring at the ceiling. Motionless. Perhaps paralysed with fear or dread. That's the aim.

Eventually I watch her get to her feet. It's clear from the way she moves that she's in a lot of pain. I'm not a monster, I do feel a twinge of something when I see her limp into the bathroom and start to run a bath. If not guilt or remorse exactly, then maybe pity, but I don't let that twinge in my gut solidify. I certainly don't let it travel to my brain. I haven't got time. I see an opportunity. I have to get moving.

38

Emma

I am struggling to get comfortable. My ribs ache, and however I try to sit or lie puts pressure on a tender blooming bruise, but I think a bath will help soothe my injuries. It will certainly distract me from the screaming silence that has settled between me and Matthew. I feel humiliated and exposed after telling him my theory that Becky is haunting me. I don't know what I was expecting from him. I just wanted him to make me feel safe. Part of me wanted him to say that he didn't for a moment believe in such things, that it was impossible. I don't want to believe it myself. But he didn't make me feel safe. His look of horror and disgust disturbed me further.

He thinks I'm a drunk. No one respects or admires drunks. Me least of all. It offends me that Matthew might think I'm the sort of person who would lose control to alcohol, be controlled by alcohol. I thought I could trust him with my thoughts, no matter how odd or intimate. I hoped he would gently laugh away my fears, reason with me or hold and comfort me. Do something, *anything*, that would keep us connected and would reassure me. But he slammed the shutters down by insinuating I am mad, unhinged, addicted. I feel locked out, like a disgraced fallen woman banging on the gates of a stately home trying to get the attention of the master who has seduced and abandoned her. Obviously he's not the wealthy one and I'm not pregnant, but I feel desperate, pathetic, somehow disgraced for trusting him. I feel oddly afraid of this hasty marriage. Not afraid of him as such, but certainly afraid of the fact that I have so dramatically changed my status quo.

I massage my eye sockets with the heel of my hand. I have to stop this train of thought. It isn't helpful. Matthew is my husband. I love him, don't I? I *do*. At least, I think I do. I must. I have to. It's practically impossible to know exactly what I think right now, when my head and body ache and desperate thoughts ricochet repeatedly around my mind.

How much do I really know about him?

I pour a generous amount of citrus-scented bath oil into the running water. I'm trying to smother the woody, deathly smell that Matthew says he can't detect and I am sure is a sign of a visitation from Becky. I shake my head, despairing at my own thoughts. How have I turned into the sort of person who thinks being haunted is a possibility, let alone a rational explanation? Yet I do, or at least I don't know what else to think. I massage the back of my neck. Fraught, exhausted.

I decide while I wait for the bath to fill that I will call Heidi. According to her socials, she arrived back in the country on Sunday evening, after the inevitable two-hour plane delay. I've been thinking of calling her all afternoon, working up the courage. I know I have to apologise and put things right. I miss her and I'm sorry, but besides that, I need my best friend. I'm scared, and despite being newly married, I feel alone, vulnerable. Before I met Heidi, I often felt lonely, but that stopped the day we became friends. Our friendship has always shielded me. If ever I was going through a hard time at work or in one of my fleeting relationships, or my brother was causing me concern, I knew I could pop round to hers, or at least pick up the phone, and she'd laugh or talk or argue me out of my fug. How did I forget that, even temporarily? I realise that I've allowed the excitement of meeting Matthew to be all-consuming. There has been new pressure on my time, a whole host of unfamiliar emotions carousing through my mind and oxytocin surging through my body. I guess there is no fool like an old fool, and I do feel both old and foolish right now. I'm not saying Matthew is a mistake; I'm simply recognising that centring everything around him so completely and swiftly was unwise.

I psych myself up to eat a huge dollop of humble pie. Heidi is the first contact saved in the favourites on my phone. I decide to make a video call, because I need to look her in the eye when I say I'm sorry. The phone rings four, five, six times. I shake a little. Is it possible that she isn't going to pick up? That she might ignore me? I brace myself, wondering how I'll absorb that blow. I'm just about to hang up when her image springs up in front of me as she answers. The moment of relief is nipped at when I see that she is sitting with Gina, in Gina's home. I know they have always met up without me to do mum or couple things, but somehow, right now, being faced with their cosy togetherness hurts. This is clearly just a girls-night social and nothing to do with the kids or husbands. This will make the apology harder too. The only thing worse than having to apologise for behaving like an idiot is other people witnessing as much.

I swiftly absorb the scene. There are mugs on the coffee table, a box of Jaffa Cakes, most likely empty, a big packet of Tyrrells crisps and an open bottle of white wine, two half-full glasses. I'm glad that at least Heidi kicks off the conversation. 'I hear congratulations are in order,' she says in a way that clearly communicates she doubts it.

I smile anyway. 'Thank you.'

She doesn't ask anything more about the wedding day, which would be usual, but I suppose nothing about this marriage is conventional. Instead she says, 'You don't look especially overjoyed. Far from the blushing bride I was expecting. Are you ill?'

It would be easy to be offended, but in fact I'm grateful to her for behaving so normally with me. Her normal is to tell me how it is. Or at least how she sees it. I find it reassuring that she's not holding back or hiding in small talk; it gives me hope that we can swiftly get back on our usual footing. 'Oh, I'm fine. I had a little accident, that's all. It's taken the wind out of my sails.'

Gina's face creases with concern. 'Oh no. What happened?'

'I was running. I just tripped.' This is a lie, obviously, but I don't have the courage to start by explaining the ladder incident. I'll get to it. I'm not hiding it from them. It's just not the place to begin this conversation.

Heidi and Gina share a look, but I don't halt to examine it. I pile in with my apology before I lose my nerve. 'I've been a dick lately. I'm sorry.'

'Yeah, you have,' says Heidi.

'That day of the walk. The things I said. I am so sorry. Can you forgive me?' My voice scrapes along my throat before it tumbles into our history. I wonder how hard she's going to make me work for this.

But then she sighs and says, 'Yes, you silly bag, of course I can.'

Just like that. No drama, no recriminations. It feels so normal, so easy.

Too easy? The thought assaults me and I'm annoyed by it. I want to sink into the moment of relief and happiness. However, after the constant drama of the last few months, I am mistrustful of things running smoothly and positively.

'We get it. You haven't been totally yourself,' adds Gina.

'What do you mean by that?' My question comes out sharper than I intended. I see Gina blink as though she's batting away some level of shock.

'Nothing,' she says soothingly. 'Just that you're going through a lot of changes at home and at work.'

The restructuring has been incredibly stressful. My CFO has been especially stringent and rigorous. I mean, that's great, that's his job, but he's forever complaining that I haven't responded to emails from him, emails that I haven't even received. When I tell him as much, he says things like 'Check your spam' before sighing laboriously and saying he'll send again. Classic BS. Obviously he's never sent the emails in the first place and is covering for his own incompetence. He's questioned my expense claims, too. Sent them back to me with certain items highlighted in red and terse notes attached: *Was this hotel used wholly and exclusively for business purposes?* I don't go into this detail with Heidi and Gina; they wouldn't get it. Instead I just mumble, 'Yes, it's been a busy time,' and then I grasp the heart of my concerns. 'I thought marriage would be easier,' I blurt.

'Did we teach you nothing?' laughs Heidi. But it's not a mean laugh; she's welcoming me back under her wing, and so I make an effort to laugh along with her.

'You're sharing your home for the first time. That takes some getting used to.' Gina spells out what I already know, but it's good to hear it anyway. Reassuring. 'You're both adapting. It must be difficult for him too. His wife has only been dead a year.'

'I'm his wife,' I mutter. I wish I didn't sound so sulky.

'Yes. Right. I meant his first wife.' Gina looks uncomfortable.

'And it's been fourteen months.'

Heidi asks, 'How are you feeling about the whole Becky thing now you're Mrs Charlton? Last time we spoke, things were intense. You chose to elope because he was so cut up about going inside churches.' I'm pretty sure she mutters 'for fuck's sake' under her breath, but I let it go.

'I'm struggling,' I confess. I want to tell them that I'm overwhelmed with emotions, that I feel awful. That I'm shocked that I've turned into this woman who feels rather than thinks or reasons. I feel my husband loves someone else more than he loves me, that he's always distracted and thinking about her. A dead woman. As she is dead, it shouldn't matter, but it does, because only the dead can be canonised. I feel hollowed. There is a throbbing between my breasts. In my heart, I guess.

I am about to tell them this, but I'm stopped in my tracks when Gina murmurs, 'Yeah, Matthew said as much.'

'Excuse me? What?'

Heidi swiftly elbows her, but Gina lifts her chin, the way she does when she's determined. 'I'm not keeping secrets from her,' she insists.

'What secrets?'

'Matthew rang me. He asked me not to mention it to you. He said there were . . .' she pauses, looks for the right words, obviously not keen to use whatever words he did. 'Issues,' she says finally.

I bristle at the idea of them having conversations behind my back. 'What issues specifically did he tell you about?'

'He's worried about you.' Gina looks worried too.

'He says you're seeing ghosts,' interrupts Heidi stonily. She doesn't look worried; more disbelieving, dumbfounded.

'No, no. I never said that.'

Heidi nods with satisfaction. 'Of course you didn't. I didn't believe him for a minute. You are literally the most sane and rational person I've ever met. You'd never believe in that sort of garbage.'

'Hey, my nana swore she had a ghost living with her,' comments Gina.

'Yeah, but your nana was ninety-three and had dementia,' retorts Heidi.

I shake my head. 'I haven't *seen* a ghost, but I do think I'm being haunted.'

There's a moment when I think we've lost connection and the screen has frozen, but then I see the images move on the muted TV behind Heidi and Gina. The screen isn't frozen; they are paralysed.

'You serious?' Heidi laughs, and then checks my expression.

'Shit, you *are* serious. Oh girl.' Her face no longer shines with humour or challenge or indignation, all those emotions it's displayed during this call. Now she simply looks creased with pity. 'OK, Emma, you know I love you, you're like a sister to me, so I'm asking this from a good place. Are you drinking when you're on your own?'

'Why are you asking me that?'

'Why aren't you giving me an answer?' We stare at one another. Shocked, saddened.

'That's why Matthew called me,' says Gina quietly. 'He said he was worried about your drinking and your mental health. It was brave of him to reach out.'

'I thought he was bullshitting,' says Heidi. I note the past tense. She thinks something different now.

I tut. 'No, I'm not drinking. Well, sometimes, a bit. No more than I ever have. Don't you drink when you're on your own?'

'I'm not the one who is being mad here. I mean, you must be kidding about the ghost thing. How does that make sense to you?' Heidi meets my gaze. Her huge brown eyes are sharp with accusation, not warm or bright as they usually are. 'If you're not kidding, then you have to be ill.'

'Sorry?' I am not sorry. I am offended. 'What are you saying exactly?'

'Why did you tell us you tripped when running when you told Matthew that you fell off a ladder?' Gina's question is asked so gently I want to cry.

'No, look, that is nothing. That's right. I just didn't want to get into it with you.' I sound flustered, unreliable.

'So you're saying now you did fall off a ladder,' Heidi probes.

'I've always said as much.'

'Not to us. You've just said you tripped when running.'

'Why a ladder? Why did you pick the same way to injure yourself as Becky died?' asks Gina. 'That worries me, Emma.'

'What? No. I didn't injure *myself*. At least not deliberately. That's madness. I was pushed off the ladder and then it was back up against the wall, but that was after it landed on me.'

'You seem really confused.'

'The bolognese. How do you explain that?' I ask. 'She threw the bolognese.'

'She?'

'Becky's ghost.'

'Oh sweetheart. You spilt the bolognese. Matthew explained. You saw a rat. Got a horrible fright and dropped the pan. The rat ran through the sauce and then around the room in panic because it was scalded.'

'No, there was no rat.' Why would Matthew say there was a rat?

'There's a colony of them. Living under your house. Matthew has had pest control out to try to sort it.'

'No, I'd know that.'

'You do know it. Or did. He said you had to go up to Scotland while it was dealt with because you were so distraught thinking about the nest under the floorboards.'

'That's why you're always hearing peculiar bangs and scratches.'

'No.'

'It is awful,' adds Heidi, shuddering. 'No one is OK with rats. We don't blame you for being freaked out.'

I look at my two best friends. They seem utterly sincere. 'No, no. I would have told you about a rats' nest.'

'Well, maybe, but you weren't speaking to us.'

My head hurts. A fat tear rolls down my face. I want to brush it away, but I don't want to draw attention to it. Heidi straightens her shoulders and stares right at me. 'Emma, think about it. Were you drunk when you fell off the ladder or when you think you heard books being thrown or when you accidentally locked yourself in the sauna? Is it likely that you've had too much to drink on occasion and have forgotten some things, imagined others? Is that more or less likely than that your new husband's dead wife is haunting you?'

I hang up.

39

I run into the bathroom and lock the door behind me. I don't want Matthew following me in here. I don't want to see him right now. He has never told me there is a rats' nest. I would remember that. Who could forget a thing like that? Why did he call my friends instead of speaking to me if he's worried about me? I turn off the taps, as the bath is almost full to the brim now. Hell, if the call had lasted any longer, it would have overflowed. I'd forgotten it was running. Another accident, another problem. Is it possible that I am losing my grip? I spot a wine glass by the basin. It's almost empty. I don't recall bringing wine upstairs with me. My God, what is wrong with me? I throw off my robe and step into the bath.

The pain is excruciating. Impossible. I want to scream and scream, but something stops me. Instinct protects me. I open my mouth wide, so wide I think my face will split in two, but I don't let out a sound. My right leg has turned scarlet. I'm out of the bath in a second, but the scald is so intense that I can already see blisters forming on my shin. I go to the shower and run cold water, but the pain shimmies through me, the hairs on the back of my neck stand tall. That bathwater was near boiling. How is that possible? It can't run from the tap at boiling point. It is *not* possible. I did not do this. I am not imagining this.

I concentrate on aiming cold water at my burnt flesh. I know that the first aid recommendation is to cool the burn under cold running water for at least twenty minutes, and that doing so will reduce pain, swelling and the risk of scarring, but with every minute that passes, I weigh up whether reducing potential scarring is a priority when I might very well be fighting for my life here. What the hell is happening? Fear and disbelief skitters down my spine. Which would be the least horrifying explanation? A vengeful spirit? An abusive husband? Or, as my eyes fall on the near-empty wine glass, I have to ask myself, am I drunk?

I curl my fingers into my palms. Clench and unclench my hands, count down from one hundred. Get to the end, count again. This act takes extraordinary self-control, extraordinary presence of mind and resilience. I want to run, I want out, but I need to let the water soothe me so I can move to the best of my ability. And I need my head to clear. What is happening here? The house is almost silent; there is no music drifting through the rooms, up the stairs. Not the cheerful Spanish salsas that Matthew favours, or the low-flow remixes that I like. There's no TV or radio, not even the sound of food being prepped or pans clattering. Just the pattering of rain on the windows and the roof again.

I pat myself dry, then pull on baggy linen trousers and a jumper. I look around for a pair of trainers but can't see any. Maybe it's better to be barefoot as I sneak downstairs. Normal practice would be to cover the burn with cling film to help prevent infection, but I believe Matthew is in the kitchen and I want to avoid him. My leg is stinging with a ferocity that makes walking difficult, this on top of the pain in my ribs, but I have to get out of this house. I have to get away from here.

Carefully, silently, I edge down the stairs. The design of my open-plan house now strikes me as exposing, not cool or clever. An icy sense of anxiety spreads through me, inching slowly from the top of my skull, enveloping my face, where it seems to pull the moisture from my throat and mouth, making it difficult to swallow. It settles in my chest like a heavy weight. I can hardly breathe. I see Matthew at the dining room table. He's not eating or drinking. He's not reading. His laptop is open in front of him; I can't see what is on the screen. Maybe he has been editing some photos, something ordinary and non-sinister. I don't know, and I don't know if I can even risk hoping for so much. He's not striking any keys. He's simply staring out into the night, his shoulders hunched, arched like a viaduct. He's so still it almost seems as though he is in a daze or a trance. The black night is framed by the window, and I see my reflection as I inch down the stairs. If he moves his focus just a fraction, he will notice me too. I have to hope that whatever is whirling around his head holds his attention just a little longer.

'Where are you going?'

I jump. His voice is cold and clear. The calmness horrifies me.

'I'm just going for a drive.'

'Don't. You shouldn't.'

I edge down another stair. My thoughts are pulled to the back door. I imagine reaching it, opening it. Then running.

'Why shouldn't I?' I try to keep my voice light.

'You've been drinking.' I haven't. I don't think I have. Have I? There was that glass. 'Plus you're injured.' How does he know I'm burnt? I didn't scream. 'Your ribs must still be aching. Are you due another painkiller?'

'I just need some air.' I walk with as much faux confidence as I can muster towards the console table where I keep the car keys. I pretend I'm feeling breezy despite the pain I'm in as I open the drawer and pick them up.

Suddenly he is bounding towards me. 'It's too wet to drive!' he shouts.

I am exhausted, depleted, but fury is a great cheerleader. I back myself. I am on my own; maybe I always have been, but that's OK. Right now is not the time for self-pity. I bolt for the back door. I feel his fingers snatch at the ends of my hair, which trail behind me; a caress, or was he grasping? Would he have taken a fistful and yanked me to the floor? Would he have straddled me, stopped me from running? I wrench open the door with all the strength I possess. I feel his breath and threat through the door as I pull it closed behind me and dash towards the car. I am barefoot, so the jagged stones on the driveway dig into my feet, stabbing like needles.

It's raining hard. I'm almost immediately drenched. The car is parked at a distance from the house, down the drive, where the charging station is. I'm pleased to see that Matthew lazily neglected to plug it in when we returned from the awkward Sunday lunch yesterday. I start to run towards it, as fast as I can manage with my injuries. My lungs burn with the effort.

I'm a good runner, and good runners are used to pushing through pain. I am grateful for all the times I've got up in the morning and run in the dark, wet and cold. I hear Matthew's footsteps behind me, heavy and firm; he must have paused to put on his shoes. I'm glad that slight delay has given me a brief advantage, but he's quickly making up ground. Instinct takes control. I just have to act. To move. To save myself. I point the key fob towards the car, press hard, my fingertips turning white. It beeps, the lights winking a welcome. I fling open the door, throw myself inside. Matthew is right behind me. He yanks at the door handle. But it's locked. He slams his hand on the window, on the car roof.

'Get out of the car!' he yells. 'Get out of the fucking car.'

The lights on the dashboard flash. I press my foot hard on the accelerator and drive. He stumbles after the car, wide skirts of rainwater arching up from the wheels as I speed through puddles, soaking him. I urgently press the button on the fob that opens the gate. It rolls back slowly, but the time it takes allows him to reach it, and he stands in front of it. Guarding it. I keep driving at speed, heading for the road. At the last second, he jumps out of the way. My heart is beating so fast, I think it will burst out of my body. Would I have ploughed into him? I don't know. I'm so scared. I just need to get away from here. From the danger, whatever it is.

My view is obscured. The world is nothing but a watery blur, the window is fogged under my breath. I scrunch my body close to the steering wheel and put my foot down heavily. I won't look back. The windscreen wipers slip right and left, a constant motion, but they're useless against the ferocity of the downpour. I can't hear myself think as the rain pelts on the roof, *bang, bang, bang, bang*, endless, like a toddler with a drum. I know these narrow, serpent-like roads well, well enough to realise that I'm driving too fast. There are warning lights blinking on the dashboard in front of me. I should slow down. I daren't. I grip the steering wheel, my knuckles transparent, ghostly. The headlights slice into the slick darkness, but I'm going at such a speed that each pothole causes the car to bounce, the lights flickering into the wet trees, revealing only a sliver of the deluged road ahead.

Suddenly I see her. She just steps out of nowhere. She's soaking and pale, her face as white as the moon. Translucent, ephemeral. I hit the brakes, press my foot hard against the floor of the car. I scream for her to get out of the way. To move. She doesn't, and I glide towards her as though on ice. Time changes. It slows and swells, it speeds and concertinas. The impact throws me forward.

And then there is nothing.

40

Two days later

Matthew

'Thank you for coming in to talk to us, Mr Charlton.' He didn't like the fake politeness. Why were they pretending he had much choice in the matter? He'd gone to the hospital to see Emma, and there was a policeman at the door to her room. He hadn't been allowed to enter. He'd been advised to go to the station. They said if he didn't go to the station, they would call in on him later that day to explain where inquiries were at. They were perfectly polite. Solicitous, even, aware that he was a devastated husband dealing with a very difficult situation.

Maybe.

Or maybe they thought something altogether different; they were holding their cards close to their chest.

He had thought of running. He could go back to Woodview, pick up anything of any value that he could carry and get the hell out of there. He was stung by the bitter memory that a simple robbery had been the first plan, way back when. So far from where they'd ended up. This thing was a mess. He could go to the train station, get to London, and from there, wherever.

Liverpool, Newcastle, Glasgow. A big city where he could vanish. Or maybe a port. He could go abroad. Disappear. But Becky was the one who knew how to offload hot valuables; he didn't know where to start. And hadn't she said stolen stuff only ever fetched a fraction of its worth? That money wouldn't last. Besides, he would look as guilty as hell if he ran, and then they would come after him. He didn't have a car, obviously, since it was wrapped around a tree. He was using Emma's Uber account, so they'd find out he had gone to the train station, and as soon as he used one of their credit cards, the police would track him. He couldn't run. He shouldn't. This was a fucking mess, yes. But he was her husband. There was nothing illegal about getting married. They couldn't prove intention; they couldn't prove he had done anything wrong. He just had to hold his nerve.

At the station, he was led into an interview room. It was exactly as he'd seen on television. Windowless, dank. The policewoman flicked on the overhead light even though it was daytime. He wondered if the room was specifically designed to be depressing. It was empty other than a table and four chairs. On the table was a hefty pile of files – that was intimidating – but there was no recording device, which was a relief. There were two police officers. A man in his mid-fifties who clearly ate and drank more than he should and as a result had a huge belly that hung over his belt. Matthew couldn't imagine him running after a criminal, but he could imagine him sitting on one. The other officer was an Indian woman in her early twenties. She had a gap between her teeth and wore her hair up in a greasy ponytail. She looked very young and he felt very old. They offered him a cup of tea, but he declined. He just wanted them to say what it was they had to say. Whatever it was, it was better to get on with it.

The female officer placed a picture of Susan, Becky's mother, on the table between them. 'Do you recognise this woman?' Her tone was firm. It surprised Matthew that she was leading the conversation. He assumed this slight disruption to the stereotype was part of their routine. They didn't want to be predictable.

He wondered what he should say. He ran through the facts in his head. Susan was his fiancée's mother. No, that wasn't right. He was married; he couldn't have a fiancée as well as a wife. Obviously. He realised that, but his head was clouded with panic. He didn't know how to reply. What would Becky tell him to say if she was here? He had known Susan for sixteen years, although it wasn't a consistent relationship. She'd tended to drift in and out of Becky's life, absent for months, sometimes years. The last few years she'd been a fixture. Something Becky was happy about; Matthew less so.

He tried to buy time by fingering the edge of the photo, peering carefully, as though really giving it his full attention. He more or less lived with Susan; she was practically family, albeit difficult, troubling, awful family. He concentrated on the fiction they had constructed. In that world, he knew this woman vaguely, barely. That was the world he had to stay in. 'Yes, I know her. She was Emma's cleaner until a few months ago. Then we had to let her go.'

'Right. According to the cleaning agency, the Mop Mob' – the policewoman paused to check her notes, and smiled whimsically, even though it couldn't be the first time she had heard the name of the company – 'Susan Morden and a second cleaner, Shyla Mahar, were both asked to leave their jobs rather suddenly after several years working for your wife. Can you explain that?'

Matthew shrugged. 'I took over the cleaning. Tried to make myself useful.'

'Nothing more?'

'More?'

'We've talked to Shyla Mahar.'

'Right.' He wondered what Shyla might have said. She'd been upset when they let her go. Felt accused, and mentioned her colour. It was nothing to do with her colour; it was nothing to do with her. Her being fired was just part of the plan. It had been awkward, though. He didn't want to get into that. Better there was no talk of unpleasantness.

'I'm sorry to tell you that Susan Morden has been formally identified, by her daughter, as the woman your wife ploughed into and killed on Monday night.'

'I see. That's very sad.' He coughed. How should he react? What was the acceptable level of distress and shock? Of course he already knew as much. Becky had called him the minute she left the morgue. When he first heard the news, he had been shocked, extremely so. And concerned. Sad. Sad for Becky, really, not himself. He'd heard Becky cry before, often. Rage, too. But nothing could have prepared him for her response to her mother's death. She'd roared. Howled like an animal. He'd been taken aback at her utter collapse, her guttural grief. She hadn't made sense, she kept talking about things 'going too far', 'not turning out as expected'. Obviously this wasn't what anyone had planned but accidents did happen. He'd told her she had to get a grip.

She'd begged him to let her come to Woodview, said she just wanted him to hold her. That she needed him. She rarely said she needed him. 'I'm on my own. I'm on my own now,' she kept repeating. He'd had to say she couldn't, of course. It was too risky. Emma's friends might pop to the house at any point before or after they visited the hospital; how would he explain Becky's presence?

'Well if they do, don't be too hospitable. We don't want to encourage people dropping in,' she'd retorted, adding, 'You're a fucking animal, my mum is on a slab.' He'd told her to go back to her mum's flat; there would be people at the pub who could comfort her. He promised he'd get there as soon as he could.

'When Susan Morden was in your employ, were you aware that she had a criminal record?' the policewoman asked.

'I'm sorry, what?'

'Can you answer the question, please, Mr Charlton?'

He sighed. 'No, I was not,' he lied. The fat fella was taking notes. Matthew thought to add, 'Although my wife may have been. Susan was employed by Emma quite a long time before we met. She will have checked her references, I imagine.'

'Well, yes, that is something we'll need to talk to your wife about when she wakes up. Susan Morden had served sixteen years in prison.'

'Goodness, sixteen years. That's a stiff sentence. Can I ask what for?' He hoped he was hitting the right note. A man mostly concerned for his wife, but compassionately interested in the woman who had met a tragic end too, of course. He was the proper sort. Decent, borderline posh. He liked playing this role. He had been doing so since he started his relationship with Emma. It suited him.

'Murder.'

'Gosh.'

'She murdered your wife's parents.'

41

The room bloated up underneath him. Morphed about him.

'What? No. That doesn't ma—' He snapped his mouth shut. He felt sweat prickle on his upper lip. That wasn't true. That wasn't right. Susan had killed her husband. Becky's abusive father. But he couldn't set them straight without revealing his connection to Susan, to Becky, to so much more. Why were they lying to him? Was this a trap?

The policewoman started to explain how thirty-five years ago, Susan Morden had been convicted of tampering with James and Helen Westly's car in order to make it unsafe to drive. The interference led directly to their deaths. There was conclusive evidence that that had been the aim.

There was a ringing in his ears. An alarm going off somewhere. He asked the police officers whether they could hear it too. Was it a fire drill, perhaps? They looked confused. They couldn't hear anything. He slapped his hand against his ear to make the ringing stop. The policewoman continued to talk. There were fingerprints, a locking wheel nut key had been found at Susan's house, there was even a friend who had testified that Susan had bragged about wanting to kill the Westlys. It was conclusive. The jury had reached a unanimous verdict in just under an hour.

Matthew stared at the table. It would be a mistake to meet their gazes. The police had all sorts of training, didn't they? In psychology and body language and stuff. They could read a person's expression. He couldn't get his head around it. They had to have it wrong. Didn't they? But no, they seemed certain. They had the files. The facts. Bloody hell, even before the shock had a chance to slow and settle, a surge of annoyance ran through his core. Why was it that with everything to do with Becky he was left feeling like he was playing catch-up? She had lied to him. Again. Bitch.

He did know that Susan had been inside. Becky hadn't kept that from him. It was one of the first things she'd told him, way back when they first met. He remembered her glaring at him, eyes shining, a defiant jut of the chin, daring him to be shocked, expecting him to walk away when she told him she'd been brought up in care because her mother was in jail. Even then he had understood it was a test. Becky had abandonment issues. No surprise. She was seeing if he was shocked, whether he would shrug her off. He didn't. There had been times, over the years since, when he wondered what his life might have been like if he had walked away from her, then or at any point. Those thoughts didn't often go very far. He didn't really have the imagination to conjure up a life without Becky. She made the plans, set the path. Paid most of the bills. She was always reminding him of that.

He never had been able to walk away from her. He had

been transfixed by her from the get-go. He was twenty and mesmerised by her looks: her face, her body, her hips, eyes, bone structure, arse. They were all amazing. She was so utterly beautiful that when he looked at her, he would get a hard-on like some thirteen-year-old boy stumbling across porn for the first time. Just *looking* at her. He was sort of powerless. And that, he reasoned, was falling in love. Wanting her all the time. Back then, he hadn't been even the slightest bit aware that there was anything else needed beyond physical attraction (which led to great sex) and having a laugh together (which also led to great sex) to add up to them being a *thing*. Without it being discussed, they were in a relationship. It was very straightforward.

He hadn't been bothered about the fact her mother was in prison. In fact, he secretly thought it was quite cool. It added a much-needed edgy vibe to his own credentials. His family were so boring in comparison. His father worked as a sales rep for a company that supplied dental equipment. He'd reached the dizzy heights of area sales manager and drove a company Volvo. His mother was a classroom assistant to Year 2 children. They lived quiet, law-abiding lives. They paid their taxes, washed the car every Sunday and took the caravan to Cornwall every July. They picked up litter, even that belonging to other people. His mother wouldn't dream of folding the corner of a page in a book; she always used a home-made, hand-stitched bookmark. He was embarrassed by their acquiescence to the accepted norms, their ability to be content with very ordinary things, and he was horrified at the idea of becoming like them. But luckily – because he had good cheekbones and had twice been given the main part in the school play – suddenly there had been chances and choices, and girls like Becky.

Although there were no other girls like Becky. Not really. He came to understand that.

She'd told him that her dad was a nasty bastard and had hurt them. Or did she say he had just hurt her mother? He wasn't absolutely sure now; she had told him the story such a very long time ago. It was one of the nights when they were high on something or other and then suddenly low. Laughs, sex, alcohol, tears. Confessions, drama, revelations, fears. They'd had a lot of nights like that back then. Becky had told him some really difficult stuff about her life. It sometimes seemed like there had only been difficult stuff. It was horrible to listen to and hard to keep track of. One horror story merged into the next. There were creeps in the care and foster homes who tried to get in her room at night. Some succeeded. She told him what it was like having to visit her mum in a high-security prison as a little girl because Susan had requested it, and then what it was like not to visit because Susan had got bored of the idea and didn't want to see Becky any more. She spoke of casting couches, lechy married men, boyfriends who told her she was ugly. None of it was good.

The day after these confessions, she was always awkward with him. Unsure as to whether he'd wake up thinking it was all a bit much. He usually just woke up with a hangover and a head full of bruised brain cells that couldn't quite recall the details she'd given him. He never asked for clarity; he didn't want to appear ghoulishly interested in her traumas. She was hot and that was enough. Then time passed and they moved on, got further away from her intensely difficult start in life, his boringly suburban one. They found their own shared space. It was OK.

Or it had been.

He could not remember whether Becky had said her father was physically or mentally cruel. He thought it was an accidental death, an impetuous crime of passion or self-defence, but maybe he'd just made that assumption. The details were fuzzy, but the story had *definitely* been that Susan had killed Becky's father in a domestic and that was why she had gone to prison. A domestic. He'd thought she must have pushed the bastard down the stairs or maybe hit him with something surprisingly fatal. He hadn't thought what. OK, he hadn't thought about it much at all. It wasn't nice to think about, was it?

He was absolutely certain, however, that there had never been any mention of a premeditated double murder of strangers. He'd have recalled that. What the actual fuck?

So it was a lie. Whose lie?

It might have been a lie that was told to Becky. Perhaps a well-meaning foster parent couldn't quite bring themselves to tell the little tot that her mother was a cold-blooded killer and so made up something to protect her; salvage the mother's memory so the child could develop some self-respect. Matthew didn't know. He had to consider the possibility that Becky knew the truth and this was *her* lie. A lie she had told him.

Susan was a convicted murderer. Convicted for the premeditated killing of two people. Not just any two people, *Emma's parents*. That was a total mind-fuck and obviously not a coincidence. Matthew thought Becky might have wanted to mention that. The sarcasm flipped into his head. A defence mechanism against the horror. It was, as usual, difficult to know what to think about Becky. He had always thought Susan was a sly bitch. He knew that conventional wisdom had it that you weren't supposed to think ill of the dead, but facts were facts. He had never liked Becky's mother. She'd scared him. She had a grim power about her; despite being only five foot four, she had always seemed threatening, evil.

'It's a lot to process,' he said carefully. That much was true. Because it wasn't just Susan and/or Becky who had lied to him, was it? He had to consider the possibility that Emma hadn't been one hundred per cent truthful either. She'd said her parents' deaths had been an accident. He sighed. Maybe she'd thought she was telling the truth. Maybe her grandparents had lied to her. Fuck, did anyone ever tell the truth about anything? Becky was always calling him naive. It was a diss, he knew it. 'So let me get this straight. You're saying that this Susan woman, Emma's ex-cleaner, had a criminal record. She murdered Emma's parents?' He tapped the photo with his forefinger.

'Yes.'

'Why?'

'She's not here to tell us, is she?' said the policeman with a wide yawn.

'That's not really the question I'm focusing on,' added the policewoman. 'What I need to establish next is the why behind *this* case.'

'You can't think Emma knew what Susan Morden had done,' Matthew spluttered. Neither officer answered nor moved a muscle. They stared at him, their eyes boring into him. It was obvious what they were thinking. This incident was no longer being viewed as an accident. This was not a question of the casualty being in the wrong place at the wrong time. Everything had shifted. Susan Morden had been a criminal, but now she was a victim. Emma had been a patient, involved in a terrible tragic accident. Now she was a suspect with a compelling motive.

All change.

'You might want to consider getting your wife a lawyer, Mr Charlton, just so you're not on the back foot. Because if we can prove that she knew Susan Morden was responsible for her parents' deaths, well then . . .' The female officer shrugged. 'I'm not a big believer in coincidences.'

42

Matthew was glad to leave the police station. As he stepped into the fresh air, he took in a deep lungful. He didn't quite feel relief – he was far from allowing himself something so clean-cut and definitive – but certainly he felt an awareness that it was better being outside than in. That thought wasn't just in his head; it ran through his blood, pulsed around his body. What the hell had he got himself into? This was out of control. He looked about him, trying to appear discreet and casual while checking he wasn't being watched or followed. He decided not to call an Uber but instead to walk to the Fox and Crown. He didn't want to leave an electronic trail of his whereabouts. He had learnt from Becky how much of a person's life could be tracked, traced, distorted, even ruined that way.

He slipped along the narrow, overgrown footpaths. Long grasses whipped his legs; he walked quickly, with his head down. He did not want to be seen, but inevitably he was, as soon as he arrived at the pub. 'All right, Mattie.' The greeting was casual, thrown out without much thought by Graham

Cadd, the landlord. Matthew felt nauseous, hit as usual by the smell of hops and barley rammed up against the incongruous smell of bleach and other cleaning fluids, as the toilets had just been swilled. He managed to nod in response.

Not for the first time, he regretted the fact that this scam had to happen so close to home. Not that the flat here *was* his home as such; it was Susan's, or had been, he acknowledged grimly. However, as he and Becky had frequently stayed there, he was known by the locals as Becky's partner. They didn't know Emma – she wasn't one for pubs – but from the moment this car crash had happened, Matthew had worried that the story would be covered in the local paper and people would start getting curious about the wealthy local woman. Any journalist worth their salt would report that she was recently married. A woman's marital status, along with her age, always seemed to be part of the story. What if he was named? Becky always called him Mattie, Emma used the more formal version of his name, but the link could easily be made. His surname was fairly unusual. If the paper ran a photo of Emma's husband – and that was a very real possibility – then he was screwed. The world was closing in. Worse yet, if the police decided this wasn't an accident, that it was a crime, then there was every chance that the story would make it into the national papers, and his connection to both women would inevitably be uncovered. The scam of him marrying Emma Westly for her money would be revealed, as that sort of scandal sold papers. Where would he run then? Getting out of Hampshire wouldn't be enough. The panicked thoughts of this inevitable exposure circled his head, round and round again, not so much gathering momentum as creating a frenzy, becoming tangled and terrifying.

'Your Becky OK?' Graham asked.

Matthew wondered what he knew. Was he aware that Susan was dead – Becky's mother, his tenant? It would be the normal and usual thing to explain this. But nothing about Matthew's life was normal or usual, so he didn't know what to say. He suddenly longed for his own mother and father, the solid regularity of them. But in the same instant that their simple dependability came into his mind, so did the claustrophobia of their overheated sitting room in the winter, their caravan holidays in the summer. His resolve stiffened.

'Yeah, she's fine, thanks, mate.'

'Only I saw her run upstairs yesterday, looked upset, hasn't come out of the flat since.'

'Just PMT,' said Matthew. He knew that would most likely shut down the conversation. It did. Graham picked up a tea towel and began polishing glasses.

Matthew bounded up the stairs and knocked loudly on the door to the flat. When Becky opened it, he was shocked. It would be going too far to say he barely recognised her – of course he did – but she was changed. So altered from Saturday night when he'd seen her last. She had aged and diminished. Sort of shrivelled. Her face was grey and wrinkled; she looked like paper that had been crumpled up and tossed away. She'd always been slim, but now she looked skinny. Fragile. He stepped into the flat and closed the door behind him; she fell into his arms. Her hair smelt greasy. Emma's hair always smelt of shampoo. Wow. That was inappropriate. He felt a sting of guilt. But he found he did that a lot. He didn't mean to, it just happened. He drew comparisons. Of course he did. It was impossible not to.

305

'I'm so sorry about your mum.'

Becky nodded, sniffed. She must have been crying hard, as her eyes were pink. He thought of a guinea pig his brother had had when they were kids; Matthew had never taken to it. A tear slipped down her face. She didn't wipe it away; he got the impression she'd stopped noticing them. She moved towards the kitchen table, sat down heavily. The kitchen was about the same size as the police interview room he had just come from. Small. It was about the same size as Emma's shoe cupboard. 'Where've you been?' She sounded sharp, angry. Nothing new there.

'I went to the hospital to see Emma.' Becky scowled and looked away from him. 'You said I had to act normal. Isn't it normal that her husband goes to see her?'

'Suppose. It's not like you can have a chat with her, though, is it?' Matthew stayed silent, didn't bite, but this just caused Becky to demand, 'You can't, can you? She hasn't come round?'

'No, she hasn't. She's still unconscious.' He tried to read her expression, but she had a good poker face and it was never easy to know her thoughts. Could she be actively pleased that Emma was lying in a coma? Was she that ruthless? He reminded himself that she was grieving, not thinking clearly. He tried to stay on track. 'Anyway, they wouldn't let me in. The police were guarding her door.'

'The police were. Why?' Becky was instantly alert. Her entire body seemed to freeze with tension. Even the tears on her cheeks stopped rolling.

'They wanted to bring me up to date with new developments.'

'Like what?'

There was something in her voice that made him uncomfortable. A catch. Not quite eagerness, not quite panic. Something that settled between the two. He didn't trust Becky any more. He hadn't for some weeks now, months, maybe years. He used to think that not entirely trusting her meant their relationship had a bit of an exciting edge. Having to always second-guess her was, in some ways, fun. Now he was exhausted by it. The edge didn't look as attractive as it used to; now it was perilous. More of a cliff edge, and people toppled over cliff edges, fell to their deaths. 'The police wanted to tell me about your mum.'

'You acted surprised, right?'

He hadn't needed to act. What they'd told him had been a surprise. He nodded. 'Again, I'm sorry that I couldn't come with you to identify her. That must have been an awful thing to do on your own.' He really was genuinely very sorry, because going with your fiancée to the morgue when she had to look at her mashed-up mother was what a decent man would do. He wanted to be a decent man, but it was out of the question.

'They haven't linked us, have they?' Becky asked tersely.

'No. No nothing like that.' He paused before adding, 'But they have linked your mum and Emma.'

'She was her cleaner. Hardly Poirot-level detection uncovering that.'

'Yes, but there's more.' He stumbled, wondering how to tackle what he had to say next. How could he explain what her mother had done? What she *was*. Becky was so fragile right now. She'd had a terrible childhood, very little to hold onto, but she'd gone all-in with her mother these last couple of years. It was obvious that she wanted to believe Susan was a good person. What would this news do to her? Before he could find the right words, Becky interrupted.

'Do they know that my mother killed Emma's parents?'

It was as though she had kicked him behind the knees. 'You knew?' His voice sounded like a fourteen-year-old boy's. High. Unsure. The shock had made him an adolescent.

Becky shrugged. 'Not until recently.'

'When did you find out?'

'Just a couple of days ago, maybe a week.'

He didn't believe her. It wasn't that she had a specific tell to give away when she was lying. If only. It was more that he had started to doubt what she said to him every time she opened her mouth. That was the thing with trust, it was like one of those soapy bubbles kids made by blowing through a hoop on a plastic stick. Iridescent and magical, wildly pretty, but incredibly delicate, and once popped, there was nothing to salvage. 'Why didn't you tell me as soon as you found out? What the hell is going on? It's obviously not a coincidence.'

'Why are you shouting at *me*? She killed my mother. You're married to a murderer. Don't shout at me.' Becky was yelling quite loudly herself, immediately on the attack. Matthew was aware that the pub below them was empty, no chatter or music or clink of glasses to drown out their noise. Graham would be able to hear them shouting, might be able to hear the specific words. '*I* am the victim here. *I* am the one who is grieving,' Becky continued. She looked harried, tiny, desperate.

Matthew sighed and turned to put the kettle on. He spotted three Red Bull cans in the bin, a half-empty bottle of vodka next to the sink. She needed a non-alcoholic drink; he needed time to think.

He suppressed the thing bouncing loudly in his head, which was that Susan had been a rubbish mother, that she was barely worth grieving for. It would be unforgivable to say that out loud. To date, they had got past a lot in their relationship. They had waded through a quagmire of complexity, shaken off anger and endured poverty, but he couldn't risk stamping on the memory of her mum. Personally, he'd thought Susan was a fairly hopeless sort of a mother when he'd believed that she had been to prison for killing Becky's violent father, because she'd left a toddler to the perils of the social care system. He'd often wondered, couldn't she have just got out from under him some other way? Run away, called the police, found a refuge? But he'd tried not to judge. He had never been in her position, couldn't really imagine it. Besides, he'd thought her crime was because she'd temporarily lost it, couldn't take one more moment of abuse. Awful, with disastrous consequences, but not her fault exactly. Everyone had a snapping point.

But now he knew that she hadn't gone to prison for killing Becky's dad. Where *was* Becky's dad? Had Susan even known who he was? There was a chance that she might not have, he thought with some judgement. Susan had not been sent to prison for a tragic crime of passion, she had been sent to prison for a premeditated double murder of strangers. She had sacrificed her daughter for what? Why did she kill the Westlys? Money? Was it a robbery? Must have been; that made sense, because Emma's family were rich. Susan had recently demonstrated that she was prepared to go horribly far for money. He thought of Emma being pushed off the ladder, and shuddered.

Another reason Matthew doubted Susan's mothering credentials was that she had barely kept in touch with her daughter while she served her time – even the minimal tokens of Christmas and birthday cards failed to land with any regularity – but she wouldn't give her up for adoption. That was a selfish move. Becky could have been adopted as a baby, slipped into a stable family who yearned for a child; she'd have been loved, settled, grounded, instead she'd had a tumultuous upbringing, being passed around, unwanted, continually disrupted and disturbed. He had lost count of how many homes she said she'd lived in. Becky romanticised this act of her mother's, said it was because Susan had hoped that one day they'd have a relation-ship. Bullshit. Matthew guessed it was that Susan knew her chance of parole was more likely if the board were reminded that she had a child on the outside. Even when she was finally released, she hadn't immediately rushed to build bridges with her daughter. She only showed up when she heard that Becky was making good money as a model, and disappeared again when the opposite was true. Matthew wished she'd stayed hidden, far away from them.

He thought about when she had reappeared in their lives. She'd offered them a home, of sorts; at least a bed settee in her tatty flat. That had been a couple of years ago, when she'd started working for Emma. Was that just a coincidence? The policewoman had said she didn't believe in coincidences, and nor did he. He wondered now whether Susan had planned to embroil them in scamming Emma two years ago. Had he been used? Becky had been delighted when her mother had got in touch. It had been a bit awkward to stomach. Becky presented as someone who was so independent, sorted and comfortably autonomous, yet as soon as her mother was back on the scene, she'd transformed into this desperate people-pleaser. At least she had around Susan. She rarely bothered to please Matthew.

'Are they going to arrest Emma?' she asked. She ignored the tea he put on the table in front of her.

'Yes, I think they are.'

'What for? Dangerous driving, drunk driving? Murder?'

'I don't know. I suppose any of them are a possibility.'

'*When* are they going to arrest her?'

'She's still unconscious. I don't know.' Matthew collapsed into the other kitchen chair, opposite Becky. His mind was still playing catch-up.

'I wonder how we can prove that she knew who my mother was and that she was responsible for her parents' deaths.'

'Can we prove that? Is it true?'

Becky cast a withering stare Matthew's way. 'Whether it's true or not, we can give them evidence that proves it.'

He shook his head, confused. 'That doesn't make sense.'

Her expression turned to one of despair; a look that yelled 'Keep up.' She often looked at him that way. It really annoyed him. He wasn't stupid, he just wasn't scheming. The things that seemed to come to her in a flash took longer to occur to him. That wasn't a bad thing.

'I can create a browsing history on her laptop that suggests she's been looking into her parents' deaths and into my mum. We could plant evidence linking Mum to the vandalism of the graves; the red paint is here in her flat, we just need the police to find it,' said Becky. She'd stopped crying.

'But your mum didn't vandalise the graves. I saw you there.'

'Yeah, that one was me, but I don't think we need to be too

squeamish about who did what at this stage. We both know Mum pushed Emma off the ladder. Once the police are sure that she was the one harassing Emma, it will be an easy jump to think that Emma found out, and then discovered my mum had murdered hers and wanted revenge. It all works beautifully. I couldn't have planned it better myself.' She looked relieved. No, more than that, she looked satisfied.

'But why bother?' Matthew asked. 'Why would we create evidence to show that Emma wanted to kill your mother? If she has done it deliberately, that will come out without us having to interfere.'

'Yes, well, maybe, but we can't count on it.'

'If she didn't mean to kill your mother it would be terrible for her to go down for a crime she didn't commit.'

'It happens. Besides, do we want Emma to be carefully investigated, or do we want this sorted in a hurry? The police will be pleased to get an open-and-shut case. You don't want them looking into all of this too closely. Not considering everything that has happened recently.'

Everything that has happened recently.

He supposed that was a euphemism for their sustained campaign to drive Emma mad, a campaign that meant Emma's property had been damaged, her peace of mind destroyed and finally her body broken. It made him uncomfortable thinking about it. He knew he was part of it, but he really didn't like admitting that, even to himself. It had all got out of hand. They'd done a terrible, extreme thing. He wanted to put distance between himself and that mess. It had escalated. It had gone too far, and now it appeared Becky wanted to take it further still. He had been bamboozled into accepting whatever it was she wanted, but there had to come a point when he called time. If Emma was sent to prison for something she had done, that was one thing, but shouldn't they just leave this to the police and the justice system? 'You want to falsify evidence? On top of everything.'

'Mattie, she killed my mother.'

'Yes, but I really think it was an accident. I don't think she knew your mother had killed her parents. She would have told me otherwise.'

'What, like you told her everything? Get real, Mattie. People don't tell their partners everything.'

But he thought Emma did. She'd even told him she believed in ghosts. That took some trust, didn't it? To appear so vulnerable. That demonstrated her faith and confidence in him. Although it was misguided. The thought shamed him. 'Emma was driving injured,' he pointed out. He didn't add that she was terrified, that he'd chased her out of the house himself. 'It was dark and wet. No one would expect a pedestrian on that bend. What was your mother doing on the road at night anyway? Obviously up to something. This could have been a genuine accident.'

'Maybe it was, but you don't go to jail for accidental death. Think about it, Mattie, if Emma is in jail, then you are free.' Becky was smiling now, her face shining like a child's in rude health, the shadow of grief fallen from her. She added, 'You know what, we can't lose. If she stays in a coma, Woodview is ours to use as we please, you'll get control of her finances and we can start the renovation of the Old Schoolhouse. If she goes to prison for murder, no one will doubt your right to divorce her. You'll get a healthy settlement.'

Matthew stared at her, horrified but also wiser. Becky was mad. It was strange to think such a thing. To *know* it. Especially as they had spent the past couple of months trying to send Emma mad, or at least make her look so. But Emma wasn't the crazy one. Becky was. Perhaps it was the grief or shock of losing her mother; perhaps it was the years of abuse and neglect as a child, or poverty and degradation as an adult. Whatever it was, she was too damaged and greedy to see clearly any more. The ideas tumbling out of her mouth were insane. It was up to him to steer the ship. Morally, emotionally, physically, he had to take charge. He tried to process exactly what this meant for him. How exposed he might be if Becky followed this plan she was suggesting, which she most likely would, with or without his agreement. That much was clear. However, before his thoughts could fully settle, his phone rang. He answered.

'Hello . . . I see, right, well, yes. Thank you.' He hit the red button and turned to Becky.

'Who was that? What is it?'

'It was the hospital. Emma is awake.'

43

It had been a very long day. The longest he'd known perhaps. He couldn't remember exactly how many hours he'd been awake; enough for everything to have changed. His world was irrevocably altered. He'd woken up at Woodview, then gone to the hospital, the police station, the Fox and Crown, Woodview, the hospital again and then back to Woodview. He felt like a hamster running on one of those wheels, achieving little, going nowhere. He was exhausted.

He had rarely been alone in the house; Becky made sure that she was here for almost every minute that Emma wasn't. It was strange to spend time here without either of them, but he quickly found it to be healing. Emma was always going on about the energy of the house, and Becky was always going on about the luxury. He was enjoying the silence, the solitariness. He didn't feel lonely, he felt relieved. Perhaps he'd go so far as to say unshackled. He padded about in bare feet, allowing the warmth of the underfloor heating to ooze through his soles, up his ankles and calves. He listened to some piano music at low volume. It was soothing. He didn't know much about classical music, but he liked it. He rarely listened to it when anyone else was around. Emma would have wanted to talk about his curation, because she was interested in everything about him, which was cool, but he didn't want to admit to her that his selection was simply the result of him searching 'relaxing classical piano music' on Spotify and being furnished with a basic playlist of tunes he largely recognised from adverts and movies.

That was the problem with meeting someone as an adult: they expected you to be fully formed and impressive. He was not what Emma believed him to be. He was not a thoughtful, deep man, touched by loss and desperate to seize the day; he did not have a particular interest in new exhibitions at galleries, or a desire to taste jellied eels, or a compunction to hike mountains. Those were all Becky's ideas, Becky's invention. He didn't know who he was. Emma's eternal intellectualising and scrutinising meant he lived under a constant threat of being exposed as duller or more ordinary than she thought him to be. That was excruciating. Maybe he was just a pretty face.

If he'd ever listened to classical music in front of Becky, she would have howled with derision and called him pretentious. That was the problem with being with someone since you were very young: they sometimes didn't allow you to grow or change. At least that was the case with him and Becky. They had roles and they stuck to them. He was the Neanderthal who struggled to finish tasks; she was the one with ambition and drive who would take them places. Maybe other couples handled things better, maybe other couples encouraged one another. Grew together.

He listened to the classical music while he took a long shower. The hot water drilled onto his back. It massaged some of the stress out of his muscles, washed away some of the filth of the day from his mind.

After he had received the call from the hospital this morning, he had walked back from the pub to Woodview, and from there he'd ordered an Uber so he could return to the hospital. He had to be so careful. This wasn't a game; this was an investigation. Not that he'd ever thought it was a game as such, it was just that all the events of these past few months had an unreal quality to them. Surreal, sometimes dreamlike. Sex with a new woman, sanctioned by his existing one, frequent visits to stunning hotels and incredibly expensive restaurants, even a trip to the Maldives had all created an other-worldly, illusory element to his life. It had been possible to tell himself it wasn't absolutely real.

He liked Emma, he hadn't anticipated that. He liked her a lot. She was good, kind, clever, fit, and even though she was eleven years older than he was, she didn't patronise him or admonish him the way Becky did. She seemed to enjoy his company, value his thoughts, respect his talent as a photographer. She didn't see him as a failed broke actor. Of course not, she had no idea about any of that. The sex was good, very good. He had been so scared these last couple of days. Terrified that she wouldn't come round, that she wouldn't survive. Terrified of what would happen if she did. Both thoughts had scared him to his core, but he had wanted her to live.

Was that love? Even before this, he had started to wonder did he love her?

He wasn't *in* love with her exactly. He wasn't even sure what that meant any more. The dizzy, can't eat, can't sleep, can't think of anyone other than your lover thing had happened with him and Becky. They'd climbed all over each other for months, they'd wanted to know every atom of one another, inside and out. That first year or so, they'd fucked so hard and so frequently that they'd often thought they might drop with exhaustion, but that was a long time ago and look where it had got him. They were young when they met. Kids. That feeling doesn't last. He couldn't imagine feeling as embroiled with anyone now as he had once been with Becky; it was infantile to hope for it. Like wanting to still believe in Father Christmas.

He and Becky still turned each other on, though. Even after sixteen years. They knew their way around one another, knew the quickest way to make sex satisfying. You might say it was efficient. He was still exploring Emma, which was fun. He did have feelings for her. He respected her, admired her. Yeah, maybe he did love her.

What did he feel for Becky now? He didn't know. Love, lust, hate, disgust? Pity, embarrassment, fear, anger? He had felt all of those just today. And right now, in this exact moment, as the water from the shower drilled into him, he felt none of them. He felt nothing.

And that was worse.

Becky had walked with him from the pub to Woodview. He'd asked her not to, said it was a risk them being seen together and that she should stay in the flat, but she had ignored him. She was becoming sloppy, not so committed to the detail of the scam or remaining undetected. It was probably because she thought the finish line was in sight. She'd talked non-stop as they walked, a stream of consciousness. It had been hard to remain tuned in to what she was saying. Most of it was self-preservation stuff. She wondered what Emma might say now she was awake, what she might remember, whether she still believed in ghosts. Had there been alcohol in her system when she crashed? What might she be charged with?

As the Uber pulled up, he told Becky once again to go back to the pub, to lie low, to wait. She said she would, but he'd doubted it. He knew she would hack Emma's computer and follow her plan to falsify evidence. She would create searches that indicated Emma was obsessed with the death of her parents and had discovered Susan Morden was responsible so had deliberately set out to kill her in revenge. Becky would use her skills to manipulate search history records so that it looked as though Emma had been plotting this for months. She would do a thorough job. He had specifically asked her not to frame Emma. He'd said she should leave things alone, that they had done enough damage, but he knew she wouldn't listen to him. She always did what she wanted. He could see that now. He wondered why it had taken him so long to work it out. To admit it to himself.

He didn't have time to argue with her at that exact moment. What he had to do was get to the hospital and see Emma. Talk to her. Wasn't that what any right-thinking husband would do? Furthermore, it was what he wanted to do. He wanted to see Emma. He wanted to know if she was OK. He wanted to know what she remembered. It was difficult to be sure which mattered to him the most. Everything about his relationship with Emma was complex. That wasn't surprising considering how it had begun, but now it struck him as sad. Part of him wished he could be who she thought he was.

His trip to the hospital turned out to be a waste of time. He'd run through the corridors at speed, only stopping at the shop to briefly consider whether he should arrive with a gift. He thought flowers would be appropriate; he could see himself dashing to her bedside with an enormous, impressive bouquet of roses, irises, maybe some eucalyptus. A bright cluster, vibrant and cheerful. He was frustrated to discover that there wasn't so much as a bunch of carnations, because hospitals discouraged taking flowers to patients. 'People have allergies, and it just makes work for the nurses, dealing with that and finding vases and such,' the shop assistant explained. She suggested a crossword puzzle book or a sandwich. He declined. Neither would make the impact he was hoping for. It didn't matter, as it happened. When he arrived at the ward, he was told that he couldn't see Emma.

'Why not?' he demanded.

The nurse who had stopped him at the ward reception looked uncomfortable, agitated. She glanced up the corridor, her eyes resting on the policeman sitting outside the door of Emma's room. It was the same policeman who had been there earlier that morning and had suggested Matthew go to the station. Matthew couldn't work out if the nurse was apologising for the policeman's presence or if she was trying to get his attention so that he could deal with Matthew. He decided to take things into his own hands. He strode towards the officer and asked, 'Is my wife under arrest?'

'No, sir, she is not. Although she is helping with police inquiries.'

Matthew tried to peer over the man's shoulder, through the small window in the door of Emma's room. He could see the corner of the foot of the bed. He could see that the police officers who had interviewed him earlier were in the room, but Emma was out of view. He was surprised by the jolt of longing he felt.

'Well in that case, I'd like to be in there with her.'

'That's not possible.'

'Is there a legal reason why not? I can't think there is if she's not under arrest. Does she have a lawyer in there with her?' He was giving himself a director's note right then: his tone should be anxiety manifesting in irritation or even anger. He had found it helpful over these last few months to pretend the entire thing was an acting job, as Becky had originally suggested. He'd often read that actors who worked on soaps for years started to blur where they ended and their characters began.

'I'm not obliged to share that information with you, sir.' The 'sir' was delivered in a way that wound up Matthew further. It struck him as the opposite of respectful, more a reminder of who was really in charge.

'If she's fit enough to speak to your boss, she must be fit enough to speak to her husband,' Matthew snapped.

'That's the issue, sir, she doesn't want you in there. We're keeping you out of her room at *her* request.'

Matthew glared at the officer. He wanted to ask why Emma didn't want to see him, but he knew the answer and it wasn't in his interest to have it articulated aloud. She was scared of him. Terrified. The last time they had been together, she had run away from him. He'd hoped that she might not recall the minutes just before the accident. He'd hoped that even if she did, she would give him a chance to explain why he was chasing her, why he was trying to stop her getting in the car. Why he didn't want her to drive anywhere. If she'd speak to him. However, as it was, there was no point in making a fuss. He turned on his heel and left the hospital. His footsteps, clip-clopping along the echoey corridor, sounded very loud.

Back at Woodview, the first thing he did was check the security footage. He thought it was highly likely Becky would have done the same after she had tampered with Emma's laptop. She was as competent with this security software as he was – more so, in fact; she had taught him how to cut, pause, loop and alter the dates of footage so that they could eradicate the evidence of her visits there.

But this time, thank fuck, she had slipped up. It was all there, everything he had expected and more. Thank fuck. She had failed to check and delete the recent footage. He supposed it was because that wasn't her goal today. She'd been focused on framing Emma, and she was perhaps in a hurry; certainly she was a mess, grieving, manic. Or maybe it was the opposite. She had been careless because she felt relaxed about monitoring the security cameras since Emma was in hospital and unable to check the recordings any time soon. Most likely she trusted Matthew to do it for her as he had on so many occasions.

Just after 4 p.m., the police came and asked if he was happy for them to search the house. 'We have a warrant if you're not happy,' the female officer said laconically. The threat, the power, spelt out.

'Be my guest, of course. We have nothing to hide. But I can't think what you imagine you'll find.' He held the door wide open. They wanted Emma's laptop, of course.

They went straight to it. He didn't doubt that they were acting on an anonymous tip-off. One that Becky would have phoned in. They also took her phone.

'Odd that she went out without it, don't you think?' mused the officer. 'Did she leave the house in a hurry?'

'Yes, she did.'

'Did she tell you where she was going?'

'No, just that she wanted to go for a drive. She wasn't at her most communicative because we'd had a bit of a disagreement.' There was no point in denying it. Chances were Emma had already said as much. A lot was going to come out. It was best if he told the truth where he could.

After the police left, he took a swim. Fifty hard lengths, front crawl and butterfly, at speed. He wanted to feel the power and potency of his own body. He wanted to exert himself. Exhaust himself. He was wired. Adrenalin charged through his blood. Despite everything going on, the undoubted drama and trauma, he felt different. He did not feel that the ground was rising and falling, sloping beneath his feet. For the first time in a long while, he felt that he at least had a plan of his own. After the swim, he took a sauna, helped himself to a very lovely full-bodied glass of red and waited.

People often complained that the police were slow, in every sense of the word. Matthew had never bought into that derisive stereotype. He'd always respected them. Not the chauvinistic, racist ones, obviously – they were an abomination – but you got those sorts of wankers in all walks of life. His upbringing was such that he held a traditional, generally unfashionable respect for the police. He thought they were doing their best in a world where they constantly encountered people who were doing their worst. He liked to believe in a world where kids could stop and ask a police officer for directions or the time. The reality was that kids nowadays carried smartphones, so that was never going to happen, but still he held onto the vague belief that it could. He accepted that the police were under-resourced, swamped with paperwork, constantly playing catch-up with the bad guys. Mistakes would be made. Shortcuts taken. Thoroughness sacrificed for expediency and results targets.

Wasn't that what Becky was counting on? Wasn't he?

He was not disappointed. At 10 p.m., he received a call informing him that the police had pressed charges against Emma. She was being charged with the murder of Susan Morden.

44

The next day

'No. That's ludicrous. Emma would never . . . How can you think that?' Matthew had travelled to the police station first thing the next morning and demanded to speak to the officer in charge. He wanted them to see his shock and outrage. He thought it was important that they witnessed his belief in his wife's good character and moral value. To be fair, this didn't require any acting talent. He one hundred per cent believed that Emma was a good person. She had not murdered Susan. She had no idea of the connection between Susan and her parents. 'She didn't do it, at least not deliberately. It was an accident,' he went on staunchly. 'She was driving at speed, yes, I can believe that. I told you we had a row. I'm as much to blame as she is.'

'You weren't in the car, sir, let alone driving it,' the officer pointed out. 'I don't think we can charge you.'

Matthew wondered if it was part of their training, this particular line in sarcasm. His old-school respect for the police was somewhat pricked, but he was determined to remain calm, cool and collected. It was important. 'Charge her with careless driving, accidental death, if you must. But murder? That's ridiculous.'

'Touching,' said the young policewoman. 'But Emma has a lawyer, and I'm sure once you talk to her, she'll tell you we have a strong case. Your wife is still in hospital, too fragile to move, but she is under arrest. Her bail has been set; she can meet it quite comfortably, apparently.'

There it was again, the advantages of money, and it seemed the policewoman was aware of it too. Aware and resentful. Did she think bail ought to have been set at a higher level? Was it fair that Emma could find the £40,000 necessary to secure her relative freedom until the trial?

'Here is a list of bail conditions. Thanks for bringing in her passport. Very helpful.'

'Well, you asked me to, not that she can go anywhere right now.'

'Once she's out of hospital, she'll have to report to the station every second day. Her lawyer will go over the details.'

Matthew hesitated. He looked around the now familiar interview room. Flat, dismal, small. Like his life had been before Emma. It smelt stale; the Old Schoolhouse had a similar stench. He thought it was something to do with the endless trail of people who would have sweated in both places. In this room, criminals fearful, brutal; in the schoolhouse, kids oppressed, filthy. Their stench had seeped into the floorboards, the brickwork.

He sighed. This wasn't the worst thing he'd ever done. Not the biggest betrayal. He could, if he put his mind to it, justify his decision. Dropping off the passport was one thing, but now he had to do what he had really come for. It was difficult when it came down to it. Sad. Sixteen years he'd been with Becky. But she'd brought this upon herself. She'd left him no choice. 'I'm between a rock and a hard place.' He dropped his head into his hands.

'What do you mean by that?' the officer asked, immediately sensing that he was about to deliver up something important. Matthew thought he saw her neck lengthen, her nose actually twitch, like a hunting dog.

'Fuck it.' He suddenly sat bolt upright, indicating his commitment to doing the hard thing but the right thing. 'I have information that will make you look at everything differently. This entire case.'

'What information is that?'

'If I tell you, I'll lose my marriage, but if I don't tell you, my wife loses her liberty.'

The police officers leaned towards him gracefully, like synchronised swimmers. 'What have you got to tell us, Mr Charlton?'

He slipped the USB across the table. 'You'll work it all out from this. Well, this and an examination of the car. I think you'll find it was tampered with. My guess is the brakes will have been damaged or a wheel loosened. A copycat scenario of how her parents were killed. I believe Emma lost control of the car, but that wasn't her fault. You're right, it wasn't an accident. A crime has been committed, but not the murder of Susan Morden. The real crime is the attempted murder of my wife. She was the victim. This is the security footage from our home. It shows who tampered with the car. It was my ex-girlfriend, Becky.'

'I see.'

There was no going back now. 'She also happens to be Susan Morden's daughter.' The police officers shared a glance. The woman raised an eyebrow. 'I know, messy.' Matthew coloured a little, aware that the phrase was inadequate. This wasn't messy, this was tragic, horrific, cruel. He couldn't bring himself to admit as much. Doing so was too big. Too much. 'I've emailed Emma's lawyer with these images too.' He'd done it as he left the house, so that he couldn't lose his nerve. 'She'll most likely be in touch very shortly. I think you'll agree this has changed everything.'

Matthew spent several more hours in the police station, giving his statement. He tried to stick as closely to the truth as possible, but obviously, self-preservation meant that it was difficult to admit everything. He told the police that he'd simply met Emma, fallen for her and ended his relationship with Becky, and that she'd taken their break-up badly. He didn't want to talk about the scam they'd planned. It would strengthen the case against Becky, yes, but it would also obliterate any chance he had of holding onto his marriage. And he found he did want the marriage to survive. He wanted that very much, if at all possible.

He told them about the sustained campaign of aggression against Emma, but he didn't mention that Emma thought she was being haunted. How could he when he didn't want to disclose the fact that he'd made up a dead wife? He held onto a sliver of hope that Emma would be too proud to reveal all their personal details to the police. The business about the existence or non-existence of a dead wife was not pertinent to the case; she might decide to keep it to herself. When she heard that he'd saved her, that he'd come forward with the evidence

328

that got the charges against her dropped, she might forgive him. Not straight away, but eventually. She loved him, didn't she? But first he had to get through this interview.

'And it's just a coincidence, is it? The fact that your ex's mother killed your wife's parents?' He could hear their scepticism.

'The world is full of strange coincidences. It comes down to geography in the end. I very much doubt it's a coincidence that Susan worked for Emma. Knowing what I do now, I think she always intended to cause trouble for Emma, and that's why she took the job – to get closer to her, find an opportunity. Maybe she and Becky were jointly responsible for the harassment that Emma has endured recently. I don't know what each of them knew about the other's situation and motivation. They never had a close mother-and-daughter relationship, obviously, since Susan Morden spent all of Becky's formative years in prison. Who knows what secrets they kept.' He shrugged. 'I certainly had no idea about any of it. I just met Emma because I lived locally. I lived locally because Becky and I had chosen to live with Becky's mother.' He raised his hands, palms open and up to the ceiling, and shrugged dramatically. 'Would it help if I took a lie detector test or something?'

The two police officers smirked at one another. Silently mocking his naivety. He didn't care. They could think him foolish, manipulated or even idiotic. He was perhaps all of those things. He just wanted them to believe him.

'I'm happy to help the investigation in any way possible.'

The police didn't give much away throughout the long hours of interviewing. He couldn't tell if they believed him or not. They offered him a lawyer. He said he didn't need one. 'I've nothing to hide. I'm telling the truth.' And he was, largely. Maybe not the whole truth and nothing but the truth, but who told that nowadays? They let him tell his entire story, including the fact that when he had checked the security camera footage, he had seen Becky going into the garage and then emerging later with something concealed under her jumper. 'I'm guessing that was the tool she used to tamper with the car.'

He didn't know how long it would take the police to digest this new evidence, and whether they would accept it. He hoped they would. Eventually they said he could go. 'But don't go too far, Mr Charlton. We'll want to talk to you again.'

'My wife is in hospital. I'm not going anywhere,' he replied.

As he left the police station, it started to pour. Sharp needles rained down on him, pricking his skin. He had decided to do one more thing: a difficult final act, but it was necessary in order to get the police to completely believe what he was saying. He needed a confession from Becky. He headed to the pub.

45

There was a scattering of afternoon drinkers in the pub, relaxing back on their chairs, pint glasses in hand and the remnants of cottage pie smeared on the plates in front of them. It was far from a gastro pub. Graham bought the pies at the local Costco and heated them up in the microwave. Still, Matthew ordered the last two, waited in silence until the microwave pinged, then carried them upstairs to the flat. He put the tray on the floor outside the door, pressed record on his phone and then knocked. He had a key, but that wasn't a fact he wanted to share with the police if he could avoid it. By arriving with a tray of food, he had a reason for not letting himself in if Becky asked. This wouldn't be easy. He had loved her once.

She was pleased to see him. Her face lit up. He might have felt guilty, but she quickly asked, with obvious glee, 'Have they arrested her?'

'Yes.'

'Whoop!' She punched the air.

'Your mother just died. They've arrested Emma for her murder. I'm not sure an air punch is the appropriate response.'

'Obviously I'm gutted about my mum. She had a shit life and I thought things were just about to change for her. I thought *I* was going to change them for her. The fact that I can't hurts.' Becky started to cry. Matthew felt awkward. He shouldn't have snapped at her. Not on top of everything else he had done, but Jesus, she could be unlikeable. How had it taken him so long to see it? Maybe he had known it for some time but hadn't done anything about it because he'd been without choice or incentive. 'I'm punching the air because this is what Mum would have wanted. It's justice.'

What did she mean by that? She didn't look well. Greasy-haired, gritty-eyed. She was wearing the same outfit she'd been wearing on Saturday night. Joggers and a T-shirt. The T-shirt had sweat stains under the arms and something spilt down the front – coffee maybe. Not pretty at all. Matthew put the tray down on the small Formica table and moved around the kitchen collecting up cutlery. He filled two glasses with tap water and then sat down. Becky sat too but didn't pick up a fork. The table was so small their knees touched; he was hopeful that her voice would be clearly picked up on the recording. He decided there was no point in stalling. Better just to dive in.

'You killed your own mother.'

'What?'

He spelt it out. 'This whole plan of yours. This greed, or lust for revenge, or whatever it was. You killed your own mother.'

'What are you talking about? I wasn't driving the car.' Becky looked surprised, shocked even, at his accusation. She obviously wasn't expecting to be called out for killing Susan.

332

'No, but you tampered with it. Made it unsafe, presumably in the hope that Emma would have an accident and die. You planned to kill Emma, but you killed your mother by mistake when Emma ploughed into her.'

She didn't refute it. She laughed. A short, violent spurt of hysteria; he wondered whether she'd taken something. 'What are you talking about. Are you mad?'

'The car was tampered with.'

'Who said?' Again she looked stunned.

He shook his head sadly, didn't answer. He had questions of his own to ask. 'The thing that bothers me, Becky, is that if everything had gone to plan for you, and Emma had been killed, the police would have investigated the accident and discovered that the car had been messed with. They'd have looked for someone to pin it on. Who did you plan that to be? Me? Was that your ultimate plan, that I went down for murdering the woman I'd fallen in love with, the woman I'd chosen over you?'

'You'd fallen in love with her?' Becky asked. She looked panicked, hunted, sweaty, sheeny. Her eyes darted about as though she was crazed or angry or amazed. He didn't know which. 'No. No. You have it all wrong. I never did that. How could you think I would want to kill her, let alone pin it on you?' He'd expected her to deny it.

'I'm not saying you planned to kill your mother. She wasn't the intended victim. Emma was,' he clarified. Becky put her hands to her head. As she lifted her arms, he got a whiff of her body, stagnant, neglected, but also alcohol on her breath. Of course she'd been drinking. She was grieving, on her own, above a pub. He knew she'd have pinched a bottle of spirits.

She seemed confused, tearful, unreliable. He wondered whether anyone listening to the recording would recognise as much. 'Admit it, Becky.'

'No, no. I didn't do that,' she insisted. Despite her drunken, grieving state, her confusion and shock, she was sticking to her story. She'd always been good under pressure. Then she alighted on an alternative theory. 'If Emma's car was messed with, that must have been my mother.'

'My God, you are unbelievable. You'd blame your dead mother for a crime you committed.'

'She knew about the prenup. I'd told her. She'd have wanted Emma out of the way so you could collect the cash.'

'That doesn't make sense. What benefit would it be to your mother if I gained financially from Emma's death?'

'Well, you'd have shared it with me,' Becky insisted.

'You're delusional,' Matthew muttered.

Becky lifted her head and met his eyes. He thought he saw a flicker of something in her expression. He wasn't sure what; it could have been a myriad of things – resignation, realisation, repugnance, even reluctant respect. She was quick to glaze over, practised at not letting him know what she was thinking. 'Why would you think I'd interfered with the car?' She asked the question quietly.

'I have evidence. Security footage.'

'That's impossible. You can't have footage of that. There are no cameras in the garage.'

'Well, not of you loosening the wheel nut exactly,' he admitted. 'But footage that shows you going into the garage the night of the accident and then emerging a little while later with a tool stuffed up your jumper. I've given the footage to the police.'

'You bastard.' She said it gently, almost a caress. He'd expected more denials, more fury. She shook her head slowly, understanding everything now. She was quick, always had been. People underestimated her brain because of her beauty, but he knew that she would have made the leap, seen the end. 'Yes, I went into the garage, but that was just to get access to the tumble dryer. I put her cashmere jumper in the dryer to shrink it. That's all.'

'That's pathetic.'

'Maybe, but that was all I was doing.'

'I mean your excuse is pathetic, not shrinking her jumper, which you've obviously just made up.' Although now he thought of it, that was pathetic too. Everything they had done. All the little cruelties, the nasty scheme to undermine, destabilise, destroy. How had he gone along with it for so long? 'Why were you shrinking her jumper?'

'I wanted her to think she'd done it when drunk, obviously.'

'But you didn't need to do that. She'd already lost the plot. She thought she was being haunted. Why were you still torturing her?'

Becky held his gaze. The years they had spent together spun across the table. All the love that had rolled between them, the hate that had erupted, the joy and pain they had brought to one another. He recalled the initial optimism that had been eroded by the endless disappointments; the poverty endured, rows fought, humiliations suffered. This was what all relationships amounted to in the end. A balance between the valuable, the miserable and the impossible. Their bad stuff had mounted up, ultimately outweighing the parts that made things worthwhile, or even bearable. The lies, deceit and betrayals had created a wall between them. He wondered, if he put out his hand, would he feel it physically manifested? What they had been, what they had become. There had been barricades and divisions in the past. Somehow they had always waded their way through, struggled on. But this time, neither of them had the energy to scramble over the wall, let alone knock it down.

Becky eyed him coldly. 'Torturing is a very strong word. I can tell you what torture is. It's spending your life with your nose pressed up against the window, watching others enjoy what should have been yours.'

'What do you mean?'

'Emma's wealth. It should have been mine.'

'No it shouldn't. Just because you want something doesn't mean you're entitled to it.'

'She owed me.'

'What do you mean by that?'

'Mum kept saying you were falling in love with her. I didn't want to believe it.'

'And that's why you planned to kill her.'

'No, I never did. You can't think that about me. A murderer? No.' The sirens of the approaching police cars were audible now. The blue lights flickered into the room. 'Our plan was working. Emma would have gone down for killing my mother. Mum would have been entirely blamed for harassing her, and tampering with the car too. No one would have looked our way.'

Matthew didn't have to answer. As the police banged on the door, he stood up and let them in.

46

One year later

Emma

The murder charge against me was dropped. Many people confirmed my account that I had no prior knowledge my parents had been murdered, let alone that Susan Morden, my ex-cleaner, was responsible. I had always believed my grandparents' story that it was an accident. Matthew testified that Becky had created the searches about my parents' deaths and Susan Morden's involvement and imprisonment that were found on my computer. Without that prior knowledge, there was no motive for me to murder her. My lawyer hired a computer security expert to forensically explore my PC. The expert concluded that a hacker with a level of competency had made all the searches after the crash, while I was in hospital, unconscious. The timeline had been manipulated so as to fool the police when making their initial investigations.

No motive, no opportunity, no case.

Perverting the course of justice was added to the charges against Becky Morden, as the prosecuting lawyer declared that no one else could have been responsible for manufacturing evidence against me. In court, Becky's defence lawyer pointed out that Matthew could have done it. This caused Heidi to mutter, 'I wouldn't put it past him. I just don't trust him. Never have.' She stopped short of saying 'I told you so'. We both know she did tell me; I didn't listen. I didn't want to hear.

Ever reasonable, Gina added, 'He's owned up to his part in everything. It's horrifying enough. If he was responsible for framing you, I think he'd say so. The defence lawyer's job is to cast reasonable doubt on the charges Becky is facing. You don't have to think the worst.'

I don't express an opinion. Staying quiet, waiting to see what the court decides is an act of discipline. I have jumped to conclusions, drawn shaky suppositions and wanted to believe lies so often since Matthew came into my life, and doing so led to nothing other than trouble. I will wait to see what the outcome of the trial is. I will believe what is decided by judge and jury. That is the sane and measured thing to do. My talent used to be my discipline. I prided myself on being rational, thorough, careful. I'm looking for that again.

Heidi and Gina have been amazing throughout the trial. Despite their own busy lives and commitments, they've ensured that one or the other or both are always with me. It has helped, as I've been hit with endless complex and shocking revelations. I'm concentrating on restoring my equilibrium. I lost myself for a while and I need to find my routines and my reason; I need to concentrate on my relationships with my friends and their families. These are the things that have sustained me in the past. I need these tools to cope as I process the facts. I had rules and routines for a reason. When they are abandoned, things start to fall apart. Children of alcoholics know this better than most; how did I forget?

Matthew is not a widower. He is someone's fiancé. Becky is not dead, yet she is still haunting me. Listening to her defence is devastating. If she is to be believed, she was in an active relationship with him throughout our meeting and our marriage. Both things were a sham, part of a long-term plan to defraud me of my wealth. Matthew told the police that he had not understood the ultimate endgame of the crime, but that the plan had been revealed to him in incremental stages that increased in seriousness and criminality. Apparently, he'd initially thought it was going to be a matter of a simple robbery; later that progressed into severe gaslighting, in order to have me committed so that he could take fiscal control. In court he said he wasn't proud of that. 'Things just got out of hand.' I thought Heidi was going to leap out of her seat, jump over the viewing gallery balcony and throttle him with her bare hands at that point. She spluttered her indignation and disbelief when he insisted he'd had no idea that attempts were being made on my life.

Everything he ever said to me was a lie.

His claim not to have known that the plan was to kill me is something Becky also asserts. Nice that they have so much in common, I suppose. She admitted to several counts of aggravated trespassing, vandalism, breaking and entering, theft, and the desecration of my parents' graves, but like Matthew she has continued to insist she is innocent in the matter of tampering with the car. Furthermore, she claims she has never physically harmed me.

'Did you lock Ms Westly in her private sauna?'

'I did not.'

'Did you interfere with the ladder when Ms Westly was clearing the gutters?'

'I did not. I was in London, with Matthew Charlton.'

'Did you fill her bath with scalding water?'

'No, I didn't.'

'Do you believe these incidents were accidents, Ms Morden?'

'No, I don't.'

'Do you have any idea who might have been responsible for them, then?'

'I think my mother might have been responsible.'

'Did she ever discuss her intention to harm Ms Westly with you?'

'No.'

I have to testify too. Part of the prosecutor's job is to establish the harm inflicted, as it dictates the sentence that is likely to be attached to the crimes. I'm expected to describe the pain I suffered when injured and the horror of the confusion as this campaign of assault unfolded. I try to remain calm and clear-minded as I answer the questions that expose me as a woman of a certain age who fell in love with a liar who was only interested in my money. I'm a private person and not one who looks for sympathy; I shy away from pity, so I don't really want to have to tell the court that I'm still in physio to correct the damage to my shoulder and back that happened in the car crash. I would rather not have to admit that at night I repeatedly check that doors are locked, the alarm is set, and it is beyond humiliating to have to admit how my reasoning was so damaged that at one point I thought I was being haunted. Giving testimony feels like a further assault, but I answer the questions fully and thoughtfully. I try not to give the headlines in the tabloids any of my attention. Although I'm aware that I'm known as the 'Haunted Hottie Heiress' because someone at work let it slip.

'At least they think you're hot,' said Edward, my PA, and then asked me not to report that to HR.

Despite trying to remain dignified and carry on, the truth is, Becky's trial absorbs me completely. Not only because it centres around whether she did or did not plan to kill me, but because I'm still processing the fact that when I met Matthew, I was told that this woman was dead. I find my gaze is glued to her nearly all the time I am in court. I watch her as though she is a miracle. A Lazarus. I now have all the answers to all the questions that have plagued me this last year. I know what she looks like. I was right to think she was beautiful. She is, even in her ill-fitting, unflattering prison uniform. She has good posture, excellent skin. I am fascinated by how she moves, speaks, thinks. I still have no idea as to what her personal style might be, but I drink in her physicality. It's fair to say he has a type. Becky is a slim, tall brunette, like me. She has eyes that are just a shade darker than mine. We both have strong cheekbones. I don't know what to make of this coincidence. It's not as though there's any reason to believe Mathew selected me or fancied me or wanted me in the real sense. I was simply a financial target. A mark. I wonder how clever she or her mother might have been. Did she consider that our general similarity would make the whole scam more palatable to him?

Becky has continued to insist that her mother was responsible for all the violence against me and that she was unaware of any of the incidents until after they had occurred. She did not

341

plan to harm me physically. This is a wise position to take, as all the other counts combined are unlikely to carry a sentence as big as attempted murder, if that is proven. On day six of the court case, the prosecuting lawyer shows video footage of her entering the garage on the night of the accident and then leaving again with something concealed under her jumper. It's suggested it was the locking wheel nut key that was used to tamper with the wheel and cause it to come off when I was driving.

'It was a shrunken cashmere sweater,' Becky claims when asked what she was carrying.

Then the prosecutor reveals that the wheel nut key was found in her mother's flat, and Becky's defence collapses. If Susan Morden had tampered with the car, how was it possible that the nut key had been returned to the flat above the pub? She died at the scene that night. Becky looks horrified. Trapped in her own lies. The court lets out a collective gasp. I'm glad to be sitting down, as I feel my body slump. I know it's over for her. A logical conclusion has been reached, even if she continues to deny her culpability.

'I just don't think she is capable of accepting responsibility; she's just too deluded or damaged or something,' comments Gina, shaking her head.

The jury only debate for a matter of hours before they return with a unanimous decision. Guilty of attempted murder. Becky is sentenced to four years. Matthew was also charged and prosecuted for intention to commit fraud and conspiracy to murder. He is found guilty of the first count and innocent of the second. I'm surprised to discover I feel some level of relief when his verdict is read out. I suppose I don't want to believe I slept with a man who wanted to kill me. No one wants to think they are fool enough to fall in love with a would-be murderer. Now the courts say I did not. He receives two hundred hours of community service.

'It was as clear-cut as it was possible to be,' comments Gina as we leave the court. We slip out of the back in order to avoid the press, who will be waiting at the front.

'Which makes it the first clear-cut thing about either of them,' Heidi retorts. She smiles at me. 'It's over. You can put it all behind you and move on with your life now.' Her face switches from serene to panicked in a heartbeat. 'Oh my God, come on, let's get into a cab.' She practically yanks my arm out of the socket in her rush to get away.

I look about me to see what she wanted me to avoid. I expect a tenacious journalist to be stalking me, but no, my eyes meet Matthew's. He too is being ushered out of the back door. I watch as he shakes hands with his lawyer.

Heidi tugs at my arm. Gina suggests, 'Let's go and get a celebratory drink.'

'I need to speak to him.'

'No, no, you don't.' Heidi looks aghast.

'I do. He's my husband.'

'Only on paper.'

What doesn't kill you makes you stronger, right? I slip out of her grip. 'You two have been amazing. Honestly, I am so grateful to you, but right now you need to go home to your families. I'll call you tonight. I'm OK, but I need to talk to him. I want to.' Heidi looks furious and Gina looks like she wants to cry as I turn from them and walk towards Matthew.

47

Matthew

Matthew watched her walk towards him. He was buoyant on fresh air and freedom. Two things he thought he might lose today, but they were his to enjoy again. He took deep breaths. He had been living under extraordinary pressure, never quite daring to believe that the justice system would come through for him. Up until now, he hadn't, if he was honest, given much thought to how Emma might be bearing up. Since the charges against her were dropped – all thanks to him – he'd known she was going to be OK. Whatever happened, she would be able to slink back to her beautiful home, get on with her life. He'd ensured that. The prosecuting lawyer had dwelt endlessly on the trauma she had been through and the physical injuries she had sustained, but Matthew hadn't had the space for empathy or sympathy, or anything really other than survival. Now, looking at her, really looking at her, he felt another whip of guilt. When they met, she had bloomed; now she looked shrivelled.

Things weren't great between them. She hadn't spoken to him directly since the crash. All communications came via her solicitors. She had insisted he move out of Woodview before she was released from hospital. He'd returned to Susan's flat, taken over the rental. Graham was glad to have him as a tenant. Once the story broke, the only other people interested in taking the place were ghouls. The sort that listened to true-crime podcasts. Graham didn't want that type of person creeping about. Matthew had seen an opportunity and negotiated the rent down a bit; he'd always thought Susan was overpaying. It would have stood empty otherwise; he was doing Graham a favour. Becky couldn't raise her bail, so she was in prison awaiting trial.

Now, as Emma walked towards him, sunshine in her hair – making it appear a little more coppery, more fiery than usual – he wondered about her. About them. Was there a chance? Even a fleeting one? An iridescent hope flickering on the horizon. How charming was he? Was there a world where they could put this behind them? Stranger things had happened.

'Hello, Matthew.' Her voice at least was crisp, certain. Like it had been at the beginning. She straightened her shoulders, tentatively taking back the space she had once owned. He found that at once intimidating and attractive. 'You must be very pleased.'

'Well, I'm not sure pleased is the right word, considering everything.' He looked at his feet. He wanted her to note his shame, his repentance. 'I'm relieved, though,' he admitted.

'Were you uncertain of the outcome?' she asked testily. She was staring at him; he could feel her hard gaze on his bent head. He forced himself to meet her eyes. Her expression settled somewhere between accusatory and challenging. Nothing good. He had to change that. He had convinced a jury of his innocence, that was one thing, but he'd never hurt the jurors personally; he hadn't lied to them while making them come. He rallied as he knew he must.

'Obviously I know what I'm guilty of and what I'm innocent of, but what is that old saying? "The law is an ass." I didn't know if I'd be believed.'

'Right.'

'Am I?' He shot out *that* look. The look lovers shared. The one he hoped she still found irresistible. The one that said he found her irresistible.

She sighed. 'I keep wondering if you have ever said anything truthful to me. Anything at all.'

'That's stupid, of course I have.'

'Like what?' It was awkward, because he wanted to fix them if he could, but at that exact moment, it was tricky articulating exactly what he had ever truly felt or thought when he was with her. He wasn't sure. She let the silence stretch into indisputable discomfort, and then barked out a harsh laugh. 'I've been thinking back to our first meeting, when you told me I was the reason you were at the conference. That, at least, was true. That meeting was the very start of your game. I think that was possibly the last true thing you said to me.'

'No. God, no.' He reached for her arm, but she moved away from him, out of reach. The pavement was narrow, and so she stepped onto the road; a cyclist had to swerve to avoid clipping her. She didn't seem to care. Her only concern was avoiding his touch. He backed up against the wall so that she could mount the pavement again, stay safe.

'The shame and humiliation of being duped scalds every cell in my body.' Her confession was simple, and he recognised in it an honesty he hadn't often experienced with Becky, certainly not for years.

'I did love you. Maybe I still do,' he blurted.

She shook her head. 'Please don't embarrass us both with more lies.'

'I mean it. Isn't there a way through this? In sickness and in health, for better, for worse and all that.'

She laughed again. The same harsh bark. Her cynicism pinched; he didn't like it about her. He liked her being sweet, compliant, malleable. This sarcasm and distrust reminded him of his relationship with Becky. The sun dipped behind a cloud; the world seemed a little darker.

'Look, I know what I did was wrong,' he began. She raised her eyebrows, widened her eyes. 'Dreadful. I admit it. But I was desperate. An idiot. And in the end, I chose you. I didn't have to tell the police about the footage I found of Becky going into the garage. I could have let you go to prison, I could have got control of your money and lived happily ever after with her.'

'Not if what I heard in the trial can be believed. The woman is damaged. The best you could have hoped for is unhappily ever after,' Emma commented drily.

Matthew smiled at the humour and the truth of the observation. Emma didn't. 'I knew that it was unlikely you'd think well of me after everything I'd done, once it came out, but I had to risk it because I couldn't let you suffer any more. I hoped, ultimately, that you'd forgive me. Please give me a second chance. Pretend we've just met.'

'You do like to pretend.'

'That's not what I mean. We could start again, a clean slate.'

Emma looked confused as she studied him carefully. 'You married me for my money.'

'No, it was more than that. You don't have to believe me, but—'

'I don't.'

'It's true.'

'Do you know, one night I added up the lies you'd told me. I started with your marital status, your nationality, your family structure, your living arrangements, and then I moved on to the more emotional things – "I'm a straightforward sort of guy", "What you see is what you get". I got to a hundred and seven and then gave up.'

'That doesn't seem very constructive.'

'That much we can agree on.'

He wanted her to fall into his arms. He wanted her to invite him back to Woodview. They could be OK. He was sure of it. They had been so happy. He wasn't pretending when they'd shared those cosy evenings, good food, wine and conversation. He'd been very comfortable, very content. But the expression on her face suggested she wasn't going to do what he wanted.

'You're one of those arseholes who believes there's such a thing as "your truth". There isn't, Matthew. There are just facts. I don't care that you "chose" me. I'm not interested in us having a second chance or a clean slate. I'm divorcing you.' Her demeanour changed in front of him. No longer shrivelled, but far from blooming. Now she appeared like vigorous climbing ivy, reaching and robust. 'I'm not going to let this ruin my life or shape anything going forward. Do you understand that? You will not have an impact on me. This past year and a half isn't going to define me or ruin me. I'm just going to carry on being who I was, but without you. I'm not the first stupid woman to fall for a financial romantic scam and I won't be the last. I'm not ashamed and nor should I be. *You* should be.' He could see her chest rising and falling, and he imagined the adrenalin coursing through her body. She obviously felt strong and complete. He felt weak and frayed.

'I *am* ashamed.' He held his arms wide, trying to convey a sense of offering himself up to her judgement. 'We were desperate. We were broke and living in such degradation—'

She cut across him. 'Read this number.' She handed him a piece of paper with a seven-figure number written on it.

'What is this?'

'I'm divorcing you, and this is the amount I'm going to settle on you.'

'It's . . . What? It's more than—'

She didn't let him finish, making the point, he had nothing to say that could be of interest to her. 'This scam of yours turned me into some sort of sad case who had effectively paid for your company. I was ashamed of that at first. Then I thought about it and decided it wasn't my problem that you decided to be someone who could be bought and sold. For you, our relationship was simply transactional. By definitively and explicitly paying you for your services, I'll be able to view it in the same way. Take this settlement. I never want to see you again. Ever. I never want to hear from you. Don't so much as like a post on my socials. Goodbye, Matthew.'

She turned away from him and walked down the street. Head held high, posture ramrod. He watched her flag down a cab. He watched the cab until it disappeared into the distance. A tiny dot.

He couldn't believe his luck.

48

Eighteen months later

Becky

When I arrived, the other women said I'd get used to it; used to the total lack of everything worthwhile – space, privacy, choice, opportunity. News flash, I already was used to it. Being in prison is a lot like being in care. I was familiar with the overly controlled structure, the smells of too many careless bodies in one place and the dissatisfaction of mass catering. I was well acquainted with the lack of hope and the intermittent bouts of overpowering rage brought on by the debilitating unfairness that this was where I'd landed. This was where I'd been put.

I was already used to enduring too. Waiting things out. Sometimes I acknowledge to myself that prison is at least warmer and cleaner than the Old Schoolhouse. I am fed. It's rent-free. Maybe it is the worst, maybe it's not. I don't know. I try not to let myself think about that because I haven't got a choice anyway. I just have to do the time.

Prison is the very embodiment of time-wasting. That is the point of the punishment. The system absorbs life's most precious commodity. I loathe time-wasting. I am being cheated.

In this place nothing can make time go faster or create the illusion that it is being usefully spent. Not the poxy education classes that are an insult to my intelligence, not the lousy food, certainly not the incessant and mind-numbing imbecilic conversation. Not even the fear. I shouldn't be here. This place is for murderers, paedophiles, terrorists. I should be on the outside doing community service, like he is. I did not physically hurt Emma Westly. I did not plan to kill her. All I did was plan for her to be institutionalised rather than me. I just wanted to even things up a bit. It was my turn to live in the posh house. When I tell my cellmate that I shouldn't be here, that I didn't do what they'd sent me down for, she laughed. 'Right. There are five hundred and sixty-nine other innocent prisoners in this place. Not one of us did the crime, bitch.'

They divide up our days into neat parcels that are designed to give the impression we have a purpose, or if that is overstating it, then at least we have routine. At 7.30 a.m., the cells are unlocked. We're given breakfast. Obviously no one asks how we'd like our eggs; we eat what we're given. It's cheap and tasteless, I doubt the nutritional value. We queue to shower, stretch, shit. It's a communal shower. I feel eyes on me constantly. I'm very used to women envying my body, resenting it and adoring it at the same time. On the outside, I used to like to linger in admiring gazes, I used to feel shored up by other women's umbrage or approval. In here I shower as quickly as possible, dress with my back to their prying looks. Being resented or admired can lead to trouble.

We start work at 9 a.m. A lot of the jobs are menial, by which I mean many of the women do whatever work they did before they landed here in prison: cook, clean, serve. The aim seems to be to keep hands busy, self-esteem low. Because I have nice hair, I was put to work in the beauty salon; this is considered a good gig. It's OK except the shampoo is cheap and my hands are chapped as they are always in and out of water. Working is classed as a purposeful activity. Other purposeful activities include library time, exercise and lessons, which all happen after communal lunch. I'm learning French. *Pourquoi pas, putain?*

Everything anybody wants to do – from buying deodorant to sending an email to visiting the art class – must be requested, conferred, arranged. Filling out paperwork is essential, and waiting for a response is an exercise in extreme patience. It's made very clear that everything that is granted can be retracted. But that's not just true in prison, and you're a fucking idiot if you believe it is. After dinner, but before 8.30 p.m. lights-out, there is a period they call association time. This was when the inmates get forced to socialise, like it's good for us. It isn't. During association, contraband alcohol, ciggies and drugs are passed from one prisoner to the next. So are rumours, insults and threats. No one sleeps well in here, despite the early lights-out situation.

Admittedly, it is not a taxing regime, but it is far from stimulating. The interesting inmates are dangerous, the non-threatening ones are stupid. Oh my God, the constant inane drivel that I endure. Some of the women just never shut up. Never. Even in their sleep they mutter relentlessly. I think it's to prove subconsciously that they are still a presence, a force; you know, still *being*, even if they are only proving this to themselves. Truly, they talk nothing but crap, and I say that as someone who has spent hours with models. Crap about

TV (it's too loud, too quiet, they've seen this show before so are bored, they've never seen it before so don't understand it), their families (they miss them, they hate them, the families are visiting them or ignoring them), the guards (fucking pervs or easily persuaded), the food (too hot, too cold, tastes like shit, not enough), the clouds (they look like rabbits or it looks like rain), their crime (they didn't do it, or they did worse and got away with it), their pimps (fuckers or salt of the earth) or their boyfriends (fuckers or fucking gods). It doesn't matter what they talk about, they talk crap. I stay silent as much as I can. This has earned me a reputation for being a stuck-up bitch, but I don't care. I don't care what these people think of me. I think nothing of them. I'm not looking for friends or companionship. I'm not looking for allies or enemies. I'd rather everyone ignored me. I'd like to disappear. I'm just looking for the end.

Days tugged into weeks, hauled into months. I passed my first-year anniversary here, for want of a better word. No one baked a cake. More days, more weeks, more months. A guard assaulted me. I reported it and he was moved to another block. A win for me, not so much for the women in C block. A prisoner assaulted me. I didn't report it. I held her head in the basin and scalded her next time she visited the salon. There was an inquiry. I maintained it was an accident, that I didn't know how hot the tap was running. In fact, I had added sugar as the water flowed over her forehead; it increases heat capacity. I got to keep my job in the hairdresser's, but the thermostat had to be adjusted; inmates have had to get used to cold washes when they come for a wash and blow-dry. People left me alone after that.

I knew he was coming in advance of his visit. There is no chance of a cheery surprise drop-in because the OK on visitors is like everything else in this place: an elaborate process that requires requests, permission granted or denied, admin and vetting. When he first wrote to me requesting a visit, I considered just ignoring him. What was the point? What did we have to say to one another? He was victorious. He was on the outside. I was on the inside. He'd outsmarted me. That stung, it really did, because he isn't as clever as I am. Least, that's what I've always thought. If he's cleverer than I am, then I must be really bloody stupid.

I guess I'm really bloody stupid.

In the end, boredom won and I agreed to his visit as I literally had nothing better to do. I was curious about what he could possibly want to say to me. Whatever it was, it had to be more interesting than listening to endless discussions about tattoo designs or squabbling about whether trading a Kit Kat for three tea bags is fair or not. I wanted to know what had made him crawl out of the woodwork.

In preparation for his visit, I washed my hair and painted my nails. Not to make myself attractive for him. No, but to show him I am still standing. The moment before the guards let me into the visitors' room, I nervously sniff under my arms and breathe into my hand.

I am glad I made the effort. He looks good. Great, actually. Bastard. He is wearing new jeans, very cool expensive-looking leather boots, a navy-blue roll-neck jumper, a trendy jacket. I can't tell for certain whether the jumper is cashmere without touching it. It's possibly something even more expensive, like vicuña wool. I am not allowed to touch him. Even if I was permitted, I wouldn't. I think of what it must feel like to be him, snuggled up to that level of comfort and luxury. For one awful moment I think he's going to tell me she's taken him back. If she has, there is a danger that I'll throw the table at him, except of course it's bolted down. Everything is bolted down, because in this stuffy, sweaty little visitors' room, news that might generate table-chucking is often delivered. Grandparents say they won't be bringing the grandkids to visit their daughter any more, partners admit to gambling debts and hocking possessions, and lawyers announce there's no case for appeal.

He doesn't bother with small talk. I'm glad. It would be embarrassing if he muttered something about me looking well or him being pleased to see me. I have bags under my eyes, my cheeks are brushed with broken veins, my actions are listless, clumsy. Possibly I'm frightening to look at. I might appear pitiful or pitiless. He sits down. The quietness is obvious, even though there is a lot of noise around us; even more so because of that. People squabble, cry, sigh, laugh and gossip. We sit in silence. I hope he can sense the threat of violence in my voicelessness, my only weapon at this point. My scalp itches with annoyance.

He coughs. 'She gave me a settlement.'

'What?'

'A ton of cash to fuck off.'

'So you're divorced?'

'Yes. You've been inside a year and a half.'

'Two and a half, actually,' I correct.

'I meant since the trial.' It's easy for him to minimise my incarceration, break it up into palpable bits. For me, it's more of a stretch. 'That's plenty of time to divorce if it's what both parties want.'

'I thought you might try and make it work.'

355

'No, I had no interest in that. Not at any point.' He says this definitively and moves his hand in a theatrical slicing gesture, which makes me doubt him.

'Right.' I wonder, just for a fleeting second, if he's going to tell me that he had no interest in making it work with Emma because he wants to be back with me, his first love, his real love. He doesn't. Instead he reaches into his jacket pocket and pulls out an envelope. He starts to lay the glossy photos out on the table between us. At first, I don't get what I'm looking at. Then I realise. The Old Schoolhouse. He's printed out the photos because visitors are not allowed to bring their phones in here. I'm surprised by this level of organisation from him. He's changed. Moved forward. At best I'm standing still; a more accurate appraisal would suggest I've moved backwards. It's not fair. I can't believe I ever imagined that life could be.

'I used the money she gave me to make these renovations.'

I drink in the images, hardly able to believe my eyes. It's every bit as beautiful as I always imagined it could be, always hoped it would be. I can't believe it exists in this finished state, after all this time, after all the longing and hoping and imagining. And scheming.

Finally.

I'm surprised to note that he must have listened to me over the years when I described what I would do with the place if we ever had any money. He has had the roof retiled with slate, and the sash windows repaired, insulated, double-glazed. He tells me that all the paint-clogged and damaged cornicing, mouldings and ceiling roses have been repaired or remoulded, and he shows me before-and-after pictures. He has taken up the floorboards, installed underfloor heating, and then replaced them restored, sanded, waxed. He says that two of the four flats are complete. He shows me pictures of the bathrooms and kitchens. The vibe in the bathrooms is glamorous retro powder room with dusty pink hues, antique dressers and William Morris wallpaper. He must have had an interior designer source the vintage pieces; ornate mirrors, brass fixtures and classic cabinets create layers of visual interest that he simply doesn't have the imagination to conjure. The kitchens boast a range of stunning, aesthetically pleasing features such as textured tiles and wooden and marble surfaces. They are dark and statement, softened by brushed champagne gold metallics. The beauty leaves me breathless.

'I need to sell the smaller flat to raise money to complete the other two.' He tells me this as though it might be news to me, rather than a plan I conceived years ago. 'I have an offer.'

'How much?'

He hesitates, then names an amount. It strikes me as the low end of what the flat must be worth. I suspect he's lying to me. I don't respond immediately, so he rushes on. 'The thing is, I've stuck a shed load of cash into the place now, but I can't sell without you signing, because the mortgage is in our joint names, right?'

'Have you got a solicitor?' I ask.

'Not yet. I've been more involved with getting the place into a fit state to sell. I wanted to get you to agree to sign first, and then I'll consult a solicitor, see how we go about it while you're inside. I mean, I don't know your rights. I'm not going to screw you over.' He so obviously is. 'I plan to settle an amount on you.'

'Sorry?'

'Like she did with me. I thought you could have half of whatever we get for the flat I sell.' He means half of whatever he says he got for the flat. 'After solicitor's fees and estate agents and other costs have been taken off, naturally.' I see my designated amount dwindling before it's even come into existence. 'When Emma settled with me, I thought it was a pretty fucking cold thing to do, but I see now it's an effective way of, you know, closing things down between us and moving on.'

I pause, meet his eyes and then ask, 'As cold as planting evidence?'

He glances about him, fidgets in his seat uncomfortably. 'Are you still going on about that?'

'I didn't tamper with the wheels.'

He tries to look bored. In fact he looks sweaty. 'Right, so you said in court.'

'But the locking wheel nut key was found in my mum's flat. My only question is, was it my mother who loosened the wheels, or was it you, Mattie? I've given it a lot of thought. That could have been either of you, but it was you who planted the nut key to incriminate me. Mum was dead by then. You must have deleted the footage of whichever one of you it was going into the garage, because it never turned up when the police checked. It was just unlucky for me that I decided to play that one last stupid trick, shrinking her jumper. I bet you were thrilled with that. I played right into your hands, didn't I?'

'What you're accusing me of demands quite a lot of planning and cunning. You've always given the impression you think I'm pretty thick. How could I possibly have come up with all of that on my own?' His sarcasm seems pathetic considering our respective positions.

'Why did you do it, Matthew?'

I don't think he's going to answer, but then he says, 'I was your trash, her treasure.'

'I see.'

'I was never enough for you.' Maybe he's right. I don't know. I loved him. But I'm here now, so I guess maybe he wasn't enough. He shrugs, seeming coolly confident, totally independent, something he hasn't been for years. 'Anyway, what's done is done. The way I see it, we need to move on. Let's sell the small flat, then I can finish the other two, and when you get out, you'll have a nest egg. We can go our separate ways. Put all of this behind us. I'll give you what you put down as a deposit.'

'In real terms, with inflation and so on, that's a loss after all these years.' Years I slept in the leaky, draughty, rat-infested work-in-progress.

'I'll chuck in an extra five grand.'

I laugh. 'Five grand? You'll make millions.'

'Well, it's my money that has meant I could get it into a fit state to sell.'

'And mine that bought it in the first place.'

'But we were stuck. My money solved this.'

I'd wanted him to have a tempting taste of the good life so that he had a crystal-clear understanding of what he was playing for. Well, I guess I taught him well; he seems to have learnt that lesson thoroughly. 'It's not your money. It's Emma's money. I'm not signing anything.'

I call the guard and tell him I want to go back to my cell.

49

Visitors are like buses, apparently. You wait around forever for one, and then two come at once. When Emma sent her request asking if she could come to see me, I did not hesitate as I had with Mattie. I wanted to see her. I longed to.

I know her. I know all about her. I know her working hours (long), the songs she likes to sing when in the shower (Taylor Swift). I know how she folds her knickers in her underwear drawer. I know she keeps a Chanel lipstick (Beige Brut, costing £46) and chewing gum (Extra peppermint) in her handbag, I know the contents of her medicine cabinet, her bank accounts and library shelves. I know how often she dyes her hair and shaves; I know when she last had a smear test. I know the expression she wears when she comes. For such a long time, the strange and powerful intimacy was one-way. It wasn't until the night she killed my mother that our relationship became in any way mutual.

She doesn't know me. The dead wife, the first wife, the not-quite wife. She must want to; she's the enquiring type. So here we are in the loud, uncomfortable, unwelcoming visitors' room, face to face. The woman who came before. The woman who came next. We are equally fascinating to each other. She sits across the table and stares at me. She stared at me in court, too. She was up in the viewing gallery most of the time, I was down in the dock. Often I felt the heat of her gaze bearing down on me, like a physical weight. I occasionally looked up, caught her eye. It was a bit like looking into the sun, blinding. I'd have to look away. In court, I thought her glare communicated a laser-sharp, ferocious sense of agony. Others might not have detected as much; the broadsheets reported that she was calm and collected, the tabloids said she was unreadable, icy. I knew she was in pain, physical and emotional. I knew from the way she pulled her top lip over her teeth. Pain as the result of anger or humiliation, I guess. Today her lips are slightly parted. She looks confused but curious.

She opens her tote bag and pulls out a baby-blue cashmere jumper. I know it's cashmere, but you can't tell by looking. It's stiff, rigid as cardboard and shrunken so that it's only fit for a doll. 'I found this,' she declares.

'When?'

'Two weeks ago. It had fallen down the back of the chest of drawers in my dressing room. I was doing a big clear-out. I guess it's been there a long time.'

I nod. 'Two and a half years in total.'

Her forehead creases. 'Why didn't you tell your solicitor where it was?' she asks, puzzled.

'I did. He said it didn't prove anything, that I could have shrunk it on another date, not the night I claimed.'

'Your own solicitor said that?' She seems shocked. 'He didn't think it might have strengthened your case? He didn't want to at least try?' Her voice is high with outrage. I guess that's a money thing, the ultimate privilege of being rich: you get to believe in the fairy tale of fairness; you think people have the energy to do the right thing, when most of us just get by doing something.

'My solicitor was paid for by legal aid. He was worth every penny I didn't pay. You pay peanuts, you get monkeys and all that,' I explain. She had the best solicitors money could buy; the charges against her were dropped before she left hospital. I mean, that's fair – she didn't plan to kill my mum, she was innocent – but it's weird how fair stuff only happens to rich people.

'I took the jumper to my solicitor,' she says.

'Why?' I shouldn't be surprised. I know she channels the paragon-of-virtue vibe and holds the belief that she can change things.

'I thought it might get the case reopened.'

'The case against me?'

'Yes.'

'Why would you do that?'

'This proves you were telling the truth.'

'Does it? Or is my solicitor right? Does it just prove I shrank your jumper at some point?'

'I believe your story,' she says quietly.

It's good to hear, even from her, but irrelevant to my legal position. 'Did your solicitor believe my story?'

Colour creeps up her neck, she sighs. 'No. He said the same as yours. The jumper doesn't validate your defence. It isn't evidence of your innocence, at least not enough to counter the fact that the nut key was found in your flat, in your bedside drawer.'

'Right.'

'Did he plant it?'

'You know the answer to that.' The blotchy redness has crawled all the way up her face now. She's probably embarrassed by her own naivety. She should be. I bet she's regretting her big theatrical gesture. The generous settlement that was supposed to buy her peace of mind will gnaw, disturbing her until her dying day now she knows what he is. At the very least, a cheat, a falsifier of evidence. Maybe a would-be murderer. 'If you're here to find out if it was him who tampered with your car or if it was my mother, I can't help you. I don't know for a fact.'

She nods stiffly. I guess she's had long enough to get used to the idea that someone wanted her dead. I suppose it still takes some processing if you're unsure who that someone is. A woman you barely knew, who you pinned to a tree and is long gone, or the man who made you lose your mind with love. I almost feel sorry for her. Fuck it, I *do* feel sorry for her. She believes so fiercely in justice and truth and fairness, the world must be hard for her. Truths like this must be mind-blowingly destructive, because they expose unfairness, they don't prop it up. It strikes me that her attitude is a waste. If I was rich, I wouldn't squander my time on expecting life to be just. I'd know better. I'd just dress beautifully and drink champagne.

'That's not why I'm here.'

'Oh. So why, then?'

'I want to know why your mother killed my parents.'

'This has just occurred to you?' She's supposed to be so

clever, so logical. But you have to wonder, is she? It's taken her a while to get to this.

'In the court case it wasn't addressed.'

'It wasn't seen as relevant to the case,' I point out.

'I can see that legally it wasn't, but in reality that one action led to everything else, this entire mess. I don't believe Susan Morden's actions were financially motivated; my parents weren't wealthy. They didn't have much money at all at that point in their lives. And why would my grandparents tell me they had died in an accident rather than being murdered, since someone was tried and convicted for their murder?'

'To protect you,' I tell her. She looks surprised. It's not her fault. We're all the same, we're all limited. We don't know what we don't know. I bet she thought her grandparents were cold and remote. I bet she had no idea they were traumatised by the truth of her parents' deaths, grief-stricken at losing their son and humiliated that his actions had led to his death. Possibly she resented being sent to that out-of-the-way boarding school, unaware that they were trying to shield her. They were doing their best for her. I still fucking hate them, though.

'Protect me from what?'

'What were you told?'

'Nothing true. Not even that they were murdered. I only found that out when I was arrested. My grandparents said there was this crazy woman who stepped out into the road and my dad swerved to avoid her but ended up ploughing into a tree. He died immediately. My mother died eight hours later in hospital.'

I shift on my seat, uncomfortable. I've never considered that it might have been anything other than instantaneous. I've never thought of the wife suffering for hours. I want to tell her the truth. I think I've always wanted her to know. 'Your father and my mother were having an affair.'

'What?'

It feels like someone has turned down the sound around us. The kids squabbling, the women gossiping, the guards bossing, it all falls away. There's just us two. 'She wanted him to leave your mother. He wouldn't. So she killed them both. If she couldn't have him, then no one would, was her thinking. She cut the brakes of their car.'

Emma shakes her head. Stunned at the wild, ludicrous nature of what I'm telling her, stunned by the perfect truth of it. Her eyes find mine and I see that they are flooded with complete understanding. She sees me properly. Perhaps for the first time. As it dawns on her, I confirm, 'She was pregnant with me. She told me she'd got pregnant on purpose. She was hoping that it would be the impetus he needed to end his marriage. But her plan didn't work. He just told her to get rid of me. She didn't. She got rid of him instead.' This is a small consolation in my scrappy, miserable start: my mother had at least chosen me, an unborn baby, over the adulterous alcoholic who wanted his mistress to abort.

'So we are . . .'

'Sisters. Yes. Well, technically half-sisters, but yes. We're one big not-so-happy family.'

50

She belonged to me first. She was mine before she was his. Even before I spent months following her, even before she 'met' Mattie, she and I were connected.

She's controlled, I'll give her that. She asks, 'When did your mother tell you this?'

'About two years before she died.'

'Around the time she started working for me.'

'Yes, that wasn't a coincidence. Nor was the fact that she invited Mattie and me to live with her in her flat.' I've had time to think about it, but I can't decide. Even now, some things will, I guess, stay forever a mystery. That is life. We're arrogant and deluded to think we can find all the answers, that we're entitled to them or that we'd know what to do with them if they were presented. I don't know if my mum was trying to gift me the legacy that I was due or whether she was manipulating us all along. Were Mattie and I just pawns? Did she play on our financial desperation? My need for a home. My need for a mother.

'Does he know this?' Emma asks.

He. She doesn't have to name him, there's only one he. There are two of us. We both know who she means. 'No.' I smile coolly. 'For him it was all about the money. He has never, as far as I'm aware, questioned why my mother might have killed your parents. He simply accepted that she did. He never really liked her. I guess it was easy for him to think the worst of her.'

Emma bangs her hand down on the table. 'We should get the case reopened. Bring all this to light.'

'My case? What's the point? I'll probably only have to serve another six months. I've kept my nose clean. I'll most likely make parole. It will take longer than that to get to court. Do you want to sell tickets to that circus again?'

She pauses. I don't doubt she's thinking about the journalists who most likely camped outside the gate to Woodview, the headlines that ruined her day time after time. 'But Matthew Charlton planted evidence. He should be tried for that.' I note the transition. 'He' no more.

'That wouldn't carry much of a sentence, most likely a few more hours' community service. What's the point?'

'What if it was him who tampered with the car?' I notice that her hands are shaking, but I don't think she's frightened. I think it's a thirst for justice and answers that's agitating her.

'You know, it was most likely my mother who did that,' I admit with a sigh. 'As I say, I don't know for a fact, it's just my opinion. She thought Matthew had fallen in love with you, that he wouldn't leave you and come back to me. My guess is that pushed her over the edge. She probably couldn't bear history repeating itself, you know?'

Emma leans towards me, exerting a keenness that's

borderline desperate. I wonder if she wants to ask me my opinion on that matter too. Do I also think he was in love with her? I don't add anything else.

'I see that you were owed, that you had a right,' she admits. 'I inherited from my grandparents, but they were your grandparents too. You must have felt cheated. You *have* been cheated, over and over again. But why didn't you just come to me? If you'd explained everything, we could have taken DNA tests, consulted lawyers, and we'd have come to an agreement. An arrangement.'

I let out a derisive laugh. This question could only be asked by someone who has been shielded by wealth, met by fairness and grown confident in their expectation of how life should work out. 'I'm not a big believer in "ask and you will receive". Look at this place.'

Emma casts her eyes around the room, which is groaning with missed opportunities, limitations and desperation. These inequalities are manifested in dangerous criminals with broken minds who are devoid of moral compasses, and pathetic criminals with broken hearts who are lacking the sense they were born with. Neither group expects generosity or understanding. They fight tooth and claw for what they have or they have nothing at all. I'm sitting with them. I'm this side of the table.

Emma processes this new information. 'I'll have my lawyer look at this. I'll make a settlement and—'

'No.' I interrupt firmly. 'I know you did that for Mattie. He told me. I don't want your money.'

'But you need it.'

'No, I don't. I've earned my own.'

'What? How?'

And I can't resist telling her. It's a risk, I know that, because if she still loves him, she could leave here and immediately relay it to him. She has the resources to get him lawyers; they could build a case that might alter my planned path before I get out of here. But I don't think she'll do that. She doesn't love him and she doesn't hate me. She might even see the beautiful justice in my plan. After all, she was married to him too for a while. Maybe she was also on occasion irritated by his lack of attention to detail, that lazy way he has of sitting back and letting it all be worked out for him.

'He's ploughed all your cash into my property, a place called the Old Schoolhouse. It was a mess. Not fit to live in. We needed money to do it up. You might remember it was mentioned in court. He thinks it's *our* property. He thinks his name is on the deeds, but he's not one for attention to detail. Around the time he was marrying you, I had it transferred into my name. He unknowingly signed the paperwork when he thought he was signing for a remortgage to cover the cost of some makeshift repairs. He was too excited about the trip to the Maldives and too irritated by your insistence on a prenup to really pay attention to what I presented him with. He trusted me.'

'So when you get out of here . . .'

'I'll simply go home, change the locks and say goodbye to him. He'll be homeless. Penniless.'

'That seems very' – she searches around for the words – 'ruthless and cruel.'

'Yes. Or ruthless and fair. I suppose it depends on your viewpoint.' I open my hands wide and gesture to my surroundings again. Reminding her of where he put me. 'Will you tell him?'

She shakes her head, slowly but emphatically, left to right

two or three times. 'No. This has nothing to do with me. This is between you two.' She stands up, and I'm surprised to feel a slight sting of disappointment. There's fifteen more minutes of visiting time on the clock; she doesn't have to leave yet. 'If there's anything you need, if it doesn't go to plan, if you need legal advice or a loan, anything at all, get in touch with me. It might not be as cut-and-dried as you think. He might not just slink away.'

'I'll keep it in mind, but I know him. I think he will just slink away. He'll probably move back in with his mum and dad. Thanks, though.' She nods. It feels good to know there's someone, that I'm not alone. Even if it's her. Especially as it's her. 'I'm sorry,' I say hurriedly.

'Are you?'

'Yes. For some of it, most of it. I just needed a home. I've got a home now.'

'I understand.' She pauses. 'I'm sorry that you thought it was the only way.'

'We're very different.'

'Some would say we have a lot in common.' She throws out something that is midway between an irreverent grin and an eye-roll. 'Would you mind if I put in another request to visit you?'

'Why would you do that?'

'I could bring you something.'

'Like what?'

'Whatever you needed. Well, not an file or a shovel, but maybe new clothes, or chocolate. Whatever is allowed in here.' I laugh. It's nice to hear someone make a joke. 'When I was at boarding school, some of the other girls received care packages from their families: comics and make-up and stuff. You know, treats. I always thought that must be fun.'

'Didn't you get care packages?' I would have imagined her grandparents sending her cloth-bound books, expensive chocolates.

'No.'

'Oh.'

'Never.'

'Did you like school?' I ask.

'Does anyone?' She smiles. 'What doesn't kill you, et cetera, et cetera, right?'

We stare at one another, my sister and I. We are shoulder-deep in a swamp of complex history; hurt and hate, injury and injustice and sheer bad luck threaten to drown us. Is she offering something here? An olive branch across our strange, dysfunctional family tree. Can I grab it, and can she drag me out of the swamp? My mother killed hers. Our father cheated us all. I tried to ruin her life and steal everything from her. We face a little more than the usual sibling rivalry. This is not just a matter of pinching her clothes or toys. But maybe she is thinking about *why* I have done what I have, rather than *what* I've done. She says, 'I will put in another request to come and visit you.' And so she takes the matter out of my hands; she decides what is best for us.

51

Six months later

Emma

I get up at 7 a.m., my new regular alarm time at the weekend. Disciplined but not 'bloody mental' (Heidi's words). Nine minutes to dress, get downstairs, swallow a vitamin, get water. I call to Odin, my German shepherd, who is not only a fabulous guard dog but is fast becoming the love of my life. We run for three quarters of an hour. Once back at the house, I feed Odin, make coffee, do a vinyasa flow class online. Heidi and Gina also join from their front rooms, and it's fun to know we are doing it together. I drink my kale juice and scoop up the enormous bouquet of flowers that I've been storing in the utility room. Then I get in the car and beg Odin to settle down and not crush the flowers. It's 9.30. I'm more measured nowadays, but I like to think I'm still very efficient. Weekends are too precious to waste. Not a lot scares me, but I am fearful of the opportunities I might miss, which is why I'm travelling to London today. I'm going to my sister's housewarming.

Becky has given me a key to the Old Schoolhouse. As she did so, she said, 'What's yours is mine.'

'Don't you mean "what's mine is yours"?' I corrected her.

'Not necessarily,' she quipped. She's funny, my little sister.

When I arrive, I let myself in and find her on her hands and knees scrubbing the kitchen in the main flat. The one Matthew lived in until a few days ago. The place is spotless, but I guess her urge to clean is nothing to do with hygiene but more to do with mental absolution. I admire her industry. Over the last six months, I've regularly visited her in prison, first monthly, then twice a month, then weekly. We're getting to know one another. During the trial, the press chose to characterise us as opposites: the ageing heiress versus the broke beauty. I was presented as an overly privileged naive (borderline kooky) woman who must have stumbled into her position of power through positive gender discrimination. I was deemed too stupid to have earned my role. My years demonstrating fiscal sense, business acumen and hard graft had been obliterated by one stupid heart-led decision. Becky was presented as a manipulative, feral (aka vicious) woman who had never done an honest day's work in her life but instead devoted herself to freeloading, debauchery and profligacy. She was painted as someone who had used her sexuality to exploit and extort. Her years of overcoming disadvantage to achieve outstanding career success in a highly competitive industry, followed by years of frugality, were discounted. Wiped out. At first it seemed we had nothing in common, and all the things we did share seemed sad: an alcoholic father, lonely childhoods, Matthew. But we wanted to discover more.

'If you had to describe yourself in three words, what would they be?' I asked Becky once when I was visiting her. She liked these getting-to-know-you games, bored of conversations about the food or TV.

'Oh, that's easy,' she replied quickly. 'Passionate, competitive and ambitious. You?'

I paused and thought about it. 'Disciplined, logical, careful.'

'I think we both demonstrate all those traits to an extent. You are competitive and ambitious, that's why you're so disciplined.'

'Maybe,' I reply, trying to reframe how I view myself, how I view her.

'And look how logical I'm being. I'm content to serve time for a crime I didn't commit as I know there was stuff that I deserve to be punished for, and anyway it will all even out when I get to move into the Old Schoolhouse.'

'Yes, I suppose I do see the logic in your thinking,' I admitted. 'But passionate is the opposite of careful.'

'I'm pretty sure marrying someone after knowing them a matter of months weighs in on the passionate side, rather than the careful,' she pointed out.

'And look where that got me.' I rolled my eyes.

'It got you me,' she said with a laugh.

Maybe she's on to something. Maybe we are not so dissimilar. It's hard to tell, as our life experiences have been very different. I decide it doesn't matter, because she's right. I got her. A barmy criminal sister to go with my unreliable addict brother. I love Tom. It isn't impossible to imagine I'll love Becky one day too. Someone has to.

Heidi is sceptical. I would be disappointed if she was anything else, but she is being supportive despite her misgivings. She understands that I need to fold Becky into my life. Gina is excited about meeting her. As is Tom. He and Becky have said hello over FaceTime.

'Those two will be a shit show,' warned Heidi. 'They might well trigger one another. Both of them are so extreme.'

'Maybe,' I admitted. 'Or they might glimmer one another.'

'Glimmer one another? What do you mean?'

'It's the opposite of trigger. It's when something or someone sparks something wonderful in another, maybe gifting a feeling of peace or purpose. Maybe Tom and Becky will feel more complete because our family has expanded.'

Heidi and Gina have both agreed to come to Becky's tiny housewarming brunch to meet her. By the time they arrive, Becky has put away her rubber gloves and is dancing around the kitchen. She's put a playlist together; it includes songs such as 'Sisters Are Doin' It for Themselves' and 'Spice Up Your Life'.

'She's not big on nuance, is she?' mutters Heidi.

'No. Nor regrets. It's one of the things I like about her,' I reply.

It's just the four of us. Neither of my friends is quite ready to introduce my jailbird sister to their families, but they will in time. I know they will, because they are good people and they will see that Becky needs support, that she *needs* good people. Heidi arrives with croissants and a fruit salad; Gina has brought orange juice and cava, so we make Buck's fizz. The fact that Becky was right about Matthew slinking off and not contesting ownership of the Old Schoolhouse has gone a long way towards endearing her to Heidi, who still believes Matthew got away too lightly. She's happy to see him punished rather than profiting. As she looks around the beautiful space, I hear her comment to Gina that she's 'glad the money Emma gave that prick is back in her family'.

I'm delighted she referred to Becky as my family. Heidi doesn't trust my little sister yet, but she tolerates her, accepting that Becky's personal circumstances have been tragic, that she is a product of her environment and so am I. Becky, Tom and I have all paid heavily for our parents' mistakes; our job is to try to make fewer mistakes of our own as we go forward.

ACKNOWLEDGEMENTS

I want to start with saying thank you to Kate Mills, my wonderful publisher. Kate, you are fabulous to work with. You are always so honest and upbeat, committed and confident. Thanks for truly understanding and delivering what I need most throughout this process (I'm not talking about champagne, although that is important and you do have a healthy respect for that fact) but I'm talking about being a true partner every step of the way. You are incredible to work with. The same goes for Lisa Milton. How lucky are we to have such a determined force for good at the top and centre of the HQ. I trust and respect you both so much. It is a total joy working with you both and it has been from the very first meeting all those years ago.

I also want to say a heartfelt thank you to Charlie Redmayne. You are a CEO who embodies drive and determination, who combines commerciality and creativity and who throws properly excellent author parties. You make HarperCollins a wonderful place for a writer to be published.

I'm so delighted to be working with an incredible team. I am thoroughly grateful for, and appreciative of, the talent and commitment of every single person involved in this book's existence. I know you all work with dedication, insight and expertise. Thank you all very much for everything you do to get my books into the hands of readers. Thank you, Emily Burns, you've blasted into my working world with incredible verve and skill. I'm so happy to welcome you to the team. They are the best, and you fit right in! Thank you, Anna Derkacz, George Green, Fliss Porter, Joanna Rose, Vicki Watson, Rachael Nazarko, Rebecca Fortuin, Angie Dobbs, Halema Begum, Noemi Vallone, Sophie Waeland, Aisling Smyth, Kate Oakley, Anna Sikorska and Laura Meyer. I can't possibly detail everything you all do (it would be another novel in itself) but please know, I'm aware and full of gratitude.

I want to send massive thanks across the seas to the brilliant teams who publish my books worldwide. You really are making my dreams come true. My North America team are absolutely tremendous and it's such a joy to be finding readers in America and Canada. Thank you Craig Swinwood, Loriana Sacilotto, Margaret Marbury O'Neill, Nicole Brebner, Sophie James and Rebecca Silver. I know there are many, many more people on this team and I appreciate every one of you. I hope to meet you all in person soon. Thank you to Sue Brockhoff in Australia. There are many other publishing teams, who I have yet to meet, but I am so grateful that incredible professionals across the globe are giving my books their love and attention. It's so ridiculously exciting finding readers in so many countries. Thank you.

Thank you to all my readers, bloggers, reviewers, retailers, librarians and fellow authors who have supported me throughout my career. I say it time and time again, without readers, there really would be no point in doing what I do at all. You are, by definition, the entire point of my career.

Thank you to Mum and Dad for nurturing a love of reading and my sister, friends and family for always supporting me by fronting up my books in supermarkets and bookstores, and in dozens of other ways.

I want to do a shout out to my yoga gang. You guys help me unfurl physically and mentally after I've spent the day bent over my desk. You help me find balance, in more ways than one and you keep me sane and smiling when my characters are dashing around my head doing diabolical stuff! I'm so grateful for our lovely little community. Thank you for your friendship, Amelia Rose Key, Clare Slater, Eleanor Bowe, Eleonora Kennedy, Kath Shaw, Naomi Begum-Inglis, Rosemary Tyler and Tim Ashworth. Namaste.

I'd like to acknowledge the wonderful generosity of Graham Cadd (who also likes to be known as Amazing Graham) who bid to name a character in this novel at a fundraiser for Children with Cancer UK. A charity that works tirelessly to fund innovative research, support families and raise awareness of cancer in children, teenagers and young adults.

Finally, obviously, forever and always thank you to Jimmy and Conrad. Can I say what I said last year as I still think it's spot on. Obviously, I'm not the most conventional wife and mother on earth. I realise you are both constantly accommodating that fact. But I know you know I'm devoted and adore you both. I hope we can agree that living with my peculiarities, passions and penchant for saying aloud literally every thought that ever enters my head is, on balance, worthwhile! I am so proud of you both.